本科"十四五"规划教材

高等院校立体化创新系列教材·外国语言文学及文化系列

英美文学与文化教程

The Literature and Culture of the United Kingdom and the United States

主　编　杜丽霞
副主编　Edward Lewis

图书在版编目(CIP)数据

英美文学与文化教程 / 杜丽霞主编 . — 西安：西安交通大学出版社，2023.7(2024.1 重印)
 ISBN 978－7－5693－3092－2

Ⅰ.①英… Ⅱ.①杜… Ⅲ.①英国文学－文学欣赏②文学欣赏－美国 Ⅳ.①I561.06②I712.06

中国国家版本馆 CIP 数据核字(2023)第 033573 号

书　　　名	英美文学与文化教程
主　　　编	杜丽霞
责 任 编 辑	庞钧颖
责 任 校 对	李　蕊
装 帧 设 计	伍　胜
出 版 发 行	西安交通大学出版社 (西安市兴庆南路 1 号　邮政编码 710048)
网　　　址	http://www.xjtupress.com
电　　　话	(029)82668357　82667874(市场营销中心) (029)82668315(总编办)
传　　　真	(029)82668280
印　　　刷	西安日报社印务中心
开　　　本	720mm×1000mm　1/16　印张 22.75　字数 511 千字
版 次 印 次	2023 年 7 月第 1 版　2024 年 1 月第 2 次印刷
书　　　号	ISBN 978－7－5693－3092－2
定　　　价	55.00 元

如发现印装质量问题，请与本社市场营销中心联系。
 订购热线:(029)82665248　(029)82667874
 投稿热线:(029)82668531

版权所有　侵权必究

前　言

这部教材是编者在讲授英美文学与文化课程十余年的基础上编写的。

英国和美国，是两个重要的西方国家。英国是欧洲的重要组成部分，美国起源于英国的海外殖民扩张，在承袭英国文化的基础上发展出了独特的美国文化。较为系统地了解英美文学与文化，对了解西方世界的历史与发展有着重要意义。

本教材分为"英国文学与文化"和"美国文学与文化"两部分，对英美两国的历史演进予以阶段性审视，聚焦各历史时期英美两国的政治、经济、社会文化、思想认知、文学艺术等方面，甄选了代表性作家及其作品供学生学习和研讨。教材特色主要体现在以下方面。

1. 英语发展历程的梳理

"英国文学与文化"和"美国文学与文化"两部分均以"简介"开篇，前者着重介绍英语在英国的形成历程，后者阐述了美国英语产生的历史背景，并比较了二者的不同之处。通过这两篇"简介"，读者可以对英国英语和美国英语的差异及联系获得较为明晰的了解。编者曾设想在"英国文学与文化"部分采用英国英语范式，在"美国文学与文化"部分采用美国英语范式，但考虑到这样会打破整部教材的统一性，便在叙述部分都采用较为流行的美国范式，仅在"英国文学与文化"部分的个别选文中保持了英国英语范式，比如狄更斯的《艰难时世》和哈代的《德伯家的苔丝》中的选文片段等。

2. 选文的宽泛性

教材中的选文不拘泥于纯文学作品，而是囊括了对于英国和美国产生重要影响的著述，比如托马斯·霍布斯的《利维坦》，亚当·斯密的《国富论》，托马斯·潘恩的《常识》，拉尔夫·爱默生的《美国学者》等。通过这些作品及传统意义上的纯文学作品选篇，学生能较为深入地理解英美两国的文学和文化。

3. 中国元素的纳入和文化对比性

英美两国有不少经典作品涉及中国文化。本教材收录了英国浪漫主义诗人塞缪尔·泰勒·柯尔律治的名诗《忽必烈汗》，美国现代主义诗人埃兹拉·庞德对李白著名诗作《长干行》的翻译"The River-Merchant's Wife：A Letter"，受到美国主流社会高度评价的美国华裔女作家汤亭亭的《女勇士》。另外，编者在思考题的设计上注重引导学生进行文化对比，比如对比英美两国几乎人人皆知的创世神话与中国盘古和女娲创世神话的异同，思考庞德对李白《长干行》的翻译处理，比较汤亭亭笔下的花木兰与中国南北朝民歌中花木兰形象的根本差异，等等。

4. 课程育人性

为中国学生开设英美文学与文化课程，绝不仅仅是让学生知晓英美两国的名家名作，而是为了拓宽学生的国际视野，在文明互鉴中丰富自我；了解文学的书写性，增强批判性思维能力；深刻理解人与自然、人与社会、人与他人及人与自我的关系，提高道德情操和审美情趣。教材在选材和思考题设计方面注重专业性和育人性二维结合与统一，体现课程思政，并将这一理念贯穿始终。

本书参阅了大量的文献资料与专业书籍，力求做到专业性与趣味性并存。在编写过程中，本书虽经反复修改与核对，但由于编者水平有限，难免存在疏漏与不足之处，敬请各位专家、学者及广大读者批评指正。

编　者

2023 年 4 月

于交通大学 127 周年校庆之际

致 谢

本教材为西安交通大学"十四五"规划教材，在编写过程中，得到了许多同仁的帮助。

首先要感谢西安交通大学教务处给予教材专项资金，让我们在总结多年教学工作的基础上，实现了按照自己的教学规划编写、出版教材的夙愿。

其次要感谢讲授过该课程的所有教师，包括刘丹翎老师、石艳蕊老师、田荣昌老师、陈大地老师。同时也要感谢研究生李元元和康晋楠同学所做的大量工作。

再者要感谢同事和亲友的勉励和支持，感谢西安交通大学出版社的各位编辑及校对人员耐心细致的工作。你们的奉献令我们怀有无限的感动。

而最为重要的感谢，要归于在编写此教材过程中我们所使用的参考书和文本的编者及作家们。没有这些作家的卓越杰作，没有这些编者的前期成果和资料，我们根本不可能编写出这本教材。

编 者

2023 年 4 月

目　录

Part Ⅰ　British Literature and Culture

Introduction ··· 2

Chapter 1

From the 5th Century to the 15th Century

The Anglo-Saxon and Medieval Ages ······················· 6

1.1　From the Anglo-Saxon Era to the Norman Conquest ············· 6

　　An Introduction to *Beowulf* ··· 7

　　　Beowulf ·· 9

1.2　From the Norman Conquest to the End of the 15th Century ······ 13

　　Geoffrey Chaucer (c. 1343 – 1400) ································ 14

　　　The Canterbury Tales ·· 16

Chapter 2

The 16th Century

The Renaissance and the Reign of Elizabeth Ⅰ ············· 20

2.1　The Renaissance and the Reformation ··························· 20

2.2　The Rise of Elizabeth Ⅰ to Sovereignty ·························· 21

2.3　Renaissance Literature ··· 23

　　Christopher Marlowe (1564 – 1593) ······························· 24

　　　The Tragic History of Doctor Faustus ························· 26

　　William Shakespeare (1564 – 1616) ································ 29

Sonnet 18 31
Hamlet 32

Chapter 3

The 17th Century

The Bourgeois Revolution and the Early Enlightenment 35

3.1 The Bourgeois Revolution 35
3.2 The Early Enlightenment 37
3.3 Representative Writers and Works 37
    King James Bible 38
        Genesis 39
    Francis Bacon (1561 – 1626) 42
        Of Studies 43
    Thomas Hobbes (1588 – 1679) 45
        Leviathan 46
    John Locke (1632 – 1704) 49
        Two Treatises of Government 50

Chapter 4

From 1700 to 1789

The Industrial Revolution and the Age of Reason 53

4.1 The Industrial Revolution and Imperial Expansion 53
4.2 The Age of Reason 54
4.3 Representative Writers and Works 54
    Alexander Pope (1688 – 1744) 55
        An Essay on Man 56
    Jonathan Swift (1667 – 1745) 59
        A Modest Proposal 60
    Joseph Addison (1672 – 1719) 64
        The Royal Exchange 65

  Adam Smith (1723 – 1790) ·· 68
   The Wealth of Nations ·· 69

Chapter 5

From 1789 to the 1830s

The Development of Industrialisation and the Age of Romanticism
··· 73

5.1 The Revolutionary and Napoleonic Wars ·································· 73
5.2 The Development of the Industrial Revolution ·························· 74
5.3 The Flowering of Romanticism ··· 74
  William Blake (1757 – 1827) ··· 76
   The Chimney-Sweeper ··· 77
   The Chimney Sweeper ··· 78
   London ·· 79
  William Wordsworth (1770 – 1850) ·· 80
   My Heart Leaps Up ··· 81
  Samuel Taylor Coleridge (1772 – 1834) ·· 82
   Kubla Khan ··· 83
  Percy Bysshe Shelley (1792 – 1822) ·· 85
   Song to the Men of England ·· 87

Chapter 6

From the 1830s to the End of the 19th Century

The Victorian Era and the Age of Realism ·································· 89

6.1 The Victorian Era: Industry and Empire ·································· 89
6.2 Marxism and the British Working-Class ·································· 90
6.3 Darwin and the Theory of Evolution ······································· 92
6.4 The Philosophy of Utilitarianism ··· 93
6.5 An Age of Fiction: Realism and Naturalism ····························· 94
  Charles Dickens (1812 – 1870) ·· 96
   Hard Times ··· 98

Thomas Hardy (1840 – 1928) ·············· 106
    Tess of the D'Urbervilles ·············· 107
Alfred, Lord Tennyson (1809 – 1892) ·············· 111
    Ulysses ·············· 111
Josef Conrad (1857 – 1924) ·············· 114
    Heart of Darkness ·············· 116

Chapter 7

From the Turn of the 20th Century to 1945

The Two World Wars and the Age of Modernism ·············· 121

7.1 The Modern Era of British Society ·············· 121
7.2 British Modernist Literature ·············· 122
    William Butler Yeats (1865 – 1939) ·············· 123
        The Second Coming ·············· 124
    T. S. Eliot (1888 – 1965) ·············· 125
        The Love Song of J. Alfred Prufrock ·············· 126
    Aldous Huxley (1894 – 1963) ·············· 130
        Brave New World ·············· 133

Chapter 8

From 1945 to the Present

The Contemporary Era and the Age of Postmodernism ·············· 136

8.1 World War II and Its Aftermath ·············· 136
8.2 Domestic Circumstances after World War II ·············· 137
8.3 Postmodernism ·············· 138
8.4 British Literature After World War II ·············· 139
    Samuel Beckett (1906 – 1989) ·············· 143
        Waiting for Godot ·············· 144
    William Golding (1911 – 1993) ·············· 149
        Lord of the Flies ·············· 152
    Benjamin Zephaniah (b. 1958) ·············· 161

Bought and Sold ········ 161

Part Ⅱ American Literature and Culture

Introduction ········ 164

Chapter 1

From 1492 to 1775

The Colonial Age and American Colonialism ········ 168

- 1.1　American Indians ········ 168
  - The Literature of Native Americans ········ 169
    - Listen! Rain Approaches! ········ 169
- 1.2　The Northern Puritans ········ 170
  - William Bradford (1590 – 1657) ········ 172
    - Of Plymouth Plantation ········ 173
  - Anne Bradstreet (1612 – 1672) ········ 175
    - Upon the Burning of Our House ········ 176
  - Jonathan Edwards (1703 – 1758) ········ 178
    - Sinners in the Hands of an Angry God ········ 178
- 1.3　The Southern Colonists ········ 180
  - John Smith (1580 – 1631) ········ 181
    - A Description of New England ········ 182
  - William Byrd (1674 – 1744) ········ 184
    - A Progress to the Mines ········ 184

Chapter 2

From 1775 to 1783

The Revolutionary Era and the American Enlightenment ········ 186

- 2.1　The American Revolution ········ 186
- 2.2　The American Enlightenment ········ 187

Thomas Paine (1737 – 1809) ·············· 189
   Common Sense ·············· 189
Thomas Jefferson (1743 – 1826) ·············· 192
   The Unanimous Declaration of the Thirteen United States of America
·············· 193
Benjamin Franklin (1706 – 1790) ·············· 195
   The Autobiography of Benjamin Franklin ·············· 197

Chapter 3

From 1783 to 1861

The New Nation and the American Renaissance ·············· 205

3.1 The New Nation: Growth, Expansion, and Sins ·············· 205
3.2 The American Renaissance ·············· 206
3.3 Representative Prose Writers and Their Works ·············· 209
   Washington Irving (1783 – 1859) ·············· 210
     Rip Van Winkle ·············· 211
   Ralph Waldo Emerson (1803 – 1882) ·············· 215
     Nature ·············· 216
     The American Scholar ·············· 220
   Nathaniel Hawthorne (1804 – 1864) ·············· 222
     The Scarlet Letter ·············· 224
3.4 Representative Poets and Their Works ·············· 230
   Henry Wadsworth Longfellow (1807 – 1882) ·············· 231
     A Psalm of Life ·············· 232
     The Tide Rises, the Tide Falls ·············· 233
   Walt Whitman (1819 – 1892) ·············· 234
     Song of Myself ·············· 235
   Emily Dickinson (1830 – 1886) ·············· 241
     Success is counted sweetest ·············· 242
     Tell all the Truth but tell it slant— ·············· 243

Chapter 4

From 1861 to 1914

American Civil War and American Realism ... 244

4.1　American Civil War and Reconstruction ... 244
4.2　Urbanization and the Gilded Age ... 245
4.3　American Realism ... 246
　　Theodore Dreiser (1871–1945) ... 249
　　　Sister Carrie ... 250
　　Edwin Arlington Robinson (1869–1935) ... 260
　　　Richard Cory ... 260

Chapter 5

From 1914 to 1941

World War Ⅰ and American Modernism ... 262

5.1　World War Ⅰ and the "Modern Temper" ... 262
5.2　American Modernism ... 264
5.3　American Interwar Literature ... 264
　　Ezra Pound (1885–1972) ... 267
　　　In a Station of the Metro ... 268
　　　The River-Merchant's Wife: A Letter ... 268
　　Robert Frost (1874–1963) ... 270
　　　The Road Not Taken ... 271
　　　Nothing Gold Can Stay ... 272
　　　Fire and Ice ... 272
　　Ernest Hemingway (1899–1961) ... 273
　　　A Farewell to Arms ... 275
　　　The Old Man and the Sea ... 281
　　F. Scott Fitzgerald (1896–1940) ... 293
　　　The Great Gatsby ... 296

Chapter 6

From 1941 to the Present

World War Ⅱ and American Postmodernism ········· 312

6.1 World War Ⅱ and Its Aftermath ················· 312
6.2 Domestic Circumstances in the United States ········· 313
6.3 The Ideas of Existentialism and Deconstruction ········· 315
6.4 American Postmodernist Literature ················· 316
    Joseph Heller (1923 – 1999) ························· 320
        Catch-22 ····································· 321
    Toni Morrison (1931 – 2019) ························· 332
        Sweetness ······································· 333
    Maxine Hong Kingston (b. 1940) ······················ 339
        The Woman Warrior: Memoirs of a Girlhood Among Ghosts ········· 340

Part I

British Literature and Culture

英美文学与文化教程
The Literature and Culture of the United Kingdom and the United States

Introduction

The full title of the nation state known as "Britain" is the United Kingdom of Great Britain and Northern Ireland. The term "Great Britain" refers to England, Scotland, and Wales, without involving Northern Ireland. The term "the British Isles" refers to both the United Kingdom and the Irish Republic (Eire).

When we talk about English Literature, we refer to all literature written in English in the British Isles, including works in English by writers from England, Scotland, Wales, and Ireland. The non-English countries of the British Isles do have their own literatures in their native languages: Welsh in the case of Wales, Scottish Gaelic① in the case of Scotland, and Irish Gaelic in the case of Ireland. English remains the primary language in all the countries in the British Isles. Of the native languages, Welsh is the most widely spoken (some 30% of the population of Wales speak Welsh). It should be noted that writers from Australia, New Zealand, Canada, and the West Indies are often included in the study of English Literature, but they are not included in this anthology, because they are not considered British literature. However, readers will note that several of the most important writers included in this collection were born in Ireland before it gained its independence from British control.

British English as it is spoken and written today is the product of a succession of invasions. The first identifiable settlers of the British Isles were the Celts② who came from what is now Germany in about 600 BCE. They left their mark on the landscape of Britain with burial mounds and

---

① Gaelic: one of the Celtic languages, especially spoken in parts of Scotland and in Ireland
② the Celts: an ancient European People

Introduction

most famously the historic site of Stonehenge. They were followed by the Romans who made a brief visit in 55 BCE under Julius Caesar (c. 100 BCE – 44 BCE). The Romans conquered most of England and Wales as wall as part of Scotland about 100 years later. That was why the Roman language of Latin had a major influence on the development of the English language.

After the Romans left in the middle of the 4th century CE, a succession of invaders conquered the whole of England, driving the Celts into Wales, Scotland, and Ireland. These Germanic invaders, who were the Angles, the Saxons, and to a lesser extent the Jutes, formed the basis of the modern English people. From them we get the term Anglo-Saxon, which not only refers to these Germanic inhabitants of England from their arrival in the 5th century up to the Norman Conquest which took place in 1066, but also denotes the language of their various kingdoms, of which the most important was Wessex, the home of Alfred the Great (849 – 899).

At the end of the 8th century CE, England was subject to raids and invasions by the Vikings① who came from Norway and Denmark. However, by the middle of the 9th century, Alfred the Great had defeated these invaders. Some Vikings remained as settlers, particularly in the North of England, and their language is remembered in the names of many cities, towns, and villages in northern England.

In 1066, England was invaded by the Normans from northern France. William, Duke of Normandy, had a claim to the English crown. He defeated Harold, the last Anglo-Saxon king of England, at the battle of Hastings to become King William I of England, usually known as William the Conqueror. The title Duke of Normandy has been handed down to all succeeding British monarchs. This was the last invasion of the British Isles, and it left a major mark on the English language as well as British culture: most importantly, the Normans introduced the European feudal system to England. Under this system the king granted land and other privileges to his

---

① the Vikings: a race of Scandinavian people in the 8th to 10th centuries who sailed in ships to attack areas along the coasts of northern and western Europe

noble supporters in return for payment in cash and kind① and an obligation to provide military forces to the king in the case of war or rebellion. It formed the basis for the English system of government until the Tudor② period (1485 – 1603). Even today, aristocratic titles like the Duke of Kent or the Marquess of Bath are linked to localities.

To facilitate the establishment of feudalism, one of William's first actions was to order a survey of all the lands and property of England, with all the statistics being recorded in what became known as *The Domesday Book*. This book also listed the populations of cities, towns, and villages as well as the numbers of cattle, pigs, and other farm animals held by communities. It was essentially the first census in England; it enabled William to calculate the number of soldiers each of his nobles were to provide, if necessary, to his army.

The Norman Conquest also led to major changes in the languages spoken in England. Over the following five or six centuries, Norman French (the language of the new ruling class) combined with Latin (the language of the Christian Catholic church) and Anglo-Saxon (the language of the common people) to form what became modern English. This combination is clear in the names that modern English gives to meat and the animals from which the meat comes. This is why English, unlike many other European languages, has different names for the live animal and the meat: beef comes from cows,③ pork from pigs, and mutton or lamb from sheep. This reflects the fact that in general the meat was eaten by the Norman rulers, but the animals were looked after by the Anglo-Saxon serfs. "Beef" comes from the French word "boeuf," "pork" from "porc," and "mutton" from "mouton" whereas "cow," "pig," and "sheep" are Anglo-Saxon words.

Although England was not invaded after 1066, successive groups from

---

① payment in kind: a method of paying someone with goods or services instead of money
② Tudor: House of Tudor, an English royal dynasty of Welsh origin
③ cow: In common usage, "cow" refers to a domestic bovine regardless of sex and age. In precise usage, the name is given to mature females of several large mammals, including cattle, elephants, sea lions, and whales.

Introduction

abroad did emigrate to Britain. Among the earliest immigrants were the Huguenots,① French Protestants who fled Catholic persecution in the 16th and 17th centuries. The slave trade brought Afro-Caribbeans to ports like Bristol and Liverpool in the 17th and 18th centuries. In the 19th century the growth of the British Empire brought more immigrants from Africa and Asia. Finally, from the late 1940s to the present day, there have been many immigrants from India, Africa, and the West Indies. Not only did these foreign cultures give British culture the diversity it possesses today, they also contributed many words to the English language, for example: "coffee" from Arabic, "bungalow" (a single-storey house) from Hindi, and "reggae"② from Jamaican patois.③

---

① Huguenot: any of the Protestants in France in the 16th and 17th centuries, many of whom suffered severe persecution for their faith
② reggae: a kind of popular music from the West Indies with a strong regular beat
③ patois: a spoken form of a language used by the people of a small area and different from the national standard language

Chapter 1

From the 5th Century to the 15th Century
The Anglo-Saxon and Medieval Ages

1.1 From the Anglo-Saxon Era to the Norman Conquest

Anglo-Saxon England was essentially a regional tribal society. These tribes developed into a series of Kingdoms, generally independent but often coming together to resist outside threats like the Vikings. The most powerful of these kingdoms was Wessex whose most influential king was Alfred the Great who led the resistance to Scandinavian invasions. His great-grandson Edgar (c.943 – 975) was the first king of all England and was crowned in Bath in 973 CE.

The Anglo-Saxons were pagans upon their arrival in Britain. In 597 Pope Gregory the Great sent St. Augustine to England to convert the Anglo-Saxons. The first converted king was King Ethelbert of Kent, and then within a century all England was Christianised. Churches were established and monks became the most learned section of society. Pagan mythology was gradually replaced by Christian religion.

In the early 11th century, England was conquered by the Danes,① who were defeated in 1042 by the Anglo-Saxons who eventually recaptured their domain. In 1066, the death of King Edward the Confessor left a power vacuum in the English state with several Anglo-Saxon nobles and more importantly William, Duke of Normandy, claiming the throne. William had been promised the throne by Harold of Wessex. However, Harold broke his promise and was crowned king himself. This prompted William to invade in

---

① Dane: a native or inhabitant of Denmark, or a person of Danish descent

1066, which resulted in the defeat and death of Harold at the Battle of Hastings. William was crowned as King William I, although he is better known in Britain as William the Conqueror. This is commonly called the Norman Conquest, which put an end to the period of Anglo-Saxon.

The Anglo-Saxon period was unsettled with Viking raids and conflict between the tribes and later kingdoms. These were not ideal conditions for literature to flourish. Written culture was centred in the monasteries, and therefore focused on religious works. Nevertheless, the Anglo-Saxons produced the literary masterpiece *Beowulf*.

An Introduction to *Beowulf*

A heroic poem believed to be composed between 700 and 750 CE, *Beowulf* is considered as the earliest European vernacular① epic. Consisting of over 3000 lines of poetry, it is often seen as the highest achievement of Anglo-Saxon (or Old English) literature. The writer remains unknown; it was possibly composed by more than one writer and from more than one source. In this respect it bears comparison with Homer, who is now generally considered to be a composite poet and whose works were composed over a long period of time. It was probably transmitted orally and then written down. The poem did not appear in print until 1815.

Written in the West Saxon dialect of Old English, *Beowulf* articulates both pagan and Christian elements. As a result of the uncertainty regarding the date of its composition, there has been some debate as to whether it was a pagan composition with Christian elements added later or a Christian composition with pagan elements added in order to give it historical veracity② for its audience.

Here is the plot of *Beowulf*. Hrothgar is the King of the southern Danes. Through success in battle, he has become rich and mighty. As a symbol of his power, he builds a magnificent mead-hall named Heorot, in which he and his loyal warriors can feast, drink, boast, and listen to the

---

① vernacular: the native language of the author's time and place
② veracity: the quality of being true

tales of the Anglo-Saxon bards. But the good time is short-lived. Grendel, a monster descended from Cain①(an example of a Biblical character inserted into the pagan narrative), raids the hall, snatching men and eating them in nightly raids until no one dares to sleep in the hall. The hall, once the symbol of the Danes' greatness, is now a place of shame and terror. This campaign of terror continues for twelve years, until Beowulf, a young warrior from southern Sweden, hears about Grendel. Determining to fight him, Beowulf sails to Hrothgar's lands.

Hrothgar, who knew Beowulf's father, accepts Beowulf's offer to fight Grendel and gives him a feast. That night, the warriors sleep in Heorot, with Beowulf keeping watch. Grendel arrives and eats one of the warriors, but when he reaches for Beowulf who is famous for his powerful grip, which is as strong as the grip of thirty men, Beowulf tears off the monster's arm at the shoulder. Grendel returns to the moor② to die.

Hrothgar gives a second feast to celebrate Beowulf's victory. At the feast, Hrothgar generously rewards Beowulf with treasure. That night, Grendel's mother comes to the hall from her home, which is at the bottom of a lake, seeking revenge for the death of her son. She kills a favourite warrior and adviser of Hrothgar's, and consumes him, then returns home. In the morning, the warriors follow her tracks to her lake; Beowulf enters the lake. He fights with Grendel's mother and kills her. When he sees Grendel's body, he removes the head and takes it back to Hrothgar. There is another celebration in the mead-hall with more gifts and promises of friendship. Hrothgar says he feels like Beowulf is his son, and weeps at Beowulf's departure. Beowulf and his men return to their homeland and he eventually becomes king, and rules in great prosperity and fame for fifty years.

In Beowulf's old age, a thief awakens a dragon, who in great anger burns the land, including Beowulf's mead-hall. Beowulf, knowing his death is near, decides to fight the dragon. When Beowulf and the dragon fight,

---

① Cain: the first-born son of Adam and Eve (Cain killed his younger brother Abel out of jealousy.)
② moor: a tract of open uncultivated country

all of Beowulf's men flee except his kinsman Wiglaf. With Wiglaf's help, Beowulf kills the dragon, but he himself is fatally wounded. Before he dies, Beowulf tells Wiglaf to rule after him, and to build him a burial chamber that overlooks the sea. Beowulf's body is burnt and his ashes are buried in the barrow, as he has hoped.

Beowulf belongs to a heroic tradition that is grounded in Germanic religion and mythology. The ethical values expressed relate to the Germanic code of loyalty to chief and tribe, and vengeance toward enemies.

Since *Beowulf* was first translated into modern English in 1805, there have been numerous versions published and a number of stage and film adaptations. The following excerpt is from the translation published in 2007. Its translator is the Irish Nobel Prize-winning poet Seamus Heaney who had himself studied Anglo-Saxon at Queen's University, Belfast. The excerpt comes from the first third of the poem. Heaney summarises the events in three subtitles: "Grendel strikes," "A Great warrior perishes," and "Beowulf fights with Grendel."

Beowulf

(Excerpt)

Grendel strikes

In off the moors, down through the mist bands①
God-cursed Grendel came greedily loping.②
The bane③ of the race of men roamed forth,
hunting for a prey in the high hall.
5 Under the cloud-murk④ he moved towards it
until it shone above him, a sheer keep⑤
of fortified gold. Nor was that the first time

---

① mist bands: low clouds
② loping: making long slow strides
③ bane: a source of harm or ruin
④ murk: dense fog
⑤ keep: fort

he had scouted the grounds of Hrothgar's dwelling—
although never in his life, before or since,
10   did he find harder fortune or hall-defenders.
Spurned and joyless, he journeyed on ahead
and arrived at the bawn.① The iron-braced door
turned on its hinge when his hands touched it.
Then his rage boiled over, he ripped open
15   the mouth of the building, maddening for blood,
pacing the length of the patterned floor
with his loathsome tread, while a baleful② light,
flame more than light, flared from his eyes.
He saw many men in the mansion,③ sleeping,
20   a ranked company of kinsmen and warriors
quartered together. And his glee was demonic,
picturing the mayhem:④ before morning
he would rip life from limb and devour them,
feed on their flesh; but his fate that night
25   was due to change, his days of ravening
had come to an end.

A Great warrior perishes

Mighty and canny,
Hygelac's kinsman was keenly watching
for the first move the monster would make.
30   Nor did the creature keep him waiting
but struck suddenly and started in;
he grabbed and mauled a man on his bench,
bit into his bone-lappings,⑤ bolted down his blood

---

① bawn: an enclosure of defensive walls about a farmhouse or castle
② baleful: sinister, malignant in intent
③ mansion: large house (here referring to the mead-hall)
④ mayhem: violent destruction or confusion
⑤ lappings: ligaments

and gorged on him in lumps, leaving the body
35 utterly lifeless, eaten up
hand and foot. Venturing closer,
his talon① was raised to attack Beowulf
where he lay on the bed; he was bearing in
with open claw when the alert hero's
40 comeback and armlock forestalled him utterly.

Beowulf fights with Grendel

The captain of evil discovered himself
in a handgrip harder than anything
he had ever encountered in any man
on the face of the earth. Every bone in his body
45 quailed and recoiled, but he could not escape.
He was desperate to flee to his den and hide
with the devil's litter,② for in all his days
he had never been clamped or cornered like this.
Then Hygelac's trusty retainer recalled
50 his bedtime speech, sprang to his feet
and got a firm hold. Fingers were bursting,
the monster back-tracking, the man overpowering.
The dread of the land was desperate to escape,
to take a roundabout road and flee
55 to his lair in the fens. The latching③ power
in his fingers weakened; it was the worst trip
the terror-monger had taken to Heorot.
And now the timbers trembled and sang,
a hall-session that harrowed every Dane
60 inside the stockade:④ stumbling in fury,

---

①talon: claw
②litter: a number of baby animals that one mother gives birth to at the same time
③latching: grip
④stockade: defensive wall usually of pointed lengths of wood

	the two contenders crashed through the building.

the two contenders crashed through the building.
The hall clattered and hammered, but somehow
survived the onslaught and kept standing:
it was handsomely structured, a sturdy frame
65   braced with the best of blacksmith's work
inside and out. The story goes
that as the pair struggled, mead-benches were smashed
and sprung off the floor, gold fittings and all.
Before then, no Shielding elder would believe
70   there was any power or person upon earth
capable of wrecking their horn-rigged① hall
unless the burning embrace of a fire
engulf it in flame. Then an extraordinary
wail arose, and bewildering fear
75   came over the Danes. Everyone felt it
who heard that cry as it echoed off the wall,
a God-cursed scream and strain of catastrophe,
the howl of the loser, the lament of the hell-serf②
keening his wound. He was overwhelmed,
80   manacled tight by the man who of all men
was foremost and strongest in the days of this life.

Questions for Discussion

1. What weapons does Beowulf use against Grendel in their fight?
2. *Beowulf* continues to be read more than a thousand years after it was composed. Why do you think people still love to read it? What heroes do we need in today's world?
3. Give examples of pagan and Christian elements in the excerpt.

---

① horn-rigged: decorated with animal horns
② hell-serf: servant of the Devil

1.2 From the Norman Conquest to the End of the 15th Century

After the Norman Conquest in 1066, William the Conqueror imposed the European feudal system on England and unified the country under the Norman crown. This system was based on the Crown's ownership of land and its leasing of areas to his vassals in return for loyalty and military service.

During the Norman period after 1066, the feudal system developed and then defined English society for the next five or six hundred years. The class structure, especially of the nobility, arose from the conquest. "Barons" were given land in return for providing soldiers to the king in case of war. They in turn gave land to "knights" who would also fight and provide soldiers to fulfil the barons' liabilities.① Apart from the land the king kept for himself, the church, which also held significant political power, held about a third of the land. Underneath all were the serfs and peasants, who were effectively slaves tied to the land of their overlords, paying rent for farms on which they lived and worked, or working directly for their overlord.

It should be remembered that at this point the British Isles comprised three separate countries: England and Wales, Scotland, and Ireland. After three hundred years of Norman rule, England had developed its own special characteristics, of which the most significant was the English language, now an amalgam② of Norman French and Anglo-Saxon with some words of Latin and Greek origin. However, there were political tensions in England, caused by several factors, usually made worse by a weak or young king. These sorts of political tensions had led to the overthrow of Edward Ⅱ who reigned between 1307 and 1327, which was followed by a period of about three years' rule by the Barons under Roger Mortimer (1327 – 1330). Mortimer was himself overthrown by the 17-year-old Edward Ⅲ, the son of

---

①liabilities: debts or obligations

②amalgam: a mixture of different elements

Edward II.

Considered as one of England's greatest kings, Edward III reigned for about fifty years. He started to modernize the English state, exercising greater control over his lords, and establishing the first modern English Parliament. Changes were driven by several factors including the Black Death in 1348, which had decimated the population, with 30%–60% of the population dying. This meant that the serfs gained more power as their labor was in demand. There were several peasant revolts. During the Great Revolt of 1381, clergyman John Ball's rhetoric question "When Adam delved and Eve span, who then was the gentleman?" became a popular phrase. Around this period, a new middle class of merchants, lawyers, and clerks arose while the authority of the Church was challenged by groups such as the Lollards, predecessors of the Protestant religion.

For about two hundred years after the Norman Conquest, most of the literature in England was of a religious nature, predominantly written in Latin. By the 13th and 14th centuries, however, romance literature was being introduced from France and Italy to the upper classes. These are usually tales in verse written in the vernacular rather than in Latin, and the stories deal with knightly virtues and therefore are about love, chivalry, and the effect of religion on such behaviors. In England, the stories are often concerned with the legendary King Arthur and his Knights of the Round Table. Perhaps the most famous of these Arthurian romances is that known as *Sir Gawain and the Green Knight*, published in the late 14th century. The author is now unknown and the manuscript is untitled. However, Chaucer's *The Canterbury Tales* is the literary masterpiece of this period.

Geoffrey Chaucer (c. 1343 – 1400)

Geoffrey Chaucer was born in London to a rich wine-merchant's family. This means he was a member of the emergent middle-class. He served as a minor court official all his life and married an attendant to the Queen, becoming an Esquire.① He was captured by the French during the

---

①Esquire: a nobleman who worked for and helped a knight or king

Hundred Years War, an intermittent struggle between England and France in the 14th and 15th centuries. Following his release, he served as a spy for Edward III and travelled around Europe. As a result of his travels, he was influenced by European literary traditions, and *The Canterbury Tales* demonstrates this influence.

Chaucer was so renowned that in British literary history the latter half of the 14th century, which roughly paralleled his lifetime, has been alternatively called the Age of Chaucer. His portrayal of English society as well as his contribution to the English language made him truly deserve this special honour. Since the Norman Conquest the French language had been the language of the court and the upper classes, and Latin was the language of the learned and the Church. Chaucer was taught in French when he was at school, not in English. But as with Dante (1265-1321) who chose Italian in preference to Latin for *The Divine Comedy*, Chaucer used the London dialect of his day. He greatly increased the prestige of the English language.

The Canterbury Tales begins with "The General Prologue," in which Chaucer introduces a group of pilgrims who meet at the Tabard Inn in Southwark, London. They plan to go to the shrine of St. Thomas Becket in Canterbury Cathedral, a journey of about 100 miles. These pilgrims are a cross section of 14th century society. The Knight and the Squire represent the higher levels of society; the Prioress① and the Monk stand for upper-class members of the Church; the Friar,② the Summoner, and the Pardoner are all corrupt members of the Church, with the Parson③ being perhaps the only honest representative of the Church; the Merchant, the Man of Laws, the Franklin,④ the Wife of Bath, and the Reeve represent the newly emergent middle-class; the Miller and the Host represent ordinary people.

One of the pilgrims, the unnamed narrator, claims that after the pilgrims meet, the host of the Tabard Inn suggests that, to pass the time of

---

① prioress: a woman who is in charge of a priory, which is a building where nuns live, work and pray
② friar: a member of one of several Roman Catholic religious communities of men who in the past travelled around teaching people about Christianity and lived by asking others for food
③ parson: a priest
④ franklin: a landowner of free but not noble birth in the 14th and 15th centuries in England

the journey, they each tell four stories, two on the way down and two on the way back. The format is derived from European writers such as Boccaccio(1313 – 1375), in particular from his *The Decameron*, in which ten lords and ladies tell stories to entertain themselves while avoiding the plague in Florence. It is likely that Chaucer got much of his source material from *The Decameron* as he had spent time travelling around Europe for Edward Ⅲ. Given that there are 30 pilgrims, that would make a total of 120 stories. However, *The Canterbury Tales* was unfinished on Chaucer's death, with only 24 stories being completed.

Although the framework is religious and the pilgrims are on their way to Canterbury Cathedral, they are not all the most pious of pilgrims; for some, it is like a tourist trip. The Catholic Church was a major force in medieval society, both economically rich and politically powerful. Its wealth came from collecting "tithes"① from all sections of society. The religious figures in *The Canterbury Tales*, except for the poor Priest, are presented as hypocrites.

Chaucer is often considered as the father of English poetry. Each character has a distinctive voice and justification for their story.

The Canterbury Tales have been adapted for theatre, film, and television many times and in many languages. The extract that follows is a modernized translation made by A. S. Kline in 2007.

The Canterbury Tales
The General Prologue
(Excerpt)

When that April with his showers sweet
The drought of March has pierced root deep,
And bathed each vein with liquor of such power
That engendered from it is the flower,

...

---

①tithe: a tenth part of someone's produce or income that they give or pay as a tax to the Church

5	Then people long to go on pilgrimage,
	And palmers① who seek out foreign strands,
	To far-off shrines, renowned in sundry lands;
	And specially, from every shire's end
	Of England, down to Canterbury they wend,②
10	The holy blissful martyr there to seek,
	Who had aided them when they were sick.
	It befell that in that season on a day,
	In Southwark at *The Tabard* as I lay,
	Ready to set out on my pilgrimage
15	To Canterbury with pious courage,
	There came at night to that hostelry
	Quite nine and twenty in a company
	Of sundry folk who had chanced to fall
	Into a fellowship, and pilgrims all,
20	That towards Canterbury meant to ride.
	The chambers and the stables were full wide,
	And we housed at our ease, and of the best;
	And shortly, when the sun had gone to rest,
	I had such speech with each and every one,
25	That of their fellowship I soon made one,
	Agreeing I would make an early rise,
	To take our way there, as I now advise.
	Nonetheless while I have time and space,
	Before a step more of my tale I pace,
30	It seems to me in full accord with reason,
	To tell you everything of their condition,
	Of each of them, as they appeared to me,

---

① palmer: pilgrim (It is so called because in Medieval Europe, a pilgrim bore a palm branch as a sign of his visit to the Holy Land.)
② wend: go in a specified direction

And who they were, and of what degree,①
And what apparel② they were travelling in;
35   And with a knight then I will first begin.
...
With him③ there rode a noble **PARDONER**
Of Charing Cross,④ his friend and his peer,
Returned directly from the Court of Rome.
He sang out loud: 'Come hither, love, to me!'
40   The Summoner sang a powerful bass around;
Never a trumpet of half so great a sound.
The Pardoner had hair as yellow as wax,
But smooth it hung like a hank of flax.
In clusters hung the locks he possessed,
45   With which his shoulders he overspread;
But thin they fell, in strands, one by one.
But hood, to adorn them, he wore none,
For it was trussed up in his wallet—
He thought he rode fashionably set;
50   Dishevelled, save his cap, he rode all bare.
Such bulging eyeballs had he as a hare.
A pilgrim badge had he sewn on his cap;
His wallet lay before him in his lap,
Brimful of pardons, come from Rome hotfoot.
55   A voice he had as small as has a goat;
No beard had he, nor ever looked to have;
As smooth it were as it were lately shaved—
I judge he was a gelding⑤ or a mare.
But of his craft, from Berwick unto Ware,⑥

---

①degree: social class
②apparel: clothes
③him: referring to "The Summoner"
④Charing Cross: an area of central London
⑤gelding: a castrated male horse
⑥from Berwick unto Ware: Berwick and Ware were two towns in the North (Berwick on the Scottish border) and South (Ware near London) of England.

60	Never was such another Pardoner.
	And in his bag a pillow-case was there,
	Which he claimed was Our Lady's veil;
	He said he had a fragment of the sail
	That Saint Peter used, when he skimmed
65	Upon the sea till Jesus summoned him.
	He had a cross of brass set with stones,
	And in a glass, he had pigs' bones.
	And with these relics, when he had to hand
	Some poor parson living on the land,
70	In one day he gathered in more money
	Than the parson in a month of Sundays.
	And thus with feigned flattery, his japes①
	Made people and the parson his apes.
	But to tell true from first to last,
75	He was in church a noble ecclesiast.②
	He read a lesson well or a story,
	But best of all he sang an Offertory.
	For well he knew, when that song was sung,
	He must preach and well tune his tongue
80	To win silver, as he well knew how;
	Therefore he sang more sweetly and loud.

Questions for Discussion

1. What is Chaucer's purpose in choosing such a wide-ranging group of people to take part in the pilgrimage?
2. Why is the Knight presented first and the first to tell a tale?
3. Why is the Pardoner such an offensive character?

---

① jape: a practical joke
② ecclesiast: a priest or member of the clergy (usually in the Christian church)

Chapter 2

The 16th Century
The Renaissance and the Reign of Elizabeth I

2.1 The Renaissance and the Reformation

As England entered the 15th century, significant changes were taking place in the world. As a result of the fall of Constantinople to the Turks in 1453, many Greek scholars fled to Italy, carrying with them influential books of classical philosophy, art, and science. This brought about the widespread cultural trend known as "Renaissance." The word "Renaissance" (French for "rebirth") is a fitting title to describe the re-awakened interest in science, art, and literature that swept across Europe. The Renaissance movement put an end to the Medieval Ages, when the Roman Catholic Church was the dominant power across Europe.

The Protestant Reformation was a key event in the 16th century. On October 31 of 1517, the German monk Martin Luther nailed his famous "The Ninety-five Theses on the Power and Efficacy of Indulgences," commonly known as "The Ninety-five Theses," to the door of the cathedral in Wittenberg, protesting against the sale of indulgences and certain other practices of the Catholic Church. He had no intent to break away from the church; he only meant to open up some topics for academic discussion. However, his ideas soon sparked a mass movement known as the Protestant Reformation. The Reformation had a revolutionary influence on the social, political, and economic structure of Europe in the 16th century.

The central watchword of the Renaissance was "Humanism." Humanism was not necessarily incompatible with a belief in God; it sought to place humankind rather than God at the centre of existence. Mankind should seek happiness in earthly existence rather than sacrifice it for a life after death. By focusing on the individual, humanism points the way away from a reliance on an authority figure (say, the Pope) and gives the individual the right to read and interpret the Bible. More importantly, the idea of individual achievement was of particular relevance to the Protestant Reformation since one of its beliefs was that through hard work and effort an individual could rise through society, and that worldly success could be seen as a sign of God's approval of not just such ambition but also the very person. The growth of education and other social changes, together with the development of proto-capitalist societies in the Protestant states of northern Europe, particularly in England, were a direct result of humanism as articulated through the Reformation. It was no coincidence that many of what are now the oldest and most prestigious educational institutions in England, such as many of the colleges of Oxford and Cambridge universities, and schools such as Eton and the King's School, were founded during this period.

2.2　The Rise of Elizabeth Ⅰ to Sovereignty

Before Queen Elizabeth Ⅰ's reign (1558 – 1603), England underwent a period of upheaval both at home and abroad. Against the background of the Hundred Years War between England and France, there were a number of dynastic struggles for the English throne culminating in the Wars of the Roses between the House of York and the House of Lancaster, which ended in 1485 with the victory of Henry, Duke of Richmond, a member of the Lancastrian faction. Richmond declared himself King Henry Ⅶ and after marrying a daughter of the Yorkist family established the Tudor dynasty, uniting the Red Rose (the symbol of Lancaster) with the Yorkist White Rose. The Tudor period (1485 – 1603) saw the development of England from a small island country into a world power and into a modern, non-feudal, unified state. Henry Ⅶ curbed① the military power of the noble

---

①curb: to restrain or control

families, dealt with early resistance to his rule, and built up the country's wealth through his economic policies. He made alliances with Spain and Scotland through the marriages of his son Prince Henry (later Henry Ⅷ) to Catherine of Aragon and his daughter Princess Margaret to the King of Scotland. Although England, Wales, and Ireland were effectively one country under the rule of the English crown (king or queen), Scotland was a separate country until the accession① of King James Ⅰ of England (who was also King James Ⅵ of Scotland) in 1603, and even then, only became fully integrated into what became known as the United Kingdom in 1707.

Most significant for the future of Britain was Henry Ⅷ's desire to produce a male heir and it was his attempt to divorce Catherine of Aragon that led to his split with the Roman Catholic Church and the establishment of the Church of England (also known as the Anglican Church), with himself as its head. Although Henry Ⅷ was not an extreme Protestant, the Anglican Church developed into the largest single Protestant church in Europe. Though he was married six times, Henry Ⅷ produced only one son, the sickly Edward (1537 – 1553), and two daughters, Mary (1516 – 1558) by Catherine of Aragon and Elizabeth (1533 – 1603) by Anne Boleyn, for whom he divorced Catherine.

His son Edward, like Elizabeth, was raised a Protestant. Edward, at the age of nine, became King Edward Ⅵ on his father's death. Though Edward Ⅵ died only six years later, it was during these six years that he and his advisers laid the foundations for England to become a Protestant country despite the efforts of Mary, his half-sister, who succeeded him as queen on his premature death. Queen Mary Ⅰ (more usually known as Mary Tudor or by her Protestant opponents as "Bloody Mary") was a fervent Catholic. She used repressive measures to try to restore England to the Catholic faith. This led to widespread opposition to her rule. The opposition grew much fiercer when she married King Philip Ⅱ of Spain, because people feared that England would become a Spanish province. She died childless and was

---

①accession: the attainment or acquisition of a position of rank or power, typically that of monarch or president

succeeded by her half-sister, Elizabeth, who has often been regarded as England's greatest ever ruler.

Queen Elizabeth I, often known as "The Virgin Queen" or in her lifetime as "Gloriana," never married although she was courted by several foreign kings and princes as well as some English aristocrats. Guided by her main advisors, she consolidated the religious authority of the Church of England, becoming its head (a position that all English and British kings and queens since have held, up to and including the present King Charles III). She also encouraged the growth of what would become the first British Empire focused on North America; she enhanced foreign trade and friendly relations with several Muslim states which sent ambassadors to her court. She did not see her gender as a handicap to effective rule. Rather, she often referred to herself as a "prince." One of her most famous speeches, made just before the defeat of the Spanish attempt to invade England (the Spanish Armada[①]), included the following statement:

I know I have the body but of a weak and feeble woman, but I have the heart and stomach of a king, and of a King of England too.

In addition to political, military, and economic successes, her reign saw the flowering of English theatre and the growth of humanism in its Protestant form.

2.3 Renaissance Literature

Between the death of Chaucer in 1400 and the accession of Queen Elizabeth I in 1558, there were few major developments in English literature. Although ballads recounting the lives and adventures of legendary figures from British history and stories of the mythical King Arthur and his Knights of the Round Table remained popular during this period, it was in the field of drama that the most important developments took place. Medieval

---

[①] the Spanish Armada: the enormous 130-ship naval fleet dispatched by Spain in 1588 as part of a planned invasion of England

English drama took two main forms: Miracle (or Mystery) Plays and Morality Plays. Miracle Plays were based on the Bible and other religious stories; the form probably originated with priests acting out Bible stories for an illiterate audience on important religious holidays. The Miracle Plays lasted well into the last years of the 16th century when Shakespeare and his contemporaries were writing.

Morality Plays existed in parallel with the Miracle Plays but dealt with more general moral lessons. They were acted by professionals who moved around the country in troupes,① going from place to place performing at markets, fairs, and carnivals,② etc. In the course of time, many of the troupes reformed themselves to perform new plays and became part of the structure that developed into Renaissance theatre in England.

During the 16th century, England saw the development of a rich theatrical tradition now based more in theatre buildings in London than on touring companies. The first modern theatre building in England was The Theatre built in 1576 near Bishopsgate in London. In the next twenty-five years at least six more theatres were built just outside the walls of the City of London, of which the most famous was The Globe (1599) in Southwark, south of the river Thames. The theatres were built outside the city walls because the City was controlled by Puritans who had religious objections to theatrical performances and the like.

There was a great demand for new plays, and a whole playwriting industry established itself in London. Few plays were published in print, with the result that many scripts have been lost and the names of lesser-known writers have been forgotten. The two most important playwrights were Christopher Marlowe and William Shakespeare.

Christopher Marlowe (1564 – 1593)

Christopher Marlowe was born in Canterbury, Kent, England. After graduating from Cambridge at the age of twenty, Marlowe went to London

---

①troupe: a group of performers such as singers or dancers who work and travel together
②carnival: an instance of merrymaking, feasting, or masquerading

to begin a career as a playwright. His life is shrouded in mystery. The traditional story about his death is that he was stabbed to death in a fight in a bar, supposedly over the bill, although some historians believe he was killed by a secret agent of the government for his active preaching of atheism① or for some other political reason.

All Marlowe's seven plays are tragedies, and they were all written in his twenties, when he had the reputation of being the most exciting playwright in London. His first play *Tamburlaine the Great* (1587) is about Timur② the Tartar. Beginning his career as a shepherd chief, Timur rebels and triumphs over the Persian king. Intoxicated by his success, he sweeps like a tempest over the East. Seated on his chariot drawn by captive kings, with a caged emperor before him, he boasts his power. Then he plans to attack the Ming Emperor but is afflicted with disease. He raves against the gods and would overcome them as he has overthrown earthly rulers. Tamburlaine represents the Renaissance desire for infinite power and authority. Arguably, *The Tragic History of Doctor Faustus* (1604) is his best-known play, which was adapted from a popular old German legend. With its emphasis on the power and ability of the individual, *The Tragic History of Doctor Faustus* ideally reflects the cultural changes of the Renaissance.

Faustus is a man who has gained academic success through his own efforts. Tired with studying the four main subjects of academic learning of his time, namely theology, philosophy, law, and medicine, he resolves to begin a study of witchcraft. Faustus conjures up Mephistopheles, a servant of the devil, and signs a contract for twenty-four years of unlimited powers during which Mephistopheles will act as his servant; then, at the end of the time Faustus's soul will be taken into Hell. The remainder of the play follows Faustus's adventures such as making a fool of the Pope in Rome and meeting with the most beautiful women of history including Helen of Troy.

---

① atheism: the belief that God does not exist
② Timur: Timur (1336 – 1405), also spelled Timour, chiefly remembered for his conquests over vast stretches of land from India and Russia to the Mediterranean Sea and for the cultural achievements of his dynasty

Throughout the play, a Good Angel tries to get Faustus to repent and give up his ways while a Bad Angel encourages this behaviour. He fails to repent and is taken into Hell.

The Tragic History of Doctor Faustus
Scene I
(Excerpt)

Chorus: ...
Only this, gentles,①—we must now perform
The form of Faustus' fortunes, good or bad:
And now to patient judgments we appeal,
And speak for Faustus in his infancy.
5   Now is he born of parents base of stock,②
In Germany, within a town call'd Rhodes:
At riper years, to Wittenberg he went,
Whereas his kinsmen chiefly brought him up.
So much he profits in divinity,
10   That shortly he was grac'd with doctor's name,
Excelling all, and sweetly can dispute
In the heavenly matters of theology;
Till swol'n with cunning, of a self-conceit,
His waxen wings did mount above his reach,
15   And, melting, heavens conspir'd his overthrow;
For, falling to a devilish exercise,
And glutted③ now with learning's golden gifts,
He surfeits upon cursed necromancy;④
Nothing so sweet as magic is to him,

---

① gentles: good people
② base of stock: lower class
③ glutted: overfull
④ necromancy: a form of magic involving communication with the dead

20   Which he prefers before his chiefest bliss:①

And this the man that in his study sits.

[Exit.]

FAUSTUS discovered in his study.

Faustus: Settle thy studies, Faustus, and begin

To sound the depth of that thou wilt profess:

Having commenc'd, be a divine in show,

25   Yet level at the end of every art,

And live and die in Aristotle's works.

Sweet Analytics, 'tis thou hast ravish'd me!

*Bene disserere est finis logices.*②

Is, to dispute well, logic's chiefest end?

30   Affords this art no greater miracle?

Then read no more; thou hast attain'd that end:

A greater subject fitteth Faustus' wit:

Bid Economy farewell, and Galen③ come:

Be a physician, Faustus; heap up gold,

35   And be eterniz'd for some wondrous cure:

Summum bonum medicinoe sanitas,④

The end of physic is our body's health.

Why, Faustus, hast thou not attain'd that end?

Are not thy bills⑤ hung up as monuments,

40   Whereby whole cities have escap'd the plague,

And thousand desperate maladies been cur'd?

Yet art thou still but Faustus, and a man.

Couldst thou make men to live eternally,

---

① bliss: supreme happiness

② *Bene...logices*: [Latin] The purpose of logic is to argue well.

③ Galen: Galen (c. 129 – c. 216) was Greek physician, writer, and philosopher who exercised a dominant influence on medical theory and practice in Europe from the Middle Ages until the mid-17th century.

④ *Summum...sanitas*: [Latin] The purpose of medicine is health.

⑤ bills: prescriptions

           Or, being dead, raise them to life again,
45   Then this profession we're to be esteem'd.
           physic,① farewell! Where is Justinian?②
           ...
           If we say that we have no sin, we deceive ourselves,
             and there is no truth in us.
           Why, then, belike③ we must sin, and so consequently die:
50   Ay, we must die an everlasting death.
           What doctrine call you this, *Che sera, sera*,④
           What will be, shall be? Divinity,⑤ adieu!⑥
           These metaphysics⑦ of magicians,
           And necromantic books are heavenly;
55   Lines, circles, scenes, letters, and characters;
           Ay, these are those that Faustus most desires.
           O, what a world of profit and delight,
           Of power, of honour, and omnipotence,
           Is promis'd to the studious artizan!
60   All things that move between the quiet poles
           Shall be at my command: emperors and kings
           Are but obeyed in their several provinces;⑧
           But his dominion that exceeds in this,
           Stretcheth as far as doth the mind of man;
65   A sound magician is a demigod:
           Here tire, my brains, to gain a deity.⑨

---

① physic: medicine
② Justinian: Justinian Ⅰ (483-565) was Byzantine emperor who completely reformed Roman law.
③ belike: therefore
④ *Che sera, sera*: [Spanish] What will be, will be.
⑤ divinity: theology
⑥ adieu: [French] goodbye
⑦ metaphysics: philosophy that deals with the first principles of things and the nature of reality
⑧ provinces: areas that they rule
⑨ gain a deity: become a god

> Questions for Discussion
>
> 1. Why do you think Marlowe chooses the four particular areas of study for Faustus to assess and reject?
> 2. What significance is the play's location in Germany in general and Wittenberg in particular to the religious debates of the period?
> 3. Though he was warned against studying witchcraft, Doctor Faustus stubbornly pursued it, for which he lost his soul. According to your understanding, what knowledge can be identified as evil knowledge? Please name a couple of examples.

William Shakespeare (1564 – 1616)

Unlike Marlowe who went straight to London after Cambridge and carried on writing for the theatre there, William Shakespeare did not get his first mention on the London theatre scene until in 1592. Born and raised in Stratford-upon-Avon, Shakespeare left his hometown in 1585. It has been speculated that he had to leave as a result of a criminal charge of killing a local landowner's deer and that in these "lost years" he had served as a schoolmaster or as a soldier. It has also been suggested that he started his connection with theatre in London as a "horse-holder," a sort of Elizabethan car-park attendant. All of these stories are however mostly guesswork—his personal life remains shrouded in mystery.

Shakespeare's career as an actor and playwright stretched for more than twenty years. Many of his plays were popular, and quite a number of them were published in his lifetime. In all, he is known to have created at least thirty-seven plays, which can be divided into three main genres: tragedy, comedy, and history. Undoubtedly, this categorization is too straightforward, because the histories blur comedy and tragedy, while the comedies contain elements of tragedy, and tragedies, comedy. Some of Shakespeare's most famous plays are tragedies. This genre was extremely popular with Elizabethan theatre-goers, and as a conventional rule, a play of tragedy follows the rise and fall of a powerful nobleman. All of Shakespeare's tragic protagonists have a fatal flaw that propels them towards their bloody end. His popular tragedies include *Hamlet* (1603), *King Lear* (1608), and *Macbeth* (1623).

Shakespeare's comedy was driven by language and complex plots involving mistaken identity. A good rule of thumb① is if a character disguises himself/herself as a member of the opposite sex. His popular comedies include *Much Ado About Nothing* (1600) and *The Merchant of Venice* (1600), although the latter is sometimes defined as a tragi-comedy.

Shakespeare used his history plays to make social and political commentary. Therefore, they are not historically accurate in the same way we would expect in a modern historical drama. He drew from a range of historical sources and set most of his history plays during the Hundred Years' War with France. His popular history dramas include *Henry* Ⅴ (1597) and *Richard* Ⅲ (1600).

Hamlet is not only Shakespeare's most popular tragedy but also the most discussed. It is a product both of the Reformation and of the Humanism of the late Renaissance. Shakespeare voices his praise of the noble quality of Prince Hamlet as a representative of humanist thinking; he also expresses Hamlet's disillusionment with the corrupt and degenerate② society in which he lives. Hamlet's revenge is not just a personal matter; his bigger concern is the injustice, conspiracy, and betrayal in the society. His father, the old king, is murdered by his uncle who then succeeds to the crown and becomes the new king, marrying Hamlet's mother immediately after his father's death. His mother's marriage to his uncle is the first blow Hamlet receives because he has always regarded her as a virtuous woman. Then his former friends Rosencrantz and Guildenstern are despatched by the new king to spy on him. This is the second blow. Finally his girlfriend Ophelia is made a tool to find out whether or not he is really mad. This is something beyond his endurance. These incidents reveal that man is not so good as he has imagined; thus he is constantly concerned about appearance and reality and has difficulties with religious doubts directly influenced by

---

①rule of thumb: a broadly accurate guide or principle, based on experience or practice rather than theory
②degenerate: debased

humanist thought.

Besides his plays and two long poems, Shakespeare also wrote sonnets, 154 altogether in number, among which "Sonnet 18" is the most well-known. It describes the youthful beauty of a friend.

Sonnet 18

Shall I compare thee to a summer's day?
Thou art more lovely and more temperate:
Rough winds do shake the darling buds of May,
And summer's lease hath all too short a date;
5 Sometime too hot the eye of heaven shines,
And often is his gold complexion dimm'd;
And every fair from fair sometime declines,
By chance or nature's changing course untrimm'd;①
But thy eternal summer shall not fade,
10 Nor lose possession of that fair thou ow'st;
Nor shall death brag thou wander'st in his shade,
When in eternal lines to time thou grow'st:
So long as men can breathe or eyes can see,
So long lives this, and this gives life to thee.

Questions for Discussion

1. Generally speaking, what can be inferred about England's summer weather? What are some of the downsides of a summer's day?
2. According to the poem, what words can be used to describe the addressee?
3. How does the speaker guarantee that the addressee's "eternal summer shall not fade"?

---

① untrimmed: not made neat by cutting or clipping

Hamlet

Act II Scene 2
(Excerpt)

Hamlet: (*To Rosencrantz and Guildenstern*) What a piece of work is a man! How noble in reason! How infinite in faculty!① In form and moving how express and admirable! In action how like an angel! In apprehension how like a god! The beauty of the world! The paragon② of animals! And yet, to me, what is this quintessence③ of dust? Man delights not me: no, nor woman neither, though by your smiling you seem to say so.

Act III Scene 1
(Excerpt)

    Hamlet: To be, or not to be: that is the question:
    Whether 'tis nobler in the mind to suffer
    The slings④ and arrows of outrageous fortune,
    Or to take arms against a sea of troubles,
5   And by opposing end them? To die: to sleep;
    No more; and by a sleep to say we end
    The heart-ache and the thousand natural shocks
    That flesh is heir to, 'tis a consummation⑤
    Devoutly to be wish'd. To die, to sleep;
10   To sleep: perchance to dream: ay, there's the rub;
    For in that sleep of death what dreams may come
    When we have shuffled off this mortal coil,⑥
    Must give us pause: there's the respect

---

① faculty: an inherent mental or physical power
② paragon: a person or thing regarded as a perfect example or a particular quality
③ quintessence: most perfect example
④ slings: weapons that throw stones
⑤ consummation: ending or completion
⑥ mortal coil: earthly life

Chapter 2 The 16th Century — The Renaissance and the Reign of Elizabeth I

      That makes calamity of so long life;
15   For who would bear the whips and scorns of time,
      The oppressor's wrong, the proud man's contumely,①
      The pangs of despised love, the law's delay,
      The insolence of office and the spurns
      That patient merit of the unworthy takes,
20   When he himself might his quietus② make
      With a bare bodkin?③ who would fardels④ bear,
      To grunt and sweat under a weary life,
      But that the dread of something after death,
      The undiscover'd country from whose bourn⑤
25   No traveller returns, puzzles the will
      And makes us rather bear those ills we have
      Than fly to others that we know not of?
      Thus conscience does make cowards of us all;
      And thus the native hue of resolution
30   Is sicklied o'er with the pale cast of thought,
      And enterprises of great pith and moment
      With this regard their currents turn awry,⑥
      And lose the name of action.—Soft you now!
      The fair Ophelia! Nymph,⑦ in thy orisons⑧
35   Be all my sins remember'd.

---

① contumely: abuse or insult
② quietus: peaceful end, i.e. death
③ bodkin: long, sharp, narrow needle like a dagger
④ fardel: heavy baggage, burden
⑤ bourn: boundary
⑥ turn awry: turn away from the usual or expected course
⑦ Nymph: a beautiful girl (from the Greek for a beautiful fairy)
⑧ orisons: prayers

Questions for Discussion

1. What does Hamlet say concerning the question "What a piece of work is a man"?
2. How do the two extracts relate to humanism of the English Renaissance?
3. Hamlet vows to take revenge but hesitates a lot. T. S. Eliot suggests that Hamlet is a man incapable of taking action. What hinders him in taking action? What's your view regarding a person's thinking a lot before taking action?

Chapter 3

The 17th Century
The Bourgeois Revolution and the Early Enlightenment

3.1 The Bourgeois Revolution

The 17th century was one of the most extraordinary centuries in English political and intellectual history. It saw the biggest upheaval in British society since the Norman Conquest. It was a century in which conflicts between Crown and Parliament and the overlapping conflicts between Protestants, Anglicans, and Catholics swirled into civil war in the 1640s.

In 1600 England was still under the rule of Elizabeth Ⅰ, a Tudor, but on her death only three years later, James Ⅵ of Scotland, a Stuart, united England and Scotland under his personal rule as James Ⅰ. Slightly over a hundred years later, the English Parliament had established its authority over the crown and in 1707, after the Scottish parliament voted to abolish itself, England and Scotland were officially united as Great Britain. The country was well on its way to becoming the constitutional monarchy it is today.

The long reign of Elizabeth and that of her chosen successor James Ⅰ had established England, Scotland, and Wales as Protestant countries, although Ireland, with the exception of Ulster (what is now Northern Ireland), was overwhelmingly Roman Catholic, a fact that led to sporadic① rebellions until they attained independence in the 1920s. It is worth mentioning that James's successor Charles I, who reigned from 1625 to 1649, though publicly a Protestant, was married to a Catholic and privately

---

① sporadic: happening only occasionally

followed her faith, which was a contributory factor to the outbreak of the English Civil Wars (1642 – 1651) and his subsequent deposal and execution in 1649.

However, more important were the demands made by the emergent bourgeoisie for political power. As Marx has pointed out, when those holding economic power do not control the political structure, then a crisis occurs which will lead to revolution. The English Civil Wars were Britain's bourgeois revolution in nature, the first in the world, about 140 years ahead of the French Revolution. Charles Ⅰ, like most monarchs in Europe, believed in the "Divine Right of Kings" which he thought allowed him to pass laws and levy taxes as he wished. This brought him into conflict with the English and Scottish Parliaments which, although not fully democratic, elected predominantly bourgeois representatives who held economic power. Charles Ⅰ was also opposed by the City of London, which was the financial powerhouse that it has remained to this day. When he attempted to raise taxes, Parliament rebelled and was therefore dissolved by Charles, who attempted to rule alone. This led to the English Civil Wars.

After some initial failures on the battlefield, the Parliamentary forces (popularly known as "Roundheads" on account of their hairstyles) were reorganised by Oliver Cromwell as the New Model Army, which comprehensively defeated the "Cavaliers" (the nickname for the Royalists). The New Model Army became the basis of the modern British Army. Charles was charged with and convicted of treason and was executed to be replaced by The Commonwealth (essentially a republic) under Cromwell as Lord Protector (president).

Following Cromwell's death in 1658, Parliament in 1660 invited the late king's elder son, also called Charles, to take the throne as King Charles Ⅱ, in what became known as the Restoration, on condition that he agreed that political power would remain with Parliament. He died childless and was succeeded by his brother James Ⅱ, who was secretly a Catholic and also believed in Divine Right of Kings. After his wife gave birth to a son, Parliament, in fear of a return to Catholicism, in 1688 deposed and exiled James Ⅱ and replaced him with his sister Mary and her husband William of

Orange, the ruler of the Netherlands, as joint rulers in what became known as Glorious Revolution. William and Mary accepted the authority of Parliament which passed laws (which remain in force to this day) to prevent a Catholic becoming king or queen of Britain and therefore the Protestant ascendancy and a constitutional monarchy were finally firmly established.

3.2 The Early Enlightenment

The Bourgeois Revolution was inspired and made possible by "The Enlightenment," which could be viewed as continuation of the Renaissance. Enlightenment thinking encouraged rational scientific inquiry, humanitarian tolerance, and the idea of universal human rights, thus the Enlightenment was an intellectual liberation which emancipated human beings from the self-incurred immaturity. Britain took a leading role in the Enlightenment, with Newton being undoubtedly the leader in science, while Bacon and Locke being the leaders in philosophy. These Enlightenment thinkers emphasised the power of human reason and claimed that human beings not only need—but also can—use human reason to clear away ancient superstition, prejudice, dogma, and injustice. In religion, they rejected revealed religion and were in favor of "Deism" (Natural Religion): they deduced the existence of a supreme being from the construction of the universe rather than from the Bible. They argued that the universe was an orderly system and by the application of reason humanity could comprehend its laws. Because the world seemed more comprehensible, people paid less attention to revealed religion.

3.3 Representative Writers and Works

In literature, the early 17th century was dominated by poetry and drama, particularly the work of Shakespeare. Following his death in 1616, Shakespeare became more widely accessible due to the efforts of his fellow playwright Ben Jonson, who had Shakespeare's collected works published: *The First Folios* of 1623 are the basis of all subsequent editions of

Shakespeare's plays. John Milton's epic poem *Paradise Lost* (1667) established the author as one of the greatest poets in the world. Nevertheless, it has been almost universally agreed that the greatest single work of literature was *The King James Bible* of 1611, which, irrespective of① religious belief, can be read as a major work of literature.

What is worth mentioning is that essays on philosophy and other subjects became more widely circulated, with Francis Bacon being a worldwide renowned essayist, as well as Britain's first great philosopher of the 17th century. Thomas Hobbes and John Locke, the second and third great philosophers of the century, wrote expressing their opposing philosophies that underpinned② the Bourgeois revolution.

King James Bible

It is true that the Bible has been read by Christians for religious messages, but overall speaking, it is an account of the birth and growth of the Hebrew people (also known as the people of Israel), about the people's later decline and ill fortune as well as their hopes for a better life during a long-continued time of trouble. Along this central storyline, we find in the Bible Israel's literary production of various genres, including myths, historical narratives, proverbs, poetry, and personal stories. The word "Bible" itself is derived from the Greek word *biblia*, which simply means "books."

The Reformation and Renaissance played a decisive role in the Bible's translation into European vernacular languages, with the most well-known example being Martin Luther's translation of the Bible from the original Greek and Latin into German. Completed in 1534, it became the first real literary work in modern German prose, and it created the vocabulary of literary German.

In 1604, King James Ⅰ called a conference to consider some petitions of the Puritans. The outcome of this conference was far different from all expectations. The final result was the King James Bible of 1611. Forty-

---

①irrespective of: regardless of, in spite of
②underpin: support or form the basis of something.

seven scholars participated in the translation work under the leadership of Archbishop Lancelot Andrews.

The King James Bible has been widely celebrated as one of the major literary accomplishments of early modern England. British critic T.B. Macaulay (1800 – 1859) claimed: "Suppose all the things written in English were destroyed except the English Bible, this book would be good enough to display all the beauty and power in English to us."

What follows is the Hebrew creation myth as appears in the King James Bible's opening book named Genesis. ①

Genesis

Chapter 1

(Excerpt)

¹ In the beginning God created the heaven and the earth.

² And the earth was without form, and void; and darkness was upon the face of the deep. And the Spirit of God moved upon the face of the waters.

³ And God said, Let there be light: and there was light.

⁴ And God saw the light, that it was good: and God divided the light from the darkness.

⁵ And God called the light Day, and the darkness he called Night. And the evening and the morning were the first day.

⁶ And God said, Let there be a firmament② in the midst of the waters, and let it divide the waters from the waters.

⁷ And God made the firmament, and divided the waters which were under the firmament from the waters which were above the firmament: and it was so.

⁸ And God called the firmament Heaven. And the evening and the morning were the second day.

⁹ And God said, Let the waters under the heaven be gathered together unto one place, and let the dry land appear: and it was so.

---

①Genesis: meaning "beginning" or "origin", Genesis is the first book of the Bible.
②firmament: the sky

¹⁰ And God called the dry land Earth; and the gathering together of the waters called he Seas: and God saw that it was good.

¹¹ And God said, Let the earth bring forth grass, the herb yielding seed, and the fruit tree yielding fruit after his kind, whose seed is in itself, upon the earth: and it was so....

¹⁶ And God made two great lights; the greater light to rule the day, and the lesser light to rule the night: he made the stars also....

²⁰ And God said, Let the waters bring forth abundantly the moving creature that hath life, and fowl that may fly above the earth in the open firmament of heaven.

²¹ And God created great whales, and every living creature that moveth, which the waters brought forth abundantly, after their kind, and every winged fowl after his kind: and God saw that it was good.

²² And God blessed them, saying, Be fruitful, and multiply, and fill the waters in the seas, and let fowl multiply in the earth.

²³ And the evening and the morning were the fifth day.

²⁴ And God said, Let the earth bring forth the living creature after his kind, cattle, and creeping thing, and beast of the earth after his kind: and it was so....

²⁶ And God said, Let us make man in our image, after our likeness: and let them have dominion over the fish of the sea, and over the fowl of the air, and over the cattle, and over all the earth, and over every creeping thing that creepeth upon the earth.

²⁷ So God created man in his own image, in the image of God created he him; male and female created he them.

²⁸ And God blessed them, and God said unto them, Be fruitful, and multiply, and replenish① the earth, and subdue it: and have dominion over the fish of the sea, and over the fowl of the air, and over every living thing that moveth upon the earth....

³¹ And God saw every thing that he had made, and, behold, it was very good. And the evening and the morning were the sixth day.

---

① replenish: fill (something) up again

Chapter 2
(Excerpt)

¹ Thus the heavens and the earth were finished, and all the host① of them.

² And on the seventh day God ended his work which he had made; and he rested on the seventh day from all his work which he had made.

³ And God blessed the seventh day, and sanctified② it: because that in it he had rested from all his work which God created and made....

⁷ And the Lord God formed man of the dust of the ground, and breathed into his nostrils the breath of life; and man became a living soul.

⁸ And the Lord God planted a garden eastward in Eden; and there he put the man whom he had formed....

¹⁵ And the Lord God took the man, and put him into the garden of Eden to dress it and to keep it.

¹⁶ And the Lord God commanded the man, saying, Of every tree of the garden thou mayest freely eat:

¹⁷ But of the tree of the knowledge of good and evil, thou shalt not eat of it: for in the day that thou eatest thereof thou shalt surely die.

¹⁸ And the Lord God said, It is not good that the man should be alone; I will make him an help meet for him.

¹⁹ And out of the ground the Lord God formed every beast of the field, and every fowl of the air; and brought them unto Adam to see what he would call them: and whatsoever Adam called every living creature, that was the name thereof.

²⁰ And Adam gave names to all cattle, and to the fowl of the air, and to every beast of the field; but for Adam there was not found an help meet for him.

²¹ And the Lord God caused a deep sleep to fall upon Adam, and he slept: and he took one of his ribs, and closed up the flesh instead thereof;

²² And the rib, which the Lord God had taken from man, made he a

---

① host: a great number or multitude
② sanctify: make (something) holy

woman, and brought her unto the man.

²³ And Adam said, This is now bone of my bones, and flesh of my flesh: she shall be called Woman, because she was taken out of Man.

²⁴ Therefore shall a man leave his father and his mother, and shall cleave unto his wife:① and they shall be one flesh....

Questions for Discussion

1. According to Chapter 1, what was the first thing God created and how did God create everything? What did God instruct man to do with the fish of the sea and the fowl of the air and every living creature that moves on the ground?
2. It has been widely agreed by literary theorists that creation myths, though being fictional tales, address questions deeply meaningful to the society and reveal people's central worldview. What central worldview of the Hebrew people can be inferred?
3. Please compare Hebrew creation myth with Chinese mythological story about how Pan Gu(盘古) and Nüwa(女娲) create the world and human beings.

Francis Bacon (1561 – 1626)

Francis Bacon was born in London, the son of a civil servant in Queen Elizabeth's court. Trained as a lawyer, Bacon held a series of government posts and was knighted in 1603. As a supporter of King James I, he rose to the position of Lord Chancellor of England, the highest honour in the British legal profession. Yet Bacon was later convicted of taking bribes to support his extravagant lifestyle. After resigning in disgrace, Bacon pursued his scholarly interests.

Bacon contributed to such fields as philosophy, biology, physics, chemistry,

---

① cleave unto sb.: stick close to sb.

and architecture. As one of the developers of the modern scientific method, Bacon introduced many concepts and methods used today, such as observation, hypothesis, and inductive reasoning.① He also developed the concept of a scientific research establishment that would work collaboratively in methodical fashion to give material benefits to humankind.

At the age of sixty-five, Bacon decided to test the powers of refrigeration and carried a dead chicken out into the snow to freeze it. He died from bronchitis② a few days later.

Bacon will be lastingly remembered for his concise, beautiful, and forceful essays such as "Of Truth," "Of Friendship," "Of Riches," "Of High Place," and "Of Studies," to name but a few.

Of Studies

(Excerpt)

Studies serve for delight, for ornament, and for ability. Their chief use for delight is in privateness and retiring; for ornament, is in discourse;③ and for ability, is in the judgment and disposition of business. For expert men can execute, and perhaps judge of particulars, one by one; but the general counsels, and the plots and marshalling of affairs, come best from those that are learned. To spend too much time in studies is sloth; to use them too much for ornament, is affectation; to make judgment wholly by their rules, is the humour④ of a scholar. They perfect nature, and are perfected by experience: for natural abilities are like natural plants, that need pruning,⑤ by study; and studies themselves do give forth directions too much at large, except they be bounded in by experience. Crafty men contemn studies, simple⑥ men admire them and wise men use them; for they

---

① inductive reasoning: a type of reasoning that involves drawing a general conclusion from a set of specific observations
② bronchitis: an infection of the main airways of the lungs (bronchi), causing them to become irritated and inflamed
③ discourse: discussion, speech
④ humor: attitude, inclination
⑤ prune: to cut back in order to encourage growth
⑥ simple: uneducated

teach not their own use; but that is a wisdom without them, and above them, won by observation. Read not to contradict and confute,① nor to believe and take for granted, nor to find talk and discourse, but to weigh and consider. Some books are to be tasted, others to be swallowed, and some few to be chewed and digested; that is, some books are to be read only in parts; others to be read, but not curiously;② and some few to be read wholly, and with diligence and attention. Some books also may be read by deputy,③ and extracts made of them by others; but that would be only in the less important arguments, and the meaner sort of books, else distilled books are like common distilled waters, flashy things. Reading maketh a full man; conference④ a ready man; and writing an exact man. And therefore, if a man write little, he had need have a great memory; if he confer little, he had need have a present wit; and if he read little, he had need have much cunning, to seem to know that he doth not. Histories make men wise; poets witty; the mathematics subtle; natural philosophy⑤ deep; moral grave; logic and rhetoric able to contend. *Abeunt studia in mores*.⑥ Nay, there is no stond⑦ or impediment⑧ in the wit but may be wrought out by fit studies; like as diseases of the body may have appropriate exercises. Bowling is good for the stone⑨ and reins, shooting for the lungs and breast, gentle walking for the stomach, riding for the head, and the like. So if a man's wit be wandering, let him study the mathematics; for in demonstrations, if his wit be called away never so little, he must begin again. If his wit be not apt to distinguish or find differences, let him study the Schoolmen,⑩ for they are

---

① confute: to argue against
② curiously: with much attention
③ deputy: a person appointed to act for another
④ conference: discussion with others
⑤ natural philosophy: natural science, especially physical science
⑥ *Abeunt studia in mores*: [Latin] Studies pass into and influence manners.
⑦ stond: dialectal English variant of "stand," meaning "blockage"
⑧ impediment: hindrance or obstruction in doing something
⑨ stone: kidney or gall stones
⑩ Schoolmen: scholastic philosophers

cymini sectores.① If he be not apt to beat over matters, and to call up one thing to prove and illustrate another, let him study the lawyers' cases. So every defect of the mind may have a special receipt.

Questions for Discussion

1. What benefits does Bacon list of studying history, poetry, mathematics, philosophy, logic, and rhetoric? Please summarize in your own words.
2. What analogy, or comparison, does Bacon make between different kinds of study and different kinds of physical exercise? Restate his argument in your own words.
3. In your opinion, how valid is Bacon's statement that books should be either tasted, swallowed, or chewed and digested? Explain your argument.
4. Did Bacon change your opinion of studies? Why or why not?

Thomas Hobbes (1588 – 1679)

Thomas Hobbes is best known for his political philosophy, especially as articulated in his masterpiece *Leviathan*②(1651).

Hobbes was born in Westport, Wiltshire, in southern England. His father was a quick-tempered vicar of a local parish church. Disgraced after engaging in a brawl at his own church door, he disappeared and abandoned his three children to the care of his brother, a well-to-do tradesman and alderman. After graduating from Oxford, Hobbes served as tutor and secretary to various noblemen, including several members of the Cavendish family. Through his association with the aristocrats, Hobbes entered circles where the activities of the king, members of Parliament, and other wealthy landowners were discussed, which enabled him to observe the influence and

---

① *cymini sectores*: "splitters of hairs," meaning over-precise in their definitions and answers
② Leviathan: Leviathan is presented in the Old Testament of the Bible as a mighty sea monster.

structures of power and government.

Hobbes argues that war is the natural state of humankind and that only a strong government united around a great supreme ruler, one with the power of the biblical Leviathan, could counterweigh chaos. Thus he has usually been seen as supporting the Royalist position during the English Civil Wars between the Royalists and Parliamentarians. In 1640, with the growing anti-royalist sentiment, Hobbes left England for his safety and lived in exile in Paris, and he did not return to England until 1651, shortly after his masterpiece *Leviathan* was published. *Leviathan* has four parts: "Of Man," "Of Commonwealth," "Of a Christian Commonwealth," and "Of the Kingdom of Darkness." He wrote *Leviathan* during the latter half of the English Civil Wars. Many elements of the text were inspired by the current unrest and disagreements in England.

After his return to England, Hobbes continued to write on philosophy. In his later years, Hobbes published translations of Homer's *The Odyssey* and *The Iliad*.

The importance of Hobbes's political philosophy cannot be overstated; it went on to influence John Locke, Jean-Jacques Rousseau, and Immanuel Kant, to name but a few.

Leviathan

Chapter 13 Of the Natural Condition of Mankind as Concerning Their Felicity[①] and Misery
(Excerpt)

Nature has made men so equal in the talents of body and mind that, though one man is sometimes manifestly[②] stronger in body or of quicker mind than another, yet when all is reckoned together the difference between men is not so considerable as that one man can thereupon claim to himself any benefit to which another may not also claim. For as to the strength of body, the weakest has strength enough to kill the strongest,

---

① felicity: happiness
② manifestly: clearly

The 17th Century — Chapter 3
The Bourgeois Revolution and the Early Enlightenment

either by secret machination① or by confederacy with others that are in the same danger with himself ...

From this equality of ability arises equality of hope in the attaining of our ends. And therefore if any two men desire the same thing, which they cannot both enjoy, they become enemies; and in the way to their goal, they endeavour to destroy or subdue one another. And from this, it comes to pass that where an invader has no more to fear than another man's single power, if one plant, sow, build, or possess a convenient seat, others may probably be expected to come prepared with forces united to dispossess and deprive him, not only of the fruit of his labour, but also of his life or liberty. And the invader again is in the like danger of another ...

Hereby it is manifest that during the time men live without a common power to keep them all in awe, they are in that condition which is called war; and such a war as is of every man against every man ... the nature of war consists not in actual fighting, but in the known disposition thereto during all the time there is no assurance to the contrary. All other time is peace.

Whatsoever therefore is consequent to a time of war, where every man is enemy to every man, the same is consequent to the time wherein men live without other security than what their own strength and their own invention shall furnish them withal. In such condition there is no place for industry, because the fruit thereof is uncertain: and consequently no culture of the earth... no arts; no letters; no society; and which is worst of all, continual fear, and danger of violent death; and the life of man, solitary, poor, nasty, brutish, and short.

It may seem strange to some man that has not well weighed these things that Nature should thus dissociate and render men apt to invade and destroy one another: and he may therefore, not trusting to this inference, made from the passions, desire perhaps to have the same confirmed by experience. Let him therefore consider with himself: when taking a journey, he arms himself and seeks to go well accompanied; when going to sleep, he locks his doors; when even in his house he locks his chests; and

---

① machination: plotting

this when he knows there be laws and public officers, armed, to revenge all injuries shall be done him; what opinion he has of his fellow subjects, when he rides armed; of his fellow citizens, when he locks his doors; and of his children, and servants, when he locks his chests. Does he not there as much accuse mankind by his actions as I do by my words?

To this war of every man against every man, this also is consequent; that nothing can be unjust. The notions of right and wrong, justice and injustice, have there no place. Where there is no common power, there is no law; where no law, no injustice. Force and fraud are in war the two cardinal virtues. Justice and injustice are none of the faculties① neither of the body nor mind. If they were, they might be innate in a man that were alone in the world, as well as his senses and passions. They are qualities that relate to men in society, not in solitude. It is consequent also to the same condition that there be no propriety, no dominion, no mine and thine distinct; but only that to be every man's that he can get, and for so long as he can keep it. And thus much for the ill condition which man by mere nature is actually placed in; though with a possibility to come out of it, consisting partly in the passions, partly in his reason.

The passions that incline men to peace are: fear of death, desire for a comfortable life, and the hope of attaining a comfortable life by hard work. And reason suggests convenient articles of peace upon which men may be drawn to agreement.

Questions for Discussion

1. According to the passage, why do people harm each other?
2. According to Hobbes, what "condition" do men live in when they live without a common power to keep them all in awe?
3. How does Hobbes describe life without common security? According to Hobbes, what inclines men to peace?

---

①faculties: plural form of "faculty," which means a natural ability for a particular kind of action

The 17th Century | Chapter 3
The Bourgeois Revolution and the Early Enlightenment

John Locke (1632 – 1704)

John Locke is best remembered for his role in laying much of the groundwork for the Enlightenment as well as for his central contributions to the development of liberalism characterized by opposition to authoritarianism.

Locke was born in Somerset in southwestern England. His father was a lawyer and small landowner who had fought on the Parliamentarian side at the early stages of the English Civil Wars. Thanks to his father's wartime connections, in 1647 Locke was able to enroll at Westminster School in London. His outstanding performance there enabled him to enter Oxford, where he stayed between 1652 and 1667, first as student then as lecturer, with his studies focusing on philosophy and the sciences, especially medicine. In 1667, he was appointed physician to Anthony Ashley Cooper (later the First Earl of Shaftesbury). That year he supervised a dangerous liver operation on Shaftesbury that likely saved the latter's life.

For the next two decades, Locke's fortunes were tied to Shaftesbury, who, among various political activities, is best remembered for leading the 1679 "exclusion" campaign to bar the Catholic Duke of York (the future James II) from the royal succession. When that endeavour failed, Shaftesbury began to plot armed resistance, and was forced to flee to Holland in 1682. One year later, Locke went in exile in Holland, and returned only after the Glorious Revolution, which was a watershed in English history, for it marked the point at which the balance of power in English government passed from the Crown to the Parliament.

Locke's important works include *An Essay Concerning Human Understanding* (1689), *Two Treatises of Government* (1689), and *Some Thoughts Concerning Education* (1693).

It is widely agreed that *Two Treatises of Government* was substantially composed some years before its publication in 1689 as a response to the political situation as it existed in England at the time of the "exclusion" controversy—the debate over whether a law could be passed to forbid (exclude) James, the Roman Catholic brother of King Charles II, from succeeding to the English throne. Undoubtedly, the message is of lasting significance: it is the major statement of Locke's political philosophy.

Two Treatises of Government
From Second Treatise on Government
Chapter 2　Of the State of Nature
(Excerpt)

　　Sec. 6.　...The state of nature has a law of nature to govern it, which obliges every one: and reason, which is that law, teaches all mankind, who will but consult it, that being all equal and independent, no one ought to harm another in his life, health, liberty, or possessions: for men being all the workmanship of one omnipotent,① and infinitely wise maker; all the servants of one sovereign master, sent into the world by his order, and about his business; they are his property, whose workmanship they are, made to last during his, not one another's pleasure: and being furnished with like faculties, sharing all in one community of nature, there cannot be supposed any such subordination among us, that may authorize us to destroy one another, as if we were made for one another's uses, as the inferior ranks of creatures are for ours. Every one, as he is bound to preserve himself, and not to quit his station wilfully, so by the like reason, when his own preservation comes not in competition, ought he, as much as he can, to preserve the rest of mankind, and may not, unless it be to do justice on an offender, take away, or impair② the life, or what tends to the preservation of the life, the liberty, health, limb, or goods of another....

Chapter 9　Of the Ends of Political Society and Government
(Excerpt)

　　Sec. 123. If man in the state of nature be so free, as has been said; if he be absolute lord of his own person and possessions, equal to the greatest, and subject to no body, why will he part with his freedom? Why will he give

---

①omnipotent: all-powerful
②impair: spoil something or make it weaker so that it is less effective

up this empire, and subject himself to the dominion and control of any other power? To which it is obvious to answer, that though in the state of nature he hath such a right, yet the enjoyment of it is very uncertain, and constantly exposed to the invasion of others: for all being kings as much as he, every man his equal, and the greater part no strict observers of equity and justice, the enjoyment of the property he has in this state is very unsafe, very unsecure. This makes him willing to quit a condition, which, however free, is full of fears and continual dangers: and it is not without reason, that he seeks out, and is willing to join in society with others, who are already united, or have a mind to unite, for the mutual preservation of their lives, liberties and estates, which I call by the general name, property.

Sec. 124. The great and chief end, therefore, of men's uniting into commonwealths,① and putting themselves under government, is the preservation of their property. To which in the state of nature there are many things wanting. First, There wants an established, settled, known law, received and allowed by common consent to be the standard of right and wrong, and the common measure to decide all controversies between them: for though the law of nature be plain and intelligible to all rational creatures; yet men being biased by their interest, as well as ignorant for want of study of it, are not apt to allow of it as a law binding to them in the application of it to their particular cases.

Sec. 125. Secondly, In the state of nature there wants a known and indifferent② judge, with authority to determine all differences according to the established law: for everyone in that state being both judge and executioner of the law of nature, men being partial to themselves, passion and revenge is very apt to carry them too far, and with too much heat, in their own cases; as well as negligence, and unconcernedness, to make them too remiss③ in other men's....

Sec. 131. But though men, when they enter into society, give up the

---

①commonwealths: countries
②indifferent: unbiased
③remiss: negligent in the performance of work or duty

equality, liberty, and executive power they had in the state of nature, into the hands of the society, to be so far disposed of by the legislative, as the good of the society shall require; yet it being only with an intention in every one the better to preserve himself, his liberty and property; (for no rational creature can be supposed to change his condition with an intention to be worse) the power of the society, or legislative constituted by them, can never be supposed to extend farther, than the common good; but is obliged to secure every one's property, by providing against those three defects above mentioned, that made the state of nature so unsafe and uneasy. And so whoever has the legislative or supreme power of any commonwealth, is bound to govern by established standing laws, promulgated① and known to the people, and not by extemporary decrees;② by indifferent and upright judges, who are to decide controversies by those laws; and to employ the force of the community at home, only in the execution of such laws, or abroad to prevent or redress foreign injuries, and secure the community from inroads③ and invasion. And all this to be directed to no other end, but the peace, safety, and public good of the people.

Questions for Discussion

1. What is the law of nature that should govern humankind? Who created this law of nature?
2. Why would a person voluntarily give up some of his freedom to join society and submit to laws and rules of that society?
3. What role should judges play in a commonwealth of men?
4. What common views did Hobbes and Locke have concerning government and human nature?

---

① promulgate: to spread beliefs or ideas among a lot of people
② extemporary decrees: done or said without any preparation or thought
③ inroad: a sudden attack on and entrance into hostile territory

Chapter 4

From 1700 to 1789
The Industrial Revolution and the Age of Reason

4.1 The Industrial Revolution and Imperial Expansion

The 18th century saw the gradual rise of Great Britain's position as the greatest economic and military power in the world. Although it was at war with France for most of the century, Britain's naval power ensured the conditions at home remained stable enough for the development of trade and industry, and allowed the scientific and technological advances which brought about the world's first Industrial Revolution, making the century an age of capitalism and trade. In 1707, England, Wales, and Scotland were formally unified as Great Britain with one parliament in London. This established the basis of the modern United Kingdom.

The only major set-back for Great Britain was the loss of the American colonies as a result of the American War of Independence. After losing the American colonies, the British government looked eastward rather than westward, to India rather than North America, for its colonies. By the end of the century the British Indian Empire was firmly established, which exercised control over the whole of the sub-continent, a control that lasted for nearly two hundred years until 1947.

One of the most significant developments in Britain during the 18th century was the progressive abolition of the slave trade. Although slavery throughout the British Empire was not legally abolished until 1833, in Great Britain proper, slavery was declared illegal by a High Court decision in 1706. Another decision in 1772 ruled that a slave could not be forcibly removed from Britain. The slave trade was formally abolished throughout the British Empire by the Slave Trade Act of 1807. It has been argued that the abolition of slavery was a major influence on the growth of industrial capitalism in Britain.

4.2 The Age of Reason

The 18th century before the outbreak of the French Revolution (1789) experienced the extending and deepening of the influence of the Enlightenment. Following the Enlightenment pioneers such as Newton and Locke, the 18th century English men of letters did their utmost to propagate Enlightenment thought. The Enlightenment was a continuation and extension of many of the ideas of the Renaissance and Reformation. If the Renaissance was more associated with advances in literature, architecture, humanism, and a world economy, then the Enlightenment concerned more with the scientific method, industrialisation, rationality, astronomy, and calculus. That is why the period of the Enlightenment has also been called the Age of Reason. Enlightenment thinkers were not interested in theology, rather they were fascinated with humankind's own nature. The famous couplet in "An Essay on Man" by Alexander Pope (1688 – 1744) well conveys the Enlightenment thinking:

> *Know then thyself, presume not God to scan,*
> *The proper study of mankind is man.*

4.3 Representative Writers and Works

The 18th century saw the growth of the English novel as a dominant form, although poetry, drama, and especially the essay form remained popular. These developments in printed works were the result of a number of social, economic, and technical changes. The taxes on paper were reduced; printing became cheaper and more efficient; the newly started magazines and journals such as *The Tatler* and *The Spectator* created a demand for new writing; and the newly important middle-class sought written works to consume during the freetime that their new occupations allowed. Theatre and poetry remained the domain of the aristocracy, but the novel and essays were important to the bourgeoisie. During the 1700s the expansion of the number of coffee-houses, which became places where business could be conducted and politics and other social issues be discussed, was phenomenal and the popularity of publications containing essays helped stimulate this expansion.

The most accomplished novelists were Daniel Defoe (1660 – 1731), Jonathan Swift (1667 – 1745), and Henry Fielding (1707 – 1754). Defoe is best remembered for his *Robinson Crusoe* and *Moll Flanders*, each novel narrating the protagonist's travelling far and adventurously, echoing the nation's colonialism. Swift's masterpiece is *Gulliver's Travels*, which, taking the guise of travel narrative, mocks English customs and politics of the day in a most savage satire; however, he is lastingly remembered, especially in Ireland, for writing on behalf of the Irish people. Henry Fielding's masterpiece is *The History of Tom Jones, a Foundling*.

Perhaps the most prominent poet of the century was Alexander Pope, whose "An Essay on Man" best expresses the Enlightenment ideas in neoclassical form. Neoclassicism was a revival of the Greek and Roman classical forms, which emphasise order, balance, harmony, clarity, and restraint.

Undoubtedly, Joseph Addison (1672 – 1719) and Richard Steele (1672 – 1729) were the most influential essayists of the century. In the periodicals *The Tatler* and *The Spectator*, titles that still exist today, they shared their observations on fashion and the elite of wits of London in order to educate the middle-classes in the morals and politics of the day as well as to entertain them. *The Wealth of Nations* by Adam Smith (1723 – 1790), beyond any doubt, is one of the most important books ever written, because it introduced new economic principles, which continue to govern the world today.

Alexander Pope (1688 – 1744)

Alexander Pope encountered many obstacles in his life. Being afflicted with tuberculosis of the spine[①] since childhood, he was crippled and under

---

[①] tuberculosis of the spine: a pathological condition of the backbone

five feet tall, which left him an object of ridicule for the rest of his life. His parents were Roman Catholic in religion, and he kept the faith all his life even when England was ruled by Protestants. As a student, he suffered discrimination because anti-Catholic laws kept him from attending England's universities. However, Pope did not let disability or discrimination stand in his way. He read widely on his own, so that he gained a profound knowledge of the classics and the craft of writing.

Pope published "An Essay on Criticism" when he was in his early twenties. This work outraged many critics who flared up with anger that a twenty-three-year-old would dare attack the literary establishment in print. But the poem's wittiness and style won Pope some powerful friends, including influential writers such as Joseph Addison, Richard Steele, and Jonathan Swift. He followed the success with "The Rape of the Lock," a satiric poem describing a man's theft of a woman's lock of hair. In his thirties, he translated Homer's Epic poems *The Iliad* and *The Odyssey* into modern verse.

His later works, such as "An Essay on Man," display a thoughtfulness that even some of his enemies came to respect.

An Essay on Man

(Excerpt)

Epistle I

3

Heav'n from all creatures hides the book of fate,
All but the page prescrib'd, their present state:
From brutes what men, from men what spirits know:
Or who could suffer being here below?
5   The lamb thy riot dooms to bleed today,
Had he thy reason, would he skip and play?
Pleas'd to the last, he crops the flow'ry food,
And licks the hand just rais'd to shed his blood.
Oh blindness to the future! kindly giv'n,
10   That each may fill the circle mark'd by Heav'n:
Who sees with equal eye, as God of all,

A hero perish, or a sparrow fall,
Atoms or systems into ruin hurl'd,
And now a bubble burst, and now a world....

Epistle II

1

Know then thyself, presume not God to scan;
The proper study of mankind is man.
Plac'd on this isthmus① of a middle state,
A being darkly wise, and rudely great:
5   With too much knowledge for the sceptic side,
With too much weakness for the stoic's pride,
He hangs between; in doubt to act, or rest;
In doubt to deem himself a god, or beast;
In doubt his mind or body to prefer;
10   Born but to die, and reas'ning but to err;
Alike in ignorance, his reason such,
Whether he thinks too little, or too much:
Chaos of thought and passion, all confus'd;
Still by himself abus'd, or disabus'd;
15   Created half to rise, and half to fall;
Great lord of all things, yet a prey to all;
Sole judge of truth, in endless error hurl'd:
The glory, jest, and riddle of the world!
Go, wondrous creature! mount where science guides,
20   Go, measure earth, weigh air, and state the tides;
Instruct the planets in what orbs to run,
Correct old time, and regulate the sun;
Go, soar with Plato to th' empyreal② sphere,
To the first good, first perfect, and first fair;
25   Or tread the mazy round his follow'rs trod,
And quitting sense call imitating God;

---

①isthmus: a narrow strip of land, with water on each side, that joins two larger pieces of land
②empyreal: relating to the highest heaven in the cosmology of the ancients

As Eastern priests in giddy circles run,
And turn their heads to imitate the sun.
Go, teach Eternal Wisdom how to rule—
30   Then drop into thyself, and be a fool!...

2

Two principles in human nature reign;
Self-love, to urge, and reason, to restrain;
Nor this a good, nor that a bad we call,
Each works its end, to move or govern all:
5   And to their proper operation still,
Ascribe all good; to their improper, ill.

Self-love, the spring of motion, acts the soul;
Reason's comparing balance rules the whole.
Man, but for that, no action could attend,
10   And but for this, were active to no end:
Fix'd like a plant on his peculiar spot,
To draw nutrition, propagate, and rot;
Or, meteor-like, flame lawless through the void,
Destroying others, by himself destroy'd....

Questions for Discussion

1. According to Epistle Ⅰ: Section 3, what an orderly universe is the world? What's the speaker's view of this order?
2. To what is the human condition compared in line 3 of Epistle Ⅱ: Section 1? What does the metaphor tell you about humanity's "middle state"? Then what does the speaker urge man to do and what does the speaker warn man against?
3. According to Epistle Ⅱ: Section 2, what two principles in man reign? What would happen if they function improperly? Give a couple of examples either in real life or in history to show the consequences of their proper as well as improper workings.
4. Do you agree with Pope's description of people? In your opinion, does the description still apply today?

Jonathan Swift (1667 – 1745)

Jonathan Swift was born of English parents in Dublin, Ireland. His father died before his birth. This left the family to rely on the aid of relatives to survive. Thanks to the generosity of an uncle, he received the best education possible, getting his BA degree at Trinity College in Dublin. After that, he moved to England and took up a job working as secretary to Sir William Temple, a retired diplomat. This job gave Swift opportunities to become acquainted with a number of politically influential people. Using his influential connections, Sir William Temple helped Swift gain admission into Oxford University, from which Swift graduated with MA degree in 1692. About 1696 to 1697 he wrote his powerful satires on corruptions in religion and learning, *A Tale of a Tub* and *The Battle of the Books*, which were published in 1704 and reached their final form in 1710.

In 1700 Swift returned to Ireland as chaplain① to the Lord Justice, the Earl of Berkeley. For the rest of his life, he devoted his talents to politics and religion, which were not clearly separated at the time. Thence he wrote most of his works in prose to further a specific cause. In 1710 he abandoned the Whigs, because he disapproved its indifference to the welfare of the Anglican Church in Ireland and of its desire to repeal② the Test Act, which required all holders of offices of state to take the Sacrament③ according to the Anglican rites, thus excluding Roman Catholics and Dissenters. In 1713 he was appointed Dean of St. Patrick's Cathedral in Dublin.

Swift's life in Ireland gave him an intimate knowledge of the miserable condition of the people. Though English landlords possessed large tracts of land in Ireland, they mostly lived in England. These absentees cruelly exploited the Irish people. Swift wrote a number of pamphlets criticising the oppression and exploitation of the Irish people by the absentee landlords and

---

① chaplain: a priest who is responsible for the religious needs of people in a institution such as hospital, prison, a branch of armed forces, etc.
② repeal: abandon or call off
③ Sacrament: (in Christianity) the holy bread and wine eaten at an important religious ceremony

the English government. Among them *The Drapier's Letters* (1724) and "A Modest Proposal" (1729) are the most famous.

In Ireland, he became not only an efficient ecclesiastical① administrator, but also, in 1724, the intellectual leader of Irish resistance to English oppression. He is still venerated in Ireland as a national hero.

Swift published his masterpiece *Gulliver's Travels* in 1726. The book contains four parts that deal with the four voyages of its hero to strange places, demonstrating the author's extraordinary imagination and wit.

Swift once proclaimed himself a misanthrope.② He declared that though he loved individuals, he hated "that animal called man" in general. He defined man not as "a rational animal" but merely as "an animal capable of reason," and he claimed that this was the great foundation upon which his "misanthropy" was erected. Actually, Swift was stating not his hatred of his fellow creatures, but his antagonism to the current optimistic view that human nature is essentially good.

A Modest Proposal
For Preventing the Children of Poor people in Ireland from Being a Burden to Their Parents or Country, and for Making Them Beneficial to the Publick
(Excerpt)

It is a melancholy object to those who walk through this great town or travel in the country, when they see the streets, the roads, and cabin doors, crowded with beggars of the female sex, followed by three, four, or six children, all in rags and importuning every passenger for an alms.③ These mothers, instead of being able to work for their honest livelihood, are forced to employ all their time in strolling to beg sustenance for their helpless infants: who as they grow up either turn thieves for want of work,

---

① ecclesiastical: belonging to or connected with the Christian religion
② misanthrope: someone who dislikes and avoids other people
③ importune every passenger for an alms: demand every passenger urgently or persistently for money or food

or leave their dear native country to fight for the Pretender in Spain,① or sell themselves to the Barbadoes.②

I think it is agreed by all parties that this prodigious number of children in the arms, or on the backs, or at the heels of their mothers, and frequently of their fathers, is in the present deplorable state of the kingdom a very great additional grievance; and, therefore, whoever could find out a fair, cheap, and easy method of making these children sound, useful members of the commonwealth, would deserve so well of the public as to have his statue set up for a preserver of the nation.

But my intention is very far from being confined to provide only for the children of professed beggars;③ it is of a much greater extent, and shall take in the whole number of infants at a certain age who are born of parents in effect as little able to support them as those who demand our charity in the streets. As to my own part, having turned my thoughts for many years upon this important subject, and maturely weighed the several schemes of other projectors,④ I have always found them grossly mistaken in the computation. It is true, a child just dropped from its dam⑤ may be supported by her milk for a solar year, with little other nourishment; at most not above the value of 2 shillings, which the mother may certainly get, or the value in scraps, by her lawful occupation of begging; and it is exactly at one year old that I propose to provide for them in such a manner as instead of being a charge upon their parents or the parish, or wanting food and raiment⑥ for the rest of their lives, they shall on the contrary contribute to the feeding, and partly to the clothing, of many thousands.

---

①the Pretender in Spain: James Francis Edward Stuart (1688 – 1766), the son of James II. He had claim to the throne of England, but the Glorious Revolution had barred his succession. Catholic Ireland was loyal to him and many Irishmen joined him in his exile on the Continent.

②sell themselves to the Barbadoes: The Barbadoes is an island chain in the West Indies. Because of the poverty in Ireland, many Irishmen emigrated to the West Indies. They paid their passage by working for a stated period for the planter.

③professed beggars: professional beggars ("professed" means "openly declared")

④projectors: devisers of plans or schemes

⑤dam: the female parent of an animal, especially a horse

⑥raiment: clothing

There is likewise another great advantage in my scheme, that it will prevent those voluntary abortions, and that horrid practice of women murdering their bastard children, alas! too frequent among us! sacrificing the poor innocent babes I doubt more to avoid the expense than the shame, which would move tears and pity in the most savage and inhuman breast....

I am assured by our merchants, that a boy or a girl before twelve years old is no saleable commodity; and even when they come to this age they will not yield above three pounds, or three pounds and half a crown at most on the Exchange; which cannot turn to account either to the parents or kingdom, the charge of nutriment and rags having been at least four times that value.

I shall now therefore humbly propose my own thoughts, which I hope will not be liable to the least objection.

I have been assured by a very knowing American of my acquaintance in London, that a young healthy child well nursed is at a year old a most delicious, nourishing, and wholesome food, whether stewed, roasted, baked, or boiled; and I make no doubt that it will equally serve in a fricassee① or a ragout.②

I do therefore humbly offer it to public consideration that of the hundred and twenty thousand children already computed, twenty thousand may be reserved for breed, whereof only one-fourth part to be males; which is more than we allow to sheep, black cattle or swine; and my reason is, that these children are seldom the fruits of marriage, a circumstance not much regarded by our savages, therefore one male will be sufficient to serve four females. That the remaining hundred thousand may, at a year old, be offered in the sale to the persons of quality and fortune through the kingdom; always advising the mother to let them suck plentifully in the last month, so as to render them plump and fat for a good table. A child will make two dishes at an entertainment for friends; and when the family dines alone, the fore or hind quarter will make a reasonable dish, and seasoned

---

①fricassee: a dish of stewed or fried pieces of meat served in a thick white sauce
②ragout: a highly seasoned stew of meat and vegetables

with a little pepper or salt will be very good boiled on the fourth day, especially in winter.

I have reckoned upon a medium that a child just born will weigh 12 pounds, and in a solar year, if tolerably nursed, increaseth to 28 pounds.

I grant this food will be somewhat dear, and therefore very proper for landlords, who, as they have already devoured most of the parents, seem to have the best title to the children.

Infant's flesh will be in season throughout the year, but more plentiful in March, and a little before and after; for we are told by a grave author, an eminent French physician, that fish being a prolific diet, there are more children born in Roman Catholic countries about nine months after Lent① than at any other season; therefore, reckoning a year after Lent, the markets will be more glutted than usual, because the number of popish② infants is at least three to one in this kingdom: and therefore it will have one other collateral advantage, by lessening the number of papists③ among us....

Supposing that one thousand families in this city would be constant customers for infants flesh, besides others who might have it at merry meetings, particularly at weddings and christenings, I compute that Dublin would take off annually about twenty thousand carcasses, and the rest of the Kingdom (where probably they will be sold somewhat cheaper) the remaining eighty thousand.

I can think of no one objection, that will possibly be raised against this proposal, unless it should be urged, that the number of people will be thereby much lessened in the Kingdom. This I freely own, and 'twas indeed one principal design in offering it to the world. I desire the reader will observe, that I calculate my remedy for this one individual kingdom of Ireland, and for no other that ever was, is, or I think, ever can be upon Earth. Therefore let no man talk to me of other expedients④...

---

① Lent: the period including 40 weekdays extending from Ash-Wednesday to Easter eve
② popish: (offensive) of Roman Catholicism
③ papist: an offensive word for Roman Catholic
④ expedient: something that one uses to accomplish an end especially when the usual means is not available

Therefore I repeat, let no man talk to me of these and the like expedients, till he hath at least some glimpse of hope, that there will ever be some hearty and sincere attempt to put them into practice....

I profess, in the sincerity of my heart, that I have not the least personal interest in endeavouring to promote this necessary work, having no other motive than the public good of my country, by advancing our trade, providing for infants, relieving the poor, and giving some pleasure to the rich. I have no children by which I can propose to get a single penny; the youngest being nine years old, and my wife past child-bearing.

Questions for Discussion

1. What problem does Swift describe in the opening paragraphs? What solution does he propose?
2. Does Swift analyze the causes of Ireland's problem? Why not?
3. Swift wrote "A Modest Proposal" in reaction to unjust English economic policies. The essay is highly satirical. What strategies does Swift use to let his readers know his intentions?

Joseph Addison (1672 – 1719)

The name of Joseph Addison is often coupled with that of Richard Steele, with whom he formed his lifelong friendship when he was still an early teenager studying in London. They both went on to the University of Oxford and became Whig members of Parliament, though Addison served in the government, while Steele was more business orientated and founded the periodicals *The Tatler* and *The Spectator*. In these two periodicals they collaboratively produced many essays. The essay that follows is from *The Spectator*. It informs its readership of the form and function of The Royal Exchange, a major trading institution that still exists today, although in a different location.

From 1700 to 1789 | Chapter 4

The Industrial Revolution and the Age of Reason

The Royal Exchange

(Excerpt)

There is no place in the town which I so much love to frequent as the Royal Exchange. It gives me a secret satisfaction, and in some measure, gratifies my vanity, as I am an Englishman, to see so rich an assembly of countrymen and foreigners consulting together upon the private business of mankind, and making this metropolis a kind of emporium① for the whole earth. I must confess I look upon high-change② to be a great council, in which all considerable nations have their representatives. Factors③ in the trading world are what ambassadors are in the politick world; they negotiate affairs, conclude treaties, and maintain a good correspondence between those wealthy societies of men that are divided from one another by seas and oceans, or live on the different extremities of a continent. I have often been pleased to hear disputes adjusted between an inhabitant of Japan and an alderman④ of London, or to see a subject of the Great Mogul⑤ entering into a league with one of the Czar of Muscovy.⑥ I am infinitely delighted in mixing with these several ministers of commerce, as they are distinguished by their different walks and different languages: sometimes I am justled⑦ among a body of Armenians; sometimes I am lost in a crowd of Jews; and sometimes make one in a group of Dutchmen. I am a Dane, Swede, or Frenchman at different times; or rather fancy myself like the old philosopher, who upon being asked what countryman he was, replied, that he was a citizen of the world.

Though I very frequently visit this busy multitude of people, I am

---

① emporium: a large shop selling many different items; shopping centre
② high-change: when the Exchange is at its busiest
③ factors: agents
④ alderman: a member of the City of London's ruling council
⑤ the Great Mogul: the sovereign of the empire founded in India by the Moguls in the 16th century, here meaning "an Indian prince"
⑥ Muscovy: Russia
⑦ justle: jostle

known to nobody there but my friend, Sir Andrew, who often smiles upon me as he sees me bustling in the crowd, but at the same time connives at my presence without taking any further notice of me. There is indeed a merchant of Egypt, who just knows me by sight, having formerly remitted me some money to Grand Cairo; but as I am not versed in the modern Coptick,① our conferences go no further than a bow and a grimace.

This grand scene of business gives me an infinite variety of solid and substantial entertainments. As I am a great lover of mankind, my heart naturally overflows with pleasure, at the sight of a prosperous and happy multitude, insomuch that at many publick② solemnities I cannot forbear expressing my joy with tears that have stolen down my cheeks. For this reason I am wonderfully delighted to see such a body of men thriving in their own private fortunes, and at the same time promoting the publick stock; or in other words, raising estates for their own families, by bringing into their country whatever is wanting, and carrying out of it whatever is superfluous.

Nature seems to have taken a particular care to disseminate her blessings among the different regions of the world, with an eye to this mutual intercourse and traffick③ among mankind, that the natives of the several parts of the globe might have a kind of dependence upon one another, and be united together by their common interest. Almost every degree produces something peculiar to it. The food often grows in one country, and the sauce in another. The fruits of Portugal are corrected by the products of Barbadoes; the infusion of a China plant sweetened with the pith of an Indian cane. The Philippick Islands give a flavour to our European bowls. The single dress of a woman of quality is often the product of a hundred climates. The muff and the fan come together from the different ends of the earth. The scarf is sent from the torrid zone, and the

---

①Coptick: the language of the Copts, which represents the final stage of ancient Egyptian
②publick: old spelling of "public"
③traffick: old spelling of "traffic," meaning "trade"

tippet① from beneath the pole. The brocade② Petticoat rises out of the mines of Peru, and the diamond necklace out of the bowels of Indostan.③

... Our ships are laden with the harvest of every climate; our tables are stored with spices, and oils, and wines; our rooms are filled with pyramids of China, and adorned with the workmanship of Japan; our morning's draught④ comes to us from the remotest corners of the earth; we repair our bodies by the drugs of America, and repose ourselves under Indian canopies. My friend Sir Andrew calls the vineyards of France our gardens, the Spice Islands our hot-beds, the Persians our silk-weavers, and the Chinese our potters. Nature indeed furnishes us with the bare necessaries of life, but traffick gives us greater variety of what is useful, and at the same time supplies us with everything that is convenient and ornamental. Nor is it the least part of this our happiness, that whilst we enjoy the remotest products of the north and south, we are free from those extremities of weather which give them birth; that our eyes are refreshed with the green fields of Britain, at the same time that our palates are feasted with fruits that rise between the tropicks.⑤

For these reasons there are no more useful members in a commonwealth than merchants. They knit mankind together in a mutual intercourse of good offices, distribute the gifts of nature, find work for the poor, add wealth to the rich, and magnificence to the great. Our English merchant converts the tin of his own country into gold, and exchanges his wool for rubies....

Trade without enlarging the British territories, has given us a kind of additional empire: it has multiplied the number of the rich, made our landed estates infinitely more valuable than they were formerly, and added to them an accession of other estates as valuable as the lands themselves.

---

① tippet: cape
② brocade: embroidery
③ Indostan: India
④ draught: drink
⑤ tropicks: old spelling of "tropics"

Questions for Discussion

1. What's your comment on Addison's remark "Factors in the trading world are what ambassadors are in the politick world"? Please Explain.
2. Explain in your own language why Addison was pleased with the operations of the Royal Exchange.
3. What do you think are the advantages and disadvantages of international trade?

Adam Smith (1723 – 1790)

Adam Smith has been regarded, along with Karl Marx (1818 – 1883) and John Maynard Keynes (1883 – 1946), as one of the three most influential economic theorists of the past four hundred years. While Marx systemised the theoretical basis of communism, and Keynes, in seeking a system half-way between free-market capitalism and communism, advocated government spending as a means of stimulating a depressed economy, Adam Smith originated the first systematic theory of the capitalist economy and in particular the concept of the free market.

Born in Scotland, Smith studied successively at the University of Glasgow and Balliol College, Oxford. He was a leader figure in the "Scottish Enlightenment" and wrote on philosophy as well as political economy. With his book *An Enquiry into the Nature and Causes of the Wealth of Nations* (usually known as *The Wealth of Nations*, 1776), he produced the first modern text of economic theory. Consequently, Smith has been called both "The Father of Economics" and "The Father of Capitalism." His influence continues to the present day.

The Wealth of Nations is a voluminous work including five books. The anthologised passage that follows is from Book IV. In the extract Smith examines the concepts of "free trade"① and "enlightened self-interest"② as the basis of a capitalist free-market economy. It should be read in conjunction with Addison's "The Royal Exchange" to get a sense of the ideas that underpinned the British economy in the 18th century, the material conditions of which would be the soil in which literature of the period grew. A more negative view of its effect is contained in later contributions to this anthology such as Dickens's *Hard Times* and Thomas Hardy's *Tess of the D'Urbervilles*.

The Wealth of Nations

Book Ⅳ   Of Systems of Political Economy

Chapter 2   Of Restraints upon the Importation from Foreign Countries of such Goods as can be produced at Home

(Excerpt)

By restraining, either by high duties or by absolute prohibitions, the importation of such goods from foreign countries as can be produced at home, the monopoly of the home market is more or less secured to the domestic industry employed in producing them. Thus the prohibition of importing either live cattle or salt provisions from foreign countries secures to the graziers③ of Great Britain the monopoly of the home market for butcher's meat. The high duties upon the importation of corn, which in times of moderate plenty amount to a prohibition, give a like advantage to the growers of that commodity. The prohibition of the importation of foreign woollens is equally favourable to the woollen manufacturers. The silk manufacture, though altogether employed upon foreign materials, has lately obtained the same advantage. The linen manufacture has not yet obtained it, but is making great strides towards it. Many other sorts of manufacturers have, in the same manner, obtained in Great Britain, either

---

①free trade: international trade without tariffs

②self-interest: the belief that an individual, group, or even a commercial entity will "do well by doing good"

③grazier: a person who grazes cattle or sheep for market; a meat farmer

altogether or very nearly, a monopoly against their countrymen. The variety of goods of which the importation into Great Britain is prohibited, either absolutely, or under certain circumstances, greatly exceeds what can easily be suspected by those who are not well acquainted with the laws of the customs.

That this monopoly of the home market frequently gives great encouragement to that particular species of industry which enjoys it, and frequently turns towards that employment a greater share of both the labour and stock of the society than would otherwise have gone to it, cannot be doubted. But whether it tends either to increase the general industry of the society, or to give it the most advantageous direction, is not, perhaps, altogether so evident.

The general industry of the society never can exceed what the capital of the society can employ. As the number of workmen that can be kept in employment by any particular person must bear a certain proportion to his capital, so the number of those that can be continually employed by all the members of a great society must bear a certain proportion to the whole capital of that society, and never can exceed that proportion. No regulation of commerce can increase the quantity of industry in any society beyond what its capital can maintain. It can only divert a part of it into a direction into which it might not otherwise have gone; and it is by no means certain that this artificial direction is likely to be more advantageous to the society than that into which it would have gone of its own accord.①

Every individual is continually exerting himself to find out the most advantageous employment for whatever capital he can command. It is his own advantage, indeed, and not that of the society, which he has in view. But the study of his own advantage naturally, or rather necessarily, leads him to prefer that employment which is most advantageous to the society.

First, every individual endeavours to employ his capital as near home as he can, and consequently as much as he can in the support of domestic industry; provided always that he can thereby obtain the ordinary, or not a

---

① of its own accord: by itself, on its own

great deal less than the ordinary profits of stock.

Thus, upon equal or nearly equal profits, every wholesale merchant naturally prefers the home trade to the foreign trade of consumption, and the foreign trade of consumption to the carrying trade.① ... every country which has any considerable share of the carrying trade becomes always the emporium, or general market, for the goods of all the different countries whose trade it carries on. The merchant, in order to save a second loading and unloading, endeavours always to sell in the home market as much of the goods of all those different countries as he can, and thus, so far as he can, to convert his carrying trade into a foreign trade of consumption. A merchant, in the same manner, who is engaged in the foreign trade of consumption, when he collects goods for foreign markets, will always be glad, upon equal or nearly equal profits, to sell as great a part of them at home as he can. He saves himself the risk and trouble of exportation, when, so far as he can, he thus converts his foreign trade of consumption into a home trade. ...

The produce of industry is what it adds to the subject or materials upon which it is employed. In proportion as the value of this produce is great or small, so will likewise be the profits of the employer. But it is only for the sake of profit that any man employs a capital in the support of industry; and he will always, therefore, endeavour to employ it in the support of that industry of which the produce is likely to be of the greatest value, or to exchange for the greatest quantity either of money or of other goods.

But the annual revenue of every society is always precisely equal to the exchangeable value of the whole annual produce of its industry, or rather is precisely the same thing with that exchangeable value. As every individual, therefore, endeavours as much as he can both to employ his capital in the support of domestic industry, and so to direct that industry that its produce may be of the greatest value; every individual necessarily labours to render the annual revenue of the society as great as he can. He generally, indeed, neither intends to promote the public interest, nor knows how much he is

---

① the carrying trade: the transportation of goods

promoting it. By preferring the support of domestic to that of foreign industry, he intends only his own security; and by directing that industry in such a manner as its produce may be of the greatest value, he intends only his own gain, and he is in this, as in many other cases, led by an *invisible hand* to promote an end which was no part of his intention. Nor is it always the worse for the society that it was no part of it. By pursuing his own interest he frequently promotes that of the society more effectually than when he really intends to promote it. I have never known much good done by those who affected to trade for the public good. It is an affectation, indeed, not very common among merchants, and very few words need be employed in dissuading them from it....

What is prudence in the conduct of every private family can scarce be folly in that of a great kingdom. If a foreign country can supply us with a commodity cheaper than we ourselves can make it, better buy it of them with some part of the produce of our own industry employed in a way in which we have some advantage. The general industry of the country, being always in proportion to the capital which employs it, will not thereby be diminished, no more than that of the above-mentioned artificers; but only left to find out the way in which it can be employed with the greatest advantage.

Questions for Discussion

1. What is Smith's attitude to the idea of public control over the sale and manufacture of goods?
2. How does Smith define what is often called "enlightened self-interest"?
3. Does Smith argue for the protection of privileged groups such as land-owners, manufacturers, or merchants?
4. How much do you go along with Smith's view of "invisible hand"? Explain.

From 1789 to the 1830s
The Development of Industrialisation and the Age of Romanticism

5.1 The Revolutionary and Napoleonic Wars

Between 1789 and 1815, Britain and France were almost continuously at war with each other. First, the French Revolution, which had resulted in the execution of King Louis XVI and his wife Marie Antoinette, led to a grand alliance between the major monarchies in Europe to remove the Republican Government of France, which became known as the French Revolutionary Wars. Following Napoleon Bonaparte's seizure of power in 1799 and his subsequent coronation as Emperor of the French in 1804, this conflict became known as the Napoleonic Wars. Napoleon was finally defeated at the Battle of Waterloo, in Belgium, in June 1815, by an allied army primarily from Britain and Prussia under the command of the British Duke of Wellington and was exiled to St. Helena, a British island in the Atlantic, where he died in 1821. Alongside Wellington, another major British military figure was Admiral Lord Nelson who ended Napoleon's ambitions in Egypt and the Middle East at the Battle of the Nile and finally, in 1805, destroyed the French fleet off Spain in the Battle of Trafalgar, which ensured British naval dominance for over one hundred years, although in the hour of his triumph, Nelson was killed by a French sniper.[①]

[①] sniper: a person who shoots from a hiding place, especially accurately and at long range

5.2 The Development of the Industrial Revolution

Alongside these military and political events, the last years of the 18th century saw the flowering in Britain of the first industrial revolution. Factors in Britain becoming the first modern industrial economy include: its geographical position as an island keeping it isolated from the upheavals in Europe; the presence on the island of natural resources such as iron ore and coal that were necessary for steam-powered factories; the Protestant religion which allowed the growth of banking and other financial institutions while Catholicism still outlawed the charging of interest on loans; the technological advances that were a product of the empiricist philosophy① that encouraged scientific advance in Great Britain; the expansion of the British Empire in the East, which not just provided raw materials but also a market for manufactured goods; the abolition of slavery, which ensured that a free market economy in employment was created. As a result, Britain not only became the most powerful military power in the world but also the most powerful economy.

This was not without costs, however. The living and working conditions of the "free" proletariat were extremely poor, trade unions were outlawed until the 1830s, and the environmental damage done to what had been rural areas of Britain kept being felt as late as the 1990s, particularly in South Wales, Yorkshire, and the Midlands. This early industrial development has also meant that in the late 20th and early 21st centuries much of the infrastructure and working methods in Britain had not kept pace with modern industries and technology.

5.3 The Flowering of Romanticism

Impacted by the French Revolution and the Industrial Revolution as well as the American War of Independence, the Age of Reason was over, succeeded by

---

①empiricist philosophy: the theory that all knowledge is based on experience derived from the senses

an age that emphasised human emotion, instincts, and imagination. In the field of literature, this new age has been called the Age of Romanticism.

The French philosopher Jean-Jacques Rousseau (1712 – 1778) has generally been regarded as the father of Romanticism. He rejects the worship of reason, maintaining that though reason has its use, it is not the whole answer, and that it is much safer for human beings to rely on instincts and emotions in the really vital problems of life. He contrasts the freedom and innocence of primitive men with the tyranny and wickedness of civilized society, even insisting that the progress in learning is destructive to human happiness. He preaches that civilized man should "return to nature." As a reaction to the order and restraint of classicism and neo-classicism that had marked the dominant ideology of the early 18th century, the Romantic Movement emphasised inspiration, subjectivity, and the cult of the individual. It rejected the rationalism of the Enlightenment, the authoritarian nature of government, and the damaging effect of industrialisation not only on the environment but also on the individual. It is important to understand that the term "Romanticism" was coined by literary critics after the event.

In British literary history, the time from the publication of *Lyrical Ballads* in 1798 to the 1830s has generally been called the Age of Romanticism. This age witnessed the emergence of an impressive number of great poets, including William Blake (1757 – 1827), William Wordsworth (1770 – 1850), Samuel Taylor Coleridge (1772 – 1834), George Gordon Byron (1788 – 1824), Percy Bysshe Shelley (1792 – 1822), and John Keats (1795 – 1821). It also saw Sir Walter Scott (1771 – 1832) make his name by his novels which not only are rich with romantic elements in spite of its realistic description of historical events. There were many other novelists whose works contain elements of romanticism, something that continued in English literature well into the 19th century, for instance, the Brontës' novels contain passages that are clearly influenced by the Romantic movement, and towards the end of the century Thomas Hardy's novels and poetry also show that influence.

The "Romantic poets" would have acknowledged shared concerns and themes in their work. Several of them were mutual friends, but they would not have described themselves as members of a coherent movement. This means that the Romantics demonstrated the diversity of romanticism. Indeed, Blake would probably have denied that he was a romantic though, his poem "London" reflects Romantic concerns regarding the influence of modern life on individuals, especially on children. Byron and Shelley both supported the French Revolution and the former went on to die supporting the Greeks in their fight for independence from the Ottoman Empire (Byron is still remembered in Greece as a folk hero). There are, however, exceptions, for example, William Wordsworth who rejected revolutionary ideas following Robespierre's① "Reign of Terror," became increasingly illiberal in his opinions, and ended his life as a major establishment figure accepting the post of Poet Laurate from Queen Victoria.

The following anthologised poets—namely Blake, Wordsworth, Coleridge, and Shelley—represent different strands in Romanticism, displaying a wide range of the genre, dealing respectively with the urban environment, nature worship, mythical landscape, and contemporary politics.

William Blake (1757 – 1827)

William Blake should better be described as influencing the Romantics rather than as a Romantic.

Born in London, Blake's family were dissenters.② He had little formal schooling but was educated by his mother. His parents bought him books on art and poetry and he was sent to study art and engraving. Throughout his life he combined his writing, especially his poetry, with painting, drawing, and engraving. In 1789 he published *Songs of Innocence*, which contained both texts of poems and hand-coloured illustrations whose designs were in amazing harmony with the beautiful lyrics. In 1794 Blake published *Songs of Innocence and of Experience: Shewing the Two Contrary States of the Human*

---

①Robespierre: Maximilien Robespierre (1758 – 1794), a leader of the French Revolution arrested and executed on the orders of the National Convention for his leadership of the Great Terror

②dissenter: A person who dissents, as from an established church, political party, or majority opinion. In the text, it means Blake's family challenged the authority of the Church of England.

Soul. It contained a slightly rearranged version of *Songs of Innocence* with the addition of *Songs of Experience*, which are bitter, ironic replies to those poems of the earlier volume, for instance, the tone of "The Chimney-Sweeper" in *Songs of Innocence* sharply differs from that in *Songs of Experience*, and "The Lamb" is the key symbol of *Songs of Innocence* whereas in *Songs of Experience* its rival image is "The Tyger," the embodiment of energy, strength, lust, and aggression.

William Blake had a peculiarly mystical view of religion and science, talking in terms of a "Great Architect,"① and opposing organised religion. He was a social radical, opposing slavery; a supporter of women's rights and arguing for freedom in sexual matters. In the 1950s – 60s he was taken up by the counter-culture, with writers and musicians like Aldous Huxley (1894 – 1963) and Bob Dylan② being influenced by his ideas.

The Chimney-Sweeper

(*from* Songs of Innocence)

When my mother died I was very young,
And my father sold me while yet my tongue
Could scarcely cry "Weep! weep! weep! weep!"
So your chimneys I sweep, and in soot I sleep.

5   There's little Tom Dacre, who cried when his head,
That curled like a lamb's back, was shaved; so I said,
"Hush, Tom! never mind it, for, when your head's bare,
You know that the soot cannot spoil your white hair."

And so he was quiet, and that very night,
10   As Tom was a-sleeping, he had such a sight!—
That thousands of sweepers, Dick, Joe, Ned, and Jack,

---

①Great Architect: here it means "god."
②Bob Dylan: the pen name of Robert Zimmerman (born 1941), American singer, songwriter, poet, and winner of the Nobel Prize for Literature in 2016

Were all of them locked up in coffins of black.

And by came an angel, who had a bright key,
And he opened the coffins, and set them all free;
15   Then down a green plain, leaping, laughing, they run
And wash in a river, and shine in the sun.

Then naked and white, all their bags left behind,
They rise upon clouds, and sport in the wind;
And the angel told Tom, if he'd be a good boy,
20   He'd have God for his father, and never want① joy.

And so Tom awoke, and we rose in the dark,
And got with our bags and our brushes to work.
Though the morning was cold, Tom was happy and warm;
So, if all do their duty, they need not fear harm.

The Chimney Sweeper

(*from* Songs of Experience)

A little black thing among the snow,
Crying "'weep! 'weep!" in notes of woe!
"Where are thy father and mother? say?"
"They are both gone up to the church to pray.

5   Because I was happy upon the heath,②
And smil'd among the winter's snow,
They clothed me in the clothes of death,
And taught me to sing the notes of woe.

And because I am happy and dance and sing,

---

① want: lack
② heath: a tract of wasteland

10   They think they have done me no injury,
       And are gone to praise God and his Priest and King,
       Who make up a heaven of our misery."

London

(*from* Songs of Innocence and of Experience)

I wander thro' each charter'd street,①
Near where the charter'd② Thames does flow.
And mark in every face I meet
Marks of weakness, marks of woe.

5   In every cry of every Man,
       In every Infants cry of fear,
       In every voice: in every ban,
       The mind-forg'd manacles③ I hear.

       How the Chimney-sweepers cry
10   Every black'ning Church appals,
       And the hapless④ Soldiers sigh
       Runs in blood down Palace walls.

       But most thro' midnight streets I hear
       How the youthful Harlots curse
15   Blasts⑤ the new-born Infants tear,
       And blights⑥ with plagues the Marriage hearse.⑦

---

①chartered street: street which is mapped out and documented as private property
②chartered: here it means "marked on a map."
③mind-forged manacles: mind-controlled devices
④hapless: unlucky, unfortunate
⑤blast: ruin or make something dry up and die
⑥blight: destroy or affect something (especially a plant) with a disease or injury
⑦hearse: a vehicle for carrying the coffin at a funeral

Questions for Discussion

1. Please compare the narrators of the two "The Chimney Sweeper" poems. How are they similar and different? Please explain what the first "The Chimney Sweeper" poem suggest about the prospects of the chimney sweepers, and what the second "The Chimney Sweeper" poem suggests about those "adults" who are referred to.
2. What sights and sounds does Blake experience in London? Based on what he sees and hears, what do you think is his view of London?
3. According to the three poems, how were the children affected by the society they lived in?

William Wordsworth (1770 – 1850)

William Wordsworth was one of the most important figures of English Romanticism. He was born and grew up near the Lake District, a beautiful scenic area in north-western England. From his very early years, he had a profound love for nature, which characterizes all his works. His parents died when he was very young, and he was taken care of by relatives. From 1787 to 1791 he studied at Cambridge. In 1791 he went to France to learn French in preparation for a career as a tutor. He was so greatly impressed by the French revolutionary zeal that he would have joined in the revolution if his relatives had not urgently called him back. His revolutionary enthusiasm died down as he was shocked at the massacres during the Reign of Terror under the rule of Robespierre. From 1799 to his death, he became more and more conservative and lived in retirement in the Lake District in the company of his sister Dorothy Wordsworth and his friend Coleridge. He was made Poet Laureate in 1843.

Wordsworth began writing poetry as a young boy in grammar school, and his tour of Mainland Europe deepened his love for nature and his sympathy for the common man; both being major themes in his poetry.

He is often remembered as a poet speculating on spiritual and epistemological① issues, a poet concerned with the human relationship to nature, and a fierce advocate of using common people's vocabulary and speech patterns in poetry.

My Heart Leaps Up

My heart leaps up when I behold
  A rainbow in the sky:
So was it when my life began;
So is it now I am a man;
So be it when I shall grow old,
  Or let me die!
The Child is father of the Man;
And I could wish my days to be
Bound each to each by natural piety.

Questions for Discussion

1. According to lines 1-2, what greatly excites the speaker? And what makes him feel he would rather die?
2. What's your understanding of the seemingly contradictory statement "The Child is father of the Man"? In what sense is it true?
3. What does line 9 suggest about the speaker's piety? Does he worship a rainbow as the sign of covenant between God and humankind as stated in the Bible in the episode of Noah's story, or does he worship the rainbow as a sign of nature?

---

① epistemological: relating to the part of philosophy that is about the study of how human beings know things

Samuel Taylor Coleridge (1772 – 1834)

Samuel Taylor Coleridge was born in Devon, a county in south-west England. His father was vicar of the parish and headmaster of the local grammar school. Coleridge was educated at Christ's Hospital① and Jesus College, Cambridge, but never completed his degree.

Coleridge was one of the founders of the Romantic Movement and a friend of Wordsworth. He suffered from bouts of insanity, probably as a result of bi-polar disorder that was treated with laudanum,② which led to his opium addiction. This addiction threw him into a life of poverty. He died of heart failure that was likely linked to his addiction.

Coleridge is best remembered for his long narrative poem written in ballad form named "The Rime of the Ancient Mariner" as well as his fantastic poem "Kubla Khan." The composition of "Kubla Khan" has an interesting story attached to it. The story suggests that when Coleridge was living in a cottage in Somerset, one day he fell asleep after dosing himself with laudanum while reading about the Khan Kubla③ in a travel book called *Purchas His Pilgrimage* (1613). Amazingly, during his profound sleep of about three hours he dreamed of Kubla Khan. On awaking, he instantly wrote down the lines that are here preserved. However, he was interrupted by an unnamed visitor on undefined business. After the visitor left, Coleridge was unable to remember the rest of the dream and finally the work was published with his own definition as a "fragment."

Purcha His Pilgrimage was written by Samuel Purchas (1577 – 1626)

---

①Christ's Hospital: the name of a famous English school which was specially devoted to fatherless and motherless children

②laudanum: a mixture of opium dissolved in alcohol used until the early 20th century as a pain-killer (Its use is now generally illegal in most countries because of its addictive properties but in the 19th century it was used to treat a wide range of ailments from toothache to period pains and was even given to babies to make them sleep)

③the Khan Kubla: Kubla Khan, also spelled Kublai Khan, the founder of the Yuan Dynasty in China, the ruler that Marco Polo encountered, worked for, and wrote about

who described Xanadu① as the historical capital of Kublai Khan's empire. It has been suggested that Xanadu indeed existed and it was none other than Shangdu in Inner Mongolia, China. After the foundations of the real palace were excavated there, Shangdu was made a World Heritage site in 2012.

Although uncompleted, the poem is one of the most famous in the English language and has inspired many other artists, musicians, and writers. It is an excellent example of romantic poetry in its use of a unique location, its subjectivity, spontaneity, and mystic elements.

Kubla Khan

Or, a vision in a dream. A Fragment

  In Xanadu did Kubla Khan
  A stately pleasure-dome decree:
  Where Alph,② the sacred river, ran
  Through caverns③ measureless to man
5 Down to a sunless sea.
  So twice five miles of fertile ground
  With walls and towers were girdled④ round;
  And there were gardens bright with sinuous rills,⑤
  Where blossomed many an incense-bearing tree;
10 And here were forests ancient as the hills,
  Enfolding sunny spots of greenery.

  But oh! that deep romantic chasm⑥ which slanted

---

①Xanadu: Also called Shangdu, Xanadu received lasting fame in the western world thanks to Marco Polo's description of it in his celebrated book *Travels* (c. 1298). Its reputation was further boosted by Coleridge's romantic poem *Kubla Khan*, which makes Xanadu come to represent an idyllic, exotic, or luxurious place.
②Alph: a fictitious river
③cavern: a big cave
④girdled: surrounded
⑤sinuous rills: winding streams
⑥chasm: a deep canyon

        Down the green hill athwart a cedarn cover!①
        A savage place! as holy and enchanted
15   As e'er beneath a waning moon was haunted
        By woman wailing for her demon-lover!
        And from this chasm, with ceaseless turmoil seething,②
        As if this earth in fast thick pants were breathing,
        A mighty fountain momently was forced:
20   Amid whose swift half-intermitted burst
        Huge fragments③ vaulted like rebounding hail,
        Or chaffy grain beneath the thresher's flail:
        And mid these dancing rocks at once and ever
        It flung up momently the sacred river.
25   Five miles meandering with a mazy motion
        Through wood and dale the sacred river ran,
        Then reached the caverns measureless to man,
        And sank in tumult to a lifeless ocean;
        And 'mid this tumult Kubla heard from far
30   Ancestral voices prophesying war!
        The shadow④ of the dome of pleasure
        Floated midway on the waves;
        Where was heard the mingled measure
        From the fountain and the caves.
35   It was a miracle of rare device,
        A sunny pleasure-dome with caves of ice!

        A damsel⑤ with a dulcimer⑥
        In a vision once I saw:

---

①hill athwart a cedarn cover: hill covered with cedar trees
②seething: as if boiling
③fragments: rocks
④shadow: reflection
⑤damsel: an old word for a young woman
⑥dulcimer: a stringed musical instrument played with two hammers

It was an Abyssinian① maid
40　　And on her dulcimer she played,
Singing of Mount Abora.②
Could I revive within me③
Her symphony and song,
To such a deep delight 'twould win me,
45　　That with music loud and long,
I would build that dome in air,
That sunny dome! those caves of ice!
And all who heard should see them there,
And all should cry, Beware! Beware!
50　　His flashing eyes, his floating hair!
Weave a circle round him thrice,④
And close your eyes with holy dread
For he on honey-dew hath fed,
And drunk the milk of Paradise.

Questions for Discussion

1. What do you find in the pleasure dome Kubla Khan decreed to construct?
2. What part of the poem do you find especially imaginative?
3. What would your vision of a pleasure dome look like? What kinds of decorations or furniture would appear inside such a place?

Percy Bysshe Shelley (1792 – 1822)

Percy Bysshe Shelley was born of noble blood. His ancestors had been

---

① Abyssinian: old name for a native of Ethiopia
② Abora: a fictional mountain
③ revive within me: remember
④ thrice: three times (It was believed that drawing such circles could defend against demonic possession.)

Sussex aristocrats since early in the 17th century, and his father was a Member of Parliament. At the age of 18, he graduated from Eton and entered Oxford University, but he was expelled from his college for writing the atheistic pamphlet *The Necessity of Atheism* (1811). Shelly has often been seen as the epitome of the romantic poets: wild, reckless, and radical. His work reflects his unconventional lifestyle and beliefs. He was an atheist, a political radical (though he generally advocated non-violence), an advocate of free-love, and a vegetarian, all unusual beliefs for the time. The poem that follows reflects his radical politics. He was influential on many later writers including George Bernard Shaw (1856 – 1950) and he also influenced Karl Marx, and possibly Gandhi (1869 – 1948).

It may be safe to proclaim that Shelley is better known in China through his powerful poem "Ode to the West Wind" whose opening and ending stanzas are as follows:

> *O wild West Wind, thou breath of Autumn's being,*
> *Thou, from whose unseen presence the leaves dead*
> *Are driven, like ghosts from an enchanter fleeing,*
> ...
> *The trumpet of a prophecy! O, Wind,*
> *If winter comes, can Spring be far behind?*

"Song to the Men of England" was written in 1819 while Shelly was in exile in Italy to avoid legal action over his debts and his relationships. It was a response to the "Peterloo Massacre." In English history, the Peterloo Massacre refers to the brutal dispersal by cavalry of a political protest held on St. Peter's Fields in Manchester on August 16, 1819. Over a dozen people were killed and several hundred were wounded.

"Song to the Men of England" is a good example of the romantics' belief in radical change.

From 1789 to the 1830s | Chapter 5
The Development of Industrialisation and the Age of Romanticism

Song to the Men of England

Men of England, wherefore① plough
For the lords who lay ye low?
Wherefore weave with toil and care
The rich robes your tyrants wear?

5 Wherefore feed and clothe and save
From the cradle to the grave
Those ungrateful drones② who would
Drain your sweat—nay, drink your blood?

Wherefore, Bees of England,③ forge
10 Many a weapon, chain, and scourge,④
That these stingless drones may spoil
The forced produce of your toil?

Have ye leisure, comfort, calm,
Shelter, food, love's gentle balm?⑤
15 Or what is it ye buy so dear
With your pain and with your fear?

The seed ye sow, another reaps;
The wealth ye find, another keeps;
The robes ye weave, another wears;
20 The arms ye forge, another bears.

Sow seed—but let no tyrant reap;

---

①wherefore: why
②drones: bees that do not work (This is a metaphor for the idle ruling class.)
③bees of England: a metaphor for the proletariat
④scourge: whip
⑤balm: a fragrant ointment used to heal or soothe the skin

  Find wealth—let no imposter heap;
  Weave robes—let not the idle wear;
  Forge arms—in your defence to bear.

25 Shrink to your cellars, holes, and cells—
  In hall ye deck① another dwells.
  Why shake the chains ye wrought? Ye see
  The steel ye tempered glance on ye.

  With plough and spade and hoe and loom
30 Trace your grave and build your tomb
  And weave your winding-sheet—till fair
  England be your Sepulchre.②

Questions for Discussion

1. According to the first stanza, for whom did men of England plough and weave?
2. In the second stanza, to what does Shelley compare the lords and tyrants?
3. What message is conveyed through the use of irony in the last two stanzas?
4. Why do you think Shelley called the poem "a song"?

---

①deck: decorate
②sepulchre: tomb

From the 1830s to the End of the 19th Century
The Victorian Era and the Age of Realism

6.1 The Victorian Era: Industry and Empire

During the 19th century, for more than six decades Britain was reigned over by Queen Victoria (1819 – 1901) who came to the throne in 1837. That is why the latter period of the 19th century has been called the Victorian Age.

As has been stated in the previous chapter, by the end of the 18th century Britain had become the first industrialised nation in the world. The invention of practical steam power by James Watt enabled the growth of the factory system. The presence of coal and iron ore in the Midlands and North of England, Scotland, and South Wales meant that the factory system could develop around these areas. The major industries were the textile industry, coal mining, iron and steel manufacture, and shipbuilding, all of which allowed the growth of demand for the manufacture of consumer goods. The development of industry throughout the 19th century boosted British international trade, with Britain importing mainly raw materials as well as food, and exporting industrial products.

The 19th century also saw the expansion of the British Empire into the largest the world had known. This Second British Empire was based on India rather than North America and the Caribbean after the United States gained its independence from British rule in 1783, though Canada was finally established as a permanent part of the British Empire following Britain's defeat of the United States in the War of 1812.

6.2　Marxism and the British Working-Class

In spite of the prosperity brought by the growth of trade as well as by industry and the empire, the living conditions of the British working-class—particularly in the industrial towns and cities—were extremely bad. Housing was crowded and unsanitary, prostitution and alcoholism were rife, and child mortality was high. Even upper-class families, though financially powerful, were not immune from disease and death, especially among women in childbirth and shortly after. This features in Dickens's *Dombey and Son* and in many other novels of the period.

The shockingly widening gap between the rich and poor was the backdrop of *The Communist Manifesto* (1848) co-authored by Karl Marx and Friedrich Engels (1820 – 1895). Though they were both born in Germany, they spent much of their lives in Britain. Engels's family owned factories in Manchester, which facilitated Engels's writing of *The Condition of the Working Class in England* (1845), the product of his own observations of proletarian life in Manchester in the early 1840s.

The Communist Manifesto resulted from a meeting held in London participated by leaders of Communist organizations from across Europe. Neither Marx nor Engels would have claimed to have invented Communism. Without doubt, in *The Communist Manifesto* and his later work *Capital* (1867), Marx laid the foundation for the development of communist economic and social theory. Using the process of scientific investigation to analyse the political economy of western capitalism, Marx proposes solutions to the inequalities created by capitalism.

The Communist Manifesto opens with the following remarks:

A spectre① is haunting Europe—the spectre of Communism.
All the Powers of old Europe have entered into a holy alliance to

---

① spectre: ghost

exorcise this spectre: Pope and Tzar,①　Metternich and Guizot,② French Radicals and German police-spies.

It argues:

The history of all hitherto existing societies is the history of class struggles.

Freeman and slave, patrician③ and plebeian,④ lord and serf, guild-master⑤ and journeyman,⑥ in a word, oppressor and oppressed, stood in constant opposition to one another, carried on an uninterrupted, now hidden, now open fight, a fight that each time ended, either in a revolutionary re-constitution of society at large, or in the common ruin of the contending classes....

The modern bourgeois society that has sprouted from the ruins of feudal society has not done away with class antagonisms. It has but established new classes, new conditions of oppression, new forms of struggle in place of the old ones.

Our epoch, the epoch of the bourgeoisie, possesses, however, this distinctive feature: it has simplified the class antagonisms. Society as a whole is more and more splitting up into two great hostile camps, into two great classes directly facing each other—Bourgeoisie and Proletariat.

Also, it claims:

The discovery of America, the rounding of the Cape,⑦ opened up fresh ground for the rising bourgeoisie. The East-Indian and

---

① Pope and Tzar: the head of the Roman Catholic Church and the ruler of Russia, both notoriously reactionary figures
② Metternich and Guizot: Klemens von Metternich (1773 – 1859) was conservative Foreign Minister of Austria, while François Guizot (1787 – 1874) was liberal Prime Minister of France who later reviled for adopting conservative repressive measures when in power.
③ patrician: aristocrat
④ plebeian: proletarian
⑤ guild-master: senior member of an organisation of craftsmen
⑥ journeyman: ordinary craftsman
⑦ the Cape: the Cape of Good Hope in South Africa

Chinese markets, the colonisation of America, trade with the colonies, the increase in the means of exchange and in commodities generally, gave to commerce, to navigation, to industry, an impulse never before known, and thereby, to the revolutionary element in the tottering feudal society, a rapid development.

The Communist Manifesto closes with the phrase: "Workers of all lands, unite!" This spirit of struggle conforms to Marx's belief as outlined in his "Thesis on Feuerbach" (1845), which states "The philosophers have only interpreted the world, in various ways; the point is to change it." This is the very phrase engraved on his tombstone in Highgate Cemetery.

The Communist Manifesto led to revolutions across Europe but not in Britain. Many explanations have been given regarding this lack of action in Britain, including the influence of non-conformist① protestant religion such as Methodism among the working classes, the legalisation of trade unions, and the gradual extension of the vote to all males by the end of the century. Due to this parliamentary outlet for political discontent and the birth of the Labour Party in the late 19th century as a democratic socialist party directly representing the interests of the working-classes, reformism rather than revolution became the major route in Britain, so that the living conditions of the working classes would be bettered.

Apart from novels such as Dickens's *Hard Times*, Engels's *The Condition of the Working Class in England* gives the best description of working-class life in Britain.

6.3　Darwin and the Theory of Evolution

Besides Marx and Engels's history-changing political document *The Communist Manifesto*, the 19th century also witnessed the publication of Darwin's *On the Origin of Species*, one of the most influential theoretical works of the century.

---

① non-conformist: a person who does not conform to a generally accepted pattern of thought or action (Here it means "one who does not conform to the Church of England.")

In the mid-19th century, the expansion of the British Empire and the development of steam-powered travel both on land and sea made long-distance travel much easier. This led to specimens of flora and fauna[①] being brought to England from all over the world.

During this period there also developed an interest in the study of fossils, which complemented the overall increased interest in the natural world. Charles Darwin (1809 – 1882) is often considered as the greatest biologist in history. He initially studied medicine at Edinburgh University but became more interested in natural history and transferred to Cambridge University where he gained a BA degree. After graduating in 1831 he joined a naval expedition on HMS *Beagle*. During the five years the voyage lasted, Darwin collected a vast quantity of practical evidence of variation in birds and animals which he was able to use in the development of his Theory of Evolution. He published widely on geology as well as on natural history; his *The Voyage of the Beagle* (1839), which described his discoveries, established him as a leading biologist. Twenty years later, in 1859, he finally completed *On the Origin of Species* outlining his years of research into evolutionary development. In 1871 he published *The Descent of Man*, applying evolutionary theory to humankind.

Upon its publication, *On the Origin of Species* caused major debate, with Christian churchmen suggesting that it challenged the existence of God as creator of the world. Darwin was defended by many scientists and theologians including his friend and fellow biologist Thomas Huxley (1825 – 1895). In Chapter Ⅳ of *On the Origin of Species*, Darwin writes: "This preservation of favourable individual differences and variations, and the destruction of those which are injurious, I have called Natural Selection, or the Survival of the Fittest."

6.4 The Philosophy of Utilitarianism

One of the most influential philosophies of the period was Utilitarianism. It

---

①flora and fauna: plants and animals

stems from Jeremy Bentham (1748 – 1832) and John Stuart Mill (1806 – 1873), both being English philosophers, economists, and political thinkers. Utilitarian theory is a reason-based theory that determines right from wrong by focusing on outcomes, thus the theory is a form of consequentialism. A maxim of utilitarianism is "the greatest good for the greatest number." Given that human reason is the only approach to determining whether a matter does "the greatest good for the greatest number," apparently this philosophy underestimates feelings, emotions, culture, and justice, etc. However, the industrial capitalists welcomed the philosophy; they argued that what they were doing to the working people was for the greatest happiness of the greatest number.

Despite its influence, many thinkers and writers of the period were opposed to utilitarian philosophy, such as Thomas Carlyle (1795 – 1881), Charles Dickens (1812 – 1870), and Benjamin Disraeli (1804 – 1881), to name but a few.

6.5 An Age of Fiction: Realism and Naturalism

Although poetry and the essay continued to play an important role in English literature, the novel overtook them as the most popular form. Novels were often published in serial form in weekly or monthly journals available at low cost compared with a hard-back book, although most were later published in book form in various editions acceptable and affordable to different social groups.

Realism and naturalism came into vogue as a result of a number of reasons. First of all, the 1820s and the 1830s saw the passing of the prominent romantics: Keats in 1821, Shelley in 1822, Byron in 1824, Coleridge in 1834. Though Wordsworth outlived the 1830s, his literary productivity declined dramatically. More importantly, Darwin's Theory of Evolution led to a reassessment of humankind's position in the universe, and it was under the influence of Darwinism that naturalism arose. Initially known as realism, naturalism first became popular in continental Europe in the 1850s with painters such as Courbet① and the publication of Flaubert's② *Madam Bovary* (1856). Realist artists and writers found their subjects in the average person going about their everyday life.

Realism deals with individuals rather than character types. It required new literary conventions and methods to express this new perspective. Imagination became less important than a detailed and truthful representation of the characters and their lives. Towards the end of the 19th century, a split developed between realism and naturalism, with the former seeking to show how society actually operated, while the latter seeking to apply the tools of the natural sciences to literature. The following excerpt from *The Experimental Novel* (1880) by Émile Zola (1840 – 1902), the influential French theorist and novelist, vividly describes the mechanism of naturalism:

> *In short, we must operate with characters, passions, human and social data as the chemist and the physicist work on inert bodies, as the physiologist works on living bodies. Determinism governs everything. It is scientific investigation; it is experimental reasoning that combats one by one the hypotheses of the idealists and will replace novels of pure imagination by novels of observation and experiment.*

In sum, naturalism holds the view that humans were animals whose existence was shaped by such main factors as heredity, environment, and the pressures of the moment, and that the course of human lives was determined by compulsive instincts such as hunger or sex as well as by economic and social conditions.

Britain in this era saw the appearance of a galaxy of brilliant novelists. Besides Dickens, Hardy, and Conrad, whose works are anthologised in this collection, other representative writers and titles include William M.

---

①Courbet: Gustave Courbet (1819 – 1877), French realist painter
②Flaubert: Gustave Flaubert (1821 – 1880), French novelist best remembered for his naturalist fiction *Madam Bovary*

Thackeray's *Vanity Fair*, George Eliot's *Adam Bede*, and the Brontë sisters' *Jane Eyre*, *Wuthering Heights*, and *Agnes Grey* respectively by Charlotte, Emily, and Anne.

Alfred Tennyson (1809 – 1892) and Robert Browning (1812 – 1889) were two of the most prestigious poets of the Victorian Age. For his exceptional achievements in poetry, Tennyson was appointed Poet Laureate following the death of Wordsworth. Browning was an expert at dissecting the hearts and minds of his characters, and that was why sometimes he has been called the "poet of men's souls." His poem "My Last Duchess" is a classic example of his innovative "soul-revealing" poems.

George Bernard Shaw was, without doubt, the best playwright of the period and he is often considered the greatest British playwright apart from Shakespeare. Shaw was born in Dublin, Ireland, and moved to London in 1876. He was a socialist and one of the founders of the Fabian Society, which later became the British Labour Party.① In his long life he wrote over sixty plays, most of which contain social and political comment. While the style of his plays is essentially naturalistic, using realistic scenery and generally believable and rounded characters, the political element in his works places them firmly in the category of social realism. Social realism seeks not simply to show the external reality of life in a scientific manner as naturalism does, but to explore the underlying structure of society and its politics. Shaw's plays are moralistic but take the side of the oppressed and underprivileged in society. His major works are *Widowers' Houses* (1892), *Mrs Warren's Profession* (1893), *Arms and the Man* (1894), *Major Barbara* (1905), and *Pygmalion* (1913). Besides his plays he wrote books and pamphlets on numerous social and political issues.

Charles Dickens (1812 – 1870)

Charles Dickens is considered by many to be a master story-teller and the greatest novelist of the 19th century writing in English. During his

---

① the British Labour Party: one of the two major political parties in Britain, with the other being the Conservative Party

lifetime he was, in a modern phrase, a "megastar." His works, which contained much social criticism, influenced changes in British society. Through works such as *A Christmas Carol* (1843), Dickens was responsible for the transformation of Christmas in Britain and its colonies from a church and community-based festival to the family celebration it has become today. He wrote fifteen major novels, several novellas, hundreds of short-stories and non-fiction pieces, as well as a few plays and non-fiction books.

Dickens was born in Portsmouth—a major port on the South coast of England—into a lower-middle class family, his father being a minor government official. His childhood was disrupted, in part because of his father's pitiful ability to manage money effectively, which led to the poor man's imprisonment for debt in London. Dickens's background coloured his writing. He drew on his own experiences and empirical observations of society, particularly of the life of the poor, for his work. His descriptions of the appalling conditions in which the majority of the population lived are both moving and accurate.

Like most 19th century English novels, Dickens's work was first published in serial form in weekly or monthly magazines. Dickens himself founded and edited a number of these magazines, with the most famous being *Household Words*. Apart from publishing his own novels, short stories, and observational pieces, these journals enabled Dickens to encourage other writers by publishing their early works.

The shortest of Dickens's novels, *Hard Times* (1854) was first published in *Household Words*. Set in a northern industrial town named Coketown, the story presents a description of the life of the industrial proletariat and its employers in the mid-19th century. It is a bitter indictment[①] of industrialisation, with its dehumanising effects on workers and communities in mid-19th century England. From the very beginning of the story, Dickens establishes himself within a contemporary debate on the nature of learning, knowledge, and education, criticising utilitarianism. The novel is divided into three "books" entitled "Sowing," "Reaping," and

---

① indictment: a formal charge or accusation of a serious crime

"Garnering." Mr. Gradgrind, "the speaker" in the opening chapter, a man of "facts and calculations," epitomises the philosophy of utilitarianism.

Hard Times
Chapter I   The One Thing Needful
(Excerpt)

'Now, what I want is, Facts. Teach these boys and girls nothing but Facts. Facts alone are wanted in life. Plant nothing else, and root out everything else. You can only form the minds of reasoning animals upon Facts: nothing else will ever be of any service to them. This is the principle on which I bring up my own children, and this is the principle on which I bring up these children. Stick to Facts, sir!'

The scene was a plain, bare, monotonous vault of a school-room, and the speaker's square forefinger emphasised his observations by underscoring every sentence with a line on the schoolmaster's sleeve. The emphasis was helped by the speaker's square wall of a forehead, which had his eyebrows for its base, while his eyes found commodious cellarage① in two dark caves, overshadowed by the wall. The emphasis was helped by the speaker's mouth, which was wide, thin, and hard set. The emphasis was helped by the speaker's voice, which was inflexible, dry, and dictatorial. The emphasis was helped by the speaker's hair, which bristled on the skirts of his bald head, a plantation of firs to keep the wind from its shining surface, all covered with knobs, like the crust of a plum pie, as if the head had scarcely warehouse-room for the hard facts stored inside. The speaker's obstinate carriage, square coat, square legs, square shoulders, nay, his very neckcloth, trained to take him by the throat with an unaccommodating grasp, like a stubborn fact, as it was,—all helped the emphasis.

'In this life, we want nothing but Facts, sir; nothing but Facts!'

The speaker, and the schoolmaster, and the third grown person present, all backed a little, and swept with their eyes the inclined plane of

---

① commodious cellarage: spacious cellars (This is a metaphor for the speaker's deep-set eyes.)

little vessels then and there arranged in order, ready to have imperial gallons of facts poured into them until they were full to the brim.

Chapter Ⅱ　Murdering the Innocents
(Excerpt)

Thomas Gradgrind, sir. A man of realities. A man of facts and calculations. A man who proceeds upon the principle that two and two are four, and nothing over, and who is not to be talked into allowing for anything over. Thomas Gradgrind, sir—peremptorily① Thomas—Thomas Gradgrind. With a rule and a pair of scales,② and the multiplication table always in his pocket, sir, ready to weigh and measure any parcel of human nature, and tell you exactly what it comes to. It is a mere question of figures, a case of simple arithmetic. You might hope to get some other nonsensical belief into the head of George Gradgrind, or Augustus Gradgrind, or John Gradgrind, or Joseph Gradgrind (all supposititious,③ non-existent persons), but into the head of Thomas Gradgrind—no, sir!

In such terms Mr. Gradgrind always mentally introduced himself, whether to his private circle of acquaintance, or to the public in general. In such terms, no doubt, substituting the words 'boys and girls,' for 'sir,' Thomas Gradgrind now presented Thomas Gradgrind to the little pitchers④ before him, who were to be filled so full of facts.

Indeed, as he eagerly sparkled at them from the cellarage before mentioned, he seemed a kind of cannon loaded to the muzzle⑤ with facts, and prepared to blow them clean out of the regions of childhood at one discharge. He seemed a galvanizing apparatus, too, charged with a grim mechanical substitute for the tender young imaginations that were to be stormed away.

'Girl number twenty,' said Mr. Gradgrind, squarely pointing with his

---

① peremptorily: in a commanding manner
② scales: handheld device for weighing things
③ supposititious: invented, imaginary
④ pitchers: jars
⑤ muzzle: the open end of a weapon

square forefinger, 'I don't know that girl. Who is that girl?'

'Sissy Jupe, sir,' explained number twenty, blushing, standing up, and curtseying.

'Sissy is not a name,' said Mr. Gradgrind. 'Don't call yourself Sissy. Call yourself Cecilia.'

'It's father as calls me Sissy, sir,' returned the young girl in a trembling voice, and with another curtsey.

'Then he has no business to do it,' said Mr. Gradgrind. 'Tell him he mustn't. Cecilia Jupe. Let me see. What is your father?'

'He belongs to the horse-riding,① if you please, sir.'

Mr. Gradgrind frowned, and waved off the objectionable calling with his hand.

'We don't want to know anything about that, here. You mustn't tell us about that, here. Your father breaks horses,② don't he?'

'If you please, sir, when they can get any to break, they do break horses in the ring, sir.'

'You mustn't tell us about the ring, here. Very well, then. Describe your father as a horsebreaker. He doctors sick horses, I dare say?'

'Oh yes, sir.'

'Very well, then. He is a veterinary surgeon, a farrier,③ and horsebreaker. Give me your definition of a horse.'

(Sissy Jupe thrown into the greatest alarm by this demand.)

'Girl number twenty unable to define a horse!' said Mr. Gradgrind, for the general behoof④ of all the little pitchers. 'Girl number twenty possessed of no facts, in reference to one of the commonest of animals! Some boy's definition of a horse. Bitzer, yours.'

The square finger, moving here and there, lighted suddenly on Bitzer, perhaps because he chanced to sit in the same ray of sunlight which, darting

---

① the horse-riding: the circus
② break horses: tame wild horses for riding
③ farrier: a blacksmith who specialises in the shoeing of horses
④ behoof: benefit

in at one of the bare windows of the intensely white-washed room, irradiated Sissy. For, the boys and girls sat on the face of the inclined plane in two compact bodies, divided up the centre by a narrow interval; and Sissy, being at the corner of a row on the sunny side, came in for the beginning of a sunbeam, of which Bitzer, being at the corner of a row on the other side, a few rows in advance, caught the end. But, whereas the girl was so dark-eyed and dark-haired, that she seemed to receive a deeper and more lustrous colour from the sun, when it shone upon her, the boy was so light-eyed and light-haired that the self-same rays appeared to draw out of him what little colour he ever possessed. His cold eyes would hardly have been eyes, but for the short ends of lashes which, by bringing them into immediate contrast with something paler than themselves, expressed their form. His short-cropped hair might have been a mere continuation of the sandy freckles on his forehead and face. His skin was so unwholesomely deficient in the natural tinge, that he looked as though, if he were cut, he would bleed white.

'Bitzer,' said Thomas Gradgrind. 'Your definition of a horse.'

'Quadruped.[①] Graminivorous.[②] Forty teeth, namely twenty-four grinders, four eye-teeth, and twelve incisive. Sheds coat in the spring; in marshy countries, sheds hoofs, too. Hoofs hard, but requiring to be shod[③] with iron. Age known by marks in mouth.' Thus (and much more) Bitzer.

'Now girl number twenty,' said Mr. Gradgrind. 'You know what a horse is.'

She curtseyed again, and would have blushed deeper, if she could have blushed deeper than she had blushed all this time. Bitzer, after rapidly blinking at Thomas Gradgrind with both eyes at once, and so catching the light upon his quivering ends of lashes that they looked like the antennae of busy insects, put his knuckles to his freckled forehead, and sat down again.

The third gentleman now stepped forth. A mighty man at cutting and

---

① quadruped: four-legged
② graminivorous: of an eater of grass
③ shod: past tense of "to shoe"

drying, he was; a government officer; in his way (and in most other people's too), a professed pugilist;① always in training, always with a system to force down the general throat like a bolus,② always to be heard of at the bar of his little Public-office, ready to fight all England ...

'Very well,' said this gentleman, briskly smiling, and folding his arms. 'That's a horse. Now, let me ask you girls and boys, Would you paper a room with representations of horses?'

After a pause, one half of the children cried in chorus, 'Yes, sir!' Upon which the other half, seeing in the gentleman's face that Yes was wrong, cried out in chorus, 'No, sir!'—as the custom is, in these examinations.

'Of course, No. Why wouldn't you?'

A pause. One corpulent③ slow boy, with a wheezy manner of breathing, ventured the answer, Because he wouldn't paper a room at all, but would paint it.

'You *must* paper it,' said the gentleman, rather warmly.

'You must paper it,' said Thomas Gradgrind, 'whether you like it or not. Don't tell *us* you wouldn't paper it. What do you mean, boy?'

'I'll explain to you, then,' said the gentleman, after another and a dismal pause, 'why you wouldn't paper a room with representations of horses. Do you ever see horses walking up and down the sides of rooms in reality—in fact? Do you?'

'Yes, sir!' from one half. 'No, sir!' from the other.

'Of course no,' said the gentleman, with an indignant look at the wrong half. 'Why, then, you are not to see anywhere, what you don't see in fact; you are not to have anywhere, what you don't have in fact. What is called Taste, is only another name for Fact.' Thomas Gradgrind nodded his approbation.④

'This is a new principle, a discovery, a great discovery,' said the

---

① pugilist: boxer
② bolus: old word for a large pill
③ corpulent: fat, fleshy
④ approbation: approval, praise

gentleman. 'Now, I'll try you again. Suppose you were going to carpet a room. Would you use a carpet having a representation of flowers upon it?'

There being a general conviction by this time that 'No, sir!' was always the right answer to this gentleman, the chorus of No was very strong. Only a few feeble stragglers said Yes: among them Sissy Jupe.

'Girl number twenty,' said the gentleman, smiling in the calm strength of knowledge.

Sissy blushed, and stood up.

'So you would carpet your room—or your husband's room, if you were a grown woman, and had a husband—with representations of flowers, would you?' said the gentleman. 'Why would you?'

'If you please, sir, I am very fond of flowers,' returned the girl.

'And is that why you would put tables and chairs upon them, and have people walking over them with heavy boots?'

'It wouldn't hurt them, sir. They wouldn't crush and wither, if you please, sir. They would be the pictures of what was very pretty and pleasant, and I would fancy①—'

'Ay, ay, ay! But you mustn't fancy,' cried the gentleman, quite elated by coming so happily to his point. 'That's it! You are never to fancy.'

'You are not, Cecilia Jupe,' Thomas Gradgrind solemnly repeated, 'to do anything of that kind.'

'Fact, fact, fact!' said the gentleman. And 'Fact, fact, fact!' repeated Thomas Gradgrind.

'You are to be in all things regulated and governed,' said the gentleman, 'by fact. We hope to have, before long, a board of fact, composed of commissioners of fact, who will force the people to be a people of fact, and of nothing but fact. You must discard the word Fancy altogether. You have nothing to do with it. You are not to have, in any object of use or ornament, what would be a contradiction in fact. You don't walk upon flowers in fact; you cannot be allowed to walk upon flowers in carpets. You don't find that foreign birds and butterflies come and perch

---

① fancy: imagine

upon your crockery;① you cannot be permitted to paint foreign birds and butterflies upon your crockery. You never meet with quadrupeds going up and down walls; you must not have quadrupeds represented upon walls. You must use,' said the gentleman, 'for all these purposes, combinations and modifications (in primary colours) of mathematical figures which are susceptible of proof and demonstration. This is the new discovery. This is fact. This is taste.'

The girl curtseyed, and sat down. She was very young, and she looked as if she were frightened by the matter-of-fact prospect the world afforded.

'Now, if Mr. M'Choakumchild,' said the gentleman, 'will proceed to give his first lesson here, Mr. Gradgrind, I shall be happy, at your request, to observe his mode of procedure.'

Mr. Gradgrind was much obliged. 'Mr. M'Choakumchild, we only wait for you.'

So, Mr. M'Choakumchild began in his best manner. He and some one hundred and forty other schoolmasters, had been lately turned at the same time, in the same factory, on the same principles, like so many pianoforte② legs. He had been put through an immense variety of paces, and had answered volumes of head-breaking questions. Orthography,③ etymology,④ syntax,⑤ and prosody,⑥ biography, astronomy, geography, and general cosmography,⑦ the sciences of compound proportion,⑧ algebra, land-surveying and levelling, vocal music, and drawing from models, were all at the ends of his ten chilled fingers. He had worked his stony way into Her

---

①crockery: earthenware, pottery
②pianoforte: formal term for "piano"
③orthography: the conventional spelling system of a language
④etymology: the study of the origin of words and the way in which their meanings have changed throughout history
⑤syntax: the ways in which words can be used to make sentences
⑥prosody: the study of all the elements of language that contribute toward rhythmic and sound effects, chiefly in poetry but also in prose
⑦cosmography: the study of the universe or a general description of the world or of the universe
⑧compound proportion: complex fractions

Majesty's most Honourable Privy Council's① Schedule B, and had taken the bloom off the higher branches of mathematics and physical science, French, German, Latin, and Greek. He knew all about all the Water Sheds of all the world (whatever they are), and all the histories of all the peoples, and all the names of all the rivers and mountains, and all the productions, manners, and customs of all the countries, and all their boundaries and bearings on the two and thirty points of the compass. Ah, rather overdone, M'Choakumchild. If he had only learnt a little less, how infinitely better he might have taught much more!

He went to work in this preparatory lesson, not unlike Morgiana② in the Forty Thieves: looking into all the vessels ranged before him, one after another, to see what they contained. Say, good M'Choakumchild. When from thy boiling store, thou shalt fill each jar brim full by-and-by, dost thou think that thou wilt always kill outright the robber Fancy lurking within—or sometimes only maim him and distort him!

Questions for Discussion

1. What major problems does the excerpt show about the social abuses in school? How would you argue against the opinion that "the one thing needful" for students to learn in school is facts? What do you think are crucial for students to learn in school?
2. How do the first two chapters foreshadow the "hard times" that are ahead?
3. What lesson can we 21st century people learn from the work concerning education in order to avoid the emergence of "hard times"?

---

① Her Majesty's most Honourable Privy Council: Usually known as the Privy Council, it is a formal body of advisers to the Sovereign in the United Kingdom. Its membership is mostly made up of senior politicians who are (or have been) members of the House of Commons or the House of Lords.
② Morgiana: the servant of Ali Baba who discovers the thieves hiding in the oil-jars and kills them

Thomas Hardy (1840 – 1928)

Thomas Hardy was born in Dorset, a county of south-west England, which inspired his fictitious Wessex works. The son of a stonemason, Hardy trained as an architect. He wrote in his spare time until in 1874 his *Far from the Madding Crowd* achieved success. He then gave up architecture for writing.

Hardy was a prolific author producing novels, short stories, plays, and poems. Most of his works are set in the fictional county of Wessex, which is broadly the area of the Alfred the Great's Anglo-Saxon kingdom of Wessex. Unfolding against a rural background drawn as an elegy for vanishing country ways, his novels contain some of the greatest descriptions written of the English countryside, though those such as *Far from the Madding Crowd*, *The Mayor of Casterbridge* (1886), and *Tess of the D'Urbervilles* (1891) recognise the negative effect of economic factors and modern developments in machinery (for example the steam-powered threshing machine) on rural life in general and on agricultural workers' lives in particular. They also express his concern with the position of women in society, especially the double standards Victorian society applied in sexual matters. He questioned the traditional Christian view of God. His works often demonstrate his Fatalist beliefs, showing the inexorability① of human destiny.

Towards the end of the 19th century, Britain's economic pre-eminence was being challenged by newly emergent industrial powers, such as the United States and Germany, which, united under Prussia in 1870, was the home of much industrial innovation.

Britain's economic power was based on its empire, which not just provided a huge market for industrial products but also supplied raw materials for its factories. Britain had become a net importer of food, mainly from the newly established dominions of Canada, Australia, and New Zealand, all of which enjoyed self-government under the British Crown. As a result of this importation of food, the agricultural economy of

---

①inexorability: mercilessness

Britain suffered a depression, made worse by "Imperial Preference," an economic policy that ensured tariff-free trade between the countries of the Empire. The industrial sector of the British economy, particularly the textile industry, also suffered from the importation of cheap products, especially from India. It is against this economic background that Hardy's novels of rural life in the southwest of England are set.

Tess of the D'Urbervilles is Hardy's masterpiece. Subtitled *A Pure Woman Faithfully Presented*, the novel is about the tragic life of Tess Durbeyfield. After her impoverished family learns of its noble lineage, naive Tess is sent by her slothful① father and ignorant mother to make an appeal to a nearby wealthy family who bear the ancestral name of d'Urberville. Seduced by Alec, the son of the family, Tess gives birth to a child, who dies in infancy. Then Tess goes to work on a dairy farm, where she is engaged to Angel Clare, a man of liberal mind and the son of a clergyman. On the wedding night, Tess confesses to Angel her sexual past. On hearing his wife's tale, Clare regards Tess as an impure woman and abandons her. After going through a long train of misfortunes and a period of hard work on the Flintcomb-Ash farm, Tess meets Clare again, who has repented and come back to find her. But it turns out to be too late. Tess murders Alec whom she once again has been compelled to reunite with after her abandonment by Angel. In Angel's company, after hiding for a short while, Tess is arrested, tried, and hanged. The book ends with the remark "Justice was done, and the President of the Immortals had ended his sport with Tess." The following excerpt is selected from Chapter 43 when Tess is working in harsh conditions on the Flintcomb-Ash farm.

Tess of the D'Urbervilles
Chapter 43
(Excerpt)

There was no exaggeration in Marian's definition of Flintcomb-Ash

---

①slothful: lazy

farm as a starve-acre place. The single fat thing on the soil was Marian herself; and she was an importation. Of the three classes of village, the village cared for by its lord, the village cared for by itself, and the village uncared for either by itself or by its lord (in other words, the village of a resident squire's tenantry, the village of free or copy-holders, and the absentee-owner's village, farmed with the land) this place, Flintcomb-Ash, was the third.

But Tess set to work. Patience, that blending of moral courage with physical timidity, was now no longer a minor feature in Mrs Angel Clare; and it sustained her.

The swede①-field in which she and her companion were set hacking was a stretch of a hundred odd acres, in one patch, on the highest ground of the farm, rising above stony lanchets or lynchets②—the outcrop③ of siliceous veins in the chalk formation, composed of myriads of loose white flints in bulbous, cusped, and phallic shapes. The upper half of each turnip had been eaten off by the live-stock, and it was the business of the two women to grub up the lower or earthy half of the root with a hooked fork called a hacker, that it might be eaten also. Every leaf of the vegetable having already been consumed, the whole field was in colour a desolate drab; it was a complexion without features, as if a face, from chin to brow, should be only an expanse of skin. The sky wore, in another colour, the same likeness; a white vacuity④ of countenance with the lineaments⑤ gone. So these two upper and nether visages confronted each other all day long, the white face looking down on the brown face, and the brown face looking up at the white face, without anything standing between them but the two girls crawling over the surface of the former like flies.

Nobody came near them, and their movements showed a mechanical

---

① swede: a large round yellow root vegetable
② lanchet or lynchet: both "lanchet" and "lynchet" mean the same thing, which is a ridge or ledge formed along the downhill side of a plot by ploughing in ancient times.
③ outcrop: a rock formation that is visible on the surface
④ vacuity: empty space or emptiness
⑤ lineament: a distinctive feature or characteristic, especially of the face

regularity; their forms standing enshrouded in Hessian① "wroppers"—sleeved brown pinafores, tied behind to the bottom, to keep their gowns from blowing about—scant skirts revealing boots that reached high up the ankles, and yellow sheepskin gloves with gauntlets. The pensive character which the curtained hood lent to their bent heads would have reminded the observer of some early Italian conception of the two Marys.

They worked on hour after hour, unconscious of the forlorn aspect they bore in the landscape, not thinking of the justice or injustice of their lot. Even in such a position as theirs it was possible to exist in a dream. In the afternoon the rain came on again, and Marian said that they need not work any more. But if they did not work they would not be paid; so they worked on. It was so high a situation, this field, that the rain had no occasion to fall, but raced along horizontally upon the yelling wind, sticking into them like glass splinters till they were wet through. Tess had not known till now what was really meant by that. There are degrees of dampness, and a very little is called being wet through in common talk. But to stand working slowly in a field, and feel the creep of rain-water, first in legs and shoulders, then on hips and head, then at back, front, and sides, and yet to work on till the leaden light diminishes and marks that the sun is down, demands a distinct modicum② of stoicism, even of valour. Yet they did not feel the wetness so much as might be supposed. They were both young, and they were talking of the time when they lived and loved together at Talbothays Dairy, that happy green tract of land where summer had been liberal in her gifts; in substance to all, emotionally to these. Tess would fain not have conversed with Marian of the man who was legally, if not actually, her husband; but the irresistible fascination of the subject betrayed her into reciprocating Marian's remarks. And thus, as has been said, though the damp curtains of their bonnets flapped smartly into their faces, and their wrappers clung about them to wearisomeness, they lived all this afternoon in memories of green, sunny, romantic Talbothays.

'You can see a gleam of a hill within a few miles o'Froom Valley from

---

① Hessian: a type of strong rough brown cloth, used especially for making sacks
② modicum: a small amount

here when 'tis fine,' said Marian.

'Ah! Can you!' said Tess, awake to the new value of this locality.

So the two forces were at work here as everywhere, the inherent will to enjoy, and the circumstantial will against enjoyment. Marian's will had a method of assisting itself by taking from her pocket as the afternoon wore on a pint bottle corked with white rag, from which she invited Tess to drink. Tess's unassisted power of dreaming, however, being enough for her sublimation at present, she declined except the merest sip, and then Marian took a pull herself from the spirits.

'I've got used to it,' she said, 'and can't leave it off now. 'Tis my only comfort—You see I lost him: you didn't; and you can do without it, perhaps.'

Tess thought her loss as great as Marian's, but upheld by the dignity of being Angel's wife, in the letter at least, she accepted Marian's differentiation.

Amid this scene Tess slaved in the morning frosts and in the afternoon rains. When it was not swede-grubbing it was swede-trimming, in which process they sliced off the earth and the fibres with a bill-hook before storing the roots for future use. At this occupation they could shelter themselves by a thatched hurdle if it rained; but if it was frosty even their thick leather gloves could not prevent the frozen masses they handled from biting their fingers. Still Tess hoped. She had a conviction that sooner or later the magnanimity which she persisted in reckoning as a chief ingredient of Clare's character would lead him to rejoin her....

Questions for Discussion

1. In the 3rd paragraph of the extract, what are the images that strike you most forcibly? Please explain why Tess and Marian are called "flies."
2. How do Tess and Marian seek escape from the present harshness?
3. According to your understanding, what victimizes Tess?
4. How much do you agree that an individual's fate is determined by the environment?

Alfred, Lord Tennyson (1809 – 1892)

Alfred Tennyson was born into a clergyman's family. Living almost through the Victorian Age, he has seemed the embodiment of his age more than any other Victorian-era writer. Tennyson, who was appointed as Poet Laureate following the death of Wordsworth, wrote lots of extremely popular lyric poems on classical themes. His interest in classical literature was in part prompted by the nature of education in the public schools which taught Greek and Latin as part of what is called a "classical education." The British also saw their empire as mirroring and surpassing that of the Romans, thus they often used Latin and Ancient Greek imagery in its self-presentation. Tennyson's poem "Ulysses" shows his use of classical mythology. Ulysses is the Roman name for the Greek hero Odysseus in Homer's *The Odyssey*, king of Ithaca, husband of Penelope, and father of Telemachus. After the Greeks' victory over the Trojans, Ulysses wanders at sea for ten years before he returns home. In the poem, Tennyson moves the story of Odysseus beyond Homer's *Odyssey*, presenting the thoughts of an aging hero who longs for one last adventure: despite his old age, Ulysses is planning to put out to sea again. Tennyson himself stated that this poem expressed his own "need of going forward and braving the struggle of life."

Tennyson was raised to the peerage in 1884, which is why he is often referred to as Alfred, Lord Tennyson. He died in 1892 and was buried in Westminster Abbey.

Ulysses

It little profits that an idle king,
By this still hearth,① among these barren crags,②
Match'd with an aged wife, I mete and dole
Unequal laws③ unto a savage race,
5   That hoard, and sleep, and feed, and know not me.

---

① hearth: fireplace
② crag: a steep or rugged cliff or rock face
③ met and dole unequal laws: measure out rewards and punishments and deal out accordingly

I cannot rest from travel: I will drink
Life to the lees:① All times I have enjoy'd
Greatly, have suffer'd greatly, both with those
That loved me, and alone, on shore, and when
10 Thro' scudding drifts the rainy Hyades
Vext the dim sea:② I am become a name;
For always roaming with a hungry heart
Much have I seen and known; cities of men
And manners, climates, councils, governments,
15 Myself not least, but honour'd of them all;
And drunk delight of battle with my peers,
Far on the ringing plains of windy Troy.
I am a part of all that I have met;
Yet all experience is an arch wherethro'
20 Gleams that untravell'd world whose margin fades
For ever and forever when I move.
How dull it is to pause, to make an end,
To rust unburnish'd, not to shine in use!
As tho' to breathe were life! Life piled on life
25 Were all too little, and of one to me
Little remains: but every hour is saved
From that eternal silence, something more,
A bringer of new things; and vile it were
For some three suns③ to store and hoard myself,
30 And this gray spirit yearning in desire
To follow knowledge like a sinking star,

---

① lees: "Lees" means "dregs." "Drink life to the lees" means "exhaust all the possibilities of life or live life to the fullest."
② scudding drifts the rainy Hyades vext the dim sea: It means "driving showers of spray and rain that violently hit the dim sea." The "Hyades" are a group of stars whose rising was assumed to be followed by rain. "Vext" is the old form of "vexed," meaning annoyed.
③ three suns: three years

Beyond the utmost bound of human thought.

 This is my son, mine own Telemachus,
To whom I leave the sceptre and the isle,—
35 Well-loved of me, discerning to fulfil
This labour, by slow prudence to make mild
A rugged people, and thro' soft degrees
Subdue them to the useful and the good.
Most blameless is he, centred in the sphere
40 Of common duties, decent not to fail
In offices① of tenderness, and pay
Meet adoration to my household gods,
When I am gone. He works his work, I mine.

 There lies the port; the vessel puffs her sail:
45 There gloom the dark, broad seas. My mariners,
Souls that have toil'd, and wrought, and thought with me—
That ever with a frolic welcome took
The thunder and the sunshine, and opposed
Free hearts, free foreheads—you and I are old;
50 Old age hath yet his honour and his toil;
Death closes all: but something ere the end,
Some work of noble note, may yet be done,
Not unbecoming men that strove with Gods.
The lights begin to twinkle from the rocks:
55 The long day wanes: the slow moon climbs: the deep
Moans round with many voices. Come, my friends,
'T is not too late to seek a newer world.
Push off, and sitting well in order smite
The sounding furrows; for my purpose holds
60 To sail beyond the sunset, and the baths

---

① offices: duties

        Of all the western stars①, until I die.
        It may be that the gulfs will wash us down:
        It may be we shall touch the Happy Isles②,
        And see the great Achilles③, whom we knew.
65   Tho' much is taken, much abides; and tho'
        We are not now that strength which in old days
        Moved earth and heaven, that which we are, we are;
        One equal temper of heroic hearts,
        Made weak by time and fate, but strong in will
70   To strive, to seek, to find, and not to yield.

Questions for Discussion

1. In the poem, Tennyson expresses the idea "I am a part of all that I have met" (line 18). How far do you agree? Explain.
2. How do you interpret lines 65 – 70 of the poem?
3. Everyone ages and loses physical strength and vitality. What's your picture of your old-age life? What's your idea of an ideal state of old years?

Josef Conrad (1857 – 1924)

Josef Conrad is another non-English born writer who is considered a great figure in English literature. He was born in Poland and was an orphan by the age of 12. His parents died after being sent to Siberia for plotting against the Russian Czar. He started work as a sailor when he was 17 and after sailing on British ships he became a British citizen in 1886. He worked

---

① the baths of all the western stars: the outer ocean or river that, in Greek cosmology, surrounded the flat circle of the earth and into which the stars descended
② the Happy Isles: In Greek myth the Islands of the Blessed, a paradise of perpetual summer, were thought to be located in the far-western ocean. The Greek myth has it that the Islands of the Blessed were peopled by great heroes who had been translated there by the gods and made immortal.
③ Achilles: Greek hero killed at Troy

on ships until 1894. His sailing experiences included commanding a steamship in the Belgian Congo, which inspired his well-known novella *Heart of Darkness* (1899). He wrote his best-known works before and just after the turn of the 20th century: *Lord Jim* (1900), *Nostromo* (1904), and *The Secret Agent* (1907). He died of a heart attack in 1924.

Heart of Darkness tells a story within a story. The novella begins with a group of passengers aboard a boat floating on the River Thames. One of them, Charlie Marlow, relates to his fellow passengers—with the narrator being one of them—an experience of his that took place on another river altogether—the Congo River in Africa. Marlow is sent to Africa to work for a European shipping company. He hears about a manager called Kurtz, who is both efficient and moral, but is feared by the other managers. They set off up-river to find Kurtz who turns out to have become a brutal tyrant and almost a god to the natives. Kurtz threatens to tell the natives to attack the steamer, but Marlow persuades him against it. Kurtz dies on the way back. His last words are "The horror! The horror!" When Marlow gets back to Europe, instead of telling the truth, he tells Kurtz's fiancée that his last words were her name. As Marlow falls silent, the narrator feels that the Thames also leads "into the heart of an immense darkness." The narrative style of the novella is in the first person: both Marlow and the narrator use the first-person.

The bulk of the story takes place in the Belgian Congo, the most brutal colony in Africa. The novella depicts the wastefulness and cruelty of the colonial agents. In this it shows the hypocrisy of the colonial project. The colonisers claim to be bringing civilisation to the Africans, but in reality they are stealing the wealth of the country. The novella also focuses on the damage that colonisation does to the souls of the white colonisers. *Heart of Darkness* can be regarded as a work that attacks colonialism, a deeply flawed project run by corrupt white men.

The following extract comes from the first chapter. It describes Marlow's arrival in the African colony.

Heart of Darkness
Chapter 1
(Excerpt)

"I left in a French steamer, and she called in every blamed port they have out there, for, as far as I could see, the sole purpose of landing soldiers and custom-house officers. I watched the coast. Watching a coast as it slips by the ship is like thinking about an enigma.① There it is before you—smiling, frowning, inviting, grand, mean, insipid, or savage, and always mute with an air of whispering, 'Come and find out.' This one was almost featureless, as if still in the making, with an aspect of monotonous grimness. The edge of a colossal jungle, so dark-green as to be almost black, fringed with white surf, ran straight, like a ruled line, far, far away along a blue sea whose glitter was blurred by a creeping mist. The sun was fierce, the land seemed to glisten and drip with steam. Here and there greyish-whitish specks showed up clustered inside the white surf, with a flag flying above them perhaps. Settlements some centuries old, and still no bigger than pinheads on the untouched expanse of their background. We pounded along, stopped, landed soldiers; went on, landed custom-house clerks to levy toll in what looked like a God-forsaken wilderness, with a tin shed and a flag-pole lost in it; landed more soldiers—to take care of the custom-house clerks, presumably. Some, I heard, got drowned in the surf; but whether they did or not, nobody seemed particularly to care. They were just flung out there, and on we went. Every day the coast looked the same, as though we had not moved; but we passed various places—trading places—with names like Gran' Bassam, Little Popo; names that seemed to belong to some sordid farce acted in front of a sinister back-cloth. The idleness of a passenger, my isolation amongst all these men with whom I had no point of contact, the oily and languid② sea, the uniform sombreness of the coast, seemed to keep me away from the truth of things, within the toil of a

---

①enigma: an unanswerable question
②languid: without energy or spirit or interest

mournful and senseless delusion. The voice of the surf heard now and then was a positive pleasure, like the speech of a brother. It was something natural, that had its reason, that had a meaning. Now and then a boat from the shore gave one a momentary contact with reality. It was paddled by black fellows. You could see from afar the white of their eyeballs glistening. They shouted, sang; their bodies streamed with perspiration; they had faces like grotesque masks—these chaps; but they had bone, muscle, a wild vitality, an intense energy of movement, that was as natural and true as the surf along their coast. They wanted no excuse for being there. They were a great comfort to look at. For a time I would feel I belonged still to a world of straightforward facts; but the feeling would not last long. Something would turn up to scare it away. Once, I remember, we came upon a man-of-war anchored off the coast. There wasn't even a shed there, and she was shelling the bush. It appears the French had one of their wars going on thereabouts. Her ensign① dropped limp like a rag; the muzzles of the long six-inch guns stuck out all over the low hull; the greasy, slimy swell swung her up lazily and let her down, swaying her thin masts. In the empty immensity of earth, sky, and water, there she was, incomprehensible, firing into a continent. Pop, would go one of the six-inch guns; a small flame would dart and vanish, a little white smoke would disappear, a tiny projectile would give a feeble screech—and nothing happened. Nothing could happen. There was a touch of insanity in the proceeding, a sense of lugubrious② drollery③ in the sight; and it was not dissipated by somebody on board assuring me earnestly there was a camp of natives—he called them enemies! —hidden out of sight somewhere.

"We gave her her letters (I heard the men in that lonely ship were dying of fever at the rate of three a day) and went on. We called at some more places with farcical names, where the merry dance of death and trade

---

①ensign: flag, banner
②lugubrious: mournful, gloomy, sad
③drollery: something whimsically amusing or funny

goes on in a still and earthy atmosphere as of an overheated catacomb;① all along the formless coast bordered by dangerous surf, as if Nature herself had tried to ward off intruders; in and out of rivers, streams of death in life, whose banks were rotting into mud, whose waters, thickened into slime, invaded the contorted mangroves,② that seemed to writhe at us in the extremity of an impotent despair. Nowhere did we stop long enough to get a particularized impression, but the general sense of vague and oppressive wonder grew upon me. It was like a weary pilgrimage amongst hints for nightmares.

"It was upward of thirty days before I saw the mouth of the big river. We anchored off the seat of the government. But my work would not begin till some two hundred miles farther on. So as soon as I could I made a start for a place thirty miles higher up.

"I had my passage on a little sea-going steamer. Her captain was a Swede, and knowing me for a seaman, invited me on the bridge. He was a young man, lean, fair, and morose,③ with lanky hair and a shuffling gait. As we left the miserable little wharf, he tossed his head contemptuously at the shore. 'Been living there?' he asked. I said, 'Yes.' 'Fine lot these government chaps—are they not?' he went on, speaking English with great precision and considerable bitterness. 'It is funny what some people will do for a few francs a month. I wonder what becomes of that kind when it goes upcountry?' I said to him I expected to see that soon. 'So-o-o!' he exclaimed. He shuffled athwart, keeping one eye ahead vigilantly. 'Don't be too sure,' he continued. 'The other day I took up a man who hanged himself on the road. He was a Swede, too.' 'Hanged himself! Why, in God's name?' I cried. He kept on looking out watchfully. 'Who knows? The sun too much for him, or the country perhaps.'

"At last we opened a reach. A rocky cliff appeared, mounds of turned-

---

① catacomb: underground burial chamber
② mangrove: a tropical tree that grows in mud or at the edge of rivers and sends roots down from its branches
③ morose: ill-tempered and gloomy

up earth by the shore, houses on a hill, others with iron roofs, amongst a waste of excavations, or hanging to the declivity.① A continuous noise of the rapids above hovered over this scene of inhabited devastation. A lot of people, mostly black and naked, moved about like ants. A jetty projected into the river. A blinding sunlight drowned all this at times in a sudden recrudescence② of glare. 'There's your Company's station,' said the Swede, pointing to three wooden barrack-like structures on the rocky slope. 'I will send your things up. Four boxes did you say? So. Farewell.'

"I came upon a boiler wallowing in the grass, then found a path leading up the hill. It turned aside for the boulders, and also for an undersized railway-truck lying there on its back with its wheels in the air. One was off. The thing looked as dead as the carcass of some animal. I came upon more pieces of decaying machinery, a stack of rusty rails. To the left a clump of trees made a shady spot, where dark things seemed to stir feebly. I blinked, the path was steep. A horn tooted to the right, and I saw the black people run. A heavy and dull detonation shook the ground, a puff of smoke came out of the cliff, and that was all. No change appeared on the face of the rock. They were building a railway. The cliff was not in the way or anything; but this objectless blasting was all the work going on.

"A slight clinking behind me made me turn my head. Six black men advanced in a file, toiling up the path. They walked erect and slow, balancing small baskets full of earth on their heads, and the clink kept time with their footsteps. Black rags were wound round their loins, and the short ends behind waggled to and fro like tails. I could see every rib, the joints of their limbs were like knots in a rope; each had an iron collar on his neck, and all were connected together with a chain whose bights③ swung between them, rhythmically clinking. Another report from the cliff made me think suddenly of that ship of war I had seen firing into a continent. It was the same kind of ominous voice; but these men could by no stretch of

---

①declivity: a descending slope
②recrudescence: the recurrence of an undesirable condition
③bight: a slack part or loop in a rope

imagination be called enemies. They were called criminals, and the outraged law, like the bursting shells, had come to them, an insoluble mystery from the sea. All their meagre breasts panted together, the violently dilated nostrils quivered, the eyes stared stonily uphill. They passed me within six inches, without a glance, with that complete, deathlike indifference of unhappy savages. Behind this raw matter one of the reclaimed, the product of the new forces at work, strolled despondently, carrying a rifle by its middle. He had a uniform jacket with one button off, and seeing a white man on the path, hoisted his weapon to his shoulder with alacrity.① This was simple prudence, white men being so much alike at a distance that he could not tell who I might be. He was speedily reassured, and with a large, white, rascally grin, and a glance at his charge, seemed to take me into partnership in his exalted trust. After all, I also was a part of the great cause of these high and just proceedings....

Questions for Discussion

1. What does the extract reveal about Marlow's attitude to the native Africans and to the European colonists who manage them?
2. What is Conrad's attitude to the French actions described by Marlow?
3. Why do you think that Conrad chooses to set the novella in the Belgian Congo? Do you think that the governance of the Belgian Congo was worse than that of other European colonies?

---

①alacrity: great willingness, enthusiasm

Chapter 7

From the Turn of the 20th Century to 1945
The Two World Wars and the Age of Modernism

7.1 The Modern Era of British Society

Despite the death of Queen Victoria in 1901, the years before the outbreak of the First World War in many respects saw, in Britain, a continuation of the ideas and culture of the Victorian Age. Upon the passing of Queen Victoria, Britain entered "the Edwardian era," the reign of King Edward Ⅶ from 1901 to 1910, who was succeeded by George Ⅴ who reigned up to 1936.

From 1910 (when George Ⅴ came to the throne) until World War Ⅰ broke out in 1914, Britain seemed peculiarly golden. The British Empire still appeared stable, with the exception of pressure for independence, or at least Home Rule, in Ireland. When the Irish demand was answered with intransigence,① this led to the Easter Rising in Dublin in 1916 and the eventual independence and division of Ireland in 1921.

The outbreak of World War Ⅰ shattered the old order and ushered in the new, modern era. To a great extent, signs of "modernity" did not clearly appear until the end of World War Ⅰ in 1918 when the major upheavals happened. The period that followed, known in Britain as "the inter-war" years, essentially saw an extension of the kinds of social conflicts between labour and capital of the previous century, and is often seen by modern historians as a hiatus② between the two wars.

---

①intransigence: refusal to change one's views or to agree about something
②hiatus: a pause or gap

In social terms, the influence of socialism on trade unions and the establishment of the Labour Party, coupled with universal male suffrage, led to more progressive Liberal Party governments, which established some elements of a Welfare State. Constitutional change was achieved with the reduction of the powers of the House of Lords in 1910. Female suffrage was achieved, on a limited scale in 1918 (for women over the age of 28) and finally full universal suffrage for all men and women over the age of 21 was achieved in 1928.

7.2 British Modernist Literature

Before talking about British modernist literature, it is essential to point out three things:

(1) Before World War Ⅰ, the works of writers such as Hardy, Conrad, and Shaw exemplified the social and political concerns of many artists.

(2) Modernism, together with naturalism, constituted the dominant cultural movements of the first half of the 20th century. Both cultural forms still have a major influence in the arts up to and including the present day.

(3) The emergence of modernist literature was not unique to Britain. Rather it was an international phenomenon.

The large-scale slaughter and massive destruction of World War Ⅰ enormously shocked people around the world, opening their eyes to the powerlessness of individuals in the face of such a brutal war, and further challenging their view of humanity. People in general had a feeling of fear, disorientation, and disillusionment; they felt a sharp "break" with the past. Intellectuals of the era were heavily influenced by the psychoanalytical theory of Sigmund Freud (1856 – 1839) and the "stream of consciousness" theory formulated by American philosopher William James (1842 – 1910). Under these circumstances, artists and writers experimented with creating works that looked very different from the past. Consequently, movements in all the arts overlapped and succeeded one another with amazingly rapid speed, such as Imagism, Cubism, Vorticism, Symbolism, Futurism, Expressionism, Dadaism, Surrealism, and many others. The new artists shared a desire to capture the variety and complexity of modern life, and to express the pressures and feeling of emptiness. The fragmented① nature of the work forces the reader to build meaning from these broken forms.

Like many literary terms, Modernism was coined after the event. It is an umbrella term which is also applied to music, painting, sculpture, architecture, drama, film, etc.

The most outstanding British Modernist novelists include James Joyce (1882 – 1941), who was Irish, and Virginia Woolf (1882 – 1941), who was from England. They both adopted "stream of consciousness" techniques to reflect the alienation and separation caused by life in the modern industrial city.

In the inter-war years, especially in the 1930s, many writers and thinkers were concerned with what might happen in the future. Due to their experience of World War Ⅰ their thoughts were often negative. *Brave New World* (1932) by Aldous Huxley is a classic example of dystopian fantasy and one which has influenced many later writers' works including George Orwell's *Nineteen Eighty-four* (1949) and the Canadian Margaret Atwood's *The Handmaid's Tale* (1985). Many of Huxley's predictions have come true, not necessarily in the exact form that he describes but in similar forms, e.g. personal computers, virtual reality, and artificial intelligence.

In poetry, the logical expression of thoughts present in most 19th century poetry was replaced by collages and complicated allusions, which often cause modern poems difficult to understand. The leading exponents were Ezra Pound (1885 – 1972) and T.S. Eliot (1885 – 1965), both Americans living in Britain. Joyce's *Ulysses* (1922) and Eliot's *The Waste Land* (1922) have been regarded as land-mark Modernist works, the former in prose, the latter in poetry. Besides the above-mentioned authors and their works, William Butler Yeats also deserves special attention.

William Butler Yeats (1865 – 1939)

Born into an Anglo-Irish Protestant family in Dublin, William Butler

---

① fragmented: broken up

Yeats finished most of his education there and began to learn about Irish folklore and mythology. In his teens, Yeats started writing poetry; his early work was influenced by the Romantics, particularly William Blake.

When he was 23 years old, Yeats published his first book of verse, which won him the admiration of a beautiful girl named Maud Gonne, an actress and Irish patriot who inspired him to join the fight for Irish independence. Yeats combined his passions for literature and Irish nationalism by joining the Celtic Revival, a cultural and political movement dedicated to Irish independence as well as the use of Irish folklore in literature. He strongly hoped to unite Catholics and Protestants through a national literature that rose above religious differences.

In his fifties, Yeats served as a senator in the newly established Irish Free State. In 1923 he was awarded the Nobel Prize for Literature, and he continued writing until he died at the age of 73. "The Second Coming," written in 1919 soon after the end of World War Ⅰ, is one of his most famous poems.

The Second Coming①

Turning and turning in the widening gyre②
The falcon③ cannot hear the falconer;
Things fall apart; the centre cannot hold;
Mere anarchy is loosed upon the world,
5 The blood-dimmed tide is loosed, and everywhere
The ceremony of innocence is drowned;
The best lack all conviction, while the worst
Are full of passionate intensity.

Surely some revelation is at hand;
10 Surely the Second Coming is at hand.

---

①The Second Coming: the poem expresses Yeats's sense of the dissolution of the civilization of his time, the end of one cycle of history and the approach of another.
②gyre: circular form or motion
③falcon: hawk

The Second Coming! Hardly are those words out
When a vast image out of *Spiritus Mundi*①
Troubles my sight: somewhere in sands of the desert
A shape with lion body and the head of a man,
15   A gaze blank and pitiless as the sun,
Is moving its slow thighs, while all about it
Reel shadows of the indignant desert birds.
The darkness drops again; but now I know
That twenty centuries of stony sleep
20   Were vexed to nightmare by a rocking cradle②,
And what rough beast, its hour come round at last,
Slouches towards Bethlehem③ to be born?

Questions for Discussion

1. How does the speaker describe the state of the world? How does he describe the state of human affairs in the first stanza?
2. How does the poem reflect the cyclical theory of history? What's your opinion of this theory?
3. Yeats wrote this poem shortly after the end of World War Ⅰ. What relationship can you see between the devastation of war and the events described in the poem?

T. S. Eliot (1888 – 1965)

    T. S. Eliot was born in St. Louis, USA, into a distinguished family that provided him with the best education available. He was educated at Harvard University, The Sorbonne in Paris, and at Oxford University. From 1915

---

① *Spiritus Mundi*: this Latin phrase means "Spirit of the World" or "Soul of the Universe."
② cradle: the cradle of the infant Jesus Christ
③ Bethlehem: the birthplace of Jesus according to the Christian Bible

till his death, he spent most of his lifetime in England and became a British citizen in 1927. He worked successively as a teacher, in banking, and then from 1925 until his retirement, for the publishers Faber & Faber. In 1948 he was awarded the Nobel Prize for Literature.

Eliot, like many other English-language poets, thought that a new approach was needed to describe and comment on the 20th century, particularly after the horrors of World War I. He was mentored by one of the other major proponents of Modernism, Ezra Pound, who was also a friend of James Joyce's. In 1915 through Pound's effort, *Poetry* magazine published Eliot's "The Love Song of J. Alfred Prufrock." Often called the first Modernist poem, this poem captures the emptiness and alienation many people felt living in modern, impersonal cities. However, when it first came out, the poem baffled, even angered, many readers. They found its subject matter "un-poetic," its fragmented structure off-putting, and its allusions difficult to understand.

Eliot, despite his reputation as a leading figure in Modernist poetry, produced a relatively small body of work. This probably was because he spent long periods working on his poems, especially the dense poems such as *The Waste Land*. Apart from *The Waste Land*, his best-known works are: "The Love Song of J. Alfred Prufrock" (1915), "The Hollow Men" (1925), *Four Quartets* (1936 – 1942), and *Old Possum's Book of Practical Cats* (1939), his most popular work which provides the lyrics for the modern popular musical *Cats*.

The Love Song of J. Alfred Prufrock
(Excerpt)

S'io credesse che mia risposta fosse
A persona che mai tornasse al mondo,
Questa fiamma staria senza piu scosse.
Ma percioche giammai di questo fondo
Non torno vivo alcun, s'i'odo il vero,

Senza tema d'infamia ti rispondo. ①

    Let us go then, you and I,
    When the evening is spread out against the sky
    Like a patient etherized② upon a table;
    Let us go, through certain half-deserted streets,
5   The muttering retreats
    Of restless nights in one-night cheap hotels
    And sawdust restaurants with oyster-shells:
    Streets that follow like a tedious argument
    Of insidious③ intent
10   To lead you to an overwhelming question...
    Oh, do not ask, "What is it?"
    Let us go and make our visit.

    In the room the women come and go
    Talking of Michelangelo.

15   The yellow fog that rubs its back upon the window-panes,
    The yellow smoke that rubs its muzzle on the window-panes,
    Licked its tongue into the corners of the evening,
    Lingered upon the pools that stand in drains,
    Let fall upon its back the soot that falls from chimneys,
20   Slipped by the terrace, made a sudden leap,
    And seeing that it was a soft October night,
    Curled once about the house, and fell asleep.

---

① The stanza in Italian is quoted by T. S. Eliot from Dante's *Inferno*. The meaning is "If I thought my reply were being made to someone who would ever return to the world, this flame would shake no more; but since, if what I hear is true, none ever did return alive from this depth, I answer you without fear of dishonor." The utterance is made to the poet Dante by one of the condemned spirits in Hell. The spirit believed—wrongly—that Dante would be unable to return to the world from Hell.
② etherized: made insensitive with ether, as before an operation
③ insidious: waiting to entrap or trick; deceitful

And indeed there will be time

For the yellow smoke that slides along the street,

25   Rubbing its back upon the window-panes;

There will be time, there will be time

To prepare a face to meet the faces that you meet;

There will be time to murder and create,

And time for all the works and days of hands

30   That lift and drop a question on your plate;

Time for you and time for me,

And time yet for a hundred indecisions,

And for a hundred visions and revisions,

Before the taking of a toast and tea.

35   In the room the women come and go

Talking of Michelangelo.

And indeed there will be time

To wonder, "Do I dare?" and, "Do I dare?"

Time to turn back and descend the stair,

40   With a bald spot in the middle of my hair—

(They will say: "How his hair is growing thin!")

My morning coat, my collar mounting firmly to the chin,

My necktie rich and modest, but asserted by a simple pin—

(They will say: "But how his arms and legs are thin!")

45   Do I dare

Disturb the universe?

In a minute there is time

For decisions and revisions which a minute will reverse.

For I have known them all already, known them all:

50   Have known the evenings, mornings, afternoons,

I have measured out my life with coffee spoons;

I know the voices dying with a dying fall

Beneath the music from a farther room.

  So how should I presume?

55 And I have known the eyes already, known them all—

The eyes that fix you in a formulated phrase,

And when I am formulated, sprawling on a pin,

When I am pinned and wriggling on the wall,

Then how should I begin

60 To spit out all the butt-ends of my days and ways?

  And how should I presume?...

And would it have been worth it, after all,

After the cups, the marmalade, the tea,

Among the porcelain, among some talk of you and me,

65 Would it have been worthwhile,

To have bitten off the matter with a smile,

To have squeezed the universe into a ball

To roll it towards some overwhelming question,

To say: "I am Lazarus,① come from the dead,

70 Come back to tell you all, I shall tell you all"—

If one, settling a pillow by her head

  Should say: "That is not what I meant at all;

  That is not it, at all."...

I grow old...I grow old...

75 I shall wear the bottoms of my trousers rolled.

Shall I part my hair behind? Do I dare to eat a peach?

I shall wear white flannel trousers, and walk upon the beach.

---

① Lazarus: The reference is to John 11: 1-4, in which Lazarus was miraculously brought back to life by Jesus.

I have heard the mermaids singing, each to each.

I do not think that they will sing to me.

80 I have seen them riding seaward on the waves
Combing the white hair of the waves blown back
When the wind blows the water white and black.
We have lingered in the chambers of the sea
By sea-girls wreathed with seaweed red and brown
85 Till human voices wake us, and we drown.

Questions for Discussion

1. How do the opening quotation from Dante, the descriptions of fog, and the simile in line 3 suggest about Prufrock's feelings of living in a kind of hell?
2. What does Prufrock tell, in his monologue, about his private self that he hides from acquaintances? If you are required to use a handful of adjectives to describe Prufrock's life and personality, what words do you think suit? Explain why you choose them.
3. In what way is Prufrock's love song unlike traditional love songs? Judging from the last stanza of the poem, does his relationship succeed? What advice would you offer him to make him feel better?

Aldous Huxley (1894 – 1963)

Aldous Huxley was part of a family of famous scientists and writers. His grandfather, Thomas Huxley was known as "Darwin's Bulldog" for his defence of evolutionary theory, while his father was an editor and his mother related to Thomas Arnold (1795 – 1842), the prominent educator who had much influence on public school education in England. Huxley was educated at Eton and Oxford University and was known for his knowledge of both literature and science. An eye disease that almost blinded him, when he was sixteen, prevented a planned career in medicine. He turned to writing and for the rest of his life published a wide range of essays, sketches, non-fiction books, and four novels.

Influenced by the trauma of World War I, Huxley wrote *Brave New World* in Paris in 1931. It was also a response to the totalitarianism of the fascist states in Europe as well as his concern that another war seemed imminent. Earlier in the century, Henry Ford had implemented assembly line production and Huxley uses him to symbolise the effect of modern industrialisation and mass production that produces standardised food, fuel, and appliances. Huxley extends this idea to predict a future where human beings are also standardised. The title of the fiction comes from Shakespeare's *The Tempest* where Miranda comments on the new visitors to the island:

> *O brave new world that has such people in it.*

The early 20th century produced a number of "predictive" and science fiction novels, however Huxley's work is more directly related to the utopian work of writers such as Thomas More (1478 – 1535). Huxley gives a fuller view of the dystopian[①] world he extrapolates[②] from the technological, scientific, and political conditions of the 1930s. It is most similar to George Orwell's novel *Nineteen Eighty-four*, although that world is more the product of political dystopia than technological advances.

As well as *Brave New World*, Huxley wrote ten other novels. His early works, published in the 1920s, such as *Crome Yellow* (1921) and *Antic Hay* (1923) were social satires on the aimless life of the young rich in the years following the First World War. After the publication of *Brave New World* in 1932, Huxley moved to the United States in order to avoid compromising his pacifist principles. He continued writing on a range of subjects and earned a

---

①dystopian: of an imperfect world; the opposite of utopian

②extrapolate: to predict based on existing circumstances

good income writing screenplays for Hollywood. But he remains best known for one novel, *Brave New World*.

Brave New World is a fundamentally satiric novel that vividly expresses Huxley's distrust of 20th-century trends in both politics and technology. The novel is set in 2540 CE, which is identified as the year AF 632, with AF standing for "after Ford," as Henry Ford's assembly line is revered as god-like; this era began when Ford introduced his Model T.① The novel examines a futuristic society, called the World State, which revolves around science and efficiency. In this society, emotions and individuality are conditioned out of children at a young age, and there are no lasting relationships because "every one belongs to every one else" (a common World State dictum). The story begins at the Central London Hatchery and Conditioning Centre, where children are created outside the womb and cloned in order to increase the population, and the children are conditioned into predetermined classes, which form immutable caste system. These classes, in order from highest to lowest, are Alpha, Beta, Gamma, Delta, and Epsilon.

Bernard Marx, an Alpha, is one of the main characters of the story. He and his love interest, Lenina Crowne, travel to a "savage reservation," where Marx's boss (the Director) supposedly lost a female companion some years ago. When the two arrive, they see people living there engaging in unfamiliar rituals. They also stumble upon a woman (Linda) and her son (John, also referred to as the Savage) whom Marx correctly assumes to be the lost family mentioned by the Director. The Director had recently been threatening to send Marx away for his antisocial behavior, so Marx decides to bring the two people home with him.

Marx presents Linda and John to the Director, and John, the son the Director never knew he had, calls the Director "father." This provokes the Director's resignation, as procreation between persons is outlawed, and his crime has been exposed. John is kept in the "brave new world," as he calls it, as a sort of experiment. Linda, however, is sent to a hospital because of

---

① Model T: Henry Ford's Model T was the first successful "world car"—a car that suited to quantity production and could be sold around the world with only minor modifications to its basic platform and parts.

her addiction to "soma," a drug used by citizens to feel calmer. She eventually dies because of it, which causes John to go on an anti-soma rampage in the hallway of the hospital.

John becomes angrier and angrier with this society, until eventually he runs away to a lighthouse to live in isolation. He is able to evade tourists and reporters for a while, but eventually they find him and gawk① as he engages in self-flagellation.② The intensity of the crowd increases when John whips not only himself but a woman as well. Crowds descend from helicopters to witness the spectacle. Another woman appears (who is implied to be Lenina), and John attempts to whip her too. John is soon overcome with passion, and, after coming under the influence of soma, he falls asleep. The next morning, appalled at his complicity in the system, he hangs himself.

The novel has 18 chapters, and the anthologised extract is from the second chapter.

Brave New World
Chapter II
(Excerpt)

'Silence, silence,' whispered a loud speaker as they③ stepped out at the fourteenth floor, and 'Silence, silence,' the trumpet mouths indefatigably repeated at intervals down every corridor. The students and even the Director himself rose automatically to the tips of their toes. They were Alphas, of course, but even Alphas have been well conditioned. 'Silence, silence.' All the air of the fourteenth floor was sibilant with the categorical imperative.

Fifty yards of tiptoeing brought them to a door which the Director cautiously opened. They stepped over the threshold into the twilight of a shuttered dormitory. Eighty cots stood in a row against the wall. There was a sound of light regular breathing and a continuous murmur, as of very faint voices remotely whispering.

---

① gawk: stare openly and stupidly
② flagellation: whipping or beating
③ they: the D. H. C. (Director of the Hatchery and Conditioning Centre) and his students

A nurse rose as they entered and came to attention before the Director.

'What's the lesson this afternoon?' he asked.

'We had Elementary Sex for the first forty minutes,' she answered. 'But now it's switched over to Elementary Class Consciousness.'

The Director walked slowly down the long line of cots. Rosy and relaxed with sleep, eighty little boys and girls lay softly breathing. There was a whisper under every pillow. The D. H. C. halted and, bending over one of the little beds, listened attentively.

'Elementary Class Consciousness, did you say? Let's have it repeated a little louder by the trumpet.'

At the end of the room a loudspeaker projected from the wall. The Director walked up to it and pressed a switch.

'...all wear green,' said a soft but very distinct voice, beginning in the middle of a sentence, 'and Delta Children wear khaki. Oh no, I don't want to play with Delta children. And Epsilons are still worse. They're too stupid to be able to read or write. Besides, they wear black, which is such a beastly colour. I'm so glad I'm a Beta.'

There was a pause; then the voice began again.

'Alpha children wear grey. They work much harder than we do, because they're so frightfully clever. I'm really awfully glad I'm a Beta, because I don't work so hard. And then we are much better than the Gammas and Deltas. Gammas are stupid. They all wear green, and Delta children wear khaki. Oh no, I don't want to play with Delta children. And Epsilons are still worse. They're too stupid to be able ...'

The Director pushed back the switch. The voice was silent. Only its thin ghost continued to mutter from beneath the eighty pillows.

'They'll have that repeated forty or fifty times more before they wake; then again on Thursday, and again on Saturday. A hundred and twenty times three times a week for thirty months. After which they go on to a more advanced lesson.'

Roses and electric shocks, the khaki of Deltas and a whiff of asafoetida[①]— wedded indissolubly before the child can speak. But wordless conditioning is crude

---

[①] asafoetida: a gum derived from a plant, used in herbal medicine and cooking

and wholesale; cannot bring home the finer distinctions, cannot inculcate the more complex courses of behaviour. For that there must be words, but words without reason. In brief, hypnopaedia.①

'The greatest moralizing and socializing force of all time.'

The students took it down in their little books. Straight from the horse's mouth. Once more the Director touched the switch. '... so frightfully clever,' the soft, insinuating, indefatigable voice was saying. 'I'm really awfully glad I'm a Beta, because ...'

Not so much like drops of water, though water, it is true, can wear holes in the hardest granite; rather, drops of liquid sealing-wax, drops that adhere, incrust, incorporate themselves with what they fall on, till finally the rock is all one scarlet blob.

'Till at last the child's mind is these suggestions, and the sum of the suggestions is the child's mind. And not the child's mind only. The adult's mind too—all his life long. The mind that judges and desires and decides— made up of these suggestions. But all these suggestions are our suggestions!' The Director almost shouted in his triumph. 'Suggestions from the State.' He banged the nearest table. 'It therefore follows ...'

A noise made him turn round.

'Oh, Ford!' he said in another tone, 'I've gone and woken the children.'

Questions for Discussion

1. In the extract given, how are the children educated in a mechanized and standardized way? Are human traits like individuality, free will, creativity, emotions, and natural instincts still attainable to children thus trained?
2. We tend to celebrate scientific advances and progresses. In your opinion, what would become of man and the world if people excessively depend on science and technology?
3. How are Charles Dickens's *Hard Times* and Aldous Huxley's *Brave New World* comparable?

---

① hypnopaedia: conveying information to a sleeping person

Chapter 8

From 1945 to the Present
The Contemporary Era and the Age of Postmodernism

8.1 World War Ⅱ and Its Aftermath

As the Depression of the 1930s worsened, some countries turned to menacing dictators for leadership: Benito Mussolini in Italy, Adolf Hitler in Germany, and a military government in Japan. Soon Japanese troops invaded China, and Hitler's army stormed through Europe. World War Ⅱ broke out.

Five years after the outbreak of World War Ⅱ, America dropped two—the first two, and the only two—atomic bombs on Japan in August 1945, which brought the war to an abrupt end.

The post-World War Ⅱ years saw the disintegration① of the British Empire, which led to new independent countries across the world. In 1947, following many years of demands for independence backed by campaigns of civil disobedience, led by Gandhi and supported by the British Labour Party, the newly elected Labour government granted independence to British India as the countries of India, Pakistan (now Pakistan and Bangladesh) and Sri Lanka (formerly known as Ceylon). This stimulated the push for independence among other British colonies: Britain's mandate over Palestine was revoked by the United Nations in 1948; Malaya gained independence in 1957; Ghana became Britain's first African colony to reach independence in 1957. By 1967, more than 20 British territories were independent. By the 1970s the British Empire was no more. Britain finally

①disintegration: the act of breaking up

returned Hong Kong to China on 1 July, 1997.

In 1957 the Treaty of Rome created the European Economic Community (EEC, also known as the "Common Market" in English-speaking countries) with six member countries. Britain joined the EEC in 1973 and then left what is now known as the European Union, in 2020.

8.2 Domestic Circumstances after World War II

The landslide victory of the Labour Party in the 1945 general election led to massive social change in Britain. Most significant was the implementation of the Education Act of 1944 which modernised schooling in Britain and laid the foundation for succeeding generations of working-class people. The creation of a "cradle to grave" social security system based on the Beveridge Report published in 1942 and the enactment of a "free at point of delivery" National Health Service, made the UK a "welfare state" in order to reduce poverty and hardship.

The 1950s was a period of rebuilding after the war. It saw the decline of Britain as a world power, although the possession of nuclear weapons maintained its position at the top table of world diplomacy. During the 1960s, further social changes modernised British society. The opening of new universities and the provision of financial support to all university students widened participation among working-class children. In the field of culture, Britain became a centre of innovation, particularly in popular music, literature, and the fine arts.

During the 1970s, Britain suffered from an economic decline, which eventually resulted in the election in 1979 of Margaret Thatcher on a neo-liberal economic and social platform. The Conservative Party remained in power until 1997, when Tony Blair's Labour Party won the largest ever parliamentary victory and remained in power until 2010, from 2007 under the leadership of Gordon Brown. Following the General Election in 2010, David Cameron and the Conservative Party were able to form a coalition government with the support of the Liberal Democrats. The Conservatives have been able to remain in power since then, dropping the Liberal

Democrats as coalition partners following Cameron's victory in the 2015 General Election. Popular demands for Britain to leave the European Union (often known as "Brexit"①) resulted in a referendum in June 2016. After years of arguments over Brexit, Britain finally left the EU in January 2020.

From the 1960s, there were increased demands from Wales and Scotland for independence. Though full independence was rejected by referenda in both countries, many local powers were devolved to a new Scottish Parliament and a Welsh Assembly. Since the Brexit referendum, in which a majority of Scots voted to remain, there have been increased pressures for Scottish independence and a desire to re-join the EU.

After Irish partition② in 1921, Northern Ireland was established with a Protestant majority and a significant Catholic minority. Its ruling body was the Northern Ireland Parliament, known as Stormont, with a Protestant Loyalist majority. For nearly fifty years, Catholics were discriminated against in jobs, education, and housing. By the 1960s a strong civil rights movement had arisen and this led to conflict between the two communities, which eventually led to what was effectively a civil war, commonly known as "the Troubles" from about 1968 onwards. Violence escalated and in 1972 Stormont was suspended and direct rule from Westminster imposed in part as an attempt to reduce discrimination against Catholics in addition to furthering a peace process.

The Troubles continued throughout the 1980s and 1990s until cease-fires led to the creation of a Northern Ireland Assembly in 1998 that guaranteed representation of both communities in a power-sharing administration.

8.3　Postmodernism

In a similar fashion to the way that Modernism developed in response to the events of World War Ⅰ, the events of World War Ⅱ, especially the holocaust and the destructive power of nuclear weapons, led to artists

---

①Brexit: the nickname for "British exit" from the EU
②partition: division, the action of parting

questioning prevailing assumptions, especially with regard to the ideas of rationality that had dominated thinking for last two centuries. If the post-World War I generation regarded the world as a fragmented and incoherent waste land, the post-World War II generation deemed the world as an irrational one, therefore people sought a new language to express the uncertainty of life in a world that might destroy itself through nuclear war.

It is important to understand that postmodernism is continuation of Modernism, which has given forms and techniques post-World War II writers find inexhaustible, for instance, postmodernism persists with Modernism's alienated mood and disorienting techniques. Postmodernist writers view language as nothing more and nothing less than a system of "signs" or "signifiers" which do not point to "the signified" in the external world, but only to themselves. To put it in another way, language only represents itself rather than truth or reality, and the so-called "truth" is only formulated and constructed with language, and the so-called "reality" is merely the product of language rather than genuine reality. That is why postmodernism is relatively coterminous① with poststructuralism and deconstruction.

It is also important to understand that postmodernism has influenced not just literature but also other forms of art, such as painting, sculpture, and architecture.

In sum, postmodernism rejects certainty and fixed meanings. The very fluidity of meaning in postmodernist work often makes its works more difficult to understand than before.

8.4 British Literature after World War II

Mainly due to the influence of postmodernism, post-World War II Britain has witnessed a variety of styles that have become accepted as part of the canon.② British literature in the late 20th century offered a wide range

---

① coterminous: having the same boundaries or extent in space, time, or meaning
② canon: a body of writings recognised by authority

of approaches and subject matters in political and social aspects. George Orwell's most influential novel, *Nineteen Eighty-four* predicted the growth of totalitarianism, whether of the right or left, and provided a stimulus for other dystopian fantasies as well as science fiction futurology.

Three main literary trends are worth our attention. They are "Angry Young Men," "Theatre of the Absurd," and "Postcolonial & Multicultural Writings."

Angry Young Men "Angry Young Men" refers to a group of British writers who produced social realist works in the 1950s as well as the protagonists of some of their novels and plays. The Angry Young Men sound a fierce note of protest or resentment against the values of the British middle class. Their leading author was playwright John Osborne. It was John Osborne's play *Look Back in Anger* (1956), which examines disillusionment with British society in the 1950s, that gave name to the group of young people. Other works that express "angry" attitudes included Kingsley Amis's campus novel *Lucky Jim* (1954) and John Braine's novel of social ambition, *Room at the Top* (1957). Undoubtedly, the most striking example of the angry young man was Jimmy Porter, the protagonist of *Look Back in Anger*. Jimmy Potter is of working-class parentage; he has received a university education; he has served in war. But after the war, despite his various efforts, he cannot find a job. He loves his wife Alison, daughter of a middle-class family, but he flings abuse at her. He is angry with all people around him. He thinks that English society is hopeless, but apart from doing mischiefs and flinging curses at the society, he does not take any constructive actions.

It is important to point out that the label is more appropriate to the anti-heroes of these works than to the authors.

Theatre of the Absurd The most remarkable influence postmodernism exerted on theatrical drama is known as "Theatre of the Absurd." The term "absurd" is derived from Albert Camus's existentialist philosophy which is best explained in his book titled *The Myth of Sisyphus* (1942), which argues that human existence is absurd and futile in nature, that modern life is purposeless, and that the universe is without meaning or value. In 1961, the critic Martin Esslin coined the phrase "Theatre of the Absurd" to refer to a number of dramatists of the 1950s (led by Samuel Beckett and Eugène Ionesco) whose works abandon logical form, character, and dialogue together with realistic illusion, so that evoke the absurd. The leading British proponents of the "Theatre of the Absurd" were Samuel Beckett and the Nobel prize-winner Harold Pinter① (1930 – 2008). The classic work of absurdist theatre is Beckett's *Waiting for Godot* (1952).

Postcolonial & Multicultural Writings In the wake of World War II, the once powerful British Empire began to dissolve. Writers from the former colonies brought fresh perspectives on language and social customs. Native and immigrant English writers also explored new approaches as they reflect on the changing modern world.

From the late 1940s through the 1950s, immigrants from the West Indies were encouraged to come to Britain to work in service industries. These immigrants have often been referred to as the "Windrush generation" after the name of the first boat which brought a large number of immigrants from Jamaica and other Caribbean islands in 1948. V. S. Naipaul (1932 – 2018), who was raised in Trinidad in the West Indies by Indian parents, moved to England at the age of 18, not to work in service industries but to attend Oxford University and subsequently settled in the UK. Many of his stories are set in developing nations that struggled to form a new national identity from what is left of native and colonial cultures. Naipaul has described himself as a rootless person, and literary critics have called him a "world writer."

In the 1960s and 1970s, a large number of Asians (mainly from India and Pakistan) as well as Africans (mainly from East Africa) also came to Britain. This is not to say that there are not racial tensions in the UK: the Black British population has suffered from both social and economic deprivation, although Asian immigrants have had more success in business and education.

---

① Harold Pinter: English playwright and screenwriter, winner of the Nobel Prize for Literature in 2005

Since English was the dominant language of the British Empire, many Black Britons spoke it as their first language. Their work reflects not only their life in Britain but also the heritage of empire and the African diaspora.① Asian immigrants were often less fluent in English and their contribution to English literature was often more marked by second generation writers. Arguably, the leading British writer of Asian ancestry is the 2017 Nobel Prize winner Sir Kazuo Ishiguro (b. 1954) who was born in Japan. In 1960 his family emigrated to Great Britain. Ishiguro's first novel, *A Pale View of Hills* (1982), details the postwar memories a Japanese woman named Etsuko trying to deal with the suicide of her daughter Keiko. With the publication of *The Remains of the Day* (1989), Ishiguro became one of the best-known European novelists at just 35 years of age. In 2005 Ishiguro published *Never Let Me Go*, which was filmed in 2010 and the film became an instant hit. He was knighted in 2019.

The 2007 Nobel Prize winner Doris Lessing (1919 – 2013) should also be mentioned. Lessing was born in Persia (now Iran) to English parents and she lived in Southern Rhodesia (now Zimbabwe) from age 5 until she settled in England in 1949. Lessing brought to England the manuscript of her first novel *The Grass Is Singing*, which tells a story about the violent relationship between white people and black people. Its publication in 1950 brought her instant success as a novelist. *Children of Violence* (1952 – 1969), a five-novel sequence that centres on Martha Quest who grows up in southern Africa and settles in England, is one of her most substantial works. *The Golden Notebook* (1962), in which a woman writer attempts to come to terms with the life of her times through her art, is one of the most complex and the most widely read of her novels. Critics have tried to label her as both a feminist and a writer about race relations, but she seems to dislike such labels.

In this chapter, three writers' works are anthologised. They are Samuel

---

①diaspora: the dispersal of an ethnic group across the world, usually as a result of slavery or oppression

Beckett's *Waiting for Godot*, William Golding's *Lord of the Flies*, and Benjamin Zephaniah's poem "Bought and Sold."

Samuel Beckett (1906 – 1989)

Samuel Beckett is a key figure in the long line of Irish giants of English literature. Born in Dublin to a Protestant family, he studied English, French, and Italian at Trinity College Dublin, which is the most prestigious university in Ireland and the alma mater of Jonathan Swift. Beckett travelled widely in Europe. Meeting James Joyce in Paris, Beckett decided to move to Paris permanently in 1937. During World War Ⅱ he remained in France and fought against the Nazis with the Resistance. He was awarded the Nobel Prize for Literature in 1969.

Beckett wrote a number of Modernist novels but became most famous for his play *Waiting for Godot* which is considered one of the seminal works of the Theatre of the Absurd. He knew Sartre[①] and was probably influenced by his existentialist philosophy and his play *No Exit* (1944), which was the first play performed in Paris after its liberation. Beckett wrote in French which he believed helped him to develop the plain style of his works and translated them into English himself.

Waiting for Godot was written between 1948 and 1949. But it was not performed until 1953, in its original French in Paris and then in English in London in 1955. It was initially badly received, but it is now regarded as one of the most significant plays in English of the 20th century.

The play consists of conversations between Vladimir and Estragon, who are waiting for the arrival of the mysterious Godot, who continually sends word that he will appear but never does. They encounter Lucky and Pozzo, and they discuss their miseries and their lots in life. They consider hanging themselves, and yet they wait. Set in an indeterminate time and place, Beckett always refused to explain its meaning but it is generally taken to reflect the horrors of modernity in its pessimistic and nihilistic[②] concept of

---

① Sartre: Jean-Paul Sartre (1905 – 1980), French existentialist philosopher, playwright, and novelist
② nihilistic: a philosophical point of view that holds that life is devoid of meaning

the world. The characters talk nonsensically and seem to suffer from amnesia.① It is impossible to know whether it is meant to be tragic or comic. The play is often seen as a response to a world emptied of meaning and significance. It is this that makes it set in a universe that may only be described as absurd.

The following three extracts come respectively from the beginning of Act Ⅰ, the beginning of Act Ⅱ, and the end of the play.

Waiting for Godot

(Excerpt)

ACT Ⅰ

A country road. A tree. Evening.

Estragon, sitting on a low mound, is trying to take off his boot. He pulls at it with both hands, panting. He gives up, exhausted, rests, tries again.

As before.

Enter Vladimir.

Estragon: (*Giving up again.*) Nothing to be done.

Vladimir: (*Advancing with short, stiff strides, legs wide apart.*) I'm beginning to come round to that opinion. All my life I've tried to put it from me, saying Vladimir, be reasonable, you haven't yet tried everything. And I resumed the struggle. (*He broods, musing on the struggle. Turning to Estragon.*) So there you are again.

Estragon: Am I?

Vladimir: I'm glad to see you back. I thought you were gone forever.

Estragon: Me too.

Vladimir: Together again at last! We'll have to celebrate this. But how? (*He reflects.*) Get up till I embrace you.

Estragon: (*Irritably.*) Not now, not now.

Vladimir: (*Hurt, coldly.*) May one inquire where His Highness spent the

---

①amnesia: loss of memory usually due to brain injury or shock or depression

From 1945 to the Present | Chapter 8
The Contemporary Era and the Age of Postmodernism

	night?
Estragon:	In a ditch.
Vladimir:	(*Admiringly.*) A ditch! Where?
Estragon:	(*Without gesture.*) Over there.
Vladimir:	And they didn't beat you?
Estragon:	Beat me? Certainly they beat me.
Vladimir:	The same lot as usual?
Estragon:	The same? I don't know.
Vladimir:	When I think of it ... all these years ... but for me ... where would you be ... (*Decisively.*) You'd be nothing more than a little heap of bones at the present minute, no doubt about it.
Estragon:	And what of it?
Vladimir:	(*Gloomily.*) It's too much for one man. (*Pause. Cheerfully.*) On the other hand what's the good of losing heart now, that's what I say. We should have thought of it a million years ago, in the nineties.
Estragon:	Ah stop blathering① and help me off with this bloody thing....

* * *

ACT Ⅱ

Next day. Same time. Same place.

Estragon's boots front centre, heels together, toes splayed.

Lucky's hat at same place.

The tree has four or five leaves.

Enter Vladimir agitatedly.

He halts and looks long at the tree, then suddenly begins to move feverishly about the stage. He halts before the boots, picks one up, examines it, sniffs it, manifests disgust, puts it back carefully. Comes and goes. Halts extreme right and gazes into distance off, shading his eyes with his hand. Comes and goes. Halts extreme left, as before. Comes and goes. Halts suddenly and begins to sing loudly.

---

① blathering: talking foolishly at length without making any sense

Vladimir: A dog came in—

  Having begun too high he stops, clears his throat, resumes:

A dog came in the kitchen
And stole a crust of bread.
Then cook up with a ladle①
And beat him till he was dead.
Then all the dogs came running
And dug the dog a tomb—

  He stops, broods, resumes:

Then all the dogs came running
And dug the dog a tomb
And wrote upon the tombstone
For the eyes of dogs to come:
A dog came in the kitchen
And stole a crust of bread.
Then cook up with a ladle
And beat him till he was dead.
Then all the dogs came running
And dug the dog a tomb—

  He stops, broods, resumes:

Then all the dogs came running
And dug the dog a tomb—

  He stops, broods. Softly.

And dug the dog a tomb ...

He remains a moment silent and motionless, then begins to move feverishly about the stage. He halts before the tree, comes and goes, before the boots, comes and goes, halts extreme right, gazes into distance, extreme left, gazes into distance.

Enter Estragon right, barefoot, head bowed. He slowly crosses the stage.

Vladimir turns and sees him.

---

①ladle: a deep-bowled long-handled spoon used especially for dipping up and conveying liquids

Vladimir: You again! (*Estragon halts but does not raise his head. Vladimir goes towards him.*) Come here till I embrace you.

Estragon: Don't touch me!

Vladimir holds back, pained.

Vladimir: Do you want me to go away? (*Pause.*) Gogo! (*Pause. Vladimir observes him attentively.*) Did they beat you? (*Pause.*) Gogo! (*Estragon remains silent, head bowed.*) Where did you spend the night?

Estragon: Don't touch me! Don't question me! Don't speak to me! Stay with me!

Vladimir: Did I ever leave you?

Estragon: You let me go.

Vladimir: Look at me. (*Estragon does not raise his head. Violently.*) Will you look at me!

Estragon raises his head. They look long at each other, then suddenly embrace, clapping each other on the back. End of the embrace.

Estragon, no longer supported, almost falls.

* * *

Vladimir: We have to come back tomorrow.

Estragon: What for?

Vladimir: To wait for Godot.

Estragon: Ah! (*Silence.*) He didn't come?

Vladimir: No.

Estragon: And now it's too late.

Vladimir: Yes, now it's night.

Estragon: And if we dropped him? (*Pause.*) If we dropped him?

Vladimir: He'd punish us. (*Silence. He looks at the tree.*) Everything's dead but the tree.

Estragon: (*Looking at the tree.*) What is it?

Vladimir: It's the tree.

Estragon: Yes, but what kind?

Vladimir: I don't know. A willow.

     Estragon draws Vladimir towards the tree.
     They stand motionless before it.
       Silence.

Estragon: Why don't we hang ourselves?
Vladimir: With what?
Estragon: You haven't got a bit of rope?
Vladimir: No.
Estragon: Then we can't.

       Silence.

Vladimir: Let's go.
Estragon: Wait, there's my belt.
Vladimir: It's too short.
Estragon: You could hang onto my legs.
Vladimir: And who'd hang onto mine?
Estragon: True.
Vladimir: Show me all the same. (*Estragon loosens the cord that holds up his trousers which, much too big for him, fall about his ankles. They look at the cord.*) It might do in a pinch. But is it strong enough?
Estragon: We'll soon see. Here.

   They each take an end of the cord and pull. It breaks. They almost fall.

Vladimir: Not worth a curse.

       Silence.

Estragon: You say we have to come back tomorrow?
Vladimir: Yes.
Estragon: Then we can bring a good bit of rope.
Vladimir: Yes.

       Silence.

Estragon: Didi?
Vladimir: Yes.
Estragon: I can't go on like this.

Vladimir: That's what you think.

Estragon: If we parted? That might be better for us.

Vladimir: We'll hang ourselves tomorrow. (*Pause.*) Unless Godot comes.

Estragon: And if he comes?

Vladimir: We'll be saved.

Vladimir takes off his hat (Lucky's), peers inside it, feels about inside it, shakes it, knocks on the crown, puts it on again.

Estragon: Well? Shall we go?

Vladimir: Pull on your trousers.

Estragon: What?

Vladimir: Pull on your trousers.

Estragon: You want me to pull off my trousers?

Vladimir: Pull ON your trousers.

Estragon: (*Realising his trousers are down.*) True. He pulls up his trousers.

Vladimir: Well? Shall we go?

Estragon: Yes, let's go.

They do not move.

CURTAIN.

Questions for Discussion

1. How does *Waiting for Godot* reflect Beckett's view of the modern world?
2. Who do you think is Godot and why does he never appear in the play?
3. What problem do you think Estragon and Vladimir have in their way of life? What advice would you give them?

William Golding (1911 – 1993)

William Golding was one of the leading British novelists of the late 20th century, winning the most prestigious British literary award, The Booker

Prize, in 1980 for *Rites of Passage* and being awarded the Nobel Prize for Literature in 1983. He served in the Royal Navy during World War II and what he witnessed clearly influenced his view of human nature. Apart from *Lord of the Flies* (1954) he is best-known for the "sea trilogy": *Rites of Passage* (1980), *Close Quarters* (1987) and *Fire Down Below* (1989), published in one volume titled *To the Ends of the Earth* (1990).

Golding held a pessimistic view of human nature, one rooted in the Christian concept of "original sin" and the Hobbesian belief that without a controlling power, life would be "nasty, brutish and short."

Lord of the Flies was Golding's first novel. Although publishers initially rejected it, it has been generally well-received and has become a standard text in English literature courses, both in schools and universities. It tells the story of a group of English public-school① boys who are marooned② on a desert island after their plane crashes during a nuclear war. Devoid of adult control, the majority revert to primitive, savage and tribal behaviour; they conduct ritual sacrifice and kill several members of the group.

Golding drew inspiration from the Victorian novelist Ballantyne's③ *The Coral Island* (1858), popular reading for boys in Golding's youth, however, in Ballantyne's book the boys create an idyllic society.

Here is an overview of the plot of *Lord of the Flies*.

After the crashing of a plane in the middle of a war, a group of English schoolboys get caught on a jungle island with no adults. Two of the boys, Ralph and Piggy, find a conch④ shell. Ralph blows into it like a horn, and all the boys on the island assemble. At the assembly, a boy named Jack mocks Piggy for being fat and runs against Ralph to become chief of the group. Ralph wins the election, and declares Jack the leader of the group's hunters. Soon after, Ralph, Jack, and another boy named Simon explore

---

① public-school: In Britain, a public-school is a fee-charging private school usually attended by upper-middle class pupils.
② maroon: leave (someone) trapped and isolated in an inaccessible place, especially an island
③ Ballantyne: full name of Robert Michael Ballantyne (1825 – 1894), Scottish author of over one hundred juvenile fiction books
④ conch: a tropical sea animal that looks like a snail

From 1945 to the Present | Chapter 8

The Contemporary Era and the Age of Postmodernism

the island and discover wild pigs. At a second assembly, the boys set up rules to govern themselves. The first rule is that whoever wants to speak at an assembly must hold the conch. At the meeting, one young boy claims he saw a "beastie" in the jungle, but Ralph dismisses it as just the product of a nightmare. Ralph then suggests that they build a signal fire at the top of a mountain so any passing ships will see the smoke and rescue them. The boys use Piggy's glasses to light a fire, but they're careless, and accidentally set part of the forest on fire. The boy who saw the "beastie" vanishes during the fire and is never seen again.

Time passes. Tensions rise. Ralph becomes frustrated when no one helps him build shelters. Lots of the boys goof off, while Jack obsesses about hunting and takes every opportunity to mock Piggy, who is smart but weak. Simon, meanwhile, often wanders off into the forest to meditate. The rivalry between Ralph and Jack erupts when Jack, the leader of the hunting group, forces the boys who were supposed to watch the signal fire come hunting with him. They kill their first pig, but a ship passes while the signal fire is out, which causes a tremendous argument between Ralph and Jack.

Ralph calls an assembly hoping to set things right. But the meeting soon becomes chaotic as several younger boys talk about the beast. Now even the bigger boys are fearful. That night, after a distant airplane battle, a dead parachutist lands on the mountaintop next to the signal fire. The boys on duty at the fire think it's the beast. Soon Ralph and Jack lead an expedition to search the island for the beast. While searching, they find a rock outcropping[①] that would make a great fort, but no beast. Tempers between the two boys soon flare up, and they climb the mountain in the dark to prove their courage. They spot the shadowy parachutist and think he's the beast.

The next morning, Jack challenges Ralph's authority at an assembly. Ralph wins, but Jack leaves the group, and most of the older boys join him. Jack's tribe paint their faces, hunt, and kill a pig. They then leave its head as an offering to the beast. Simon comes upon the head, and sees that it's the Lord of the Flies—the beast within all men. While Jack invites everyone

---

① outcropping: a rock formation that is visible on the surface

to come to a feast, Simon climbs the mountain and sees the parachutist. However, when Simon returns to tell everyone the truth about the "beast," the boys at the feast have become a frenzied mob, acting out a ritual killing of a pig. The mob thinks Simon is the beast and kills him.

Jack's tribe moves to the rock fort. They steal Piggy's glasses to make fire. Ralph and his last allies, Piggy and the twins Samneric (short for Sam and Eric but so called because they speak and act as one), go to get the glasses back. Jack's tribe captures the twins, and a boy named Roger rolls a boulder from the fort that smashes the conch and kills Piggy. The next day the tribe sets fire to the forest in order to hunt Ralph. He evades them as best as he can, and becomes a kind of animal that thinks only of survival and escape. Eventually the boys corner Ralph on the beach where they first set up their society when they landed on the island. But the burning jungle has attracted a British Naval ship, and an officer is standing on the shore. The boys stop, stunned, and stare at the man. He jokingly asks if the boys are playing at war, and whether there were any casualties. When Ralph says yes, the officer is shocked and disappointed that English boys would act in such a manner. Ralph starts to cry, and soon the other boys start crying too. The officer, uncomfortable, looks away toward his warship.

The book has 12 chapters in all. The following excerpt is from Chapter 8.

Lord of the Flies

Chapter 8 Gift for the Darkness
(Excerpt)

He[①] held the conch against his chest with one hand and stabbed the air with his index finger.

'Who thinks Ralph oughtn't to be chief?'

He looked expectantly at the boys ranged round, who had frozen. Under the palms there was deadly silence.

'Hands up,' said Jack strongly, 'whoever wants Ralph not to be chief?'

---

① he: Jack

The silence continued, breathless and heavy and full of shame. Slowly the red drained from Jack's cheeks, then came back with a painful rush. He licked his lips and turned his head at an angle, so that his gaze avoided the embarrassment of linking with another's eye.

'How many think—'

His voice tailed off. The hands that held the conch shook. He cleared his throat, and spoke loudly.

'All right then.'

He laid the conch with great care in the grass at his feet. The humiliating tears were running from the corner of each eye.

'I'm not going to play any longer. Not with you.'

Most of the boys were looking down now, at the grass or their feet. Jack cleared his throat again.

'I'm not going to be part of Ralph's lot—'

He looked along the right-hand logs, numbering the hunters that had been a choir.

'I'm going off by myself. He can catch his own pigs. Anyone who wants to hunt when I do can come too.'

He blundered out of the triangle towards the drop to the white sand.

'Jack!'

Jack turned and looked back at Ralph. For a moment he paused and then cried out, high-pitched, enraged.

'—No!'

He leapt down from the platform and ran along the beach, paying no heed to the steady fall of his tears; and until he dived into the forest Ralph watched him....

Piggy was speaking now with more assurance and with what, if the circumstances had not been so serious, the others would have recognized as pleasure.

'I said we could all do without a certain person. Now I say we got to decide on what can be done. And I think I could tell you what Ralph's going to say next. The most important thing on the island is the smoke and you can't have no smoke without a fire.'

Ralph made a restless movement.

'No go, Piggy. We've got no fire. That thing① sits up there—we'll have to stay here.'

Piggy lifted the conch as though to add power to his next words.

'We got no fire on the mountain. But what's wrong with a fire down here? A fire could be built on them rocks. On the sand, even. We'd make smoke just the same.'

'That's right!'

'Smoke!'

'By the bathing-pool!'

The boys began to babble. Only Piggy could have the intellectual daring to suggest moving the fire from the mountain.

'So we'll have the fire down here,' said Ralph. He looked about him. 'We can build it just here between the bathing-pool and the platform. Of course—'

He broke off, frowning, thinking the thing out, unconsciously tugging at the stub of a nail with his teeth.

'Of course the smoke won't show so much, not be seen so far away. But we needn't go near; near the—'

The others nodded in perfect comprehension. There would be no need to go near.

'We'll build the fire now.'

The greatest ideas are the simplest. Now there was something to be done they worked with passion. Piggy was so full of delight and expanding liberty in Jack's departure, so full of pride in his contribution to the good of society, that he helped to fetch wood. The wood he fetched was close at hand, a fallen tree on the platform that they did not need for the assembly; yet to the others the sanctity of the platform had protected even what was useless there. Then the twins realized they would have a fire near them as a comfort in the night and this set a few littluns② dancing and clapping

---

① that thing: refers to the so-called beast
② littluns: contraction of "little ones," meaning the younger ones

hands....

The littluns who had seen few fires since the first catastrophe became wildly excited. They danced and sang and there was a partyish air about the gathering.

At last Ralph stopped work and stood up, smudging the sweat from his face with a dirty forearm.

'We'll have to have a small fire. This one's too big to keep up.'

Piggy sat down carefully on the sand and began to polish his glass.

'We could experiment. We could find out how to make a small hot fire and then put green branches on to make smoke. Some of them leaves must be better for that than the others.'

As the fire died down so did the excitement. The littluns stopped singing and dancing and drifted away towards the sea or the fruit trees or the shelters.

Ralph flopped down in the sand.

'We'll have to make a new list of who's to look after the fire.'

'If you can find 'em.'

He looked round. Then for the first time he saw how few biguns[①] there were and understood why the work had been so hard.

'Where's Maurice?'

Piggy wiped his glass again.

'I expect ... no, he wouldn't go into the forest by himself, would he?'

Ralph jumped up, ran swiftly round the fire and stood by Piggy, holding up his hair.

'But we've got to have a list! There's you and me and Samneric and—'

He would not look at Piggy but spoke casually.

'Where's Bill and Roger?'

Piggy leaned forward and put a fragment of wood on the fire.

'I expect they've gone. I expect they won't play either.'

Ralph sat down and began to poke little holes in the sand. He was surprised to see that one had a drop of blood by it. He examined his bitten

---

① biguns: contraction of "big ones", meaning the older boys

nail closely and watched the little globe of blood that gathered where the quick was gnawed away.

Piggy went on speaking.

'I seen them stealing off when we was gathering wood. They went that way. The same way as he went himself.'

Ralph finished his inspection and looked up into the air. The sky, as if in sympathy with the great changes among them, was different to-day and so misty that in some places the hot air seemed white. The disc of the sun was dull silver as though it were nearer and not so hot, yet the air stifled.

'They always been making trouble, haven't they?'

The voice came near his shoulder and sounded anxious.

'We can do without 'em. We'll be happier now, won't we?'

Ralph sat. The twins came, dragging a great log and grinning in their triumph. They dumped the log among the embers so that sparks flew.

'We can do all right on our own can't we?'

For a long time while the log dried, caught fire and turned red hot, Ralph sat in the sand and said nothing. He did not see Piggy go to the twins and whisper with them, nor how the three boys went together into the forest.

'Here you are.'

He came to himself with a jolt. Piggy and the other two were by him. They were laden with fruit.

'I thought perhaps,' said Piggy, 'we ought to have a feast kind of.'

The three boys sat down. They had a great mass of the fruit with them and all of it properly ripe. They grinned at Ralph as he took some and began to eat.

'Thanks,' he said. Then with an accent of pleased surprise—'Thanks!'

'Do all right on our own,' said Piggy. 'It's them that haven't no common sense that make trouble on this island. We'll make a little hot fire—'...

Far off along the beach, Jack was standing before a small group of boys. He was looking brilliantly happy.

'Hunting,' he said. He sized them up. Each of them wore the remains

From 1945 to the Present | Chapter 8
The Contemporary Era and the Age of Postmodernism

of a black cap and ages ago they had stood in two demure rows and their voices had been the song of angels.

'We'll hunt. I'm going to be chief.'

They nodded, and the crisis passed easily.

'And then—about the beast.' They moved, looked at the forest.

'I say this. We aren't going to bother about the beast.'

He nodded at them.

'We're going to forget the beast.'

'That's right!'

'Yes!'

'Forget the beast!'

If Jack was astonished by their fervour he did not show it.

'And another thing. We shan't dream so much down here. This is near the end of the island.'

They agreed passionately out of the depths of their tormented private lives.

'Now listen. We might go later to the castle rock. But now I'm going to get more of the biguns away from the conch and all that. We'll kill a pig and give a feast.' He paused and went on more slowly. 'And about the beast. When we kill we'll leave some of the kill for it. Then it won't bother us, maybe.'

He stood up abruptly.

'We'll go into the forest now and hunt.'

He turned and trotted away and after a moment they followed him obediently.

They spread out, nervously, in the forest. Almost at once Jack found the dung and scattered roots that told of pig and soon the track was fresh. Jack signalled the rest of the hunt to be quiet and went forward by himself. He was happy and wore the damp darkness of the forest like his old clothes. He crept down a slope to rocks and scattered trees by the sea....

They raced along the pig-track, but the forest was too dark and tangled so that Jack, cursing, stopped them and cast among the trees. Then he said nothing for a time but breathed fiercely so that they were awed by him and looked at each other in uneasy admiration. Presently he stabbed down at the ground with his finger.

'There—'

Before the others could examine the drop of blood, Jack had swerved off, judging a trace, touching a bough that gave. So he followed, mysteriously right and assured, and the hunters trod behind him.

He stopped before a covert.①

'In there.' They surrounded the covert but the sow got away with the sting of another spear in her flank. The trailing butts hindered her and the sharp, cross-cut points were a torment. She blundered into a tree, forcing a spear still deeper; and after that any of the hunters could follow her easily by the drops of vivid blood. The afternoon wore on, hazy and dreadful with damp heat; the sow staggered her way ahead of them, bleeding and mad, and the hunters followed, wedded to her in lust, excited by the long chase and the dropped blood. They could see her now, nearly got up with her, but she spurted② with her last strength and held ahead of them again. They were just behind her when she staggered into an open space where bright flowers grew and butterflies danced round each other and the air was hot and still.

Here, struck down by the heat, the sow fell and the hunters hurled themselves at her. This dreadful eruption from an unknown world made her frantic; she squealed and bucked and the air was full of sweat and noise and blood and terror. Roger ran round the heap, prodding with his spear whenever pig-flesh appeared. Jack was on top of the sow, stabbing downward with his knife. Roger found a lodgement for his point and began to push till he was leaning with his whole weight. The spear moved forward inch by inch and the terrified squealing became a high-pitched scream. Then Jack found the throat and the hot blood spouted over his hands. The sow collapsed under them and they were heavy and fulfilled upon her. The butterflies still danced, preoccupied in the centre of the clearing.

At last the immediacy of the kill subsided. The boys drew back, and

---

①covert: a term used in hunting to mean a small group of trees or bushes
②spurt: move with a sudden burst of speed

Jack stood up, holding out his hands.

'Look.' He giggled and flicked them while the boys laughed at his reeking palms. Then Jack grabbed Maurice and rubbed the stuff over his cheeks. Roger began to withdraw his spear and boys noticed it for the first time. Robert stabilized the thing in a phrase which was received uproariously.

'Right up her arse!'

'Did you hear?'

'Did you hear what he said?'

'Right up her arse!' This time Robert and Maurice acted the two parts; and Maurice's acting of the pig's efforts to avoid the advancing spear was so funny that the boys cried with laughter. At length even this palled. Jack began to clean his bloody hands on the rock. Then he started work on the sow and paunched① her, lugging out the hot bags of coloured guts, pushing them into a pile on the rock while the others watched him. He talked as he worked.

'We'll take the meat along the beach. I'll go back to the platform and invite them to a feast. That should give us time.'

Roger spoke.

'Chief—'

'Uh—?'

'How can we make a fire?'

Jack squatted back and frowned at the pig.

'We'll raid them and take fire. There must be four of you; Henry and you, Robert and Maurice. We'll put on paint and sneak up; Roger can snatch a branch while I say what I want. The rest of you can get this back to where we were. We'll build the fire there. And after that—'

He paused and stood up, looking at the shadows under the trees. His voice was lower when he spoke again.

'But we'll leave part of the kill for ...'

He knelt down again and was busy with his knife. The boys crowded round him. He spoke over his shoulder to Roger.

'Sharpen a stick at both ends.'

---

① paunch: remove the inner organs out of the fat belly (of the pig)

Presently he stood up, holding the dripping sow's head in his hands.

'Where's that stick?'

'Here.'

'Ram one end in the earth. Oh—it's rock. Jam it in that crack. There.'

Jack held up the head and jammed the soft throat down on the pointed end of the stick which pierced through into the mouth. He stood back and the head hung there, a little blood dribbling down the stick.

Instinctively the boys drew back too; and the forest was very still. They listened, and the loudest noise was the buzzing of flies over the spilled guts.

Jack spoke in a whisper.

'Pick up the pig.'

Maurice and Robert skewered[①] the carcass, lifted the dead weight, and stood ready. In the silence, and standing over the dry blood, they looked suddenly furtive.

Jack spoke loudly.

'This head is for the beast. It's a gift.'

The silence accepted the gift and awed them. The head remained there, dim-eyed, grinning faintly, blood blackening between the teeth. All at once they were running away, as fast as they could, through the forest toward the open beach....

Questions for Discussion

1. What leads to the boys' splitting into two distinct factions? What are the two factions' respective top concern? What may these top concerns symbolize?
2. Why does Jack succeed in winning over many boys' support? What does this symbolize in the end?
3. Do you think a group of girls would behave differently in similar circumstances?

---

① skewer: fasten together or pierce with a skewer, which is a long piece of wood or metal used for holding pieces of food, typically meat, together during cooking

Benjamin Zephaniah (b. 1958)

Benjamin Zephaniah was born in Birmingham to a Barbadian post-man and a Jamaican nurse. Due to an inborn learning disorder, he was unable to read or write until after he was 13. His first works were in the dub poetry① genre and he has become a leading activist for the black community. In 2003 he was offered an OBE② but publicly refused it and wrote the following poem in response.

Bought and Sold

     Smart big awards and prize money
     Is killing off black poetry
     It's not censors or dictators that are cutting up our art.
     The lure of meeting royalty
5   And touching high society
     Is damping creativity and eating at our heart.
     The ancestors would turn in graves
     Those poor black folk that once were slaves would wonder
     How our souls were sold
10   And check our strategies,
     The empire strikes back and waves
     Tamed warriors bow on parades
     When they have done what they've been told
     They get their OBEs.

15   Don't take my word, go check the verse
     Cause every laureate gets worse
     A family that you cannot fault as muse will mess your mind,
     And yeah, you may fatten your purse
     And surely they will check you first when subjects need to be amused
20   With paid for prose.

---

①dub poetry: performance poetry based on musical form
②OBE: Officer of the Order of the British Empire, a British honour awarded by the Queen

Take your prize, now write more,
Faster,
F**k the truth
Now you're an actor do not fault your benefactor
25   Write, publish and review,
You look like a dreadlocks Rasta,①
You look like a ghetto blaster,②
But you can't diss③ your paymaster
And bite the hand that feeds you.
30   What happened to the verse of fire
Cursing cool the empire
What happened to the soul rebel that Marley④ had in mind,
This bloodstained, stolen empire rewards you and you conspire,
(Yes Marley said that time will tell)
35   Now look they've gone and joined.
We keep getting this beating
It's bad history repeating
It reminds me of those capitalists that say
'Look you have a choice,'
40   It's sick and self-defeating if our dispossessed keep weeping
And we give these awards meaning
But we end up with no voice.

Questions for Discussion

1. What is Zephaniah's attitude to the British Empire?
2. What does the poet think is the real danger to black poets?

---

① a dreadlocks Rasta: a Rastafarian who customarily wears dreadlocks, which are long hair braids worn by Rastafarians
② blaster: a large portable stereo
③ diss: disrespect
④ Marley: Robert Nesta Marley (1945 – 1981), usually known as Bob Marley, Jamaican pioneer of reggae music

Part II

American Literature and Culture

Introduction

The full title of the nation state known as "America" is the United States of America, often abbreviated as the US. Lying in the continent of North America, it is a part of the New World, which was not discovered until the late 15th century when on October 12, 1492, Christopher Columbus and his fleet sponsored by the Spanish Crown arrived at the island of San Salvador in the modern day Bahamas.① Because Columbus and his associates thought they were landing in the "Indies," or the Far East, they called the natives "Indians." About 1502, the Italian explorer Amerigo Vespucci demonstrated to Europeans that instead of being Asia's eastern outskirts as Columbus and his fellow sailors had thought, the New World was a separate continent. Thus, the New World was named after him as "America." Of course, now we know that this New World actually is comprised of two continents, namely North America and South America. Therefore the term America may either mean the United States of America or the continents of America.

Columbus's discovery of the New World ushered in the era of European exploration and settlement in the Americas. From the beginning of the 16th century, European settlers gradually came to North America. They were Spanish, French, Dutch, Swedish, German, Italian, Portuguese, and English. In the 17th century, the majority of colonists were English. The first successful English settlement was set up in today's American South. It was Jamestown, Virginia, established in 1607 when a group of 105 colonists landed there. The first permanent settlement in today's American North was

---

①Bahamas: the nation state officially known as Commonwealth of the Bahamas (Lying at northwestern edge of the West Indies, it consists of about 700 islands and numerous cays.)

Plymouth, Massachusetts, established in 1620 by a group of 102 passengers known as the Pilgrims, who crossed the Atlantic Ocean aboard the famous ship *Mayflower*.

Through British colonization, the English language was introduced to the land. Prior to the American Revolutionary War (1775 – 1783) which resulted in American independence from British rule, the English language used by the Americans was similar to the British English. They were both *rhotic*, meaning that speakers pronounced the letter *R* in *hard*. Even after the thirteen colonies gained independence as the United States of America, their schools still used textbooks imported from England. However, Noah Webster, an American lexicographer①, nationalist, and prolific political writer, disliked Britain's influence and control over the English language used in the new republic. To show cultural independence from Britain, in the 1780s Webster wrote and published *A Grammatical Institute of the English Language*, a compendium② that consisted of a speller, a grammar, and a reader, which were published respectively in 1783, 1784, and 1785. Webster changed the spellings in the book to be more phonetic—he believed that the spelling of words should match their pronunciation as much as possible (e.g., *color* instead of *colour*, *check* instead of *cheque*). His changes made the American version of words different from the British. The speller became very popular and over time, this influence was further solidified by Webster's dictionaries. His grammar books were also very popular. They were used in schools throughout the country. As a result, English used in America and in Britain started diverging from each other in various aspects, including spelling, pronunciation, vocabulary, grammar, punctuation, and way of formatting dates and numbers.

Regarding word-spelling, here are some more examples: British *analyse* is transformed into *analyze*, *centre* into *center*, *dialogue* into *dialog*, *fulfil* into *fulfill*, *grey* into *gray*, *disc* into *disk*.

Regarding the use of prepositions, the British would play *in* a team,

---

① lexicographer: a person who compiles dictionaries
② compendium: a collection of things, especially one systematically gathered

while Americans would play *on* a team; the British would go out *at* the weekend, but Americans would go out *on* the weekend.

Regarding the use of the past tense, Americans would use *dreamed* while Brits would use *dreamt* as the past tense of *dream*. The same applies to *learned* and *learnt* as the past tense of *learn*.

The Americans and the British also have some words that differ from each other. For instance, *trousers*, *postbox*, *biscuit*, and *football* in British English are *pants*, *mailbox*, *cookies*, and *soccer* in American English.

Regarding collective nouns, in British English, they are often considered plural (e.g., the band *are* playing), while in American English, they are often considered singular (e.g., the band *is* playing). In British English, collective nouns take either singular or plural verb forms. Hence, the British will say and write *Napoleon's army is/are on their way*. In American English, all collective nouns take the singular verb form. Therefore, in American English it will be said and written as *Napoleon's army is on the way*.

Regarding quotation marks, in American English, double quotation marks (") are always used for initial quotations, then single quotation marks (') for quotations within the initial quotation, while in British English, it is the exact reverse. Moreover, American style places commas and periods inside the quotation marks, even if they are not in the original material.

For example:

> I remember telling the Hawaiian teacher, "We Chinese can't sing 'land where our fathers died.'" She argued with me about politics, while I meant because of curse.

The British style of the same passage would be as follows:

> I remember telling the Hawaiian teacher, 'We Chinese can't sing "land where our fathers died"'. She argued with me about politics, while I meant because of curse.

The style of writing the date is different, too. In British English, the date precedes the month, such as "1 October, 2023," and it would be abbreviated as 1/10/23, while in American English, the month precedes the date, such as "October 1, 2023," and it would be abbreviated as 10/1/23.

Despite the endeavors Americans took to build up American identity, one undeniable thing was that American writers had long taken European literature, especially British literature, as a model. For instance, American poetry, namely the poetry of the United States, arose first as efforts by early Americans to add their voices to English poetry. Unsurprisingly, most of the early American poets' work relied on contemporary British models of poetic form, diction, and theme. Genuine American literature did not appear until the New England Renaissance, which lasted for several decades from around 1830s till the outbreak of the Civil War in 1861. Incidentally, the word *Renaissance* is pronounced differently in British English and American English, as [rɪˈneɪsns] vs. [ˈrenəsɑːns].

American literature begins with American experiences. From the very beginning, the American natives, the European explorers and colonists, as well as enslaved African blacks were creators of early American literature. In time, ethnic American writers descended from immigrants from across the world significantly enriched American literature and culture.

Chapter 1

From 1492 to 1775
The Colonial Age and American Colonialism

The European exploration and colonization of North America opened up the trans-Atlantic ties between the two continents, incorporating America into the European economic and political environment. Jamestown, Virginia, the first English colony established in 1607 was named after the English King James I. In 1620, the *Mayflower*, after taking 66 days beating its way across the Atlantic, put the Pilgrims ashore at Plymouth, Massachusetts. A highly noteworthy thing is that these two colonies were established and inhabited by colonists who had come to the New World with distinct aspirations in mind. This accounts for the subsequent North-South cultural difference and long-standing tensions, which had been so sharp and irreconcilable that the Civil War broke out between the two parts of the nation more than two centuries later.

American literature and culture, as a whole, begins with American experiences. To have a better understanding of the making of the United States of America, it is essential to have a close look at the following three groups of people: American Indians/Native Americans, the Puritans in the North and the plantation owners and settlers in the South.

1.1 American Indians

Before Columbus discovered the New World, the American Indians had been native to the land for thousands of years. According to modern archaeology and anthropology,[①] they were descendants of Asians who

---

[①] anthropology: the science of human beings

crossed the land-bridge known as the Bering Strait to America some 25,000 years ago. In spite of the fact that Columbus gave them a collective name "Indians," no one name could adequately describe the variety of cultures that flourished from one end of the continent to the other. Today, ethnographers[①] call them "Native Americans" and a lot of people call them "American Indians." Some native peoples also refer to themselves as "American Indians."

The Literature of Native Americans

Generation after generation these Native Americans had told stories, sung songs, and recited tales that embodied their past and told of their close relationship with the natural world. However, very few tribes had written signs—though some tribes, such as the Delaware Indians, did develop forms of writing. Therefore, most of the Native Americans' works of literature survived through an oral tradition, each generation transmitting its literature to its young people by word of mouth. The result is a literature created by no one author, but by its people.

The following is a traditional Navaho song. The Navaho, an agricultural people, are a large and varied group who settled in the American Southwest, where their culture still flourishes.

Listen! Rain Approaches!

    Truly in the East
    The white bean
    And the great corn plant
    Are tied with the white lightning.
5   Listen! It approaches!
    The voice of the bluebird is heard.

    Truly in the East

---

①ethnographer: the branch of anthropology that deals with the description of specific human cultures, using methods such as close observation and interviews

	The white bean
	And the great squash
10	Are tied with the rainbow.
	Listen! It approaches!
	The voice of the bluebird is heard.

> Questions for Discussion
>
> 1. Suppose you live in a community that has only oral language but no written signs. What challenges and advantages do you think there would be in interpersonal communication and cultural transmission?
> 2. What view of nature is reflected in "Listen! Rain Approaches!"?

1.2　The Northern Puritans

In 1620, the ship *Mayflower* that carried about one hundred Pilgrims sailed from Southampton, England and dropped anchor at Plymouth, Massachusetts. Not all the Pilgrims were Puritans, however, they were dominated by the religious views of the Puritans. These Puritans were known as "Separatists" because unlike the majority of Puritans, they saw no hope of reforming the Church of England from within. They not only wanted to purify their lives of what they saw as the corruptions of English society, but also desired to purify their church of what they saw as the corruptions of the state religion, the Church of England. They chose to withdraw from the Church of England and even from England itself in order to worship as they saw fit. Actually, prior to voyaging to the New World, these Separatists had settled in Holland for many years. Fearing that they would eventually lose their identity as a religious community living as strangers in foreign land, they applied to settle in the New World. Among this group, the leading figure was William Bradford (1590－1657).

| From 1492 to 1775 | Chapter 1 |
| The Colonial Age and American Colonialism |

In 1630, another group of Puritans arrived at the Massachusetts Bay Colony under the leadership of John Winthrop (1588 – 1649). Compared with the Pilgrims, their attitude toward the Church of England was less radical: they were dissenters but non-separatist Puritans. In this group were many urban people, particularly of the rising middle class. Economically, many of them were men of substance. Some had been members of the House of Commons, and a very few were even from the nobility. They had had all sorts of vested interests in England and no desire to leave home, its comforts, and its privileges. Yet, with the accession of Charles I in 1625 and his dissolution of Parliament in 1629, it seemed that a civil war could possibly happen. Thus, they joined the Massachusetts Bay Colony. One highly noteworthy thing was that only about 7 years after, the colony established Harvard University, the first college in the American colonies.

With regard to these two groups of Puritans, no matter what differences they might have in their attitude toward the Church of England, their basic beliefs were identical: they both held with Martin Luther that no pope or bishop had a right to impose any law on a Christian soul without consent, and they both agreed with John Calvin that God chose freely those He would save and those He would damn eternally. Plymouth was eventually absorbed into the Massachusetts Bay Colony in 1691.

These Puritans compared themselves to the Israelites① of old, who had believed they had been given the promise of a new land. John Winthrop was viewed as the Puritan Moses whose education had prepared him to fulfill the "noble design of carrying a colony of chosen people into an American wilderness." When John Winthrop addressed the immigrants to the Massachusetts Bay Colony aboard the flagship *Arbella* in 1630, he told them that the eyes of the world were on them and that they would be an example for all, a "city upon a hill."②

---

① Israelites: a member of the ancient Hebrew nation, especially in the period from the Exodus to the Babylonian Captivity (c. 12th to 6th centuries BCE)
② a city upon a hill: The phrase refers to a community that others will look up to and emulate as a shining example of perfection. It is derived from the Bible's Matthew 5:14, which reads "You are the light of the world. A city that is set on an hill cannot be hid."(King James Version)

For the Puritans, everything ideally aimed at personal salvation and the building of a new, God-centered society. They had a passionate desire to establish a New Jerusalem Life. They worked long and hard so that their farms and trading enterprises would prosper, which they deemed as a sign of God's special favor. They kept reminding themselves that their souls were the constant battlegrounds of God and Satan and that every act and thought had to be judged according to whether it truly glorified God. In America, Puritan moralism and its sense of an elect people in a covenant① with God deeply shaped the national character, at least in name.

Writing was an important part of Puritan life: it was often an extension of religion. The first book published in America was the *Bay Psalm Book* (1640), a translation of the Biblical Psalms.② Many Puritans kept journals to help them carefully examine their spiritual lives. They also wrote spiritual autobiographies.

The most well-known titles of the Puritan writings include William Bradford's *Of Plymouth Plantation* composed between 1630 and 1651, Anne Bradstreet's poetic book *The Tenth Muse Lately Sprung Up in America* (1650), and Jonathan Edwards's sermon "Sinners in the Hands of an Angry God"(1741).

William Bradford (1590 – 1657)

William Bradford is best remembered as the Governor of the Plymouth Colony and the author of *Of Plymouth Plantation*. He epitomized the spirit of determination and self-sacrifice that was characteristic of the first "Pilgrims" who navigated on the *Mayflower* and settled in Plymouth, Massachusetts.

Bradford was born in Yorkshire of parents who were modestly well off. After his father died while he was an infant and his mother remarried in 1593, he was brought up by his paternal grandparents and uncles. He did not receive a university education; he was taught the arts of farming. When he was twelve or thirteen, he heard the sermons that changed his life.

---

①covenant: a usually formal, solemn, and binding agreement
②Biblical Psalms: Psalms is one of the 66 books of the Bible. It contains 150 independent psalms.

Later, against the oppositions of his uncles and grandparents, he left home and joined the small community of believers known as the "Separatists."

When the Separatists took up residence in the Netherlands, Bradford jointed them in 1609 and there he learned to be a weaver. Later he went into business for himself.

Before the pilgrims disembarked from the *Mayflower* to settle in Plymouth, Massachusetts, they signed the Mayflower Compact and decided to form a government and follow an elected leader. When the first governor died in 1621, Bradford was chosen to take his place. He was so successful that he was reelected thirty times. In 1630 he began writing *Of Plymouth Plantation*, the history of these early Americans and their long geographical and spiritual pilgrimage.

Of Plymouth Plantation

Chapter 9 Of their Voyage, and How They Passed the Sea; and of Their Safe Arrival at Cape Cod
(Excerpt)

September 6, 1620. These troubles being blown over, and now all being compact together in one ship, they put to sea again with a prosperous wind, which continued divers days together, which was some encouragement unto them; yet, according to the usual manner, many were afflicted with seasickness....

Being thus arrived in a good harbor, and brought safe to land, they fell upon their knees and blessed the God of Heaven who had brought them over the vast and furious ocean, and delivered them from all the perils and miseries thereof, again to set their feet on the firm and stable earth ...

But here I cannot but stay and make a pause, and stand half amazed at this poor people's present condition; and so I think will the reader, too, when he well considers the same. Being thus passed the vast ocean, and a sea of troubles before in their preparation (as may be remembered by that which went before), they had now no friends to welcome them, nor inns to entertain or refresh their weatherbeaten bodies; no houses or much less towns to repair to, to seek for succor.① It is recorded in Scripture② as a mercy to the Apostle③ and his shipwrecked company, that the barbarians showed them no small kindness in refreshing them, but these savage barbarians, when they met with them (as after will appear) were readier to fill their sides full of arrows than otherwise. And for the season it was winter, and they that know the winters of that country know them to be sharp and violent, and subject to cruel and fierce storms, dangerous to travel to known places, much more to search an unknown coast. Besides, what could they see but a hideous and desolate wilderness, full of wild beasts and wild men? And what multitudes there might be of them they knew not. Neither could they, as it were, go up to the top of Pisgah④ to view from this wilderness a more goodly country to feed their hopes; for which way soever they turned their eyes (save upward to the heavens) they could have little solace or content in respect of any outward objects. For summer being done, all things stand upon them with a weatherbeaten face, and the whole country, full of woods and thickets, represented a wild and savage hue. If they looked behind them, there was the mighty ocean which they had passed and was now as a main bar and gulf to separate them from all the civil parts of the world. If it be said they had a ship to succor them, it is true; but what heard they daily from the master⑤ and company? But that with speed they should look out a place with their shallop,⑥ where they would be at some near distance; for the season was such as he would not stir from thence till a safe harbor was discovered by them where they would be, and he might go without danger; and that victuals consumed apace, but he must and would keep sufficient for themselves and their return. Yea, it was muttered by some that if they got not a place in time, they would turn them

---

①succor: help or aid
②Scripture: the Bible
③the Apostle: "The Apostle" refers to Paul. In the Bible, Acts of Apostles 28:2 tells how strangers helped Paul after he was shipwrecked.
④go up to the top of Pisgah: According to the Bible, in Deuteronomy 34:1, from the summit of Mount Pisgah Moses viewed the Promised Land.
⑤master: the captain of the *Mayflower*
⑥shallop: small boat

and their goods ashore and leave them. Let it also be considered what weak hopes of supply and succor they left behind them, that might bear up their minds in this sad condition and trials they were under; and they could not but be very small. It is true, indeed, the affections and love of their brethren at Leyden① was cordial and entire towards them, but they had little power to help them or themselves; and how the case stood between them and the merchants at their coming away hath already been declared.

What could now sustain them but the Spirit of God and His grace? ...

Questions for Discussion

1. What terms did William Bradford use to call the Natives? Do you think he was justifiable calling them this way? Why or why not?
2. What is the picture of the New World based on William Bradford's description?

Anne Bradstreet (1612 – 1672)

Anne Bradstreet was born and educated in England. Her father was the estate manager of the Earl of Lincoln. She voyaged with her family to Massachusetts when she was 16 years old. Her husband was later elected governor of the Massachusetts Bay Colony. In spite of caring for eight children, she composed poems on subjects from daily life which expressed her personal feeling for family life and the new world. Some of her poems were taken by her sister's husband to England and published in 1650, which was the first published poetry book by an American. Her book *The Tenth Muse Lately Sprung Up in America* shows she was influenced by English writers. In her poem "To My Dear and Loving Husband," she expressed the profound love for her husband. But her most famous poem is "Upon the Burning of Our House."

---

①Leyden: city in Netherlands where the Pilgrims lived before coming to America

Upon the Burning of Our House

   In silent night when rest I took,
   For sorrow near I did not look,
   I waken'd was with thund'ring noise
   And piteous shrieks of dreadful voice.
5 That fearful sound of "fire!" and "fire!"
   Let no man know is my desire.

   I, starting up, the light did spy,
   And to my God my heart did cry
   To straighten me in my Distress
10 And not to leave me succourless.
   Then, coming out, beheld a space
   The flame consume my dwelling place.

   And when I could no longer look,
   I blest His name that gave and took,
15 That laid my goods now in the dust.
   Yea, so it was, and so 'twas just.
   It was His own; it was not mine.
   Far be it that I should repine①.

   He might of all justly bereft,
20 But yet sufficient for us left.
   When by the ruins oft I past,
   My sorrowing eyes aside did cast,
   And here and there the places spy
   Where oft I sat and long did lie:

25 Here stood that trunk, and there that chest,
   There lay that store I counted best,

---

① repine: complain

My pleasant things in ashes lie,
And them behold no more shall I.
Under the roof no guest shall sit,
30   Nor at thy table eat a bit.

No pleasant tale shall e'er be told,
Nor things recounted done of old.
No candle e'er shall shine in Thee,
Nor bridegroom's voice e'er heard shall be.
35   In silence ever shalt thou lie.
Adieu, Adieu, all's vanity.

Then straight I 'gin my heart to chide:
And did thy wealth on earth abide?
Didst fix thy hope on mould'ring dust?
40   The arm of flesh didst make thy trust?
Raise up thy thoughts above the sky
That dunghill mists away may fly.

Thou hast a house on high erect
Framed by that mighty Architect,
45   With glory richly furnished
Stands permanent, though this be fled.
It's purchased and paid for too
By Him who hath enough to do.

A price so vast as is unknown
50   Yet by His gift is made thine own.
There's wealth enough; I need no more.
Farewell, my pelf; farewell, my store.
The world no longer let me love;
My hope and treasure lies above.

> **Questions for Discussion**
>
> 1. How did the speaker feel at first about the loss of her house and possessions in the fire? How did she come to terms with the loss?
> 2. How have you accepted or dealt emotionally with losing items of great value?

Jonathan Edwards (1703 – 1758)

Jonathan Edwards was one of the most important theologians and preachers in early America. Edwards was born in Connecticut and died in New Jersey. In 1729 he succeeded his grandfather as minister in Northampton, Massachusetts. He is best known, even notorious, for his sermon "Sinners in the Hands of an Angry God," which he preached in 1741. As a preacher, he made his people fear the power of God. Actually, in 1750 some of Northampton Puritans began to disagree with their famous minister and removed him from his post. However, it is unfair to accuse him, since sermons such as this had been traditional for hundreds of years.

Sinners in the Hands of an Angry God
(Excerpt)

Your wickedness makes you as it were heavy as lead, and to tend downwards with great weight and pressure towards hell; and if God should let you go, you would immediately sink and swiftly descend and plunge into the bottomless gulf, and your healthy constitution,① and your own care and prudence, and best contrivance,② and all your righteousness, would have no more influence to uphold you and keep you out of hell, than a spider's web would have to stop a falling rock ... There are the black clouds of God's wrath now hanging directly over your heads, full of the dreadful storm, and

---

① constitution: the physical makeup of the individual especially with respect to the health, strength, and appearance of the body
② contrivance: artificial arrangement

big with thunder; and were it not for the restraining hand of God, it would immediately burst forth upon you. The sovereign pleasure of God, for the present, stays his rough wind; otherwise it would come with fury, and your destruction would come like a whirlwind, and you would be like the chaff of the summer threshing floor.

The wrath of God is like great waters that are dammed for the present; they increase more and more, and rise higher and higher, till an outlet is given; and the longer the stream is stopped, the more rapid and mighty is its course, when once it is let loose. It is true, that judgment against your evil works has not been executed hitherto; the floods of God's vengeance have been withheld; but your guilt in the mean time is constantly increasing, and you are every day treasuring up more wrath; the waters are constantly rising, and waxing more and more mighty; and there is nothing but the mere pleasure of God, that holds the waters back, that are unwilling to be stopped, and press hard to go forward. If God should only withdraw his hand from the flood-gate, it would immediately fly open, and the fiery floods of the fierceness and wrath of God, would rush forth with inconceivable fury, and would come upon you with omnipotent power; and if your strength were ten thousand times greater than it is, yea, ten thousand times greater than the strength of the stoutest, sturdiest devil in hell, it would be nothing to withstand or endure it.

The bow of God's wrath is bent, and the arrow made ready on the string, and justice bends the arrow at your heart, and strains the bow, and it is nothing but the mere pleasure of God, and that of an angry God, without any promise or obligation at all, that keeps the arrow one moment from being made drunk with your blood ...

The God that holds you over the pit of hell, much as one holds a spider, or some loathsome insect over the fire, abhors you, and is dreadfully provoked; his wrath towards you burns like fire; he looks upon you as worthy of nothing else, but to be cast into the fire; he is of purer eyes than to bear to have you in his sight; you are ten thousand times more abominable① in his eyes, than the most

---

①abominable: worthy of or causing disgust or hatred

hateful venomous serpent is in ours....

O sinner! Consider the fearful danger you are in: it is a great furnace of wrath, a wide and bottomless pit, full of the fire of wrath, that you are held over in the hand of that God, whose wrath is provoked and incensed as much against you, as against many of the damned in hell. You hang by a slender thread, with the flames of divine wrath flashing about it, and ready every moment to singe it, and burn it asunder; and you have no interest in any Mediator, and nothing to lay hold of to save yourself, nothing to keep off the flames of wrath, nothing of your own, nothing that you ever have done, nothing that you can do, to induce God to spare you one moment ...

Questions for Discussion

1. Puritan theology asserts the basic sinfulness of humankind. Though Chinese philosopher Xunzi also claims that human nature is wicked, Confucius and Mencius hold the view that human nature is basically good. The 20th century existentialist philosophers Sartre and Camus deny the notion of predetermined human nature, claiming that existence precedes essence, not the reverse. What's your argument?
2. Jonathan Edwards's sermon "Sinners in the Hands of an Angry God" does its utmost to arouse people's fear. What do you think is the unwholesome effect of fear? Do you think a sense of fear has positive effect too? Why or why not?

1.3 The Southern Colonists

The southern colonies began in 1607 with Jamestown, Virginia. Different from the northern colonies in New England that featured Puritan culture, the southern colonies were culturally and religiously diverse. The southern English settlers came to pursue economic opportunities instead of religious freedom. There were also French, Dutch, Swiss, German, and Irish settlers. Much of the southern population lived on farms or plantations that were distant from one another. Often these plantations were largely self-sufficient. For the most part, southern gentlemen and ladies carried on correspondence with friends who often lived at great distances from them, as well as with family and friends back in England. Many of the southern colonists belonged to the Church of England, which the Puritans had attempted to reform. In contrast to the Puritans' dream of building the "city upon a hill," the southern people dreamed of finding a "vale of plenty," which was proposed by Captain John Smith, leader of Jamestown Colony. They pursued material wealth and some of them lived an aristocratic life with large plantations.

The southern literature was secular and characterized by a sense of satire and humor. In their letters, journals, and public reports, southern writers recorded the details of their way of life, for instance William Byrd's *The History of the Dividing Line* (1728) and *A Progress to the Mines* (1732). Of course, not all the residents of the southern colonies were prosperous owners of plantations; most were hard working tradespeople, artisans, small farmers, indentured servants,① and slaves. Yet the sophisticated gentleman and lady dominate many people's sense of the early southern colonies as we meet them in literature.

John Smith (1580 – 1631)

John Smith was an English adventurer and explorer. In 1607, the twenty-seven-year-old Captain John Smith led one hundred men and four boys to found the first permanent English settlement, Jamestown, Virginia. After two years, he returned to England. In 1614, he came back to New England and explored the coast from Maine to Cape Cod, made maps, traded with Indians, and went back to England, never to return to America. In 1616, his *A Description of New England* was published.

---

① indentured servant: a person who signs and is bound by indentures to work for another for a specified time especially in return for payment of travel expenses and maintenance

A Description of New England
(Excerpt)

  Who can desire more content, that has small means or but only his merit to advance his fortune, than to tread and plant that ground he has purchased by the hazard① of his life? If he have but the taste of virtue and magnanimity, what to such a mind can be more pleasant than planting and building a foundation for his posterity, got from the rude earth by God's blessing and his own industry, without prejudice to any? If he have any grain of faith or zeal in religion, what can he do less hurtful to any or more agreeable to God than to seek to convert those poor savages to know Christ and humanity?...What so truly suits with honor and honesty as the discovering things unknown, erecting towns, peopling countries, informing the ignorant, reforming things unjust, teaching virtue, and gain to our native mother-country a kingdom to attend her, find employment for those that are idle because they know not what to do? [This is] so far from wronging any as to cause posterity to remembering thee ...

  Here nature and liberty afford us that freely which in England we want,② or it costs us dearly. What pleasure can be more than (being tired with any occasion ashore, in planting vines, fruits, or herbs, in contriving their own grounds, to the pleasure of their own minds, their fields, gardens, orchards, buildings, ships, and other works, etc.) to recreate themselves before their own doors, in their own boats upon the sea, where man, woman, and child, with a small hook and line, by angling may take divers sorts of excellent fish at their pleasures? And is it not pretty sport to pull up two pence, six pence, and twelve pence as fast as you can haul and veer③ a line? He is a very bad fisher [who] cannot kill in one day with his hook and line, one, two, or three hundred cods ... If a man work but three days in seven he may get more than he can spend, unless he will be excessive....

---

① hazard: risk, danger
② want: lack
③ haul and veer: pull in and let out

For hunting also, the woods, lakes, and rivers afford not only chase sufficient for any that delight in that kind of toil or pleasure, but such beasts to hunt that besides the delicacy of their bodies for food, their skins are so rich as may well recompense thy daily labor with a captain's pay....

My purpose is not to persuade children from their parents, men from their wives, nor servants from their masters, only such as with free consent may be spared. But [if] each parish or village, in city or country, that will but apparel their fatherless children of thirteen or fourteen years of age, or young married people that have small wealth to live on, here by their labor [they] may live exceeding well, provided always that first there be a sufficient power to command them, houses to receive them, means to defend them, and meet① provisions for them, for any place may be overlain② and it is most necessary to have a fortress and sufficient masters (as, carpenters, masons, fishers, fowlers, gardeners, husbandmen,③ sawyers, smiths, spinners, tailors, weavers, and such like) to take ten, twelve, or twenty, or as there is occasion, for apprentices. The masters by this may quickly grow rich; these [apprentices] may learn [by] their trades themselves to do the like, to a general and an incredible benefit for king and country, master and servant.

Questions for Discussion

1. In the first paragraph, who were in John Smith's mind when he referred to "those poor savages"? How would you argue for or against his view?
2. How is John Smith's narrative in *A Description of New England* different from William Bradford's description in *Of Plymouth Plantation*? In your opinion, what caused this difference?

---

①meet: (old English) proper, fitting
②overlain: (the past participle of "overlie") overwhelmed by an enemy
③husbandmen: farmers

William Byrd (1674 – 1744)

William Byrd was one of the most brilliant of the southern landowning aristocracy. These southern gentry modeled themselves on the English upper classes, taking pride in stately homes furnished with fine china, paintings, and books. Though hard-working and religious, they were not afraid of some of the worldly pleasures that the Puritans shunned.

Byrd was born in Jamestown, which John Smith had helped establish sixty-seven years earlier. When he was seven years old, his father sent him to England for his education. There he met high class people including men of letters. He was fifty-two before he returned to Virginia. There he read his Greek and Latin classics every day; owned the second largest library in America which numbered 3,600 books; entertained and visited his neighbors; and managed his huge estate, upon which he founded the city of Richmond.

Byrd's writings include diaries, travel books, and poems. One of his best-known works, *The History of the Dividing Line* recounts his experiences on a surveying trip that defined the border between Virginia and North Carolina. His other well-known work, *A Progress to the Mines*, is Byrd's account of a trip to the iron-mining territory of western Virginia, where he visited the estate of a friend identified as "the Colonel." His writings showed how the southerners loved the material world of land, animals, plants, and the local Indians.

A Progress to the Mines

(Excerpt)

September 30 The sun rose clear this morning and so did I, and finished all my little affairs by breakfast. It was then resolved to wait on the ladies on horseback, since the bright sun, the fine air, and the wholesome exercise all invited us to it. We forded the river a little above the ferry and rode six miles up the neck to a fine level piece of rich land, where we found about twenty plants of ginseng, with the scarlet berries growing on the top of the middle stalk. The root of this is of wonderful virtue in many cases, particularly to raise the spirits and promote perspiration, which makes it a specific in colds and coughs. The colonel complimented me with all we found in return for my telling him the virtues of it. We were all pleased to find so much of this king of plants so near the colonel's habitation and growing, too, upon his own land, but were, however, surprised to find it upon level ground, after we had been told it grew only upon the north side of stony mountains. I carried home this treasure with as much joy as if every root had been a graft① of the tree of life, and washed and dried it carefully.

This airing made us as hungry as so many hawks, so that, between appetite and a very good dinner, 'twas difficult to eat like a philosopher.

Questions for Discussion

1. What aspect of southern life does William Byrd's description show? How does it differ from the northern Puritans' life?
2. With William Byrd's undertaking of the Virginia and North Carolina border project in mind, please explain why many states in the United States have straight lines as boundaries.

---

① graft: a transplant or a piece of living tissue that is transplanted surgically

Chapter 2

From 1775 to 1783

The Revolutionary Era and the American Enlightenment

2.1 The American Revolution

The American Revolution, also called the American War of Independence, broke out in 1775 and ended in 1783. It happened more than one and a half centuries after the first English colonists settled in Jamestown Colony and Plymouth Colony.

By the 1770s, the number of English colonies in America had risen to thirteen. These colonies had begun to prosper; they had looked less and less like insecure settlements on the edge of a wilderness. They had communicated more with one another and grown aware of their mutual problems and feelings. They shared their anger over the oppressive political and economic policies imposed by the British government. However, at first, no one was thinking of revolution.

What immensely infuriated the colonies were a series of intolerable laws and taxes, for instance, the Quartering Act of 1765 forced colonists to feed and house British soldiers in their own homes, and the Townshend Acts in 1767 taxed tea, glass, lead, and paper. When some of the colonial assemblies refused to abide by the new laws, the British government declared those assemblies "dissolved." Violence soon followed. In 1773 the British Parliament insisted again on its right and power to tax Americans, which triggered the famous Boston Tea Party: adopting the dress of Native Americans, protesters boarded a ship and dumped its load of British tea into Boston Harbor. The Boston Tea Party became a symbol—a symbol of American resistance.

Americans protested and petitioned King George Ⅲ for "no taxation without representation." They said they wanted only what was reasonable: they wanted to share in their own government. Britain replied with the Coercive Acts of 1774, known as the Intolerable Acts in the American colonies, designed to punish Massachusetts for the Boston Tea Party. Many more rights that had been granted to the colonists were revoked. Then on April 19, 1775, when a group of American Minutemen[①] faced British redcoats[②] on their way to seize American arms at the village of Concord, Massachusetts, Americans responded with force. However, it was not until January 1776 that a widely heard public voice demanded a complete break with England. The voice came from Thomas Paine, whose pamphlet *Common Sense* generated the growing demand for separation and pointed the way toward the July 4th 1776 Declaration of Independence, which officially announced the Thirteen States' independence from the English rule. With French military support, the united colonies achieved their victory in 1783.

One of the fundamental driving forces behind the American Revolution was the intellectual revolution called the Enlightenment, and Locke's ideas of a social contract were a significant influence on the American "Founding Fathers."

2.2 The American Enlightenment

The American Enlightenment was inspired and influenced by the European Enlightenment, which was the movement of intellectual liberation developing in Western Europe from the late 17th century to the late 18th century. This period has often been called the "Age of Reason," for

---

[①] American Minutemen: In U.S. history, American Minutemen were Revolution militiamen who agreed to be ready for military duty "at a minute's warning." They were selected from militia muster rolls by their commanding officers and they were chosen for their enthusiasm, reliability, and physical strength.

[②] British redcoats: British soldiers of the 18th and early 19th centuries and especially during the American Revolution. They were so called because of the red overcoat they wore.

Enlightenment thinkers re-examined all aspects of society (such as religion, government, justice and women's rights) through the application of reason, and they believed that reason is a main source of all knowledge. With its forerunners in science and philosophy being Bacon, Descartes, Newton, and Locke, the European Enlightenment culminated with the writings of Rousseau, Diderot, and Kant. Its central idea was the need for, and the capacity of, human reason to clear away ancient superstition, prejudice, dogma, and injustice. Descartes, the father of modern rationalism, is well known for his motto "I think, therefore I am", which means that he would only accept those things his reason said were true. Enlightenment thinking emphasized rationality and scientific research rather than tradition and religious dogma. The Enlightenment thinkers were not interested in theology. Rather they were fascinated with humankind's own nature.

Enlightenment thinking also championed the idea of universal human rights. John Locke said that all people possessed the natural rights to life, liberty, and property. He believed in the equality and independence of people. In his opinion, the governed should consent to be governed, and government should represent the interests of the people. Rousseau thought that people should have the ultimate power in government; that if necessary, they could withdraw their support of their government. He held that the least amount of government was the best.

The ideas of the Enlightenment spread to the New World and influenced the reading public. The Americans began to break through the limitations of traditional Puritanism and accept the progressive ideas of justice, equality, and liberty. They believed that education could propel personal growth and social progress. Accordingly, American Enlightenment thinkers composed writings to educate the public and defend their revolutionary cause.

The prose of the great philosopher-statesmen made up a prominent part of 18th century American literature, with the best-known titles being Thomas Paine's *Common Sense*, Thomas Jefferson's Declaration of Independence, and Benjamin Franklin's *The Autobiography of Benjamin*

Franklin. As in England, this was the great age of the newspaper and the moral essay; Benjamin Franklin said that he modeled his own style after the English essayists Joseph Addison and Richard Steele.

Thomas Paine (1737 – 1809)

Thomas Paine was born in 1737 in England, the son of a Quaker.① After a short, basic education, he started to work. In 1774, he met Benjamin Franklin in London, who advised and helped him to immigrate to America.

Paine landed at Philadelphia in November of 1774. Starting over as a publicist,② he first published his African Slavery in America in the spring of 1775, criticizing the practice in America as being unjust and inhumane.

Paine is best remembered as the author of two of the most popular writings in the 18th century America: *Common Sense* (the first pamphlet published in America to urge immediate independence from Britain) and *Rights of Man*, which he wrote in England.

Common Sense

III. Thoughts on the Present State of American Affairs

(Excerpt)

In the following pages I offer nothing more than simple facts, plain arguments, and common sense; and have no other preliminaries to settle with the reader, than that he will divest himself of prejudice and prepossession, and suffer③ his reason and his feelings to determine for themselves; that he will put on, or rather that he will not put off, the true character of a man, and generously enlarge his views beyond the present day.

Volumes have been written on the subject of the struggle between England and America. Men of all ranks have embarked in the controversy,

---

① Quaker: a member of a Christian religious group whose members dressed simply, were against violence, and had meetings without any special ceremony or priests
② publicist: an expert or commentator on public affairs
③ suffer: allow

from different motives, and with various designs; but all have been ineffectual, and the period of debate is closed. Arms, as the last resource, decide the contest; the appeal was the choice of the king, and the continent hath accepted the challenge....

As much hath been said of the advantages of reconciliation, which, like an agreeable dream, hath passed away and left us as we were, it is but right, that we should examine the contrary side of the argument, and inquire into some of the many material injuries which these colonies sustain, and always will sustain, by being connected with, and dependent on Great-Britain. To examine that connection and dependence, on the principles of nature and common sense, to see what we have to trust to, if separated, and what we are to expect, if dependent.

I have heard it asserted by some, that as America has flourished under her former connection with Great Britain, the same connection is necessary towards her future happiness, and will always have the same effect. Nothing can be more fallacious than this kind of argument. We may as well assert that because a child has thrived upon milk, that it is never to have meat, or that the first twenty years of our lives is to become a precedent for the next twenty. But even this is admitting more than is true; for I answer roundly① that America would have flourished as much, and probably much more, had no European power taken any notice of her. The commerce by which she hath enriched herself are the necessaries of life, and will always have a market while eating is the custom of Europe....

It hath lately been asserted in parliament, that the Colonies have no relation to each other but through the Parent Country , i.e. that Pennsylvania and the Jerseys and so on for the rest, are sister Colonies by the way of England; this is certainly a very roundabout way of proving relationship, but it is the nearest and only true way of proving enmity (or enemyship, if I may so call it.) France and Spain never were, nor perhaps ever will be, our enemies as AMERICANS, but as our being the SUBJECTS

---

① roundly: forcefully, emphatically

| From 1775 to 1783 | Chapter 2 |

The Revolutionary Era and the American Enlightenment

OF GREAT BRITAIN.

But Britain is the parent country, say some. Then the more shame upon her conduct. Even brutes do not devour their young, nor savages make war upon their families.... Europe, and not England, is the parent country of America. This new world hath been the asylum for the persecuted lovers of civil and religious liberty from EVERY PART of Europe. Hither have they fled, not from the tender embraces of the mother, but from the cruelty of the monster; and it is so far true of England, that the same tyranny which drove the first emigrants from home, pursues their descendants still....

Europe is too thickly planted with Kingdoms to be long at peace, and whenever a war breaks out between England and any foreign power, the trade of America goes to ruin, BECAUSE OF HER CONNECTION WITH BRITAIN. The next war may not turn out like the last, and should it not, the advocates for reconciliation now will be wishing for separation then, because neutrality in that case would be a safer convoy than a man of war. Everything that is right or reasonable pleads for separation. The blood of the slain, the weeping voice of nature cries, 'TIS TIME TO PART. Even the distance at which the Almighty hath placed England and America is a strong and natural proof that the authority of the one over the other, was never the design of Heaven.... The Reformation was preceded by the discovery of America: As if the Almighty graciously meant to open a sanctuary① to the persecuted in future years, when home should afford neither friendship nor safety....

A government of our own is our natural right: And when a man seriously reflects on the precariousness of human affairs, he will become convinced that it is infinitely wiser and safer to form a constitution of our own in a cool deliberate manner, while we have it in our power, than to trust such an interesting event to time and chance....

---

①sanctuary: a place of refuge or safety

> Questions for Discussion
>
> 1. What were the main reasons why some Americans wanted to reconcile with the British instead of fighting? How did Paine refute them?
> 2. Compare Jonathan Edwards's sermon excerpt of "Sinners in the Hands of an Angry God" in the forgoing chapter with the extracted text from Thomas Paine's *Common Sense*. Which do you think is an example of reasoned argument for persuasion? Which is an emotional appeal? What are the advantages and the disadvantages of a reasoned argument and an emotional appeal? Please use textual proofs to support your position.

Thomas Jefferson (1743 – 1826)

Thomas Jefferson was a Virginian. His father Peter Jefferson died when Thomas was fourteen. Jefferson remained an agrarian aristocrat all his life.

In 1760 Jefferson entered the College of William & Mary in Williamsburg, where he was fortunate enough to make the acquaintance of three men who strongly influenced his life: Governor Francis Fauquier, a fellow of the Royal Society; George Wythe, one of the best teachers of law in the country; and Dr. William Small, an immigrant from Scotland who taught mathematics and philosophy and who introduced Jefferson "to the invigorating realm of the Scottish Enlightenment."

Upon graduation from college, Jefferson practiced law for a short time. In 1775, he attended the Continental Congress, and in the following year, he was requested to draft the Declaration of Independence, which was edited by the Second Continental Congress and adopted in its final form on July 4, 1776.

During his lifetime, Jefferson played many roles. Though a man of many talents and achievements including serving as the third President of the United States, he once said that he wished to be remembered for only three things: drafting the Declaration of Independence, writing and supporting the Virginia Statute for Religious Freedom (1786), and founding the University of Virginia.

The Declaration of Independence was announced on July 4, 1776, which was later proclaimed Independence Day. The writing is eloquent, clear, direct, and forceful. It served effectively for the American call for independence.

The Unanimous Declaration of the Thirteen United States of America

(Excerpt)

When in the Course of human events, it becomes necessary for one people to dissolve the political bands which have connected them with another, and to assume among the powers of the earth, the separate and equal station to which the Laws of Nature and of Nature's God entitle them, a decent respect to the opinions of mankind requires that they should declare the causes which impel them to the separation.

We hold these truths to be self-evident, that all men are created equal, that they are endowed by their Creator with certain unalienable Rights, that among these are Life, Liberty and the pursuit of Happiness.—That to secure these rights, Governments are instituted among Men, deriving their just powers from the consent of the governed,—That whenever any Form of Government becomes destructive of these ends, it is the Right of the People to alter or to abolish it, and to institute new Government, laying its foundation on such principles and organizing its powers in such form, as to them shall seem most likely to effect their Safety and Happiness. Prudence, indeed, will dictate that Governments long established should not be changed for light and transient causes; and accordingly all experience hath shown, that mankind are more disposed① to suffer, while evils are sufferable, than to right themselves by abolishing the forms to which they

---

①disposed: having a certain inclination or disposition

are accustomed. But when a long train of abuses and usurpations, pursuing invariably the same Object evinces① a design to reduce them under absolute Despotism, it is their right, it is their duty, to throw off such Government, and to provide new Guards for their future security.—Such has been the patient sufferance of these Colonies; and such is now the necessity which constrains them to alter their former Systems of Government. The history of the present King of Great Britain is a history of repeated injuries and usurpations, all having in direct object the establishment of an absolute Tyranny over these States. To prove this, let Facts be submitted to a candid world.

He has refused his Assent to Laws, the most wholesome and necessary for the public good.

He has forbidden his Governors to pass Laws of immediate and pressing importance, unless suspended in their operation till his Assent should be obtained; and when so suspended, he has utterly neglected to attend to them....

He has called together legislative bodies at places unusual, uncomfortable, and distant from the depository of their public Records, for the sole purpose of fatiguing them into compliance with his measures.

He has dissolved Representative Houses repeatedly, for opposing with manly firmness his invasions on the rights of the people....

He has endeavoured to prevent the population of these States; for that purpose obstructing the Laws for Naturalization of Foreigners; refusing to pass others to encourage their migrations hither, and raising the conditions of new Appropriations of Lands....

He has erected a multitude of New Offices, and sent hither swarms of Officers to harass our people, and eat out their substance.

He has kept among us, in times of peace, Standing Armies without the Consent of our legislatures....

For cutting off our Trade with all parts of the world:

For imposing Taxes on us without our Consent:

... We, therefore, the Representatives of the United States of America, in General Congress, Assembled, appealing to the Supreme Judge

---

① evince: indicate or reveal the presence of sth.

of the world for the rectitude of our intentions, do, in the Name, and by Authority of the good People of these Colonies, solemnly publish and declare, That these United Colonies are, and of Right ought to be Free and Independent States; that they are Absolved from all Allegiance to the British Crown, and that all political connection between them and the State of Great Britain, is and ought to be totally dissolved; and that as Free and Independent States, they have full Power to levy War, conclude Peace, contract Alliances, establish Commerce, and to do all other Acts and Things which Independent States may of right do. And for the support of this Declaration, with a firm reliance on the protection of divine Providence, we mutually pledge to each other our Lives, our Fortunes and our sacred Honor.

Questions for Discussion

1. According to Jefferson, what human rights are unalienable? How do you interpret the phrase "pursuit of happiness"?
2. In the final sentence of the Declaration, what do the signers pledge? What do you think their fate would have been if Britain had been the victor in the war?
3. It has long been noted that the Declaration of Independence is ironic and hypocritical. It claims that "all men are created equal" and denounces the political tyranny and economic oppression imposed by Great Britain. However, a blatant fact was that blacks and women were not treated as equals in American Society. Furthermore, Thomas Jefferson, the author, like many other signers of the political document, was a slave owner. What do you make of this flagrant contradiction?

Benjamin Franklin (1706 – 1790)

Benjamin Franklin was born in Boston. His father was a poor

craftsman who could not afford to keep him long in school. He educated himself by reading widely. Proud, ambitious, and independent, Franklin left Boston at the age of seventeen and arrived penniless in Philadelphia. He soon established himself as a printer and a civic leader, became rich, and retired from business at the age of forty-two.

After retiring from business, Franklin intended to devote the rest of his life to his deepest interest—science. His work on lightning rods, earthquake, bifocal lenses, and electricity makes him world famous.

However, it was public affairs that dominated the last half of his life. Franklin spent many years in England and France, where he was a popular figure among intellectuals and aristocrats. Before the American Revolution he represented the colonies in London, trying to persuade the British government to modify its oppressive tax policies in America. In 1776, at age seventy, he joined Thomas Jefferson and others on the committee that drafted the Declaration of Independence. Later he served as the American representative in Paris, helping negotiate the peace treaty with England. In his final years he was a delegate to the Constitutional Convention① and worked for the ratification of the Constitution.

Benjamin Franklin was one of the most famous Americans in his day. At the time of his death, no other American was better known or more respected. In both the Old World and the New World, Franklin was highly complimented as the clever, prudent, self-made man, the thrifty Yankee who worked hard, took advantage of an opportunity and got ahead. His energy, curiosity, tact, charm, and practicality brought him many successes in business, literature, science, and government. His rags-to-riches experience has become the archetype of many Americans' dream of success.

The Autobiography of Benjamin Franklin was a typical embodiment of the Enlightenment. It demonstrates the Puritan's emphasis on self-improvement, self-analysis, moral and ethical values, as well as the Enlightener's weight on rationalism, order, and education.

---

①Constitutional Convention: a meeting made up of individuals who are interested in either creating a new constitution or making edits to the one currently in existence

From 1775 to 1783 | Chapter 2
The Revolutionary Era and the American Enlightenment

The Autobiography of Benjamin Franklin
(Excerpt)

It was about this time I conceived the bold and arduous project of arriving at moral perfection. I wished to live without committing any fault at any time; I would conquer all that either natural inclination, custom, or company might lead me into. As I knew, or thought I knew, what was right and wrong, I did not see why I might not always do the one and avoid the other. But I soon found I had undertaken a task of more difficulty than I had imagined. While my care was employed in guarding against one fault, I was often surprised by another; habit took the advantage of inattention; inclination was sometimes too strong for reason. I concluded, at length,① that the mere speculative conviction that it was our interest to be completely virtuous was not sufficient to prevent our slipping, and that the contrary habits must be broken, and good ones acquired and established, before we can have any dependence on a steady, uniform rectitude of conduct. For this purpose I therefore contrived② the following method.

In the various enumerations of the moral virtues I met in my reading, I found the catalogue more or less numerous, as different writers included more or fewer ideas under the same name. Temperance, for example, was by some confined to eating and drinking, while by others it was extended to mean the moderating every other pleasure, appetite, inclination, or passion, bodily or mental, even to our avarice and ambition. I proposed to myself, for the sake of clearness, to use rather more names, with fewer ideas annexed to each, than a few names with more ideas; and I included under thirteen names of virtues all that at that time occurred to me as necessary or desirable, and annexed to each a short precept, which fully expressed the extent I gave to its meaning.

These names of virtues, with their precepts were:

---

① at length: after a long time; eventually
② contrive: devise; plan with cleverness

1. Temperance

Eat not to dullness; drink not to elevation.

2. Silence

Speak not but what may benefit others or yourself; avoid trifling conversation.

3. Order

Let all your things have their places; let each part of your business have its time.

4. Resolution

Resolve to perform what you ought; perform without fail what you resolve.

5. Frugality

Make no expense but to do good to others or yourself, i.e., waste nothing.

6. Industry

Lose no time; be always employed in something useful; cut off all unnecessary actions.

7. Sincerity

Use no hurtful deceit; think innocently and justly, and, if you speak, speak accordingly.

8. Justice

Wrong none by doing injuries or omitting the benefits that are your duty.

9. Moderation

Avoid extremes; forbear resenting injuries so much as you think they deserve.

10. Cleanliness

Tolerate no uncleanness in body, clothes, or habitation.

11. Tranquility

Be not disturbed at trifles, or at accidents common or unavoidable.

12. Chastity

Rarely use venery① but for health or offspring, never to dullness, weakness, or the injury of your own or another's peace or reputation.

13. Humility

Imitate Jesus and Socrates.

My intention being to acquire the *habitude* of all these virtues, I judged it would be well not to distract my attention by attempting the whole at once, but to fix it on one of them at a time, and, when I should be master of that, then to proceed to another, and so on, till I should have gone thro' the thirteen; and, as the previous acquisition of some might facilitate the acquisition of certain others, I arranged them with that view, as they stand above. *Temperance* first, as it tends to procure that coolness and clearness of head which is so necessary where constant vigilance was to be kept up, and guard maintained against the unremitting attraction of ancient habits and the force of perpetual temptations. This being acquired and established, *Silence* would be more easy;... I gave *Silence* the second place. This and the next, *Order*, I expected would allow me more time for attending to my project and my studies. *Resolution*, once becoming habitual, would keep me firm in my endeavors to obtain all the subsequent virtues; *Frugality* and *Industry*, freeing me from my remaining debt, and producing affluence and independence, would make more easy the practice of *Sincerity* and *Justice*, etc. Conceiving, then, that, agreeably to the advice of Pythagoras in his Garden Verses, daily examination would be necessary, I contrived the following method for conducting that examination.

I made a little book, in which I allotted a page for each of the virtues. I ruled each page with red ink, so as to have seven columns, one for each day of the week, marking each column with a letter for the day. I crossed these columns with thirteen red lines, marking the beginning of each line with the first letter of one of the virtues, on which line, and in its proper column, I might mark, by a little black spot, every fault I found upon

---

①venery: the pursuit of or indulgence in sexual pleasure

examination to have been committed respecting that virtue upon that day.

	S	M	T	W	T	F	S
TEMPERANCE. *Eat Not to Dullness;* *Drink not to Elevation.*							
T							
S	* *	*		*		*	
O	*	*	*		*	*	*
R			*			*	
F		*			*		
I			*				
S							
J							
M							
Cl							
T							
Ch							
H							

I determined to give a week's strict attention to each of the virtues successively. Thus, in the first week, my great guard was to avoid every the least offense against *Temperance*, leaving the other virtues to their ordinary chance, only marking every evening the faults of the day. Thus, if in the first week I could keep my first line, marked T, clear of spots, I supposed the habit of that virtue so much strengthened, and its opposite weakened, that I might venture extending my attention to include the next, and for the following week keep both lines clear of spots. Proceeding thus to the last, I could go thro' a course complete in thirteen weeks, and four courses in a year. And like him who, having a garden to weed, does not attempt to eradicate all the bad herbs at once, which would exceed his reach and his strength, but works on one of the beds at a time, and, having accomplished the first, proceeds to a second, so I should have, I hoped, the encouraging pleasure of seeing on my pages the progress I made in virtue, by clearing successively my lines of their spots, till in the end, by a number of courses, I should be happy in viewing a clean book, after a thirteen weeks' daily examination. . . .

The precept of *Order* requiring that every part of my business should have its allotted time, one page in my little book contained the following scheme of employment for the twenty-four hours of a natural day:

The Morning Question, What good Shall I do this Day?	5	Rise, wash, and address Powerful Goodness; Contrive day's business, and take the resolution of the day; prosecute the present Study, and breakfast
	6	
	7	
	8	Work
	9	
	10	
	11	
	12	Read, or overlook my Accounts, and dine.
	1	
	2	Work.
	3	
	4	
	5	
	6	Put Things in their Places, Supper, Music, or Diversion, or Conversation, Examination of the Day.
	7	
Evening Question, What Good have I done today?	8	
	9	
	10	Sleep.
	11	
	12	
	1	
	2	
	3	
	4	

I entered upon the execution of this plan for self-examination, and continued it, with occasional intermissions, for some time. I was surprised to find myself so much fuller of faults than I had imagined; but I had the satisfaction of seeing them diminish....

My scheme of *Order* gave me the most trouble; and I found that, tho' it might be practicable where a man's business was such as to leave him the disposition of his time, that of a journeyman printer, for instance, it was not possible to be exactly observed by a master, who must mix with the world, and often receive people of business at their own hours. *Order*, too, with regard to places for things, papers, etc., I found extremely difficult to acquire. I had not been early accustomed to it, and, having an exceeding good memory, I was not so sensible of the inconvenience attending want of method....

In truth, I found myself incorrigible① with respect to *Order*; and now I am grown old, and my memory bad, I feel very sensibly the want of it. But, on the whole, tho' I never arrived at the perfection I had been so ambitious of obtaining, but fell far short of it, yet I was, by the endeavor, a better and a happier man than I otherwise should have been if I had not attempted it.

It may be well my posterity should be informed that to this little artifice, with the blessing of God, their ancestor owed the constant felicity of his life down to his seventy-ninth year, in which this is written. What reverses② may attend the remainder is in the hand of Providence; but, if they arrive, the reflection on past happiness enjoyed ought to help his bearing them with more resignation. To *Temperance* he ascribes his long-continued health and what is still left to him of a good constitution; to *Industry* and *Frugality*, the early easiness of his circumstances and acquisition of his fortune, with all that knowledge that enabled him to be a useful citizen, and obtained for him some degree of reputation among the learned; to *Sincerity* and *Justice*, the confidence of his country, and the

---

①incorrigible: incapable of being corrected or reformed
②reverse: a change in fortune from better to worse; a setback

honorable employs it conferred upon him; and to the joint influence of the whole mass of the virtues, even in the imperfect state he was able to acquire them, all that evenness of temper, and that cheerfulness in conversation, which makes his company still sought for, and agreeable even to his younger acquaintance. I hope, therefore, that some of my descendants may follow the example and reap the benefit....

My list of virtues contained at first but twelve; but a Quaker friend having kindly informed me that I was generally thought proud, that my pride showed itself frequently in conversation, that I was not content with being in the right when discussing any point, but was overbearing and rather insolent,① of which he convinced me by mentioning several instances, I determined endeavoring to cure myself, if I could, of this vice or folly among the rest, and I added *Humility* to my list, giving an extensive meaning to the word.

I cannot boast of much success in acquiring the reality of this virtue, but I had a good deal with regard to the appearance of it. I made it a rule to forbear all direct contradiction to the sentiments of others, and all positive assertion of my own. I even forbid myself, agreeably to the old laws of our Junto, the use of every word or expression in the language that imported a fixed opinion, such as *certainly*, *undoubtedly*, etc., and I adopted, instead of them, *I conceive*, *I apprehend*, or *I imagine* a thing to be so or so, or *it so appears to me at present*. When another asserted something that I thought an error, I denied myself the pleasure of contradicting him abruptly and of showing immediately some absurdity in his proposition; and in answering, I began by observing that in certain cases or circumstances his opinion would be right, but in the present case there appeared or seemed to me some difference, etc. I soon found the advantage of this change in my manner; the conversations I engaged in went on more pleasantly.

The modest way in which I proposed my opinions procured them a

---

①overbearing and rather insolent: exceedingly arrogant ("Overbearing" and "insolent" are synonyms, both meaning "domineering in manner" or "arrogant.")

readier reception and less contradiction; I had less mortification① when I was found to be in the wrong, and I more easily prevailed with others to give up their mistakes and join with me when I happened to be in the right.

> Questions for Discussion
>
> 1. What surprised Franklin when he began to follow his plan for self-examination? What satisfaction did he have? What gave him the most trouble?
> 2. Why did Franklin add "humility" to his list? How did he overcome this vice or folly? What benefits did he reap?
> 3. As a young person living in the 21st century, do you think the thirteen virtues Benjamin Franklin thought highly desirable still work well in today's world? Why or why not?
> 4. What do you think are the three most crucial virtues you most desire to acquire? Why? How would you acquire them?

---

①mortification: a feeling of shame

Chapter 3

From 1783 to 1861

The New Nation and the American Renaissance

3.1 The New Nation: Growth, Expansion, and Sins

The American Revolution ended in 1783 with the Treaty of Paris. George Washington became the first president of the new, independent nation in 1789. Despite backward modes of transportation and communication, the newly formed United States of America developed amazingly quickly. It extended its territory rapidly towards the west. The purchase of Louisiana from the hands of France in 1803 under the third president, Thomas Jefferson, vastly enlarged American territory. In 1812, due to commercial conflicts between the United States and Britain, a war was declared on Britain on the battlefield of Canada. Internal divisions occurred in the United States because the people in the West wanted to possess the land of Canada while the Southern plantation-owners hoped to grab Florida from the hands of Spain. The war ended two years later. Though the United States suffered many costly defeats, including the capture and burning of the nation's capital, Washington, D. C. , American troops were able to repulse British invasions in New York, Baltimore, and New Orleans. This greatly increased Americans' national pride and spirit of patriotism. By 1821, the total number of States had risen to twenty-three from the original thirteen. Texas, which was originally part of the Mexican Republic, was annexed in 1844. Shortly afterward, the Mexican-American War (1846 – 1848) ended with the defeat of Mexico and the acquisition of California and New Mexico.

As the United States consolidated and grew, so did its sins, which included the near-genocide of the American Indians, the enslavement of blacks, and the aggressive war against Mexico. Along with the national sins were problems such as materialism, child labor, and political corruption. Yet, the territorial expansion enhanced Americans' confidence and ambition. Adventurous people went to the West, dreaming of making a fortune. They displayed courage and optimism when confronted by various hardships and dangers. Thanks to the westward movement, roads and waterways were improved, and a new network of trade and communication was created. New factories gradually transformed the country from an agricultural economy into an increasingly urban and industrialized one. The new republic was growing into a prosperous and vital country.

3.2　The American Renaissance

Even after the 13 colonies gained independence from British control, despite their political independence, Americans acknowledged much the same literary canon as the British. Educated Americans in the new republic were more familiar with Greek, Roman, and European history and literature than with American writers of the Colonial Age and Revolutionary Age. Educated American children learned Greek and Latin literature in childhood. In 1820, it was still possible for the British critic, Sydney Smith, to ask, "In the four quarters of the globe, who reads an American book?" Smith, like many other Europeans, mocked America as well as American literature.

Yet, as Americans continued to build the nation, an increasing nationalism developed. Americans began to call for a literature that would be less dependent upon European models, one that would express their Americanism. To the pleasure of Americans, in the same year that Smith asked his mocking question, Washington Irving's *The Sketch Book*, which contained his short story masterpieces "Rip Van Winkle" and "The Legend of Sleepy Hollow," was published in England. The next year William Cullen Bryant gained fame for his poem "Thanatopsis" (a Greek word meaning "view of death"). In 1823, James Fenimore Cooper brought out the first of his

Leather-stocking novels, *The Pioneers*. In 1827 Edgar Allan Poe published his first volume of poetry. These writers began to draw international attention.

These writers and their works were special because they were belletrists① who began writing about American people in American places dealing with American problems, though they still considerably relied on European models. In spite of everything, they did take the first steps towards Americanism: they wrote about the American wilderness, the American Revolution, American pioneers, and American life; they praised American heroes and told American tales; their subjects were freedom and expansion, which definitely were not European issues.

More remarkable was Ralph Waldo Emerson (1803 – 1882). He lengthened the first steps taken by Irving, Bryant, Cooper, and Poe. His stirring lecture "The American Scholar" (1837) has often been called "America's Declaration of Intellectual Independence." In the lecture, Emerson exclaims: "Our day of dependence, our long apprenticeship to the learning of other lands, draws to a close. The millions, that around us are rushing into life, cannot always be fed on the sere remains of foreign harvests.... We have listened too long to the courtly muses of Europe. The spirit of the American freeman is already suspected to be timid, imitative, tame.... We will walk on our own feet; we will work with our own hands; we will speak our own minds." The nation listened and took the words to heart. Increasingly, American writers began to free themselves from European models. America at this era witnessed the appearance of a large group of classic writers both in prose and poetry. They wrote and published roughly between the 1820s and 1860s, with the results that this period has been called the American Renaissance.

The American Renaissance, also called New England Renaissance, saw the flourish of American Romantic literature, which was the first full-fledged American literary movement. American Romanticism had its origins in European countries like Germany, France, and England.

---

①belletrist: a writer of belles-lettres

Romanticism was a reaction to Classicism, the Age of Reason movement in the arts that attempted to duplicate the order and balance in the art of Greece and Rome. While Classicism stressed reason and social concerns, Romanticism stressed imagination, emotion, personal concerns, and individual experience. Romanticists often demonstrated a profound love of nature, a fascination with the supernatural and the mysterious, a yearning for the picturesque and exotic, a deep-rooted idealism, and a passionate nationalism.

Among the American Romantic writers, some can be further labeled as Transcendentalists, and some others Dark Romanticists.

American Transcendentalism, also known as New England Transcendentalism, was under the influence of German and British Romanticism. While affirming Kant's principle of intuitive knowledge not derived from the senses, it proclaimed the divinity of nature and celebrated the divinity in each human being. The leading Transcendentalist was Ralph Waldo Emerson. He expressed his transcendental philosophy in his work *Nature*, which was virtually the manifesto of Transcendentalism. Emerson attracted around him a number of admirers including Henry David Thoreau (1817 - 1862). The Transcendentalists held the view that the most fundamental truths about life and death could be reached only by going beyond the world of the senses. They believed that each individual person could rise above the material world and know something of the ultimate spiritual reality but could not know it through logic or the data of the senses; rather, that knowledge came through a deep, free intuition, which they recognized as the "highest power of the soul."

American Dark Romanticism can be regarded as a direct reaction to the optimism of the Transcendentalists. The outstanding examples are Poe, Hawthorne, and Melville. They viewed the universe as a more confusing and difficult place. They thought that nature is ambiguous, not easy to read, interpret, or harmonize. They believed that evil and suffering had to be accounted for and were not to be brushed airily aside. They held the idea that human nature is obstinate① and life was and would always be mysterious.

Given that this era produced a brilliant galaxy of writers, among whom many deserve close attention, we will put the authors of the era into two groups: prose-writers and poetry writers. We'll view them separately.

3.3 Representative Prose Writers and Their Works

The most prominent fiction writers of this era include Washington Irving (1783 – 1859), James Fenimore Cooper (1789 – 1851), Nathaniel Hawthorne (1804 – 1864), Herman Melville (1819 – 1891), as well as Harriet Beecher Stowe (1811 – 1896), while the most well-known nonfiction writers are Ralph Waldo Emerson and Henry David Thoreau.

Cooper was the first successful American novelist; he has been best noted for The Leather-stocking Tales which include five novels: *The Pioneers* (1823), *The Last of the Mohicans* (1826), *The Prairie* (1827), *The Pathfinder* (1840), and *The Deerslayer* (1841). In these series, Cooper gave a vital description of the life of a frontiersman named Natty Bumppo. His works contributed to people's appreciation for American life. Melville is now best remembered for his whaling story *Moby Dick* (1851), which is regarded as one of the most vital stories available to the American imagination. The novel tells the story of Captain Ahab and his crew who are searching for a monstrous white whale on the dangerous ocean. The end of the story is the tragic death of everyone except Ishmael, who survives to tell the story to the world. Stowe is best remembered as the little woman who, outraged by the evils of slavery, wrote *Uncle Tom's Cabin* (1852) that contributed to the American Civil War. Thoreau was directly inspired by Emerson. He answered Emerson's call of going to nature with experiment and practice. His masterpiece *Walden* (1854), which is a kind of autobiographical sermon against modern materialism, recounts the two years, two months, and two days he spent at Walden Pond. Another

---

①obstinate: very difficult to change or overcome

noteworthy thing about Thoreau was that he was jailed in the Concord jail for one night on account of refusing to pay a tax which might have been used to support the imperialistic Mexican War. In the wake of the event, he wrote his famous essay "Civil Disobedience" (1849).

There is no doubt that Washington Irving, Ralph Waldo Emerson, and Nathaniel Hawthorne, whose works follow, will long stand out as the most important prose writers of the age.

Washington Irving (1783 – 1859)

Washington Irving was the first American storyteller to be recognized internationally as a man of letters.

Irving was born into a wealthy New York family at the end of the Revolutionary War and named after George Washington. Following his family's wish, he began to study law when he was sixteen, but he preferred reading literary works and listening to the folktales from the rural Hudson Valley. In 1809 he published *A History of New York* under the pseudonym Diedrich Knickerbocker. The book combined old tales and the history of old New York, showing the customs and lifestyles of the early Dutch settlers. Well received by the public, it established Irving as a humorous writer.

In 1815, Irving travelled to Europe and in the next seventeen years lived in Britain, Holland, France, Germany, Spain, and Italy. He studied local traditions, customs, and tales, which were later adapted to his writing. In 1820, he published *The Sketch Book*, which included some local stories he had learned during his stay in these different countries. The most famous stories "Rip Van Winkle" and "The Legend of Sleepy Hollow" are borrowed from German folktales and retold by Knickerbocker. They have become classical American stories widely known in the world, with the former being especially provoking.

Irving returned to America in 1846 and lived at Sunnyside on the bank of the Hudson River until his death.

"Rip Van Winkle" tells the fascinating story of the title character who is a good-natured, hen-pecked farmer. In order to escape from the labor of the farm and his nagging wife, he wanders, with his hunting-gun on his shoulder and accompanied by his dog named Wolf, into the Catskill Mountains, where he comes into a group of queer-looking dwarfs playing ninepins.① After drinking some liquor the dwarfs are gulping, he falls asleep. When he awakens, he shockingly discovers he is an old man (he is unaware that 20 years has passed) and the dwarfs are nowhere in sight. When Rip returns to town, he finds that everything is changed, which completely baffles him and knocks him out.

Rip Van Winkle
(Excerpt)

He② now hurried forth, and hastened to his old resort, the village inn—but it too was gone. A large rickety③ wooden building stood in its place, with great gaping windows, some of them broken, and mended with old hats and petticoats, and over the door was painted, "The Union Hotel, by Jonathan Doolittle." Instead of the great tree that used to shelter the quiet little Dutch inn of yore, there now was reared a tall naked pole, with something on the top that looked like a red nightcap, and from it was fluttering a flag, on which was a singular assemblage of stars and stripes—all this was strange and incomprehensible. He recognized on the sign, however, the ruby face of King George, under which he had smoked so many a peaceful pipe, but even this was singularly metamorphosed.④ The red coat was changed for one of blue and buff, a sword was held in the hand instead of a sceptre,⑤ the head was decorated with a cocked hat, and underneath was painted in large characters, "GENERAL WASHINGTON."

There was, as usual, a crowd of folk about the door, but none that Rip recollected. The very character of the people seemed changed. There was a

---

①ninepins: a game similar to bowling, using nine wooden pins and played in an alley
②He: Rip Van Winkle
③rickety: in bad condition or likely to collapse
④metamorphose: change into a completely different form or type
⑤sceptre: a decorated stick that is carried by a queen or king during some official ceremonies as a symbol of their authority

busy, bustling, disputatious tone about it, instead of the accustomed phlegm① and drowsy tranquility. He looked in vain for the sage Nicholas Vedder, with his broad face, double chin, and fair long pipe, uttering clouds of tobacco-smoke, instead of idle speeches; or Van Bummel, the schoolmaster, doling forth the contents of an ancient newspaper. In place of these, a lean, bilious-looking fellow, with his pockets full of handbills, was haranguing, vehemently about rights of citizens—elections—members of Congress—liberty—Bunker's hill—heroes of seventy-six—and other words, which were a perfect Babylonish jargon to the bewildered Van Winkle.

The appearance of Rip, with his long, grizzled beard, his rusty fowling-piece, his uncouth dress, and the army of women and children at his heels, soon attracted the attention of the tavern politicians. They crowded round him, eying him from head to foot, with great curiosity. The orator bustled up to him, and drawing him partly aside, inquired "which side he voted?" Rip stared in vacant stupidity. Another short but busy little fellow pulled him by the arm, and rising on tiptoe, inquired in his ear, "whether he was Federal or Democrat." Rip was equally at a loss to comprehend the question; when a knowing, self-important old gentleman, in a sharp cocked hat, made his way through the crowd, putting them to the right and left with his elbows as he passed, and planting himself before Van Winkle, with one arm akimbo, the other resting on his cane, his keen eyes and sharp hat penetrating, as it were, into his very soul, demanded in an austere tone, "What brought him to the election with a gun on his shoulder, and a mob at his heels, and whether he meant to breed a riot in the village?"

"Alas! gentlemen," cried Rip, somewhat dismayed, "I am a poor quiet man, a native of the place, and a loyal subject of the King, God bless him!"

Here a general shout burst from the bystanders—"a tory!② a tory! a spy! a refugee! hustle him! away with him!" It was with great difficulty that the self-important man in the cocked hat restored order; and having

---

① phlegm: calmness of temperament
② tory: loyalist, meaning an American upholding the cause of the British Crown against the supporters of colonial independence during the American Revolution

assumed a tenfold austerity of brow, demanded again of the unknown culprit, what he came there for, and whom he was seeking. The poor man humbly assured him that he meant no harm, but merely came there in search of some of his neighbors, who used to keep about the tavern.

"Well—who are they? —name them."

Rip bethought himself a moment, and inquired, "Where's Nicholas Vedder?"

There was a silence for a little while, when an old man replied, in a thin piping voice, "Nicholas Vedder? Why, he is dead and gone these eighteen years! There was a wooden tombstone in the churchyard that used to tell all about him, but that's rotten and gone too."

"Where's Brom Dutcher?"

"Oh, he went off to the army in the beginning of the war; some say he was killed at the storming of Stony-Point—others say he was drowned in a squall at the foot of Antony's Nose. I don't know—he never came back again."

"Where's Van Bummel, the schoolmaster?"

"He went off to the wars, too; was a great militia general, and is now in Congress."

Rip's heart died away, at hearing of these sad changes in his home and friends, and finding himself thus alone in the world. Every answer puzzled him too, by treating of such enormous lapses of time, and of matters which he could not understand: war—Congress—Stony-Point;—he had no courage to ask after any more friends, but cried out in despair, "Does nobody here know Rip Van Winkle?"

"Oh, Rip Van Winkle!" exclaimed two or three. "Oh, to be sure! that's Rip Van Winkle yonder, leaning against the tree."

Rip looked, and beheld a precise counterpart of himself as he went up the mountain; apparently as lazy, and certainly as ragged. The poor fellow was now completely confounded. He doubted his own identity, and whether he was himself or another man. In the midst of his bewilderment, the man in the cocked hat demanded who he was, and what was his name?

"God knows!" exclaimed he at his wit's end; "I'm not myself—I'm somebody else—that's me yonder—no—that's somebody else, got into my shoes—I was myself last night, but I fell asleep on the mountain, and they've changed my gun, and everything's changed, and I'm changed, and I can't tell what's my name, or who I am!"

The by-standers began now to look at each other, nod, wink significantly, and tap their fingers against their foreheads. There was a whisper, also, about securing the gun, and keeping the old fellow from doing mischief. At the very suggestion of which, the self-important man with the cocked hat retired with some precipitation.① At this critical moment a fresh, comely woman pressed through the throng to get a peep at the gray-bearded man. She had a chubby child in her arms, which, frightened at his looks, began to cry. "Hush, Rip," cried she, "hush, you little fool; the old man won't hurt you." The name of the child, the air of the mother, the tone of her voice, all awakened a train of recollections in his mind.

"What is your name, my good woman?" asked he.

"Judith Cardenier."

"And your father's name?"

"Ah, poor man, Rip Van Winkle was his name, but it's twenty years since he went away from home with his gun, and never has been heard of since—his dog came home without him; but whether he shot himself, or was carried away by the Indians, nobody can tell. I was then but a little girl."

Rip had but one more question to ask; but he put it with a faltering voice:

"Where's your mother?"

"Oh, she too had died but a short time since; she broke a blood-vessel in a fit of passion at a New-England peddler."

There was a drop of comfort, at least, in this intelligence. The honest man could contain himself no longer. He caught his daughter and her child in his arms. "I am your father!" cried he—"Young Rip Van Winkle once—old Rip Van Winkle now—Does nobody know poor Rip Van Winkle!"

All stood amazed, until an old woman, tottering out from among the

---

① with precipitation: hastily and suddenly

crowd, put her hand to her brow, and peering under it in his face for a moment, exclaimed, "Sure enough! It is Rip Van Winkle—it is himself. Welcome home again, old neighbor. Why, where have you been these twenty long years?"

Rip's story was soon told, for the whole twenty years had been to him but as one night. The neighbors stared when they heard it; some were seen to wink at each other, and put their tongues in their cheeks; and the self-important man in the cocked hat, who, when the alarm was over, had returned to the field, screwed down the corners of his mouth, and shook his head—upon which there was a general shaking of the head throughout the assemblage.

Questions for Discussion

1. According to the passage, what changes had taken place compared with the past? Do you think the changes occur mainly to people or to the natural landscape as represented by the mountains and the Hudson River?
2. Some people claim that Rip Van Winkle stands for America's identity crisis as a new democracy. Would you argue for or against? Why?
3. Why do you think this story is so popular with Americans? If you had fallen asleep seven years ago and just woke up today, what words which are fairly popular now may sound strange and incomprehensible?

Ralph Waldo Emerson (1803 – 1882)

Ralph Waldo Emerson was born in Boston, Massachusetts, into the family of a Unitarian① minister who died when Waldo was eight years old.

---

① Unitarian: A Unitarian is a person, especially a Christian, who believes that God is one being. That is to say that a Unitarian rejects Trinity, a Christian doctrine which asserts the unity of the Father, Son, and Holy Spirit as one God in three persons.

He attended Harvard, studied theology, and became a Unitarian minister himself in 1829.

Though a minister and an eloquent speaker, Emerson was not interested in preserving and disseminating religious dogma. Emerson's skepticism toward Christianity was strengthened by his exposure to the German "higher criticism."① In 1832, for reasons of conscience, Emerson resigned his ministry and sailed to Europe.

In Europe he met the English writers Wordsworth, Coleridge, and Carlyle.

After returning from Europe, he settled in the village of Concord, Massachusetts, and began his lifelong career as lecturer and writer. It was at Concord that Emerson composed his first book, *Nature* (1836), which is a lyrical expression of the harmony Emerson felt between himself and nature and is one of Emerson's best-known and most influential works. His addressing speech "The American Scholar" has been an inspiration to generations of young Americans. His other published works list *Essays* (1841), *Essays: Second Series* (1844), *Representative Men* (1849), and *The Conduct of Life* (1860).

Emerson's essays were important influences upon so many American writers, including Thoreau, Whitman, Dickinson, and Frost. Modern literary historians see Emerson as the seminal American writer of the 19th century.

Nature

Introduction

(Excerpt)

Our age is retrospective.② It builds the sepulchers③ of the fathers. It

---

① higher criticism: Higher criticism is the name given in the 19th century to a branch of biblical scholarship concerned with establishing the dates, authorship, sources, and interrelations of the various books of the Bible, often with disturbing results for orthodox Christian dogma. It was "higher" not in status but in the sense that it required a preliminary basis of "lower" textual criticism, which reconstructed the original wording of biblical texts from faulty copies.
② retrospective: looking back on or dealing with past events or situations
③ sepulcher: tomb, burial place

writes biographies, histories, and criticism. The foregoing generations beheld God and nature face to face; we, through their eyes. Why should not we also enjoy an original relation to the universe? Why should not we have a poetry and philosophy of insight and not of tradition, and a religion by revelation to us, and not the history of theirs? Embosomed for a season in nature, whose floods of life stream around and through us, and invite us by the powers they supply, to action proportioned to nature, why should we grope among the dry bones of the past, or put the living generation into masquerade① out of its faded wardrobe? The sun shines to-day also. There is more wool and flax in the fields. There are new lands, new men, new thoughts. Let us demand our own works and laws and worship.

Chapter Ⅰ
(Excerpt)

To go into solitude, a man needs to retire as much from his chamber as from society. I am not solitary whilst I read and write, though nobody is with me. But if a man would be alone, let him look at the stars. The rays that come from those heavenly worlds will separate between him and what he touches. One might think the atmosphere was made transparent with this design, to give man, in the heavenly bodies, the perpetual presence of the sublime. Seen in the streets of cities, how great they are! If the stars should appear one night in a thousand years, how would men believe and adore; and preserve for many generations the remembrance of the city of God which had been shown! But every night come out these envoys of beauty, and light the universe with their admonishing② smile.

The stars awaken a certain reverence, because though always present, they are inaccessible; but all natural objects make a kindred impression, when the mind is open to their influence. Nature never wears a mean appearance. Neither does the wisest man extort her secret, and lose his curiosity by finding out all her perfection. Nature never became a toy to a

---

①masquerade: a social gathering of persons wearing masks and often fantastic costumes
②admonishing: expressing reproof or disapproval as a corrective

wise spirit. The flowers, the animals, the mountains, reflected the wisdom of his best hour, as much as they had delighted the simplicity of his childhood. When we speak of nature in this manner, we have a distinct but most poetical sense in the mind. We mean the integrity of impression made by manifold natural objects. It is this which distinguishes the stick of timber of the wood-cutter, from the tree of the poet. The charming landscape which I saw this morning, is indubitably made up of some twenty or thirty farms. Miller owns this field, Locke that, and Manning the woodland beyond. But none of them owns the landscape. There is a property in the horizon which no man has but he whose eye can integrate all the parts, that is, the poet. This is the best part of these men's farms, yet to this their warranty-deeds① give no title.

To speak truly, few adult persons can see nature. Most persons do not see the sun. At least they have a very superficial seeing. The sun illuminates only the eye of the man, but shines into the eye and the heart of the child. The lover of nature is he whose inward and outward senses are still truly adjusted to each other; who has retained the spirit of infancy even into the era of manhood. His intercourse with heaven and earth, becomes part of his daily food. In the presence of nature, a wild delight runs through the man, in spite of real sorrows. Nature says: He is my creature, and maugre② all his impertinent griefs, he shall be glad with me. Not the sun or the summer alone, but every hour and season yields its tribute of delight; for every hour and change corresponds to and authorizes a different state of the mind, from breathless noon to grimmest midnight. Nature is a setting that fits equally well a comic or a mourning piece. In good health, the air is a cordial③ of incredible virtue. Crossing a bare common, in snow puddles, at twilight, under a clouded sky, without having in my thoughts any occurrence of special good fortune, I have enjoyed a perfect exhilaration.④

---

① warranty-deed: a document often used in real estate that provides the greatest amount of protection to the purchaser of a property
② maugre: in spite of
③ cordial: a stimulating medicine or drink
④ exhilaration: the feeling or the state of being very happy or excitement

I am glad to the brink of fear. In the woods too, a man casts off his years, as the snake his slough,① and at what period soever of life, is always a child. In the woods, is perpetual youth. Within these plantations of God, a decorum② and sanctity reign, a perennial festival is dressed, and the guest sees not how he should tire of them in a thousand years. In the woods, we return to reason and faith. There I feel that nothing can befall me in life—no disgrace, no calamity, (leaving me my eyes,) which nature cannot repair. Standing on the bare ground—my head bathed by the blithe③ air, and uplifted into infinite space—all mean egotism vanishes. I become a transparent eye-ball; I am nothing; I see all; the currents of the Universal Being circulate through me; I am part or particle of God. The name of the nearest friend sounds then foreign and accidental: to be brothers, to be acquaintances, master or servant, is then a trifle and a disturbance. I am the lover of uncontained and immortal beauty. In the wilderness, I find something more dear and connate④ than in streets or villages. In the tranquil landscape, and especially in the distant line of the horizon, man beholds somewhat as beautiful as his own nature.

The greatest delight which the fields and woods minister,⑤ is the suggestion of an occult relation between man and the vegetable. I am not alone and unacknowledged. They nod to me, and I to them. The waving of the boughs in the storm, is new to me and old. It takes me by surprise, and yet is not unknown. Its effect is like that of a higher thought or a better emotion coming over me, when I deemed I was thinking justly or doing right.

Yet it is certain that the power to produce this delight, does not reside in nature, but in man, or in a harmony of both. It is necessary to use these pleasures with great temperance. For, nature is not always tricked in holiday attire, but the same scene which yesterday breathed perfume and

---

① slough: the cast-off skin of a snake
② decorum: propriety and good taste in conduct or appearance
③ blithe: cheerful and cheery
④ connate: innate, inborn
⑤ minister: give aid or service

glittered as for the frolic① of the nymphs,② is overspread with melancholy today. Nature always wears the colors of the spirit. To a man laboring under calamity, the heat of his own fire hath sadness in it. Then, there is a kind of contempt of the landscape felt by him who has just lost by death a dear friend. The sky is less grand as it shuts down over less worth in the population.

Questions for Discussion

1. How does Emerson describe the lover of nature?
2. What do you think is the difference between the kind of meaning Emerson finds in nature and the meaning a botanist, a geographer, or an astrophysicist finds in nature?
3. What does Emerson mean when he describes himself as a "transparent eye-ball" when in the woods? How does this state of mind affect his relationship with God?

The American Scholar

(Excerpt)

Each age, it is found, must write its own books; or rather, each generation for the next succeeding. The books of an older period will not fit this....

Meek young men grow up in libraries believing it their duty to accept the views which Cicero③, which Locke, which Bacon have given, forgetful that Cicero, Locke, and Bacon were only young men in libraries when they wrote these books.

Hence, instead of Man Thinking we have the bookworm....

---

① frolic: merry, full of fun
② nymph: (in ancient Greek and Roman stories) a spirit of nature represented as beautiful maidens dwelling in the mountains, forests, trees, and waters
③ Cicero: a Roman philosopher, statesman, lawyer, orator and political theorist

Books are the best of things, well used; abused, among the worst. What is the right use? ... They are for nothing but to inspire. I had better never see a book, than to be warped① by its attraction clean out of my own orbit, and made a satellite instead of a system. The one thing in the world, of value, is the active soul. This every man is entitled to; this every man contains within him, although, in almost all men, obstructed, and as yet unborn. The soul active sees absolute truth; and utters truth, or creates.... But genius looks forward; the eyes of man are set in his forehead, not in his hindhead; man hopes; genius creates....

...Genius is always sufficiently the enemy of genius by over-influence. The literature of every nation bears me witness. The English dramatic poets have Shakespearized now for two hundred years....

Undoubtedly there is a right way of reading, so it be sternly subordinated. Man Thinking must not be subdued by his instruments. Books are for the scholar's idle times. When we can read God directly, the hour is too precious to be wasted in other men's transcripts of their readings.

Of course, there is a portion of reading quite indispensable to a wise man. History and exact science he must learn by laborious reading. Colleges, in like manner, have their indispensable office,—to teach elements. But they can only highly serve us when they aim not to drill, but to create; when they gather from far every ray of various genius to their hospitable halls, and, by the concentrated fires, set the hearts of their youth on flame. Thought and knowledge are natures in which apparatus and pretension avail nothing. Gowns②, and pecuniary③ foundations, though of towns of gold, can never countervail④ the least sentence or syllable of wit. Forget this, and our American colleges will recede in their public importance, whilst they grow richer every year.

---

① warp: become or cause to become bent or twisted out of shape
② gowns: the body of students and faculty of a college or university
③ pecuniary: of or relating to money
④ countervail: compensate for

> **Questions for Discussion**
>
> 1. In Emerson's view, what's the right use of books? Do you agree? Why or why not? How were his attitudes similar to or different from Bacon's?
> 2. Emerson claims that "Gowns, and pecuniary foundations, though of towns of gold, can never countervail the least sentence or syllable of wit. Forget this, and our American colleges will recede in their public importance, whilst they grow richer every year." Do you agree or disagree? Why?

Nathaniel Hawthorne (1804 – 1864)

Nathaniel Hawthorne is best known today for his short stories and romance novels that explore moral issues and social responsibilities in Puritan New England.

Hawthorne was born in the port town of Salem, Massachusetts. His father was a sea captain who died when he was four years old. Supported by his maternal uncle, Hawthorne received a good education; he attended Bowdoin College in 1821, his college friends including Longfellow, a future poet, and Franklin Pierce, a future President of the United States.

One of Hawthorne's ancestors was a judge involved in the notorious witch trials of Salem in 1692. Hawthorne felt that the traits of his Puritan ancestors had "intertwined themselves" with his own character; he was concerned with human conscience, feeling of guilt, and ethical issues. After graduating from Bowdoin College he was drawn back to Salem. Yet Hawthorne was no Puritan. He looked back with distaste upon "the whole dismal severity of the Puritanic code of law." For more than ten years, he lived in semi-seclusion in his mother's house, studying the American past and writing short stories for various periodicals, but they obtained a modest success.

In Hawthorne's day, the Transcendentalist movement was a dominant force in New England intellectual circles. In 1841, Hawthorne was drawn to live among the transcendental reformers at the utopian community, Brook Farm. He invested $1500 in Brook Farm, but left disillusioned within a year.

Unable to support his family solely on his publications, from 1839 to 1849 Hawthorne earned his living in the customhouses in Boston and Salem. In 1849, he lost his Salem customhouse job when the political administration changed. After losing his job, he started to work on his long fiction *The Scarlet Letter*, a sensational story set in Puritan Boston about the hidden adultery between Puritan priest Arthur Dimmesdale and a young woman named Hester Prynne, who was married to Roger Chillingworth, a much older physician who did not show up until the very day when Hester was released from prison, with her illegitimate baby daughter in her arms and a scarlet letter A on the bosom of her gown. Hester named her daughter Pearl, "as being of great price" and "her mother's only treasure!" The story, unfolding around the complicated feelings of the characters in the following seven years, is a moral study on the issues of sin, guilt, consecration, revenge, child-raising, and the clash between man-made rules and intrinsic human needs, etc. *The Scarlet Letter*, coming out in 1850, was a great success. In the critical essay entitled "Out of the Very Heart of New England" (originally published in 1879), Henry James praised the romance, saying "The publication of *The Scarlet Letter* was in the United States a literary event of the first importance. The book was the finest piece of imaginative writing yet put forth in the country. . . . Something might at last be sent to Europe as exquisite in quality as anything that had been received, and the best of it was that the thing was absolutely American; it belonged to the soil, to the air, it came out of the very heart of New England."

The Scarlet Letter was followed by *The House of the Seven Gables* (1851), another successful novel. After his college friend Franklin Pierce was elected president in 1853, Hawthorne was appointed United States' consul in Liverpool, England. He held the position for 4 years, after which he traveled extensively in Europe and continued to write.

Hawthorne returned to the United States in 1860, lived in Concord, and devoted his remaining years to literature until a sudden death in 1864.

Hawthorne explores human limitations, like sin, guilt, egotism, pride, and isolation. He called the tales that explore these issues "allegories of the heart." Human souls and social evils are the main subjects of Hawthorne's works. To better present the story of *The Scarlet Letter*, the following extracts are from three chapters of the fiction.

The Scarlet Letter
Chapter 6　Pearl
(Excerpt)

She① knew that her deed had been evil; she could have no faith, therefore, that its result would be for good. Day after day, she looked fearfully into the child's expanding nature; ever dreading to detect some dark and wild peculiarity, that should correspond with the guiltiness to which she owed her being.

Certainly, there was no physical defect. By its perfect shape, its vigor, and its natural dexterity in the use of all its untried limbs, the infant was worthy to have been brought forth in Eden; worthy to have been left there, to be the plaything of the angels, after the world's first parents were driven out.... Her nature appeared to possess depth, too, as well as variety; but—or else Hester's fears deceived her—it lacked reference and adaptation to the world into which she was born. The child could not be made amenable② to rules. In giving her existence, a great law had been broken; and the result was a being, whose elements were perhaps beautiful and brilliant, but all in disorder; or with an order peculiar to themselves, amidst which the point of variety and arrangement was difficult or impossible to be discovered....

Pearl was a born outcast of the infantile world. An imp of evil, emblem and product of sin, she had no right among christened infants ... If the children gathered about her, as they sometimes did, Pearl would grow positively terrible in her puny wrath, snatching up stones to fling at them,

---

①She: Hester Prynne
②amenable: ready or willing to agree or yield

with shrill, incoherent exclamations that made her mother tremble, because they had so much the sound of a witch's anathemas① in some unknown tongue....

... The singularity lay in the hostile feelings with which the child regarded all these offsprings of her own heart and mind. She never created a friend, but seemed always to be sowing broadcast the dragon's teeth, whence sprung a harvest of armed enemies, against whom she rushed to battle. It was inexpressibly sad—then what depth of sorrow to a mother, who felt in her own heart the cause!—to observe, in one so young, this constant recognition of an adverse world, and so fierce a training of the energies that were to make good her cause, in the contest that must ensue.

Gazing at Pearl, Hester Prynne often dropped her work upon her knees, and cried out, with an agony which she would fain have hidden, but which made utterance for itself, betwixt speech and a groan,—"O Father in Heaven,—if Thou art still my Father,—what is this being which I have brought into the world!"...

Chapter 14   Hester and the Physician
(Excerpt)

All this while, Hester had been looking steadily at the old man, and was shocked, as well as wonder-smitten, to discern what a change had been wrought upon him within the past seven years. It was not so much that he had grown older; for though the traces of advancing life were visible, he bore his age well, and seemed to retain a wiry vigor and alertness. But the former aspect of an intellectual and studious man, calm and quiet, which was what she best remembered in him, had altogether vanished, and been succeeded by an eager, searching, almost fierce, yet carefully guarded look. It seemed to be his wish and purpose to mask this expression with a smile; but the latter played him false, and flickered over his visage so derisively,②

---

①anathemas: a formal curse by a pope or a council of the Church
②derisively: in a manner expressing contempt, ridicule or scorn

that the spectator could see his blackness all the better for it. Ever and anon,① too, there came a glare of red light out of his eyes; as if the old man's soul were on fire, and kept on smouldering duskily within his breast, until, by some casual puff of passion, it was blown into a momentary flame. This he repressed as speedily as possible, and strove to look as if nothing of the kind had happened.

In a word, old Roger Chillingworth was a striking evidence of man's faculty of transforming himself into a devil, if he will only, for a reasonable space of time, undertake a devil's office. This unhappy person had effected such a transformation by devoting himself, for seven years, to the constant analysis of a heart full of torture, and deriving his enjoyment thence, and adding fuel to those fiery tortures which he analyzed and gloated over....

"Hast thou not tortured him enough?" said Hester, noticing the old man's look. "Has he not paid thee all?"

"No! —no! —He has but increased the debt!" answered the physician; and, as he proceeded, his manner lost its fiercer characteristics, and subsided into gloom. "Dost thou remember me, Hester, as I was nine years agone? Even then, I was in the autumn of my days, nor was it the early autumn. But all my life had been made up of earnest, studious, thoughtful, quiet years, bestowed faithfully for the increase of mine own knowledge, and faithfully, too, though this latter object was but casual to the other,— faithfully for the advancement of human welfare. No life had been more peaceful and innocent than mine; few lives so rich with benefits conferred. Dost thou remember me? Was I not, though you might deem me cold, nevertheless a man thoughtful for others, craving little for himself,—kind, true, just, and of constant, if not warm affections? Was I not all this?"

"All this, and more," said Hester.

"And what am I now?" demanded he, looking into her face, and permitting the whole evil within him to be written on his features. "I have already told thee what I am! A fiend! Who made me so?"

"It was myself!" cried Hester, shuddering. "It was I, not less than he.

---

① ever and anon: from time to time, occasionally

Why hast thou not avenged thyself on me?"

"I have left thee to the scarlet letter," replied Roger Chillingworth. "If that have not avenged me, I can do no more!"...

"Woman, I could wellnigh① pity thee!" said Roger Chillingworth, unable to restrain a thrill of admiration too; for there was a quality almost majestic in the despair which she expressed. "Thou hadst great elements. Peradventure,② hadst thou met earlier with a better love than mine, this evil had not been. I pity thee, for the good that has been wasted in thy nature!"

"And I thee," answered Hester Prynne, "for the hatred that has transformed a wise and just man to a fiend! Wilt thou yet purge it out of thee, and be once more human? If not for his sake, then doubly for thine own! Forgive, and leave his further retribution to the Power that claims it! I said, but now, that there could be no good event for him, or thee, or me, who are here wandering together in this gloomy maze of evil, and stumbling, at every step, over the guilt wherewith we have strewn our path. It is not so! There might be good for thee, and thee alone, since thou hast been deeply wronged, and hast it at thy will to pardon. Wilt thou give up that only privilege? Wilt thou reject that priceless benefit?"...

Chapter 18　A Flood of Sunshine
(Excerpt)

The decision once made,③ a glow of strange enjoyment threw its flickering brightness over the trouble of his breast. It was the exhilaration effect—upon a prisoner just escaped from the dungeon of his own heart—of breathing the wild, free atmosphere of an unredeemed, unchristianised, lawless region. His spirit rose, as it were, with a bound, and attained a nearer prospect of the sky, than throughout all the misery which had kept him groveling on the earth. Of a deeply religious temperament, there was

---

①wellnigh: almost, nearly

②peradventure: (old) perhaps

③The decision once made: in the woods, Hester and Arthur Dimmesdale made a decision to leave the settlement in the New World to live elsewhere.

inevitably a tinge of the devotional in his mood.

"Do I feel joy again?" cried he, wondering at himself. "Methought the germ of it was dead in me! O Hester, thou art my better angel! I seem to have flung myself—sick, sin-stained, and sorrow-blackened—down upon these forest-leaves, and to have risen up all made anew, and with new powers to glorify Him that hath been merciful! This is already the better life! Why did we not find it sooner?"

"Let us not look back," answered Hester Prynne. "The past is gone! Wherefore should we linger upon it now? See! With this symbol, I undo it all, and make it as it had never been!"

So speaking, she undid the clasp that fastened the scarlet letter, and, taking it from her bosom, threw it to a distance among the withered leaves. The mystic token alighted on the hither verge of the stream. With a hand's breadth farther flight it would have fallen into the water, and have given the little brook another woe to carry onward, besides the unintelligible tale which it still kept murmuring about. But there lay the embroidered letter, glittering like a lost jewel, which some ill-fated wanderer might pick up, and thenceforth be haunted by strange phantoms of guilt, sinkings of the heart, and unaccountable misfortune.

The stigma gone, Hester heaved a long, deep sigh, in which the burden of shame and anguish departed from her spirit. O exquisite relief! She had not known the weight until she felt the freedom! By another impulse, she took off the formal cap that confined her hair, and down it fell upon her shoulders, dark and rich, with at once a shadow and a light in its abundance, and imparting the charm of softness to her features. There played around her mouth, and beamed out of her eyes, a radiant and tender smile, that seemed gushing from the very heart of womanhood. A crimson flush was glowing on her cheek, that had been long so pale. Her sex, her youth, and the whole richness of her beauty, came back from what men call the irrevocable past, and clustered themselves with her maiden hope, and a happiness before unknown, within the magic circle of this hour. And, as if the gloom of the earth and sky had been but the effluence of these two mortal hearts, it vanished with their sorrow. All at once, as with a sudden smile of heaven, forth burst the sunshine, pouring a very flood into the obscure forest, gladdening each green leaf, transmuting the yellow fallen ones to gold, and gleaming adown the gray trunks of the solemn trees. The objects that had made a shadow hitherto, embodied the brightness now. The course of the little brook might be traced by its merry gleam afar into the wood's heart of mystery, which had become a mystery of joy.

Such was the sympathy of Nature—that wild, heathen Nature of the forest, never subjugated by human law, nor illumined by higher truth—with the bliss of these two spirits! Love, whether newly-born, or aroused from a death-like slumber, must always create a sunshine, filling the heart so full of radiance, that it overflows upon the outward world. Had the forest still kept its gloom, it would have been bright in Hester's eyes, and bright in Arthur Dimmesdale's!

Hester looked at him with a thrill of another joy.

Questions for Discussion

1. In Chapter 6, what troubled Hester's mind with regard to Pearl? Why? And what worrisome problems did Pearl have? Was Hester capable of settling these problems?
2. In Chapter 14, what changes had come over Chillingworth in the past seven years? What effected the changes? And why didn't Chillingworth avenge him on Hester? Did his revenge on Dimmesdale produce an effective result?
3. What view of nature is reflected in Chapter 18? Do you think Pearl would own the changed Hester as her mother? Why or why not?
4. Nathaniel Hawthorne is concerned with moral and ethical problems in his *The Scarlet Letter*. What moral lesson can we readers learn through the reading of the excerpts?

3.4 Representative Poets and Their Works

American poetry arose first as efforts by early Americans to add their voices to English poetry; most of the early Americans' work relied on contemporary British models of poetic form, diction, and theme. William Cullen Bryant (1794 – 1878) was the first American lyric poet of distinction. He grew up in a small village in western Massachusetts. As a boy he spent much time exploring the mysteries of the forests and hills in the countryside. At the age of thirteen, he composed his thought-provoking poem "Thanatopsis." When the poem was sent by his father to *The North American Review*, a major literary magazine, the editors found the poem so impressive that one editor claimed, "No one on this side of the Atlantic is capable of writing such verse." His noble and romantic verses, often replete with themes of nature and solitude, established his reputation of the "father of American poetry." Bryant will be best remembered as the poet of his native Berkshire hills and streams in such poems as "Thanatopsis" and "To a Waterfowl."

Edgar Allan Poe (1809 – 1849), though leading a short, unhappy, and melodramatic life marked by poverty and restlessness, has achieved enormous success. He has been regarded not just a prominent poet, but also a master of the horror tale, a patron saint of the detective story, and a renowned literary critic. His most memorable poems include "To Helen" and "The Raven;" his most memorable horror stories include "The Fall of the House of Usher," "The Masque of the Red Death," "The Tell-Tale Heart," etc. He had extraordinary ability to create unforgettable images, musical language, fearful moods, and dreadful atmosphere. Many writers and critics, especially Europeans, have admired Poe more than any other American writer. The Irish poet W.B. Yeats considered Poe as "the greatest of American Poets."

Henry Wadsworth Longfellow (1807 – 1882) was the most beloved American poet of his day. He was strongly influenced by European Romanticism and he did much to bring European culture to America.

The emergence of a truly indigenous English-language poetry in the United States was the work of two poets, Walt Whitman (1819 – 1892) and Emily Dickinson (1830 – 1886). On the surface, these two poets could not have been less alike. What links them is their common connection to Emerson and the daring originality of their visions. Their poetry would profoundly stamp the American poetry of the 20th century, in which Robert Frost, Ezra Pound, T. S. Eliot, Edwin Arlington Robinson, Allen Ginsberg, and Robert Lowell are among the most significant American poets.

Henry Wadsworth Longfellow (1807 – 1882)

Longfellow was born into a well-to-do family in Maine. Educated at Bowdoin College, he showed great talent in English language and literature. He went to Europe a couple of times and stayed there long enough to study European languages and literature. He made a living mainly by teaching a variety of European languages and literatures at Bowdoin and then at Harvard. In 1845 he published the anthology *The Poets and Poetry of Europe*, which brought European poems to American readers.

Strongly influenced by European Romanticism, Longfellow had great success in making poetry popular in America. As the best-known and the most beloved American poet of his day, when Longfellow turned seventy-five, American people celebrated his birthday as if it were a national holiday. When he died, statues were dedicated in his honor across the country, and a memorial bust was placed in the Poet's Corner of Westminster Abbey in London—he is the only American poet who has this exceptional honor.

However, he has latterly been criticized for failing to reflect the deep and important problems of contemporary life, for lacking the depth and insight of a great artist.

Longfellow's short lyrics are popular with a large number of readers. The most popular ones are "A Psalm of Life" and "The Tide Rises, the Tide Falls."

A Psalm of Life

What the Heart of the Young Man Said to the Psalmist①

Tell me not, in mournful numbers,②
    Life is but an empty dream!—
For the soul is dead that slumbers,③
    And things are not what they seem.

5   Life is real! Life is earnest!
    And the grave is not its goal;
Dust thou art, to dust returnest,
    Was not spoken of the soul.

Not enjoyment, and not sorrow,
10   Is our destined end or way;
But to act, that each to-morrow
    Find us farther than to-day.

Art is long, and Time is fleeting,
    And our hearts, though stout and brave,
15   Still, like muffled④ drums, are beating
    Funeral marches to the grave.

In the world's broad field of battle,
    In the bivouac⑤ of Life,
Be not like dumb, driven cattle!
20   Be a hero in the strife!

---

① Psalmist: the author of, especially, biblical psalms
② numbers: the numbered verses in the Book of Psalms in the Bible
③ slumber: sleep
④ muffled: wrapped up, enveloped
⑤ bivouac: a temporary camp without tents or cover, used especially by soldiers or mountaineers

Trust no Future, howe'er pleasant!
　　Let the dead Past bury its dead!
Act,—act in the living Present!
　　Heart within, and God o'erhead!

25　Lives of great men all remind us
　　We can make our lives sublime,
And, departing, leave behind us
　　Footprints on the sands of time;

Footprints, that perhaps another,
30　　Sailing o'er life's solemn main,①
A forlorn and shipwrecked brother,
　　Seeing, shall take heart again.

Let us, then, be up and doing,
　　With a heart for any fate;
35　Still achieving, still pursuing,
　　Learn to labor and to wait.

The Tide Rises, the Tide Falls

The tide rises, the tide falls,
The twilight darkens, the curlew② calls;
Along the sea-sands damp and brown
The traveller hastens toward the town,
5　　And the tide rises, the tide falls.

Darkness settles on roofs and walls,
But the sea, the sea in the darkness calls;
The little waves, with their soft, white hands,

---

① main: (old English) the open ocean
② curlew: any of numerous medium-sized or large shorebirds

Efface the footprints in the sands,
10   And the tide rises, the tide falls.

    The morning breaks; the steeds① in their stalls
    Stamp and neigh,② as the hostler calls;
    The day returns, but nevermore
    Returns the traveler to the shore,
15   And the tide rises, the tide falls.

Questions for Discussion

1. The image of "footprints" is used in both poems. What do the footprints in "The Psalm of Life" do? What happens to the footprints in "The Tide Rises, the Tide Falls"?
2. In "The Tide Rises, the Tide Falls," what returns and what never returns? Does the action of the tide suggest permanence or impermanence? Explain.
3. Both "A Psalm of Life" (1838) and "The Tide Rises, the Tide Falls" (1879) offer large views of life. But how is the tone, or poet's attitude, different in the two poems?

Walt Whitman (1819 – 1892)

Walt Whitman was born on Long Island, New York City. In Whitman's day, Long Island was still a place of rolling hills and lush green fields. His father was a farmer-turned carpenter who moved the family to Brooklyn in 1823 during a building boom.

Whitman received five or six years of formal education, but he was also an eager reader of 19th century novels, English Romanticist poetry, the

---

① steed: a horse, especially a spirited horse
② neigh: (of a horse) make a characteristic high-pitched sound

classics of European literature, and the Bible.

Whitman took various jobs in his youth, such as an office boy, printer's devil,① journalist, country schoolmaster, and editor. He traveled briefly after stopping his work as an editor. The travels enabled Whitman to experience the frontier, the great rivers, the vast tracts of fertile land, and myriad② aspects of American life.

In 1855, Whitman self-published his first edition of *Leaves of Grass*, which contained 12 poems. However, it sold few copies and was panned by critics, who called it "poetry of barbarism." Only Emerson praised his poems highly. Whitman kept arranging, rearranging, and adding to *Leaves of Grass* throughout his lifetime, envisioning all of his work as one vast poem. The final edition of *Leaves of Grass* contained 389 titled poems. He was eventually recognized and received praise from the American public and critics.

Though nurtured by the Transcendentalists, Whitman was no country-dwelling person, not contemplating the quiet joys of nature. He had spent his early manhood in New York City, soaking up its sights and sounds. Later he traveled down the Mississippi, absorbing the variety of America. He listened to the talk of street gangs and working people, of farmers and soldiers, and saw in them the variety and liveliness of America, which he appreciated with great passion. His poetry extends the Transcendentalists' joy in nature to a love for humanity in all its manifestations.

One of the poems that most fully captures the essence of Whitman is "Song of Myself." It is his celebration of individuality as well as his oneness with the world. More than that, it is a celebration of life itself.

Song of Myself

(Excerpt)

1

I celebrate myself, and sing myself,

---

① printer's devil: an apprentice in a printing office
② myriad: innumerable

And what I assume you shall assume,

For every atom belonging to me as good belongs to you.

I loafe① and invite my soul,

5   I lean and loafe at my ease observing a spear of summer grass.

My tongue, every atom of my blood, form'd from this soil, this air,

Born here of parents born here from parents the same, and their parents the same,

I, now thirty-seven years old in perfect health begin,

10   Hoping to cease not till death.

Creeds② and schools in abeyance,③

Retiring back a while sufficed at what they are, but never forgotten,

I harbor for good or bad, I permit to speak at every hazard,④

Nature without check with original energy.

6

A child said *What is the grass*? fetching it to me with full hands;

How could I answer the child? I do not know what it is any more than he.

I guess it must be the flag of my disposition, out of hopeful green

5   stuff woven.

Or I guess it is the handkerchief of the Lord,

A scented gift and remembrancer designedly dropt,

Bearing the owner's name someway in the corners, that we may see and remark, and say *Whose*?

---

① loafe: (informal) spend time in idleness
② creed: a formal statement of religious belief
③ in abeyance: in a state of temporary inactivity
④ at every hazard: (emphasized form of "at hazard") in danger, at risk

10 Or I guess the grass is itself a child, the produced babe of the vegetation.

Or I guess it is a uniform hieroglyphic,①
And it means, Sprouting alike in broad zones and narrow zones,
Growing among black folks as among white,
15 Kanuck,② Tuckahoe,③ Congressman, Cuff,④ I give them the same, I receive them the same.

And now it seems to me the beautiful uncut hair of graves.

Tenderly will I use you curling grass,
It may be you transpire from the breasts of young men,
20 It may be if I had known them I would have loved them,
It may be you are from old people, or from offspring taken soon out of their mother's laps,
And here you are the mothers' laps.

This grass is very dark to be from the white heads of old mothers,
25 Darker than the colorless beards of old men,
Dark to come from under the faint red roofs of mouths.

O I perceive after all so many uttering tongues,
And I perceive they do not come from the roofs of mouths for nothing.

I wish I could translate the hints about the dead young men and
30 women,
And the hints about old men and mothers, and the offspring taken soon out of their laps.

What do you think has become of the young and old men?

---

① hieroglyphic: a character used in a system of pictorial writing
② Kanuck (Canuck): a French Canadian
③ Tuckahoe: a Virginian (so called because Virginians eat the American Indian food plant tuckahoe)
④ Cuff: a black

And what do you think has become of the women and children?

35   They are alive and well somewhere,
The smallest sprout shows there is really no death,
And if ever there was it led forward life, and does not wait at the end to arrest it,
And ceas'd the moment life appear'd.

40   All goes onward and outward, nothing collapses,
And to die is different from what any one supposed, and luckier.

21

I am the poet of the Body and I am the poet of the Soul,
The pleasures of heaven are with me and the pains of hell are with me,
The first I graft① and increase upon myself, the latter I translate
5   into new tongue.

I am the poet of the woman the same as the man,
And I say it is as great to be a woman as to be a man,
And I say there is nothing greater than the mother of men.

I chant the chant of dilation② or pride,
10   We have had ducking and deprecating about enough,
I show that size is only development.

Have you outstript the rest? are you the President?
It is a trifle, they will more than arrive there every one, and still pass on....

24

Walt Whitman, a kosmos, of Manhattan the son,

---

① graft: implant (living tissue) surgically
② dilation: the act or action of stretching, widening, or enlarging sth.

Turbulent, fleshy, sensual, eating, drinking and breeding,
No sentimentalist, no stander above men and women or apart from them,
5 No more modest than immodest.

Unscrew the locks from the doors!
Unscrew the doors themselves from their jambs!

Whoever degrades another degrades me,
And whatever is done or said returns at last to me.
...
10 Through me many long dumb voices,
Voices of the interminable generations of prisoners and slaves,
Voices of the diseas'd and despairing and of thieves and dwarfs,
Voices of cycles of preparation and accretion,①
And of the threads that connect the stars, and of wombs and of the
15   father-stuff,
And of the rights of them the others are down upon,
Of the deform'd, trivial, flat, foolish, despised,
Fog in the air, beetles rolling balls of dung.

Through me forbidden voices,
20 Voices of sexes and lusts, voices veil'd and I remove the veil,
Voices indecent by me clarified and transfigur'd.

I do not press my fingers across my mouth,
I keep as delicate around the bowels as around the head and heart,

Copulation② is no more rank to me than death is.
25 I believe in the flesh and the appetites,
Seeing, hearing, feeling, are miracles, and each part and tag of

---

① accretion: the process of growth or increase, typically by the gradual accumulation of additional layers or matter
② copulation: sexual intercourse

me is a miracle.

Divine am I inside and out, and I make holy whatever I touch or am touch'd from,
30　The scent of these arm-pits aroma finer than prayer,
This head more than churches, bibles, and all the creeds....

52

The spotted hawk swoops by and accuses me, he complains of my gab and my loitering.①

I too am not a bit tamed, I too am untranslatable,
I sound my barbaric yawp over the roofs of the world.

5　The last scud of day holds back for me,
It flings my likeness after the rest and true as any on the shadow'd wilds,
It coaxes me to the vapor and the dusk.

I depart as air, I shake my white locks at the runaway sun,
10　I effuse my flesh in eddies, and drift it in lacy jags.

I bequeath② myself to the dirt to grow from the grass I love,
If you want me again look for me under your boot soles.

You will hardly know who I am or what I mean,
But I shall be good health to you nevertheless,
15　And filter and fiber your blood.

Failing to fetch me at first keep encouraged,
Missing me one place search another,
I stop somewhere waiting for you.

---

① loiter: stand or wait around idly or without apparent purpose 消磨时光
② bequeath: give or leave by will

> Questions for Discussion
>
> 1. Please name as many characteristics of Whitman's "self" as you can in "Song of Myself." Which characteristics seem the most prominent?
> 2. Consider the image of the grass in sections 6 and 52 of "Song of Myself." What does the grass have to do with life and death?
> 3. By associating himself with the grass, what does the poet suggest about himself? Please summarize Whitman's attitude toward nature.

Emily Dickinson (1830 – 1886)

Emily Dickinson is now regarded as one of the greatest poets in the English Language. However, she was unknown to the public during her lifetime, with only seven poems published anonymously. After she died at the age of 56, people found in her home many small packages of her poems. Some of them had been carefully revised and neatly tied with ribbons; others had been scrawled① on scraps of paper. In all, 1,775 poems were preserved.

Emily was born in the quiet community of Amherst, Massachusetts. Being the second child of the family, Emily had an older brother, a younger sister, an authoritative father, and a mother not "emotionally accessible." Economically, politically, and intellectually, the Dickinson family was prominent in Amherst. Emily had the benefit of a good education, but severe homesickness and depression made her seldom leave home. From the age of 18 she began to dress all in white and began a life of seclusion. She was then described as "eccentric."

Emily was well-read. She read the works of contemporary American writers, among whom Emerson was her enduring favorite. She recognized a kindred spirit in the independent, nature-loving Thoreau. Her literary debts

---

① scrawl: to write or draw awkwardly, hastily, or carelessly

were also to the Bible and to British writers, including Shakespeare, Milton, Keats, Charles Dickens, the Brownings, Tennyson, and the Brontë sisters. However, no influence overshadowed her own spirit. Due to her life of solitude, she was able to focus on her world more sharply than other authors of her time.

Emily was original and innovative in her poetry. The main subjects of her poems are Love, Death, Nature, and God. In her poems, she abundantly used dashes and capital letters. Early editors of Dickinson's works deemed her style "not correct." They rewrote what Dickinson had written in order to make it "proper." Fortunately in 1955, Thomas Johnson published Dickinson's poems in their original formats in *The Complete Poems of Emily Dickinson*, thus displaying the creative genius and peculiarity of her poetry.

Success is counted sweetest

Success is counted sweetest
By those who ne'er succeed.
To comprehend a nectar①
Requires sorest need.
5   Not one of all the purple Host②
Who took the Flag today
Can tell the definition
So clear of Victory

As he defeated—dying—
10   On whose forbidden ear
The distant strains③ of triumph
Burst agonized and clear!

---

① nectar: the sweet liquid that bees collect from flowers
② host: (old English) army
③ strains: the sound of a piece of music as it is played or performed

Tell all the Truth but tell it slant—

Tell all the Truth but tell it slant—
Success in Circuit lies
Too bright for our infirm Delight
The Truth's superb surprise
5   As Lightning to the Children eased
With explanation kind
The Truth must dazzle gradually
Or every man be blind—

Questions for Discussion

1. Do you think that Emily's statement "Success is counted sweetest by those who ne'er succeed" sounds contradictory? What psychological truth do you find in this poem?
2. In "Tell all the Truth but tell it slant—" Emily advises us not to tell straight. Do you also think that the way how we tell the truth makes difference? Please explain.

Chapter 4

From 1861 to 1914
American Civil War and American Realism

4.1 American Civil War and Reconstruction

Regional economic differences helped bring about the outbreak of the American Civil War in 1861. In the South, enslaved African Americans provided the labor needed for an agricultural economy based on growing and selling cotton. In the North, free people, both white and black, worked for wages in the mines, factories, and trading companies of a growing industrial economy.

As the nation expanded westward, many Southerners wanted slavery to expand with it, but most Northerners did not. As each new western state entered the Union, a decision had to be made: would the state be a slave or free state? Compromise after compromise was reached until the tension became too great. In November 1860, Abraham Lincoln, who opposed the expansion of slavery, won the presidential election. In response, South Carolina and other Southern states—together known as the Confederacy—began to secede from the United States. Lincoln and his Republican Party treated this secession as a rebellion, and he vowed to preserve the Union. When Confederate cannons fired at Fort Sumter, South Carolina, the Civil War began.

Most of the Civil War was fought in the South. It was fought on a scale America had never seen before. During the first year of fighting, the Southern eleven states were triumphant. By the end of 1862, however, the North's naval blockades and larger armies began to bring it victories. Then, on January 1 of 1863, the events took a dramatic turn. Lincoln issued the

Emancipation Proclamation, which declared that all enslaved people in the rebellious states were free. The North's fight to save the Union became a war to end slavery.

Eventually, in April of 1865, after a long and bitter war with more than 600,000 deaths, the Confederate armies surrendered to the Union troops: the war ended in a victory for the North. The slave economy was destroyed.

For the new nation, the Civil War was a tragedy of the greatest magnitude. The loss of life and ruin of property, especially in the South, were astonishing. Nevertheless, the country prospered materially while the South went through a period known as Reconstruction.

4.2　Urbanization and the Gilded Age

The westward movement continued, driven by economics and a political ideology known as "Manifest Destiny" that held that the United States had the right to rule the whole of North America. It was the American version of colonialism as practiced by European countries, in particular Britain and France. The once isolated frontier became a memory when railroads continued to crisscross the continent: the first trans-continental railroad was completed in 1869, and by 1885 four trans-continental railroad lines were built. The railroads were powerful; the mighty engines hauled raw materials, hopeful migrants, and wealthy businessmen across the country. The great cities expanded rapidly. The population of Philadelphia tripled between 1870 and 1910 and that of New York City quadrupled. As the new capital of the Midwest, Chicago's population multiplied an astounding twenty times.

The discovery and extraction of coal, oil, iron, gold, silver, and other kinds of mineral wealth produced large numbers of vast, individual fortunes. For the first time, the nation as a whole was rich enough to capitalize its own further development. By the 1890s, there were over four thousand American millionaires and some millionaires' wealth greatly exceeded one million dollars, for instance, Andrew Carnegie who made his fortune in iron and steel, J. P. Morgan, the great financier, John Rockefeller, founder of the Standard Oil Company, and Cornelius Vanderbilt, the railroad magnate.

As wealth grew more conspicuous, poverty became exceedingly visible. In the countryside, increasing numbers of farmers who depended on the monopolistic railroads for transportation of their crops were squeezed off the land by the owners of the railroads that intercrossed the continent—in his fiction *The Octopus* (1901), Frank Norris characterized the railroads as the giant "octopus." Everywhere independent farmers were placed "under the lion's paw" of the land speculators and absentee landlords, as Hamlin Garland's story "Under the Lion's Paw" describes. Additionally, large-scale farming squeezed family farmers, though it was true that such practices increased gross agricultural yields.

In the big cities, an oversupply of labor kept wages down, which allowed industrialists to maintain inhumane and dangerous working conditions for men, women, and children who competed for jobs.

In brief, in this era the United States was wholly transformed. The main shifts in population were from country to city, from farm to factory, from foreign nations (mostly European nations) to America. This period was an age when America became urbanized and industrialized. It changed from a nation of distinct regions into a nation expanding from the Atlantic to the Pacific as a result of railroad construction. This period was also an age of extremes: rapid economic growth was in sharp contrast with moral decline, the dazzling wealth of the rich was in sour comparison with the shocking poverty of the poor. Hope and gloom went side by side. That was why this period also has been called the Gilded Age—this term was derived from Mark Twain's 1873 novel *The Gilded Age: A Tale of Today*, which satirized an era of serious social problems masked by a thin gold gilding.

4.3　American Realism

The Civil War challenged the nation's self-confidence; it thus put an end to the optimism of the mid-19th century. Responding to the brutality of the Civil War and the new conditions of American life, the literature of the decades following the Civil War turned from Romanticism and transcendental optimism toward a franker portrayal of society and human nature. Consequently, American literature entered an age of realism.

In part, realism was a reaction to Romanticism. Realism emphasized a faithful treatment of the ordinary. As the American novelist Frank Norris said, "Realism is the kind of fiction that confines itself to the type of normal life." William Dean Howells, one of the earliest exponents of realism, claimed that realism "is nothing more and nothing less than the truthful treatment of materials." Howells also said, "Let fictions cease to lie about life; let it portray men and women as they are."

American writers began studying everyday life and crafting it in realistic and detailed ways. Some writers set their literature in their own local regions which they knew best: in an age when transportation and communication were not what they are like today, regional literature was especially fascinating and popular, because regional writers fed Americans' curiosity about distinctive language, landforms, and customs in other parts of the country. For instance, Mark Twain illustrated for the whole nation the life on the Mississippi, while Kate Chopin's stories portrayed the colorful mixture of languages and cultures in Louisiana. The aim of most regional fiction was to capture the special atmosphere, the "local color." Some other writers, called Naturalists, were influenced by European scientists, philosophers, and writers such as Charles Darwin, Herbert Spencer, and Émile Zola. They focused on the powerful biological and socioeconomic forces that they believed determine and shape the lives of individuals.

Thus, it can be said that American realism, as a broader term, is inclusive of American regionalism, American local color writing, and American Naturalism.

The three figures who dominated American prose fiction in the last quarter of the 19th century were Mark Twain (1835 – 1910), William Dean Howells (1837 – 1920), and Henry James (1843 – 1916). For half a century, Howells was friend, editor, correspondent, and champion of both Twain and James. Mark Twain is best remembered for his *The Adventures of Tom*

Sawyer (1876), which established him as a master of fiction. Its sequel, *Adventures of Huckleberry Finn* (1883), confirmed him as one of the greatest novelists America has ever produced. His mastery of the native vernacular and his ability "to spin a yarn" are unrivaled; his humor is irresistible. His realism and detail influenced many later American fiction writers. That explains why Ernest Hemingway claims that "All modern American literature comes from one book by Mark Twain called Huckleberry Finn."

Henry James is best remembered for his "international theme" fictions, which tell of Americans in Europe and occasionally of Europeans in America, such as *The American* (1877), *The Europeans* (1878), *Daisy Miller* (1879), *The Portrait of a Lady* (1881), *The Wings of the Dove* (1902), *The Ambassador* (1903), and *The Golden Bowl* (1904). In his early international theme novels, which came out in the 1870s and 1880s, he wrote about naïve young Americans in tension with the traditions, customs, and values of the Old World, like Christopher Newman in *The American*, and the title character of *Daisy Miller*. *The Portrait of a Lady* has been regarded as his first masterpiece of the type. In his later international-themed novels, which came out in the early 1900s, the world is like the very atmosphere of the mind, which accounts for his being called a subtle psychological realist.

The leading Naturalist writers include Stephen Crane (1871 – 1900), Theodore Dreiser (1871 – 1945), Jack London (1876 – 1916), and Frank Norris (1870 – 1902). Stephen Crane is best noted for his *Maggie: A Girl of the Streets* (1893) and *The Red Badge of Courage*, which was serialized in 1894 and published in book form one year later. Jack London is best remembered for his enduringly popular stories that involve the primitive struggle of individuals in the context of irresistible natural forces such as the wild sea or the Arctic wasteland, with *The Call of the Wild* (1903) and *The Sea-Wolf* (1904) being the most famous. Theodore Dreiser and Edwin Arlington Robinson (1869 – 1935), who are anthologized in the following, bespeak pretty well American Realism in prose fiction and poetry.

Theodore Dreiser (1871 – 1945)

Theodore Dreiser is now best remembered as the author of *Sister Carrie* (1900) and *An American Tragedy* (1925), both being among America's greatest novels.

Dreiser was born in Indiana into a big family, being the eleventh of thirteen children. His father, a German immigrant who was severe and emotionally distant, was not particularly successful in providing for his large family. Dreiser's unhappy childhood haunted him throughout his life. The large family moved from house to house in Indiana dogged by poverty, insecurity, and internal division. From the age of 15, Dreiser was on his own, earning meager support from a variety of menial jobs.

A high-school teacher financed him to study for a year at Indiana University in 1889, but Dreiser's real education came from experience and independent reading and thinking. He read books by Charles Darwin, Thomas Huxley, Herbert Spencer, and some other late 19th-century scientists and social scientists who lent support to the view that nature and society had no divine sanction, that human beings, just as much as other species, were participants in an evolutionary process in which only those who adapted successfully to their environments survived.

Dreiser's first work is *Sister Carrie*, a novel telling the story of a young girl named Carrie Meeber. Attracted by the prospect of excitement, Carrie comes to Chicago, the rapidly growing Midwestern urban center. There she is seduced first by a traveling salesman, Charles Drouet, then by George Hurstwood, a married middle-aged manager of a saloon. After closing one night, Hurstwood steals ten thousand dollars from the safe in the saloon. He and Carrie end up settling down in New York City, where he slowly deteriorates while she becomes a successful actress. They eventually part company and, unknown to Carrie, Hurstwood commits suicide. Mainly because the novel depicts an amoral story of a "fallen" woman's success, it was virtually suppressed by its publisher. However, since its reissue in 1907, it has steadily risen in popularity and scholarly acceptance as one of the key works in the Dreiser canon. Now it is acclaimed as a prime example of

American Naturalism.

An American Tragedy, Dreiser's greatest and most successful novel, came out in 1925. The story is based on a much publicized murder in Upstate New York in 1906. Clyde Griffiths is a poor boy who dreams of a life of luxury and status. When his prospect for marrying a wealthy girl is threatened by his pregnant girlfriend, a factory worker with whom he has had a relationship, Clyde plans to murder her by drowning while they go boating. When the moment arrives, he lacks the nerve to do so. However, he leaves her to drown after their boat happened to tip over during an outing on a deserted lake so that it would seem like an accident. Much of the novel dwells on the capture of Clyde, the investigation and prosecution of the case, and the distressing details of Clyde's imprisonment and execution. The novel was an immediate best-seller. It confirmed Dreiser's status as one of the leading writers of his time.

During the last two decades of his life, Dreiser turned to polemical① writing and other genres—poetry, travel books, and autobiography. He visited the Soviet Union in 1927 and published *Dreiser Looks at Russia* the following year. In the 1930s, like many other American intellectuals and writers, Dreiser was increasingly attracted by the philosophical program of the Communist Party. He published two nonfiction books presenting a critical perspective on capitalist America, *Tragic America* (1931) and *America Is Worth Saving* (1941). He joined the Communist Party of the USA about five months before his death on December 28, 1945.

Sister Carrie

(Excerpt)

Chapter 1　The Magnet Attracting: A Waif Amid Forces

When Caroline Meeber boarded the afternoon train for Chicago, her total outfit consisted of a small trunk, a cheap imitation alligator-skin satchel, a small lunch in a paper box, and a yellow leather snap purse,

---

①polemical: using strong arguments to criticize or defend a particular idea, opinion, or person

containing her ticket, a scrap of paper with her sister's address in Van Buren Street, and four dollars in money. It was in August, 1889. She was eighteen years of age, bright, timid, and full of the illusions of ignorance and youth. Whatever touch of regret at parting characterised her thoughts, it was certainly not for advantages now being given up. A gush of tears at her mother's farewell kiss, a touch in her throat when the cars clacked by the flour mill where her father worked by the day, a pathetic sigh as the familiar green environs of the village passed in review, and the threads which bound her so lightly to girlhood and home were irretrievably broken.

To be sure there was always the next station, where one might descend and return. There was the great city, bound more closely by these very trains which came up daily. Columbia City was not so very far away, even once she was in Chicago. What, pray, is a few hours—a few hundred miles? She looked at the little slip bearing her sister's address and wondered. She gazed at the green landscape, now passing in swift review, until her swifter thoughts replaced its impression with vague conjectures① of what Chicago might be.

When a girl leaves her home at eighteen, she does one of two things. Either she falls into saving hands and becomes better, or she rapidly assumes the cosmopolitan standard of virtue and becomes worse. Of an intermediate balance, under the circumstances, there is no possibility. The city has its cunning wiles, no less than the infinitely smaller and more human tempter. There are large forces which allure with all the soulfulness of expression possible in the most cultured human. The gleam of a thousand lights is often as effective as the persuasive light in a wooing and fascinating eye. Half the undoing of the unsophisticated and natural mind is accomplished by forces wholly superhuman. A blare of sound, a roar of life, a vast array of human hives, appeal to the astonished senses in equivocal② terms. Without a counsellor at hand to whisper cautious interpretations, what falsehoods may not these things breathe into the unguarded ear! Unrecognized for what

---

①conjecture: guess, fancy
②equivocal: open to more than one interpretation; ambiguous

they are, their beauty, like music, too often relaxes, then weakens, then perverts the simpler human perceptions.

Caroline, or Sister Carrie, as she had been half affectionately termed by the family, was possessed of a mind rudimentary① in its power of observation and analysis. Self-interest with her was high, but not strong. It was, nevertheless, her guiding characteristic. Warm with the fancies of youth, pretty with the insipid prettiness of the formative period, possessed of a figure promising eventual shapeliness and an eye alight with certain native intelligence, she was a fair example of the middle American class—two generations removed from the emigrant. Books were beyond her interest—knowledge a sealed book. In the intuitive graces she was still crude. She could scarcely toss her head gracefully. Her hands were almost ineffectual. The feet, though small, were set flatly. And yet she was interested in her charms, quick to understand the keener pleasures of life, ambitious to gain in material things. A half-equipped little knight she was, venturing to reconnoiter the mysterious city and dreaming wild dreams of some vague, far-off supremacy, which should make it prey and subject—the proper penitent, groveling at a woman's slipper.

"That," said a voice in her ear, "is one of the prettiest little resorts in Wisconsin."

"Is it?" she answered nervously.

The train was just pulling out of Waukesha. For some time she had been conscious of a man behind. She felt him observing her mass of hair. He had been fidgeting, and with natural intuition she felt a certain interest growing in that quarter. Her maidenly reserve, and a certain sense of what was conventional under the circumstances, called her to forestall and deny this familiarity, but the daring and magnetism of the individual, born of past experiences and triumphs, prevailed. She answered.

He leaned forward to put his elbows upon the back of her seat and proceeded to make himself volubly agreeable.

"Yes, that is a great resort for Chicago people. The hotels are swell.

---

① rudimentary: relating to an immature or undeveloped form; unsophisticated

You are not familiar with this part of the country, are you?"

"Oh, yes, I am," answered Carrie. "That is, I live at Columbia City. I have never been through here, though."

"And so this is your first visit to Chicago," he observed.

All the time she was conscious of certain features out of the side of her eye. Flush, colorful cheeks, a light moustache, a grey fedora hat. She now turned and looked upon him in full, the instincts of self-protection and coquetry mingling confusedly in her brain.

"I didn't say that," she said.

"Oh," he answered, in a very pleasing way and with an assumed air of mistake, "I thought you did."

Here was a type of the travelling canvasser① for a manufacturing house—a class which at that time was first being dubbed by the slang of the day "drummers." He came within the meaning of a still newer term, which had sprung into general use among Americans in 1880, and which concisely expressed the thought of one whose dress or manners are calculated to elicit the admiration of susceptible young women—a "masher." His suit was of a striped and crossed pattern of brown wool, new at that time, but since become familiar as a business suit. The low crotch of the vest revealed a stiff shirt bosom of white and pink stripes. From his coat sleeves protruded a pair of linen cuffs of the same pattern, fastened with large, gold plate buttons, set with the common yellow agates known as "cat's-eyes." His fingers bore several rings—one, the ever-enduring heavy seal—and from his vest dangled a neat gold watch chain, from which was suspended the secret insignia of the Order of Elks. The whole suit was rather tight-fitting, and was finished off with heavy-soled tan shoes, highly polished, and the grey fedora hat. He was, for the order of intellect represented, attractive, and whatever he had to recommend him, you may be sure was not lost upon Carrie, in this, her first glance.

Lest this order of individual should permanently pass, let me put down

---

① canvasser: a canvasser is responsible for supporting the sales operations by researching the current market trends to know the public demands etc.

some of the most striking characteristics of his most successful manner and method. Good clothes, of course, were the first essential, the things without which he was nothing. A strong physical nature, actuated by a keen desire for the feminine, was the next. A mind free of any consideration of the problems or forces of the world and actuated not by greed, but an insatiable love of variable pleasure. His method was always simple. Its principal element was daring, backed, of course, by an intense desire and admiration for the sex. Let him meet with a young woman once and he would approach her with an air of kindly familiarity, not unmixed with pleading, which would result in most cases in a tolerant acceptance. If she showed any tendency to coquetry he would be apt to straighten her tie, or if she "took up" with him at all, to call her by her first name. If he visited a department store it was to lounge familiarly over the counter and ask some leading questions. In more exclusive circles, on the train or in waiting stations, he went slower. If some seemingly vulnerable object appeared he was all attention—to pass the compliments of the day, to lead the way to the parlor car, carrying her grip, or, failing that, to take a seat next her with the hope of being able to court her to her destination. Pillows, books, a footstool, the shade lowered; all these figured in the things which he could do. If, when she reached her destination he did not alight and attend her baggage for her, it was because, in his own estimation, he had signally failed.

A woman should some day write the complete philosophy of clothes. No matter how young, it is one of the things she wholly comprehends. There is an indescribably faint line in the matter of man's apparel which somehow divides for her those who are worth glancing at and those who are not. Once an individual has passed this faint line on the way downward he will get no glance from her. There is another line at which the dress of a man will cause her to study her own. This line the individual at her elbow now marked for Carrie. She became conscious of an inequality. Her own plain blue dress, with its black cotton tape trimmings, now seemed to her shabby. She felt the worn state of her shoes.

"Let's see," he went on, "I know quite a number of people in your town. Morgenroth the clothier and Gibson the dry goods man."

"Oh, do you?" she interrupted, aroused by memories of longings their show windows had cost her.

At last he had a clew to her interest, and followed it deftly. In a few minutes he had come about into her seat. He talked of sales of clothing, his travels, Chicago, and the amusements of that city.

"If you are going there, you will enjoy it immensely. Have you relatives?"

"I am going to visit my sister," she explained.

"You want to see Lincoln Park," he said, "and Michigan Boulevard. They are putting up great buildings there. It's a second New York—great. So much to see—theatres, crowds, fine houses—oh, you'll like that."

There was a little ache in her fancy of all he described. Her insignificance in the presence of so much magnificence faintly affected her. She realized that hers was not to be a round of pleasure, and yet there was something promising in all the material prospect he set forth. There was something satisfactory in the attention of this individual with his good clothes. She could not help smiling as he told her of some popular actress of whom she reminded him. She was not silly, and yet attention of this sort had its weight.

"You will be in Chicago some little time, won't you?" he observed at one turn of the now easy conversation.

"I don't know," said Carrie vaguely—a flash vision of the possibility of her not securing employment rising in her mind.

"Several weeks, anyhow," he said, looking steadily into her eyes.

There was much more passing now than the mere words indicated. He recognized the indescribable thing that made up for fascination and beauty in her. She realized that she was of interest to him from the one standpoint which a woman both delights in and fears. Her manner was simple, though for the very reason that she had not yet learned the many little affectations with which women conceal their true feelings. Some things she did appeared bold. A clever companion—had she ever had one—would have warned her never to look a man in the eyes so steadily.

"Why do you ask?" she said.

"Well, I'm going to be there several weeks. I'm going to study stock at our place and get new samples. I might show you 'round."

"I don't know whether you can or not. I mean I don't know whether I can. I shall be living with my sister, and—"

"Well, if she minds, we'll fix that." He took out his pencil and a little pocket note-book as if it were all settled. "What is your address there?"

She fumbled her purse which contained the address slip.

He reached down in his hip pocket and took out a fat purse. It was filled with slips of paper, some mileage books, a roll of greenbacks. It impressed her deeply. Such a purse had never been carried by any one attentive to her. Indeed, an experienced traveler, a brisk man of the world, had never come within such close range before. The purse, the shiny tan shoes, the smart new suit, and the air with which he did things, built up for her a dim world of fortune, of which he was the centre. It disposed her pleasantly toward all he might do.

He took out a neat business card, on which was engraved Bartlett, Caryoe & Company, and down in the left-hand corner, Chas. H. Drouet.

"That's me," he said, putting the card in her hand and touching his name. "It's pronounced Drew-eh. Our family was French, on my father's side."

She looked at it while he put up his purse. Then he got out a letter from a bunch in his coat pocket. "This is the house I travel for," he went on, pointing to a picture on it, "corner of State and Lake." There was pride in his voice. He felt that it was something to be connected with such a place, and he made her feel that way.

"What is your address?" he began again, fixing his pencil to write.

She looked at his hand.

"Carrie Meeber," she said slowly. "Three hundred and fifty-four West Van Buren Street, care S. C. Hanson."

He wrote it carefully down and got out the purse again. "You'll be at home if I come around Monday night?" he said.

"I think so," she answered.

How true it is that words are but the vague shadows of the volumes we mean. Little audible links, they are, chaining together great inaudible feelings and purposes. Here were these two, bandying little phrases, drawing purses, looking at cards, and both unconscious of how inarticulate all their real feelings were. Neither was wise enough to be sure of the working of the mind of the other. He could not tell how his luring succeeded.

She could not realize that she was drifting, until he secured her address. Now she felt that she had yielded something—he, that he had gained a victory. Already they felt that they were somehow associated. Already he took control in directing the conversation. His words were easy. Her manner was relaxed.

They were nearing Chicago. Signs were everywhere numerous. Trains flashed by them. Across wide stretches of flat, open prairie they could see lines of telegraph poles stalking across the fields toward the great city. Far away were indications of suburban towns, some big smokestacks towering high in the air.

Frequently there were two-story frame houses standing out in the open fields, without fence or trees, lone outposts of the approaching army of homes.

To the child, the genius with imagination, or the wholly untraveled, the approach to a great city for the first time is a wonderful thing. Particularly if it be evening—that mystic period between the glare and gloom of the world when life is changing from one sphere or condition to another. Ah, the promise of the night. What does it not hold for the weary! What old illusion of hope is not here forever repeated! Says the soul of the toiler to itself, "I shall soon be free. I shall be in the ways and the hosts of the merry. The streets, the lamps, the lighted chamber set for dining, are for me. The theatre, the halls, the parties, the ways of rest and the paths of song—these are mine in the night." Though all humanity be still enclosed in the shops, the thrill runs abroad. It is in the air. The dullest feel something which they may not always express or describe. It is the lifting of the burden of toil.

Sister Carrie gazed out of the window. Her companion, affected by her wonder, so contagious are all things, felt anew some interest in the city and pointed out its marvels.

"This is Northwest Chicago," said Drouet. "This is the Chicago River," and he pointed to a little muddy creek, crowded with the huge masted wanderers from far-off waters nosing the black-posted banks. With a puff, a clang, and a clatter of rails it was gone. "Chicago is getting to be a great town," he went on. "It's a wonder. You'll find lots to see here."

She did not hear this very well. Her heart was troubled by a kind of terror. The fact that she was alone, away from home, rushing into a great sea of life and endeavor, began to tell. She could not help but feel a little choked for breath—a little sick as her heart beat so fast. She half closed her eyes and tried to think it was nothing, that Columbia City was only a little way off.

"Chicago! Chicago!" called the brakeman, slamming open the door. They were rushing into a more crowded yard, alive with the clatter and clang of life. She began to gather up her poor little grip and closed her hand firmly upon her purse. Drouet arose, kicked his legs to straighten his trousers, and seized his clean yellow grip.

"I suppose your people will be here to meet you?" he said. "Let me carry your grip."

"Oh, no," she said. "I'd rather you wouldn't. I'd rather you wouldn't be with me when I meet my sister."

"All right," he said in all kindness. "I'll be near, though, in case she isn't here, and take you out there safely."

"You're so kind," said Carrie, feeling the goodness of such attention in her strange situation.

"Chicago!" called the brakeman, drawing the word out long. They were under a great shadowy train shed, where the lamps were already beginning to shine out, with passenger cars all about and the train moving at a snail's pace. The people in the car were all up and crowding about the door.

"Well, here we are," said Drouet, leading the way to the door. "Good-bye, till I see you Monday."

"Good-bye," she answered, taking his proffered hand.

"Remember, I'll be looking till you find your sister."

She smiled into his eyes.

They filed out, and he affected to take no notice of her. A lean-faced, rather commonplace woman recognized Carrie on the platform and hurried forward.

"Why, Sister Carrie!" she began, and there was embrace of welcome.

Carrie realized the change of affectional atmosphere at once. Amid all the maze, uproar, and novelty she felt cold reality taking her by the hand. No world of light and merriment. No round of amusement. Her sister carried with her most of the grimness of shift and toil.

"Why, how are all the folks at home?" she began; "how is father, and mother?"

Carrie answered, but was looking away. Down the aisle, toward the gate leading into the waiting-room and the street, stood Drouet. He was looking back. When he saw that she saw him and was safe with her sister he turned to go, sending back the shadow of a smile. Only Carrie saw it. She felt something lost to her when he moved away. When he disappeared she felt his absence thoroughly. With her sister she was much alone, a lone figure in a tossing, thoughtless sea.

Questions for Discussion

1. What are identified as instances of "forces" that determine Carrie's behaviors and choice-making? How does the description of the "forces" resemble Thomas Hardy's description of them in *Tess of the D'Urbervilles*?
2. *Sister Carrie* is narrated by intrusive narrator, which means an omniscient narrator who, in addition to reporting the events of the story, offers comments on characters and events. What do you think is the advantage of this narrative technique in relating this Naturalistic story?

Edwin Arlington Robinson (1869 – 1935)

Edwin Arlington Robinson is best noted for his brief "story and portrait" poems about his fictional New England "Tilbury Town" and its inhabitants. As a winner of three Pulitzer Prizes—the first came to him in 1922—he has been regarded as a major American poet.

Robinson was born in a tiny village in Maine and grew up in Gardiner, Maine, on which he modeled Tilbury Town. When he was a high school student, he practiced writing poetry and he continued to write during the two years he attended Harvard University. In 1893, financial problems forced him to leave college and return home. He did, however, manage to publish, at his own expense, two books of poems, *The Torrent and the Night Before* (1896) and *The Children of the Night* (1897).

At twenty-eight, Robinson moved to New York City, where he lived in semi-poverty and wrote without much of a readership. His life was made somewhat easier in 1902 when President Theodore Roosevelt, an admirer of his work, appointed him to a post in the New York Custom House. However, Robinson's first real success did not come until 1910, with the publication of *The Town Down the River*. In time he was awarded three Pulitzer Prizes and became the best American poet after the generation of Whitman and Dickinson, before Robert Frost and Ezra Pound came to the forefront of attention from American readers.

In technique and style, Robinson is a traditionalist, but he is daringly realistic in his subject matter. Most of his poems attempt to tell the "truth" about Tilbury Town. To a realist like Robinson, that truth mainly includes alienation, disillusionment, sadness, tragedy, frustration, and waste. The particular flavor of Robinson's best poems springs from his mixture of realism with humor and irony.

Richard Cory

Whenever Richard Cory went down town,
We people on the pavement looked at him:
He was a gentleman from sole to crown,

Clean favored,① and imperially slim.

5   And he was always quietly arrayed,
    And he was always human when he talked;
    But still he fluttered pulses when he said,
    "Good-morning," and he glittered when he walked.

    And he was rich—yes, richer than a king—
10 And admirably schooled in every grace:
    In fine, we thought that he was everything
    To make us wish that we were in his place.

    So on we worked, and waited for the light,
    And went without the meat, and cursed the bread;
15 And Richard Cory, one calm summer night,
    Went home and put a bullet through his head.

Questions for Discussion

1. Which line in the poem identifies the speaker? Which lines tell you about the economic condition of the speaker? How are "we" different from Richard Cory?
2. What do the people think of Richard Cory? What do "crown" and "imperially" indicate about the speaker's impression of Richard Cory?
3. What is the "surprise" ending? What effect does Cory's final action seem to have on everyone in the town? What does the townspeople's reaction to Cory's life and death suggest about human understanding?

---

① favored: having an appearance or features of a particular kind

Chapter 5

From 1914 to 1941
World War I and American Modernism

5.1 World War I and the "Modern Temper"

World War I, a conflict among European powers, began in 1914 and lasted four years. The United States kept out of the war until 1917, when it entered as an ally of England and France.

American participation in World War I marked a crucial stage in the nation's evolution to a world power. The brutality of the large-scale modern war in which tanks, machine guns, planes, and poison gas caused death and destruction on a scale unmatched before shocked and appalled people. It took no time for American artists and thinkers to realize that this cruel, modern worldwide war had nothing to do with imaginary heroism. American losses were not great in absolute terms (fewer men were killed than in the Civil War), and the majority of casualties had resulted from disease rather than in fighting, which never took place on American soil. Nevertheless, the sense of a great civilization being destroyed or destroying itself, the feeling of social breakdown, and the strong awareness of individual powerlessness, became part of the American experiences as a result of America's direct involvement in the war. Consequently, people in general had a feeling of fear, disorientation, and on occasion, liberation. They were certain that an old order had come to an end, but they were uncertain as to what might arise. This kind of mentality has been called the "modern temper," which was partly shaped by World War I.

The modern temper was also shaped by forces internal to the United States. Some of the forces such as urbanization, industrialization, and immigration had long been at work, but between the two World Wars the pace quickened. Technological advancement was another important force: new inventions and the use thereof at large changed the way people lived as well as the outlook people maintained. For instance, the telephone, the radio, motion pictures, and the widespread availability of books, newspapers, and magazines created a new kind of connectedness and a new kind of culture called mass culture. Of course, the most powerful technological influence came from the automobile, the "horseless carriage." Henry Ford's newly developed assembly-line techniques for producing automobiles enabled cars to become cheap enough for most Americans to own one, so that people could travel from place to place with a speed impossible before. Moreover, the car industry remarkably reshaped the structure of American industry and occupations, which altered America dramatically.

Alongside modern science and technology, the ideas of some great thinkers such as William James (1842 – 1910), Sigmund Freud (1856 – 1939), and Karl Marx produced a phenomenal impact on people. William James was American philosopher and psychologist, full brother of Henry James. He was often credited with the discovery of *the subconscious*, long before Sigmund Freud's seminal work on *the unconscious*. It is Henry James who first used the now-popular term *stream of consciousness*, which many eminent Modernist writers used in their works to capture the total flow of their characters' consciousness. Sigmund Freud invented the practice of psychoanalysis. According to Freud, the human mind is structured into two main parts: the conscious and unconscious mind. The Freudian theory shattered the old certainty that the "self" is a conscious, rational entity. This means that human beings' behaviors are not completely controlled by the conscious part of the mind, therefore, an individual is not the master of his own mind. Karl Marx believed that capitalism contained the seeds of its own destruction; that communism was the inevitable end to the process of evolution which began with feudalism and passed through capitalism and socialism; that the root of all behavior was economic and that the leading feature of economic life was the division of society into antagonistic classes based on a relation to the means of production; and that the ideas of any particular society represented the interests of its dominant class.

To sum up, life in the early 20th century seemed suddenly different. The modern mind found all the new knowledge exciting; it was bewildered by the conflicting philosophies and ways of life.

5.2　American Modernism

The literature produced under the influence of the modern temper is retrospectively called "Modernism" by literary critics. American Modernism was the phenomenon of international Modernism transplanted and transformed in the American context. For the first time in history, American writers, with Ezra Pound and T. S. Eliot in particular, served as leading driving-forces behind the international modernist Movement.

The word "Modernism" is derived from "modern," which principally means "new, different from what is traditional." This is a clear indication that Modernist literature was remarkably different compared with the writings of the previous eras.

Used in the broadest sense, the term "Modernism" is a catch-all phrase for any kind of literary production in the interwar period that deals with the modern world. More narrowly, it refers to work that represents the breakdown of traditional society under the pressures of modernity. In this sense, much Modernist literature is actually anti-modern, because it interprets modernity as an experience of loss.

5.3　American Interwar Literature

During the interwar years, American literature demonstrated the following major features.

The Integration of Modernism with American Subjects　American writers integrated Modernist ideas and methods with American subject matter. They chose to identify themselves with the American scene and to root their work in a specific region. In their works they treated their regions sometimes in a celebratory way, sometimes in a critical way. Edgar Lee

Masters (1868 – 1950), Sherwood Anderson (1876 – 1941), and Willa Cather (1873 – 1947) concerned themselves with the Midwest; Cather grounded her later work in the Southwest; John Steinbeck (1902 – 1968) wrote about California; Edwin Arlington Robinson and Robert Frost (1874 – 1963) identified their work with New England; William Faulkner (1897 – 1962) and Margaret Mitchell (1900 – 1949) wrote about the South. Some writers attempted to speak for the nation as a whole, as the title of John Dos Passos's *U.S.A.* clearly shows.

It is worth pointing out that the 1920s and 1930s saw the emergence of the Southern Renaissance, with William Faulkner being the most outstanding Southern writer. He is both an avant-garde Modernist and a writer of the agrarian American South. His complicated and vivid image of the south's past is at once a critique and celebration of the region's culture and historic legacies. He is best remembered as the creator of fictional cosmos "Yoknapatawpha County" in which his sequence of Modernist novels, *The Sound and the Fury* (1929), *As I Lay Dying* (1930), *Light in August* (1931) and *Absalom, Absalom*! (1936) are set. He was awarded the Noble Prize for Literature in 1949. Another noteworthy Southern writer was Margaret Mitchell, whose *Gone with the Wind* (1936) was the recipient of the 1937 Pulitzer Prize for fiction, which has been viewed as one of the best-known Southern novels.

The American Expatriates and the Lost Generation Many American writers of this period lived in Europe for part, if not all, of their lives. Gertrude Stein (1874 – 1946) moved to Paris in 1903 and made France her home for the remainder of her life; Ezra Pound went to London in 1908 and made his home in Italy after 1925; T.S. Eliot moved to England in 1914 and settled there permanently. These expatriates left the United States because they thought that their country lacked a tradition of high culture, and that they could not thrive artistically in their native land. As leading Modernists, they helped, encouraged, and influenced many other American expatriate writers of the time, including Robert Frost who spent years in Europe from 1912 to 1915, Ernest Hemingway (1899 – 1961) who was wounded in World War Ⅰ and stayed in Paris for years after the war, and F. Scott Fitzgerald

(1896 – 1940) who moved to Europe in 1924 and stayed there until 1931. Gertrude Stein has been said to have told the young Hemingway, "You are all a lost generation," and the term has thereafter been used again and again to label the people of the post-World-War- I years living in confusion and despair because of the war, especially the Americans who remained in Paris as a colony of expatriates. These so-called "Lost Generation" writers, including Ernest Hemingway, F. Scott Fitzgerald, John Dos Passos (1896 – 1970), and E. E. Cummings (1894 – 1962), went to Gertrude Stein's salon often. With no doubt, Hemingway was a typical representative of the Lost Generation writers. His *The Sun Also Rises* (1926) and *A Farewell to Arms* (1929) depict the sense of "loss." It is interesting to know that in Britain the term "lost generation" is applied to those Britons killed in World War I, especially those members of the officer class who often had showed promise in intellectual fields before the outbreak of the war.

Roaring Twenties: Jazz Age and the Harlem Renaissance Repulsed by the senseless slaughter of the war and perplexed by the new conditions, many Americans expressed a desperate, yet creative, hysteria in jazz rhythms, outrageous fashions, and careless motorcar driving. This accounts for why the 1920s has also been called "Roaring Twenties." The roaring of the decade served to mask a quiet pain. The spokesman of the Jazz Age is F. Scott Fitzgerald, whose *The Great Gatsby* (1925) masterfully depicts the roaring and the pain. The excitement ended in October, 1929 with the crashing of the New York stock market, which heralded a worldwide crash. Millions of Americans were unemployed; many more people lost their life savings.

The 1920s was also a decade in which African Americans made themselves a permanent part of the nation's cultural life. In 1915, as a direct result of the industrial needs of World War I, opportunities opened for African Americans in the factories of the North, therefore the so-called Great Migration out of the South began. In the 1920s African Americans who thronged to New York City's Harlem District turned Harlem into a vigorous and fertile center for black cultural activities. As W. E. B. Du Bois and others urged the expression of racial pride, black writers focused on their own lives, culture, and identity. The fresh and new subjects as well as skillful writing attracted publishers and readers to the works of many black writers, including Langston Hughes (1902 – 1967), Jean Toomer (1894 – 1967), Countee Cullen (1903 – 1946), and later, Zora Neale Hurston (1891 – 1960). However, with the economic depression of the 1930s, the Harlem Renaissance faded.

The Depression of the 1930s and the Proletarian Literature The 1930s saw Americans struggle to restore and restructure the nation's economy. Unfortunately, the dismal situation was made worse by the Dust Bowl drought in the Midwest. Depression era literature was blunt and direct in its social criticism. John Dos Passos, James T. Farrell (1904 – 1979), and John Steinbeck were the major writers highly active in this type of literature, with Steinbeck being the most eminent representative. He focused his attention on poor, working-class people who struggled against social and economic odds for a decent life. His masterpiece, *The Grapes of Wrath* (1939), won the Pulitzer Prize in 1940.

Ironically, the depression did not come to an end until World War II prompted a great expansion in industry. In a way, the outbreak of World War II was related to the worldwide Depression, because the social unrest it caused led to the rise of fascist dictators in Europe: Francisco Franco in Spain, Benito Mussolini in Italy, and Adolf Hitler in Germany. Hitler's program, which was to make Germany rich and strong by conquering the rest of Europe, led inexorably to World War II.

Ezra Pound (1885 – 1972)

Ezra Pound was one of the driving forces behind Modernist literature. He is especially remembered for his campaign for "Imagism," a name he coined for the new kind of poetry seeking clarity of expression through the use of precise images.

Born in a small town in Idaho, Pound grew up in a suburb of Philadelphia and attended the University of Pennsylvania. He wanted to become a poet when he was a college student, and this motivated his graduate studies in languages—French, Italian, Old English, and Latin—at the University of Pennsylvania, where he received his MA in 1906.

Convinced that his country had no place for him and that a country with no place for him had no place for art, at age 23 he left for Europe. In his view, the United States was a culturally backward nation, so he longed to produce a sophisticated, worldly poetry on behalf of his country. The result was his *The Cantos*, a vast, 800-page epic which Pound worked on for over fifty years from 1915.

In Europe he wrote poetry and criticism, and translated verse from different languages. He also served as an overseas editor for Chicago's *Poetry* magazine. He used this position to nurture the careers of many writers, such as Robert Frost and T. S. Eliot.

Primarily influenced by classical Chinese poetry and Japanese Haiku,① in 1912 Pound founded the literary movement of Imagism, which called for "direct treatment of the 'thing.'" Instead of having the poet tell us what we should be feeling, Pound wanted an image to produce the emotion, to "speak for itself."

"In a Station of the Metro" is a classic of Imagist poem, with "the Metro" referring to the Paris Subway. "The River-Merchant's Wife: A Letter" is his adaptation from Chinese Tang Dynasty poet Li Bai's poem "Song of Changgan."② Pound adapted Libai's poem from the papers of Ernest F. Fenollosa (1853 – 1908).③

In a Station of the Metro

The apparition of these faces in the crowd;
Petals on a wet, black bough.

The River-Merchant's Wife: A Letter

While my hair was still cut straight across my forehead

---

① Haiku: a type of Japanese unrhymed poem consisting of 17 syllables arranged in three lines of 5, 7, and 5 syllables respectively
② Song of Changgan:《长干行》
③ Ernest F. Fenollosa: American Orientalist and educator

I played about the front gate, pulling flowers.
You came by on bamboo stilts, playing horse,
You walked about my seat, playing with blue plums.
5   And we went on living in the village of Chōkan:
Two small people, without dislike or suspicion.

At fourteen I married My Lord you.
I never laughed, being bashful.
Lowering my head, I looked at the wall.
10 Called to, a thousand times, I never looked back.

At fifteen I stopped scowling,
I desired my dust to be mingled with yours
Forever and forever, and forever.
Why should I climb the look out?

15 At sixteen you departed,
You went into far Ku-tō-en, by the river of swirling eddies,
And you have been gone five months.
The monkeys make sorrowful noise overhead.

You dragged your feet when you went out.
20 By the gate now, the moss is grown, the different mosses,
Too deep to clear them away!
The leaves fall early this autumn, in wind.
The paired butterflies are already yellow with August
Over the grass in the West garden;
25 They hurt me.
I grow older.
If you are coming down through the narrows of the river Kiang,
Please let me know beforehand,
And I will come out to meet you
30 As far as Chō-fū-Sa.

Questions for Discussion

1. What two images are juxtaposed in "In a Station of the Metro"? Pound once wrote, "Painters realize that what matters is form and color. The image is the poet's pigment." In what way is this poem like a painting?
2. Compare Li Bai's original poem with Pound's "The River-Merchant's Wife: A Letter." Do you think Pound uses Imagist ideas well in his translation? If you translate the poem, how will you do the job differently?

Robert Frost (1874 – 1963)

Robert Frost, one of the most popular American poets of the 20th century, was a four-time winner of the Pulitzer Prize.

Although he identified himself with New England, Frost was born in San Francisco, California, and lived there until 11 years old, when his father died and his mother moved the family to New England, where she supported the family through teaching at school. Frost's mother wrote poetry, and it was his mother who introduced him to the works of the English Romantic writers, the New England Transcendentalists, and the poets of her native Scotland.

Frost attended Dartmouth College and Harvard during the 1890s without finishing studies in either one on account of his frustration with academic life. Preferring real-life experiences to academic learning, he thereafter worked as a mill hand, journalist, farmer, and schoolteacher.

At age 26, Frost moved to a farm in New Hampshire, where he got to know the rugged landscape and the inhabitants of rural New England. Between farm chores, he began his career as a poet. Unable to get his poems published, in 1912 Frost sold his farm and moved to England along with his wife and four children.

In London, Frost became acquainted with Ezra Pound and his

associates. Frost worked on his poetry and found a publisher for his first book, *A Boy's Will* (1913), which was reviewed favorably by Pound. Pound recommended Frost's poems to American editors and helped get his second book, *North of Boston*, published in 1914. *North of Boston* was widely praised by critics in both America and England, and the favorable reception persuaded Frost to return to America in 1915. He bought another farm in New Hampshire and prospered financially through sales of his books and papers, along with teaching and lecturing at various colleges. The success he enjoyed for the rest of his life, however, came too late to cancel the bitterness left by his earlier struggles. Moreover, he endured personal tragedy: a son committed suicide, and a daughter had a complete mental collapse.

Despite the debt of gratitude he owed Pound and other Modernists, Frost never subscribed to the tenets① of Modernism. Although he was certainly familiar with the ideas of William James and other modern psychologists, he was equally familiar with the works of Emerson, Thoreau, and other 19th century masters. His work abounds with the Romantic love of nature as well as a modern sense of irony. In his poems we find signs of Thoreau's love of isolation, we also find a hint of Hawthorne's dark vision; we find Longfellow's traditional craftsmanship and Dickinson's dry humor, we also find some realistic characterization.

The Road Not Taken

  Two roads diverged in a yellow wood,
  And sorry I could not travel both
  And be one traveler, long I stood
  And looked down one as far as I could
5 To where it bent in the undergrowth;②

  Then took the other, as just as fair,

---

①tenet: principle, belief
②undergrowth: shrubs or small trees under big trees in woodland

        And having perhaps the better claim,
        Because it was grassy and wanted wear;
        Though as for that the passing there
10   Had worn them really about the same,

        And both that morning equally lay
        In leaves no step had trodden black.
        Oh, I kept the first for another day!
        Yet knowing how way leads on to way,
15   I doubted if I should ever come back.

        I shall be telling this with a sigh
        Somewhere ages and ages hence:
        Two roads diverged in a wood, and I—
        I took the one less traveled by,
20   And that has made all the difference.

Nothing Gold Can Stay

        Nature's first green is gold,
        Her hardest hue to hold.
        Her early leaf's a flower;
        But only so an hour.
5   Then leaf subsides to leaf,
        So Eden sank to grief,
        So dawn goes down to day.
        Nothing gold can stay.

Fire and Ice

        Some say the world will end in fire,
        Some say in ice.
        From what I've tasted of desire
        I hold with those who favor fire.
5   But if it had to perish twice,

I think I know enough of hate
To say that for destruction ice
Is also great
And would suffice.

Questions for Discussion

1. In "The Road Not Taken," why does the speaker's mind stay focused on the road not taken? What are the clues that suggest that the road is more than a tangible road but rather "a road of life"? Have you ever encountered any dilemmas in your life? How did you make your final decision?
2. Do you agree with Robert Frost's point that nothing gold can stay? Why or why not?
3. In "Fire and Ice," what do the two emotions have in common? Explain the irony in the poem.

Ernest Hemingway (1899 – 1961)

Hemingway is one of the best known novelists in the world, the winner of Nobel Prize in 1954.

Hemingway's father was a successful physician enjoying hunting and fishing. Accordingly, Hemingway spent many of his boyhood summers hunting and fishing near his family's summer house, and it was then that he developed the masculine ideal reflected in much of his work. Outdoor adventures would remain a part of his life and his writing, with *The Old Man and the Sea* (1952) being the most obvious example.

After high school, Hemingway took a job on the newspaper named *Kansas City Star*. It was during the short time when Hemingway worked for the newspaper that he learned some stylistic lessons which would later influence his fiction. The newspaper advocated short sentences, short paragraphs, active verbs, authenticity, compression, clarity, and immediacy. "Those were the best rules I ever learned for the business of writing," Hemingway later said. "I've never forgotten them."

When the United States entered World War I in 1917, Hemingway was eager to fight. However, an eye problem barred him from the army. He ended up joining the ambulance corps of the Italian army and was wounded in battle. The war experience was traumatic; Hemingway returned to it in one way or another in all his later writing, with *A Farewell to Arms* being the most bespeaking example. It describes a romance between an American army officer, Frederick Henry, and a British nurse, Catherine Barkley. The two lovers run away from war, trying to make "a separate peace," but this idyll is shattered when Catherine dies in childbirth. This fiction well epitomizes the negative feelings following World War I: the meaninglessness of modern life, a sense of loss, disillusionment, grief, frustration, and despair. The anthologized section is from the last chapter of the novel.

After World War II, Hemingway made his home in Cuba, where he wrote *The Old Man and the Sea*, which is also presented in the anthology. *The Old Man and the Sea* appears to be about old fisherman Santiago's three-day fishing journey and his lonely and unremitting struggle with the sea, with the huge marlin fish he successfully catches, and with the sharks that swarm to bite off the meat of the marlin fish, which leave him nothing more than the skeleton of the catch. In reality, it is a powerful allegorical fable, demonstrating the old man's victory in defeat. The novella won a Pulitzer Prize in 1953 and was a major factor in Hemingway winning the Nobel Prize in 1954. It is important to note that in *The Old Man and the Sea*, Hemingway shifted his focus from human affairs to the vital contacts between humankind and other species, as well as the relationship between nature and living creatures.

In summary, Hemingway—himself a great sportsman—liked to portray soldiers, hunters, and bullfighters. He brought a hard-bitten realism into American fiction. His heroes live dangerously, by personal codes of honor, courage, and endurance. Hemingway's distinctively crisp, unadorned style left American literature permanently changed.

A Farewell to Arms

Chapter 41

(Excerpt)

...

"Where can I get breakfast?" I asked the nurse.

"There's a café down the street at the square," she said. "It should be open now."

Outside it was getting light. I walked down the empty street to the café. There was a light in the window. I went in and stood at the zinc bar and an old man served me a glass of white wine and a brioche. The brioche was yesterday's. I dipped it in the wine and then drank a glass of coffee.

"What do you do at this hour?" the old man asked.

"My wife is in labor at the hospital."

"So. I wish you good luck."

"Give me another glass of wine."

He poured it from the bottle slopping it over a little so some ran down on the zinc. I drank this glass, paid and went out. Outside along the street were the refuse cans from the houses waiting for the collector. A dog was nosing at one of the cans.

"What do you want?" I asked and looked in the can to see if there was anything I could pull out for him; there was nothing on top but coffee-grounds, dust and some dead flowers.

"There isn't anything, dog," I said. The dog crossed the street. I went up the stairs in the hospital to the floor Catherine was on and down the hall to her room. I knocked on the door. There was no answer. I opened the door; the room was empty, except for Catherine's bag on a chair and her dressing-gown hanging on a hook on the wall. I went out and down the hall, looking for somebody. I found a nurse....

I went out the door and down the hall to the room where Catherine was to be after the baby came. I sat in a chair there and looked at the room. I had the paper in my coat that I had bought when I went out for lunch and I read it. It was beginning to be dark outside and I turned the light on to read. After a while I stopped reading and turned off the light and watched it get dark outside. I wondered why the doctor did not send for me. Maybe it was better I was away. He probably wanted me away for a while. I looked at my watch. If he did not send for me in ten minutes I would go down anyway.

Poor, poor dear Cat. And this was the price you paid for sleeping together. This was the end of the trap. This was what people got for loving each other. Thank God for gas, anyway. What must it have been like before there were anesthetics. Once it started, they were in the mill-race. Catherine had a good time in the time of pregnancy. It wasn't bad. She was hardly ever sick. She was not awfully uncomfortable until toward the last. So now they got her in the end. You never got away with anything. Get away hell! It would have been the same if we had been married fifty times. And what if she should die? She won't die. People don't die in childbirth nowadays. That was what all husbands thought. Yes, but what if she should die? She won't die. She's just having a bad time. The initial labor is usually protracted. She's only having a bad time. Afterward we'd say what a bad time and Catherine would say it wasn't really so bad. But what if she should die? She can't die. Yes, but what if she should die? She can't, I tell you. Don't be a fool. It's just a bad time. It's just nature giving her hell. It's only the first labor, which is almost always protracted. Yes, but what if she should die? She can't die. Why would she die? What reason is there for her to die? There's just a child that has to be born, the by-product of good nights in Milan. It makes trouble and is born and then you look after it and get fond of it maybe. But what if she should die? She won't die. But what if she should die? She won't. She's all right. But what if she should die? She can't die. But what if she should die? Hey, what about that? What if she should die?

The doctor came into the room.

"How does it go, doctor?"

From 1914 to 1941 | Chapter 5

World War I and American Modernism

"It doesn't go," he said.

"What do you mean?"

"Just that. I made an examination—" He detailed the result of the examination. "Since then I've waited to see. But it doesn't go.". . .

I sat down on the chair in front of a table where there were nurses' reports hung on clips at the side and looked out of the window. I could see nothing but the dark and the rain falling across the light from the window. So that was it. The baby was dead. That was why the doctor looked so tired. But why had they acted the way they did in the room with him? They supposed he would come around and start breathing probably. I had no religion but I knew he ought to have been baptized. But what if he never breathed at all. He hadn't. He had never been alive. Except in Catherine. I'd felt him kick there often enough. But I hadn't for a week. Maybe he was choked all the time. Poor little kid. I wished the hell I'd been choked like that. No I didn't. Still there would not be all this dying to go through. Now Catherine would die. That was what you did. You died. You did not know what it was about. You never had time to learn. They threw you in and told you the rules and the first time they caught you off base they killed you. Or they killed you gratuitously like Aymo. Or gave you the syphilis like Rinaldi. But they killed you in the end. You could count on that. Stay around and they would kill you.

Once in camp I put a log on top of the fire and it was full of ants. As it commenced to burn, the ants swarmed out and went first toward the centre where the fire was; then turned back and ran toward the end. When there were enough on the end they fell off into the fire. Some got out, their bodies burnt and flattened, and went off not knowing where they were going. But most of them went toward the fire and then back toward the end and swarmed on the cool end and finally fell off into the fire. I remember thinking at the time that it was the end of the world and a splendid chance to be a messiah and lift the log off the fire and throw it out where the ants could get off onto the ground. But I did not do anything but throw a tin cup of water on the log, so that I would have the cup empty to put whiskey in before I added water to it. I think the cup of water on the burning log only steamed the ants.

So now I sat out in the hall and waited to hear how Catherine was. The nurse did not come out, so after a while I went to the door and opened it very softly and looked in. I could not see at first because there was a bright light in the hall and it was dark in the room. Then I saw the nurse sitting by the bed and Catherine's head on a pillow, and she was all flat under the sheet. The nurse put her finger to her lips, then stood up and came to the door.

"How is she?" I asked.

"She's all right," the nurse said. "You should go and have your supper and then come back if you wish."

I went down the hall and then down the stairs and out the door of the hospital and down the dark street in the rain to the café....

...Suddenly I knew I had to get back. I called the waiter, paid the reckoning, got into my coat, put on my hat and started out the door. I walked through the rain up to the hospital.

Upstairs I met the nurse coming down the hall.

"I just called you at the hotel," she said. Something dropped inside me.

"What is wrong?"

"Mrs. Henry has had a hemorrhage."[①]

"Can I go in?"

"No, not yet. The doctor is with her."

"Is it dangerous?"

"It is very dangerous." The nurse went into the room and shut the door. I sat outside in the hail. Everything was gone inside of me. I did not think. I could not think. I knew she was going to die and I prayed that she would not. Don't let her die. Oh, God, please don't let her die. I'll do anything for you if you won't let her die. Please, please, please, dear God, don't let her die. Dear God, don't let her die. Please, please, please don't

---

①hemorrhage: a rapid and heavy discharge of blood from the blood vessels let her die. God please make her not die. I'll do anything you say if you don't let her die. You took the baby but don't let her die. That was all right but don't let her die. Please, please, dear God, don't let her die.

The nurse opened the door and motioned with her finger for me to come. I followed her into the room. Catherine did not look up when I came in. I went over to the side of the bed. The doctor was standing by the bed on the opposite side. Catherine looked at me and smiled. I bent down over the bed and started to cry.

"Poor darling," Catherine said very softly. She looked gray.

"You're all right, Cat," I said. "You're going to be all right."

"I'm going to die," she said; then waited and said, "I hate it."

I took her hand.

"Don't touch me," she said. I let go of her hand. She smiled. "Poor darling. You touch me all you want."

"You'll be all right, Cat. I know you'll be all right."

"I meant to write you a letter to have if anything happened, but I didn't do it."

"Do you want me to get a priest or any one to come and see you?"

"Just you," she said. Then a little later, "I'm not afraid. I just hate it."

"You must not talk so much," the doctor said.

"All right," Catherine said.

"Do you want me to do anything, Cat? Can I get you anything?"

Catherine smiled, "No." Then a little later, "You won't do our things with another girl, or say the same things, will you?"

"Never."

"I want you to have girls, though."

"I don't want them."

"You are talking too much," the doctor said. "Mr. Henry must go out. He can come back again later. You are not going to die. You must not be silly."

"All right," Catherine said. "I'll come and stay with you nights," she said. It was very hard for her to talk.

"Please go out of the room," the doctor said. "You cannot talk."

Catherine winked at me, her face gray. "I'll be right outside," I said.

"Don't worry, darling," Catherine said. "I'm not a bit afraid. It's just a dirty trick."

"You dear, brave sweet."

I waited outside in the hall. I waited a long time. The nurse came to the door and came over to me. "I'm afraid Mrs. Henry is very ill," she said. "I'm afraid for her."

"Is she dead?"

"No, but she is unconscious."

It seems she had one hemorrhage after another. They couldn't stop it. I went into the room and stayed with Catherine until she died. She was unconscious all the time, and it did not take her very long to die.

Outside the room, in the hall, I spoke to the doctor, "Is there anything I can do to-night?"

"No. There is nothing to do. Can I take you to your hotel?"

"No, thank you. I am going to stay here a while."

"I know there is nothing to say. I cannot tell you—"

"No," I said. "There's nothing to say."

"Good-night," he said. "I cannot take you to your hotel?"

"No, thank you."

"It was the only thing to do," he said. "The operation proved—"

"I do not want to talk about it," I said.

"I would like to take you to your hotel."

"No, thank you."

He went down the hall. I went to the door of the room.

"You can't come in now," one of the nurses said.

"Yes I can," I said.

"You can't come in yet."

"You get out," I said. "The other one too."

But after I had got them out and shut the door and turned off the light it wasn't any good. It was like saying good-by to a statue. After a while I went out and left the hospital and walked back to the hotel in the rain.

Questions for Discussion

1. In this chapter, which is the closing chapter of the novel, two living creatures are mentioned alongside human beings: dog and ants. In what light are they depicted? What point is conveyed through the description?
2. What does the closing episode suggest about Henry's future? How can the fiction be justifiably called a work from the Lost Generation?

The Old Man and the Sea

(Excerpt)

He was an old man who fished alone in a skiff in the Gulf Stream and he had gone eighty-four days now without taking a fish. In the first forty days a boy had been with him. But after forty days without a fish the boy's parents had told him that the old man was now definitely and finally *salao*, which is the worst form of unlucky, and the boy had gone at their orders in another boat which caught three good fish the first week. It made the boy sad to see the old man come in each day with his skiff empty and he always went down to help him carry either the coiled lines or the gaff and harpoon and the sail that was furled around the mast. The sail was patched with flour sacks and, furled, it looked like the flag of permanent defeat.

The old man was thin and gaunt with deep wrinkles in the back of his neck. The brown blotches of the benevolent skin cancer the sun brings from its reflection on the tropic sea were on his cheeks. The blotches ran well down the sides of his face and his hands had the deep-creased scars from handling heavy fish on the cords. But none of these scars were fresh. They were as old as erosions in a fishless desert.

Everything about him was old except his eyes and they were the same color as the sea and were cheerful and undefeated.

"Santiago," the boy said to him as they climbed the bank from where the skiff was hauled up. "I could go with you again. We've made some money."

The old man had taught the boy to fish and the boy loved him.

"No," the old man said. "You're with a lucky boat. Stay with them."...

"Tomorrow is going to be a good day with this current," he said.

"Where are you going?" the boy asked.

"Far out to come in when the wind shifts. I want to be out before it is light."

"I'll try to get him to work far out," the boy said. "Then if you hook something truly big we can come to your aid."

"He does not like to work too far out."

"No," the boy said. "But I will see something that he cannot see such as a bird working and get him to come out after dolphin."

"Are his eyes that bad?"

"He is almost blind."

"It is strange," the old man said. "He never went turtle-ing. That is what kills the eyes."

"But you went turtle-ing for years off the Mosquito Coast and your eyes are good."

"I am a strange old man."

"But are you strong enough now for a truly big fish?"

"I think so. And there are many tricks."...

The sun rose thinly from the sea and the old man could see the other boats, low on the water and well in toward the shore, spread out across the current. Then the sun was brighter and the glare came on the water and then, as it rose clear, the flat sea sent it back at his eyes so that it hurt sharply and he rowed without looking into it. He looked down into the water and watched the lines that went straight down into the dark of the water. He kept them straighter than anyone did, so that at each level in the darkness of the stream there would be a bait waiting exactly where he wished it to be for any fish that swam there. Others let them drift with the current and sometimes they were at sixty fathoms when the fishermen thought they were at a hundred.

But, he thought, I keep them with precision. Only I have no luck any more. But who knows? Maybe today. Every day is a new day. It is better to be lucky. But I would rather be exact. Then when luck comes you are ready....

He had no mysticism about turtles although he had gone in turtle boats for many years. He was sorry for them all, even the great trunk backs that were as long as the skiff and weighed a ton. Most people are heartless about turtles because a turtle's heart will beat for hours after he has been cut up and butchered. But the old man thought, I have such a heart too and my feet and hands are like theirs. He ate the white eggs to give himself strength. He ate them all through May to be strong in September and October for the truly big fish....

"It was noon when I hooked him," he said. "And I have never seen him."

He had pushed his straw hat hard down on his head before he hooked the fish and it was cutting his forehead. He was thirsty too and he got down on his knees and, being careful not to jerk on the line, moved as far into the bow as he could get and reached the water bottle with one hand. He opened it and drank a little. Then he rested against the bow. He rested sitting on the un-stepped mast and sail and tried not to think but only to endure.

Then he looked behind him and saw that no land was visible. That makes no difference, he thought. I can always come in on the glow from Havana. There are two more hours before the sun sets and maybe he will come up before that. If he doesn't maybe he will come up with the moon. If he does not do that maybe he will come up with the sunrise. I have no cramps and I feel strong. It is he that has the hook in his mouth. But what a fish to pull like that. He must have his mouth shut tight on the wire. I wish I could see him. I wish I could see him only once to know what I have against me.

The fish never changed his course nor his direction all that night as far as the man could tell from watching the stars....

Then he said aloud, "I wish I had the boy. To help me and to see this."

No one should be alone in their old age, he thought. But it is unavoidable. I must remember to eat the tuna before he spoils in order to keep strong. Remember, no matter how little you want to, that you must eat him in the morning. Remember, he said to himself.

During the night two porpoises came around the boat and he could hear them rolling and blowing. He could tell the difference between the blowing noise the male made and the sighing blow of the female.

"They are good," he said. "They play and make jokes and love one another. They are our brothers like the flying fish."

Then he began to pity the great fish that he had hooked. Life is wonderful and strange and who knows how old he is, he thought. Never have I had such a strong fish nor one who acted so strangely. Perhaps he is too wise to jump. He could ruin me by jumping or by a wild rush. But perhaps he has been hooked many times before and he knows that this is how he should make his fight. He cannot know that it is only one man against him, nor that it is an old man. But what a great fish he is and what will he bring in the market if the flesh is good. He took the bait like a male and he pulls like a male and his fight has no panic in it. I wonder if he has any plans or if he is just as desperate as I am?

He remembered the time he had hooked one of a pair of marlin. The male fish always let the female fish feed first and the hooked fish, the female, made a wild, panic-stricken, despairing fight that soon exhausted her, and all the time the male had stayed with her, crossing the line and circling with her on the surface. He had stayed so close that the old man was afraid he would cut the line with his tail which was sharp as a scythe and almost of that size and shape. When the old man had gaffed her and clubbed her, holding the rapier bill with its sandpaper edge and dubbing her across the top of her head until her colour turned to a colour almost like the backing of mirrors, and then, with the boy's aid, hoisted her aboard, the male fish had stayed by the side of the boat. Then, while the old man was clearing the lines and preparing the harpoon, the male fish jumped high into the air beside the boat to see where the female was and then went down deep, his lavender wings, that were his pectoral fins, spread wide and all his wide lavender stripes showing. He was beautiful, the old man remembered, and he had stayed.

That was the saddest thing I ever saw with them, the old man thought. The boy was sad too and we begged her pardon and butchered her promptly.

"I wish the boy was here," he said aloud and settled himself against the rounded planks of the bow and felt the strength of the great fish through the line he held across his shoulders moving steadily toward whatever he had chosen.

When once, through my treachery, it had been necessary to him to make a choice, the old man thought.

His choice had been to stay in the deep dark water far out beyond all snares and traps and treacheries. My choice was to go there to find him beyond all people. Beyond all people in the world. Now we are joined together and have been since noon. And no one to help either one of us.

Perhaps I should not have been a fisherman, he thought. But that was the thing that I was born for. I must surely remember to eat the tuna after it gets light....

"He is two feet longer than the skiff," the old man said. The line was going out fast but steadily and the fish was not panicked. The old man was trying with both hands to keep the line just inside of breaking strength. He knew that if he could not slow the fish with a steady pressure the fish could take out all the line and break it.

He is a great fish and I must convince him, he thought. I must never let him learn his strength nor what he could do if he made his run. If I were him I would put in everything now and go until something broke. But, thank God, they are not as intelligent as we who kill them; although they are more noble and more able....

"...I must save all my strength now. Christ, I did not know he was so big."

"I'll kill him though," he said. "In all his greatness and his glory."

Although it is unjust, he thought. But I will show him what a man can do and what a man endures.

"I told the boy I was a strange old man," he said.

"Now is when I must prove it."

The thousand times that he had proved it meant nothing. Now he was proving it again. Each time was a new time and he never thought about the past when he was doing it.

I wish he'd sleep and I could sleep and dream about the lions, he thought. Why are the lions the main thing that is left? Don't think, old man, he said to himself, Rest gently now against the wood and think of nothing. He is working. Work as little as you can....

The sun and his steady movement of his fingers had uncramped his left hand now completely and he began to shift more of the strain to it and he shrugged the muscles of his back to shift the hurt of the cord a little.

"If you're not tired, fish," he said aloud, "you must be very strange."

He felt very tired now and he knew the night would come soon and he tried to think of other things. He thought of the Big Leagues, to him they were the Gran Ligas, and he knew that the Yankees of New York were playing the Tigres of Detroit.

This is the second day now that I do not know the result of the juegos, he thought. But I must have confidence and I must be worthy of the great DiMaggio who does all things perfectly even with the pain of the bone spur in his heel. What is a bone spur? he asked himself. Un espuela de hueso. We do not have them. Can it be as painful as the spur of a fighting cock in one's heel? I do not think I could endure that or the loss of the eye and of both eyes and continue to fight as the fighting cocks do. Man is not much beside the great birds and beasts. Still I would rather be that beast down there in the darkness of the sea.

"Unless sharks come," he said aloud. "If sharks come, God pity him and me."...

As the sun set he remembered, to give himself more confidence, the time in the tavern at Casablanca when he had played the hand game with the great negro from Cienfuegos who was the strongest man on the docks. They had gone one day and one night with their elbows on a chalk line on the table and their forearms straight up and their hands gripped tight. Each one was trying to force the other's hand down onto the table. There was much betting and people went in and out of the room under the kerosene lights and he had looked at the arm and hand of the negro and at the negro's face. They changed the referees every four hours after the first eight so that the referees could sleep. Blood came out from under the fingernails of both his and the negro's hands and they looked each other in the eye and at their hands and forearms and the bettors went in and out of the room and sat on high chairs against the wall and watched. The walls were painted bright blue and were of wood and the lamps threw their shadows against them. The negro's shadow was huge and it moved on the wall as the breeze moved the lamps.

 The odds would change back and forth all night and they fed the negro rum and lighted cigarettes for him.

 Then the negro, after the rum, would try for a tremendous effort and once he had the old man, who was not an old man then but was Santiago El Campeon, nearly three inches off balance. But the old man had raised his hand up to dead even again. He was sure then that he had the negro, who was a fine man and a great athlete, beaten. And at daylight when the bettors were asking that it be called a draw[①] and the referee was shaking his head, he had unleashed his effort and forced the hand of the negro down and down until it rested on the wood. The match had started on a Sunday morning and ended on a Monday morning. Many of the bettors had asked for a draw because they had to go to work on the docks loading sacks of sugar or at the Havana Coal Company. Otherwise everyone would have wanted it to go to a finish. But he had finished it anyway and before anyone had to go to work.

 For a long time after that everyone had called him The Champion and there had been a return match in the spring. But not much money was bet and he had won it quite easily since he had broken the confidence of the negro from Cienfuegos in the first match. After that he had a few matches and then no more. He decided that he could beat anyone if he wanted to badly enough...

---

①draw: a contest left undecided or deadlocked

It was dark now as it becomes dark quickly after the sun sets in September. He lay against the worn wood of the bow and rested all that he could. The first stars were out. He did not know the name of Rigel but he saw it and knew soon they would all be out and he would have all his distant friends. "The fish is my friend too," he said aloud. "I have never seen or heard of such a fish. But I must kill him. I am glad we do not have to try to kill the stars."

Imagine if each day a man must try to kill the moon, he thought. The moon runs away. But imagine if a man each day should have to try to kill the sun? We were born lucky, he thought.

Then he was sorry for the great fish that had nothing to eat and his determination to kill him never relaxed in his sorrow for him. How many people will he feed, he thought. But are they worthy to eat him? No, of course not. There is no one worthy of eating him from the manner of his behaviour and his great dignity.

I do not understand these things, he thought. But it is good that we do not have to try to kill the sun or the moon or the stars. It is enough to live on the sea and kill our true brothers....

For an hour the old man had been seeing black spots before his eyes and the sweat salted his eyes and salted the cut over his eye and on his forehead. He was not afraid of the black spots. They were normal at the tension that he was pulling on the line. Twice, though, he had felt faint and dizzy and that had worried him.

"I could not fail myself and die on a fish like this," he said. "Now that I have him coming so beautifully, God help me endure. I'll say a hundred Our Fathers and a hundred Hail Marys. But I cannot say them now."

Consider them said, he thought. I'll say them later. Just then he felt a sudden banging and jerking on the line he held with his two hands. It was sharp and hard-feeling and heavy....

He felt faint again now but he held on the great fish all the strain that he could. I moved him, he thought. Maybe this time I can get him over. Pull, hands, he thought. Hold up, legs. Last for me, head. Last for me. You never went. This time I'll pull him over.

But when he put all of his effort on, starting it well out before the fish came alongside and pulling with all his strength, the fish pulled part way over and then righted himself and swam away.

"Fish," the old man said. "Fish, you are going to have to die anyway. Do you have to kill me too?"

That way nothing is accomplished, he thought. His mouth was too dry to speak but he could not reach for the water now. I must get him alongside this time, he thought. I am not good for many more turns. Yes you are, he told himself. You're good for ever.

On the next turn, he nearly had him. But again the fish righted himself and swam slowly away.

You are killing me, fish, the old man thought. But you have a right to. Never have I seen a greater, or more beautiful, or a calmer or more noble thing than you, brother. Come on and kill me. I do not care who kills who.

Now you are getting confused in the head, he thought. You must keep your head clear. Keep your head clear and know how to suffer like a man. Or a fish, he thought.

"Clear up, head," he said in a voice he could hardly hear. "Clear up."

Twice more it was the same on the turns.

I do not know, the old man thought. He had been on the point of feeling himself go each time. I do not know. But I will try it once more.

He tried it once more and he felt himself going when he turned the fish. The fish righted himself and swam off again slowly with the great tail weaving in the air.

I'll try it again, the old man promised, although his hands were mushy now and he could only see well in flashes. . . .

Then the fish came alive, with his death in him, and rose high out of the water showing all his great length and width and all his power and his beauty. He seemed to hang in the air above the old man in the skiff. Then he fell into the water with a crash that sent spray over the old man and over all of the skiff.

The old man felt faint and sick and he could not see well. But he cleared the harpoon line and let it run slowly through his raw hands and, when he could see, he saw the fish was on his back with his silver belly up. The shaft of the harpoon was projecting at an angle from the fish's shoulder and the sea was discoloring with the red of the blood from his heart. First it was dark as a shoal in the blue water that was more than a mile deep. Then it spread like a cloud. The fish was silvery and still and floated with the waves.

The old man looked carefully in the glimpse of vision that he had. Then he took two turns of the harpoon line around the bitt in the bow and hid his head on his hands.

"Keep my head clear," he said against the wood of the bow. "I am a tired old man. But I have killed this fish which is my brother and now I must do the slave work."...

... Now he knew there was the fish and his hands and back were no dream. The hands cure quickly, he thought. I bled them clean and the salt water will heal them. The dark water of the true gulf is the greatest healer that there is. All I must do is keep the head clear. The hands have done their work and we sail well. With his mouth shut and his tail straight up and down we sail like brothers. Then his head started to become a little unclear and he thought, is he bringing me in or am I bringing him in? If I were towing him behind there would be no question. Nor if the fish were in the skiff, with all dignity gone, there would be no question either. But they were sailing together lashed side by side and the old man thought, let him bring me in if it pleases him. I am only better than him through trickery and he meant me no harm.

They sailed well and the old man soaked his hands in the salt water and tried to keep his head clear. There were high cumulus clouds and enough cirrus above them so that the old man knew the breeze would last all night. The old man looked at the fish constantly to make sure it was true. It was an hour before the first shark hit him.

The shark was not an accident. He had come up from deep down in the water as the dark cloud of blood had settled and dispersed in the mile deep sea. He had come up so fast and absolutely without caution that he broke the surface of the blue water and was in the sun. Then he fell back into the

From 1914 to 1941 | Chapter 5
World War I and American Modernism

sea and picked up the scent and started swimming on the course the skiff and the fish had taken.

Sometimes he lost the scent. But he would pick it up again, or have just a trace of it, and he swam fast and hard on the course. He was a very big Make shark built to swim as fast as the fastest fish in the sea and everything about him was beautiful except his jaws.... This was a fish built to feed on all the fishes in the sea, that were so fast and strong and well armed that they had no other enemy. Now he speeded up as he smelled the fresher scent and his blue dorsal fin cut the water.

When the old man saw him coming he knew that this was a shark that had no fear at all and would do exactly what he wished. He prepared the harpoon and made the rope fast while he watched the shark come on. The rope was short as it lacked what he had cut away to lash the fish.

The old man's head was clear and good now and he was full of resolution but he had little hope. It was too good to last, he thought. He took one look at the great fish as he watched the shark close in. It might as well have been a dream, he thought. I cannot keep him from hitting me but maybe I can get him. *Dentuso*, he thought. Bad luck to your mother .... He hit it with his blood mushed hands driving a good harpoon with all his strength. He hit it without hope but with resolution and complete malignancy....

When he sailed into the little harbour the lights of the Terrace were out and he knew everyone was in bed. The breeze had risen steadily and was blowing strongly now. It was quiet in the harbour though and he sailed up onto the little patch of shingle below the rocks. There was no one to help him so he pulled the boat up as far as he could. Then he stepped out and made her fast to a rock.

He unstepped the mast and furled the sail and tied it. Then he shouldered the mast and started to climb. It was then he knew the depth of his tiredness. He stopped for a moment and looked back and saw in the reflection from the street light the great tail of the fish standing up well behind the skiff's stern. He saw the white naked line of his backbone and the dark mass of the head with the projecting bill and all the nakedness between.

　　He started to climb again and at the top he fell and lay for some time with the mast across his shoulder. He tried to get up. But it was too difficult and he sat there with the mast on his shoulder and looked at the road. A cat passed on the far side going about its business and the old man watched it. Then he just watched the road.

　　Finally he put the mast down and stood up. He picked the mast up and put it on his shoulder and started up the road. He had to sit down five times before he reached his shack.

　　Inside the shack he leaned the mast against the wall. In the dark he found a water bottle and took a drink. Then he lay down on the bed. He pulled the blanket over his shoulders and then over his back and legs and he slept face down on the newspapers with his arms out straight and the palms of his hands up....

　　Finally the old man woke.

　　"Don't sit up," the boy said. "Drink this." He poured some of the coffee in a glass.

　　The old man took it and drank it.

　　"They beat me, Manolin," he said. "They truly beat me."

　　"He didn't beat you. Not the fish."

　　"No. Truly. It was afterwards."...

　　"The ocean is very big and a skiff is small and hard to see," the old man said. He noticed how pleasant it was to have someone to talk to instead of speaking only to himself and to the sea. "I missed you," he said.

　　"What did you catch?"

　　"One the first day. One the second and two the third."

　　"Very good."

　　"Now we fish together again."

　　"No. I am not lucky. I am not lucky anymore."

　　"The hell with luck," the boy said. "I'll bring the luck with me."

　　"What will your family say?"

　　"I do not care. I caught two yesterday. But we will fish together now for I still have much to learn."

"We must get a good killing lance and always have it on board. You can make the blade from a spring leaf from an old Ford. We can grind it in Guanabacoa. It should be sharp and not tempered so it will break. My knife broke."...

"You must get well fast for there is much that I can learn and you can teach me everything. How much did you suffer?"

"Plenty," the old man said.

"I'll bring the food and the papers," the boy said. "Rest well, old man. I will bring stuff from the drugstore for your hands."

"Don't forget to tell Pedrico the head is his."

"No. I will remember."

As the boy went out the door and down the worn coral rock road he was crying again....

Up the road, in his shack, the old man was sleeping again. He was still sleeping on his face and the boy was sitting by him watching him. The old man was dreaming about the lions.

Questions for Discussion

1. This novella is written as one text without breaks. In what way does this suit the text?
2. Is the old man loveable? What are his loveable qualities? What about this book moves you the most?
3. What's Hemingway's view of man? What's man's place in nature?

F. Scott Fitzgerald (1896 – 1940)

Though F. Scott Fitzgerald's life ran roughly parallel to the first four decades of the 20th century, it is with the 1920s that his reputation as a novelist is associated: he has been called "the Spokesman of the Roaring Twenties."

Fitzgerald was born into a family of little wealth but great social ambitions in St. Paul, Minnesota. He attended but never graduated from Princeton University. There he mingled with the moneyed classes from the East Coast, and he was greatly obsessed with them the remainder of his life.

In 1917 he enlisted in the army, but the Great War ended before he saw active service. While he was stationed in Alabama in 1918, he met and courted Zelda Zayre, a daughter of an Alabama Supreme Court judge. Due to his lack of promising career prospects and financial stability, he was rejected by Zelda. In 1919 he went to New York City, determined to make a fortune and win Zelda. His wish became true when his first novel *This Side of Paradise* (1920), a novel about college life came out and became an instant success. A week after the novel's publication, Scott and Zelda were married and together they embarked on a life of luxury and endless parties. They spent more than Fitzgerald made from the publication of his writings: *Flappers and Philosophers* (1921), *Tales of the Jazz Age* (1922), and *The Beautiful and Damned* (1922).

In 1924, the Fitzgeralds moved to Europe to live less expensively. They lived in Paris in the American expatriate community which included Gertrude Stein, Ezra Pound, and Ernest Hemingway, to name but a few. During this period Fitzgerald published his most successful novel *The Great Gatsby* (1925) and another book of short stories, *All the Sad Young Men* (1926). He wrote diligently, nevertheless the Fitzgeralds could not get out of debt. He became an alcoholic. Zelda broke down in 1930 and spent most of her remaining years in mental institutions.

In 1931 Fitzgerald returned to the United States, and in 1934 he published *Tender is the Night*, a novel following the decline of a young American psychiatrist whose personal energies are sapped and his career corroded by his marriage and his own weakness of character. As in *The Great Gatsby*, the protagonist begins as a disciple of the work ethic but turns into a pursuer of wealth, thus the American Dream becomes a nightmare. In 1937, a bad need for money drove Fitzgerald to Hollywood screenwriting and in 1939 he began writing a novel about Hollywood, describing the story of a studio executive who works obsessively and loses control of the studio and his life. Fitzgerald died of a heart attack in 1940 before he could complete the book.

Among all his novels and short stories, Fitzgerald is best known for *The Great Gatsby*, his masterpiece that captures the Jazz Age as only an insider could capture it. The story is set in New York City during the 1920s. Nick Carraway, the narrator, is a young Princeton man who works as a bond broker in Manhattan. He gets involved in the life of his rich and shady neighbor at Long Island, Jay Gatsby, who is entertaining hundreds of guests at lavish parties. Gatsby reveals to Nick that he and Nick's cousin Daisy Buchanan had a brief affair before the war; however, during the war Daisy married Tom Buchanan, who literally bought her love. Gatsby claims that he is still in love with her. He persuades Nick to bring him and Daisy together again. "You can't repeat the past," Nick says to Gatsby. Gatsby tries to convince Daisy to leave Tom, who, in turn, reveals that Gatsby has made his money from bootlegging. "They're a rotten crowd," Nick shouts to Gatsby. "You're worth the whole damn bunch put together." Daisy, while driving Gatsby's car, hits and kills Tom's mistress Myrtle Wilson without knowing her identity. Gatsby remains silent to protect Daisy, but Tom tells Myrtle's husband that it was Gatsby who killed his wife. Wilson murders Gatsby and then commits suicide. Nick is left to arrange Gatsby's funeral, attended only by Gatsby's father and one former guest in addition to Gatsby's home servants.

The above is the story the fiction tells. However, the way the story is narrated is far more meaningful. Nick is both moved and repelled by the tale he tells, and his attitude towards Gatsby is both sympathetic and critical. The fiction can be called a complex study of the American dream embodied by the young Gatsby, who is inspired and disillusioned by the sense of hope America promises to its youth but fails to deliver. It is Gatsby's idealist but doomed pursuit of a woman and the American dream.

The fiction has nine chapters and the anthologized text is from Chapter 3 and Chapter 9.

The Great Gatsby
Chapter 3
(Excerpt)

...As soon as I arrived I made an attempt to find my host but the two or three people of whom I asked his whereabouts stared at me in such an amazed way and denied so vehemently any knowledge of his movements that I slunk off in the direction of the cocktail table—the only place in the garden where a single man could linger without looking purposeless and alone.

I was on my way to get roaring drunk from sheer embarrassment when Jordan Baker[①] came out of the house and stood at the head of the marble steps, leaning a little backward and looking with contemptuous interest down into the garden.

Welcome or not, I found it necessary to attach myself to someone before I should begin to address cordial remarks to the passers-by.

"Hello!" I roared, advancing toward her. My voice seemed unnaturally loud across the garden.

"I thought you might be here," she responded absently as I came up. "I remembered you lived next door to—"

She held my hand impersonally, as a promise that she'd take care of me in a minute, and gave ear to two girls in twin yellow dresses who stopped at the foot of the steps.

"Hello!" they cried together. "Sorry you didn't win."

That was for the golf tournament. She had lost in the finals the week before.

"You don't know who we are," said one of the girls in yellow, "but we met you here about a month ago."

"You've dyed your hair since then," remarked Jordan, and I started but the girls had moved casually on and her remark was addressed to the premature moon, produced like the supper, no doubt, out of a caterer's

---

①Jordan Baker: a close friend of Daisy's

basket. With Jordan's slender golden arm resting in mine we descended the steps and sauntered about the garden. A tray of cocktails floated at us through the twilight and we sat down at a table with the two girls in yellow and three men, each one introduced to us as Mr. Mumble.

"Do you come to these parties often?" inquired Jordan of the girl beside her.

"The last one was the one I met you at," answered the girl, in an alert, confident voice. She turned to her companion: "Wasn't it for you, Lucille?"

It was for Lucille, too.

"I like to come," Lucille said. "I never care what I do, so I always have a good time. When I was here last I tore my gown on a chair, and he asked me my name and address—inside of a week I got a package from Croirier's with a new evening gown in it."

"Did you keep it?" asked Jordan.

"Sure I did. I was going to wear it tonight, but it was too big in the bust and had to be altered. It was gas blue with lavender beads. Two hundred and sixty-five dollars."

"There's something funny about a fellow that'll do a thing like that," said the other girl eagerly. "He doesn't want any trouble with ANYbody."

"Who doesn't?" I inquired.

"Gatsby. Somebody told me—"

The two girls and Jordan leaned together confidentially.

"Somebody told me they thought he killed a man once."

A thrill passed over all of us. The three Mr. Mumbles bent forward and listened eagerly.

"I don't think it's so much THAT," argued Lucille skeptically; "it's more that he was a German spy during the war."

One of the men nodded in confirmation.

"I heard that from a man who knew all about him, grew up with him in Germany," he assured us positively.

"Oh, no," said the first girl, "it couldn't be that, because he was in the American army during the war." As our credulity switched back to her she leaned forward with enthusiasm. "You look at him sometimes when he thinks nobody's looking at him. I'll bet he killed a man."

She narrowed her eyes and shivered. Lucille shivered. We all turned and looked around for Gatsby. It was testimony to the romantic speculation he inspired that there were whispers about him from those who found little that it was necessary to whisper about in this world.

The first supper—there would be another one after midnight—was now being served, and Jordan invited me to join her own party who were spread around a table on the other side of the garden. There were three married couples and Jordan's escort, a persistent undergraduate given to violent innuendo and obviously under the impression that sooner or later Jordan was going to yield him up her person to a greater or lesser degree. Instead of rambling this party had preserved a dignified homogeneity, and assumed to itself the function of representing the staid nobility of the countryside—East Egg condescending to West Egg, and carefully on guard against its spectroscopic gayety.

"Let's get out," whispered Jordan, after a somehow wasteful and inappropriate half hour. "This is much too polite for me."

We got up, and she explained that we were going to find the host—I had never met him, she said, and it was making me uneasy. The undergraduate nodded in a cynical, melancholy way.

The bar, where we glanced first, was crowded but Gatsby was not there.

She couldn't find him from the top of the steps, and he wasn't on the veranda. On a chance we tried an important-looking door, and walked into a high Gothic library, panelled with carved English oak, and probably transported complete from some ruin overseas.

A stout, middle-aged man with enormous owl-eyed spectacles was sitting somewhat drunk on the edge of a great table, staring with unsteady concentration at the shelves of books. As we entered he wheeled excitedly around and examined Jordan from head to foot.

"What do you think?" he demanded impetuously.

"About what?"

He waved his hand toward the book-shelves.

"About that. As a matter of fact you needn't bother to ascertain. I ascertained. They're real."

"The books?"

He nodded.

"Absolutely real—have pages and everything. I thought they'd be a nice durable cardboard. Matter of fact, they're absolutely real. Pages and— Here! Lemme show you."

Taking our skepticism for granted, he rushed to the bookcases and returned with Volume One of the "Stoddard Lectures."

"See!" he cried triumphantly. "It's a bona fide piece of printed matter. It fooled me. This fella's a regular Belasco. It's a triumph. What thoroughness! What realism! Knew when to stop too—didn't cut the pages. But what do you want? What do you expect?"

He snatched the book from me and replaced it hastily on its shelf muttering that if one brick was removed the whole library was liable to collapse.

"Who brought you?" he demanded. "Or did you just come? I was brought. Most people were brought."

Jordan looked at him alertly, cheerfully without answering.

"I was brought by a woman named Roosevelt," he continued. "Mrs. Claud Roosevelt. Do you know her? I met her somewhere last night. I've been drunk for about a week now, and I thought it might sober me up to sit in a library."

"Has it?"

"A little bit, I think. I can't tell yet. I've only been here an hour. Did I tell you about the books? They're real. They're—"

"You told us."

We shook hands with him gravely and went back outdoors.

There was dancing now on the canvas in the garden, old men pushing young girls backward in eternal graceless circles, superior couples holding each other tortuously, fashionably and keeping in the corners—and a great number of single girls dancing individualistically or relieving the orchestra for a moment of the burden of the banjo or the traps. By midnight the hilarity had increased. A celebrated tenor had sung in Italian and a notorious contralto had sung in jazz and between the numbers people were doing "stunts" all over the garden, while happy vacuous bursts of laughter rose toward the summer sky. A pair of stage "twins"—who turned out to be the girls in yellow—did a baby act in costume and champagne was served in glasses bigger than finger bowls.

The moon had risen higher, and floating in the Sound① was a triangle of silver scales, trembling a little to the stiff, tinny drip of the banjoes on the lawn.

I was still with Jordan Baker. We were sitting at a table with a man of about my age and a rowdy little girl who gave way upon the slightest provocation to uncontrollable laughter. I was enjoying myself now. I had taken two finger bowls of champagne and the scene had changed before my eyes into something significant, elemental and profound.

At a lull in the entertainment the man looked at me and smiled.

"Your face is familiar," he said, politely. "Weren't you in the Third Division during the war?"

"Why, yes. I was in the Ninth Machine-Gun Battalion."

"I was in the Seventh Infantry until June nineteen-eighteen. I knew I'd seen you somewhere before."

We talked for a moment about some wet, grey little villages in France.

Evidently he lived in this vicinity for he told me that he had just bought a hydroplane and was going to try it out in the morning.

"Want to go with me, old sport? Just near the shore along the Sound."

"What time?"

"Any time that suits you best."

It was on the tip of my tongue to ask his name when Jordan looked around and smiled.

"Having a gay time now?" she inquired.

---

①the Sound: the Sound refers to the Long Island Sound, which is a semi-enclosed arm of the North Atlantic Ocean, lying between the New York – Connecticut shore to the north and Long Island to the south.

"Much better." I turned again to my new acquaintance. "This is an unusual party for me. I haven't even seen the host. I live over there—" I waved my hand at the invisible hedge in the distance, "and this man Gatsby sent over his chauffeur with an invitation."

For a moment he looked at me as if he failed to understand.

"I'm Gatsby," he said suddenly.

"What!" I exclaimed. "Oh, I beg your pardon."

"I thought you knew, old sport. I'm afraid I'm not a very good host."

He smiled understandingly—much more than understandingly. It was one of those rare smiles with a quality of eternal reassurance in it, that you may come across four or five times in life. It faced—or seemed to face—the whole external world for an instant, and then concentrated on YOU with an irresistible prejudice in your favor. It understood you just so far as you wanted to be understood, believed in you as you would like to believe in yourself and assured you that it had precisely the impression of you that, at your best, you hoped to convey. Precisely at that point it vanished—and I was looking at an elegant young rough-neck, a year or two over thirty, whose elaborate formality of speech just missed being absurd. Some time before he introduced himself I'd got a strong impression that he was picking his words with care.

Almost at the moment when Mr. Gatsby identified himself a butler hurried toward him with the information that Chicago was calling him on the wire. He excused himself with a small bow that included each of us in turn.

"If you want anything just ask for it, old sport," he urged me. "Excuse me. I will rejoin you later."

When he was gone I turned immediately to Jordan—constrained to assure her of my surprise. I had expected that Mr. Gatsby would be a florid and corpulent person in his middle years.

"Who is he?" I demanded. "Do you know?"

"He's just a man named Gatsby."

"Where is he from, I mean? And what does he do?"

"Now YOU're started on the subject," she answered with a wan smile.

"Well,—he told me once he was an Oxford man."

A dim background started to take shape behind him but at her next remark it faded away.

"However, I don't believe it."

"Why not?"

"I don't know," she insisted, "I just don't think he went there."

Something in her tone reminded me of the other girl's "I think he killed a man," and had the effect of stimulating my curiosity. I would have accepted without question the information that Gatsby sprang from the swamps of Louisiana or from the lower East Side of New York. That was comprehensible. But young men didn't—at least in my provincial inexperience I believed they didn't—drift coolly out of nowhere and buy a palace on Long Island Sound.

"Anyhow he gives large parties," said Jordan, changing the subject with an urbane distaste for the concrete. "And I like large parties. They're so intimate. At small parties there isn't any privacy.". . .

Rather ashamed that on my first appearance I had stayed so late, I joined the last of Gatsby's guests who were clustered around him. I wanted to explain that I'd hunted for him early in the evening and to apologize for not having known him in the garden.

"Don't mention it," he enjoined me eagerly. "Don't give it another thought, old sport." The familiar expression held no more familiarity than the hand which reassuringly brushed my shoulder. "And don't forget we're going up in the hydroplane tomorrow morning at nine o'clock."

Then the butler, behind his shoulder: "Philadelphia wants you on the phone, sir."

"All right, in a minute. Tell them I'll be right there. . . . good night."

"Good night."

"Good night." He smiled—and suddenly there seemed to be a pleasant significance in having been among the last to go, as if he had desired it all the time. "Good night, old sport. . . . Good night."

But as I walked down the steps I saw that the evening was not quite over. Fifty feet from the door a dozen headlights illuminated a bizarre and tumultuous scene. In the ditch beside the road, right side up but violently shorn of one wheel, rested a new coupé which had left Gatsby's drive not two minutes before. The sharp jut of a wall accounted for the detachment of the wheel which was now getting considerable attention from half a dozen curious chauffeurs. However, as they had left their cars blocking the road a harsh discordant din from those in the rear had been audible for some time and added to the already violent confusion of the scene.

A man in a long duster① had dismounted from the wreck and now stood in the middle of the road, looking from the car to the tire and from the tire to the observers in a pleasant, puzzled way.

"See!" he explained. "It went in the ditch."

The fact was infinitely astonishing to him—and I recognized first the unusual quality of wonder and then the man—it was the late patron of Gatsby's library.

"How'd it happen?"

He shrugged his shoulders.

"I know nothing whatever about mechanics," he said decisively.

"But how did it happen? Did you run into the wall?"

"Don't ask me," said Owl Eyes, washing his hands of the whole matter.

"I know very little about driving—next to nothing. It happened, and that's all I know."

"Well, if you're a poor driver you oughtn't to try driving at night."

"But I wasn't even trying," he explained indignantly, "I wasn't even trying."

An awed hush fell upon the bystanders.

"Do you want to commit suicide?"

"You're lucky it was just a wheel! A bad driver and not even TRYing!"

"You don't understand," explained the criminal. "I wasn't driving. There's another man in the car."

The shock that followed this declaration found voice in a sustained "Ah-

---

① duster: a long lightweight overgarment to protect clothing from dust

h-h!" as the door of the coupé swung slowly open. The crowd—it was now a crowd—stepped back involuntarily and when the door had opened wide there was a ghostly pause. Then, very gradually, part by part, a pale dangling individual stepped out of the wreck, pawing tentatively at the ground with a large uncertain dancing shoe.

Blinded by the glare of the headlights and confused by the incessant groaning of the horns the apparition stood swaying for a moment before he perceived the man in the duster.

"Wha's matter?" he inquired calmly. "Did we run outa gas?"

"Look!"

Half a dozen fingers pointed at the amputated wheel—he stared at it for a moment and then looked upward as though he suspected that it had dropped from the sky.

"It came off," some one explained.

He nodded.

"At first I din' notice we'd stopped."

A pause. Then, taking a long breath and straightening his shoulders he remarked in a determined voice:

"Wonder'ff tell me where there's a gas'line station?"

At least a dozen men, some of them little better off than he was, explained to him that wheel and car were no longer joined by any physical bond.

"Back out," he suggested after a moment. "Put her in reverse."

"But the WHEEL'S off!"

He hesitated.

"No harm in trying," he said.

The caterwauling① horns had reached a crescendo and I turned away and cut across the lawn toward home. I glanced back once. A wafer of a moon was shining over Gatsby's house, making the night fine as before and surviving the laughter and the sound of his still glowing garden. A sudden emptiness seemed to flow now from the windows and the great doors,

---

①caterwauling: shrieking

endowing with complete isolation the figure of the host who stood on the porch, his hand up in a formal gesture of farewell.

Reading over what I have written so far I see I have given the impression that the events of three nights several weeks apart were all that absorbed me. On the contrary they were merely casual events in a crowded summer and, until much later, they absorbed me infinitely less than my personal affairs....

For a while I lost sight of Jordan Baker, and then in midsummer I found her again. At first I was flattered to go places with her because she was a golf champion and every one knew her name. Then it was something more. I wasn't actually in love, but I felt a sort of tender curiosity. The bored haughty face that she turned to the world concealed something—most affectations conceal something eventually, even though they don't in the beginning—and one day I found what it was. When we were on a house-party together up in Warwick, she left a borrowed car out in the rain with the top down, and then lied about it—and suddenly I remembered the story about her that had eluded me that night at Daisy's. At her first big golf tournament there was a row that nearly reached the newspapers—a suggestion that she had moved her ball from a bad lie in the semi-final round. The thing approached the proportions of a scandal—then died away. A caddy retracted his statement and the only other witness admitted that he might have been mistaken. The incident and the name had remained together in my mind.

Jordan Baker instinctively avoided clever shrewd men and now I saw that this was because she felt safer on a plane where any divergence from a code would be thought impossible. She was incurably dishonest.

She wasn't able to endure being at a disadvantage, and given this unwillingness I suppose she had begun dealing in subterfuges① when she was very young in order to keep that cool, insolent smile turned to the world and yet satisfy the demands of her hard jaunty body.

It made no difference to me. Dishonesty in a woman is a thing you

---

①subterfuge: deceit used in order to achieve one's goal

never blame deeply—I was casually sorry, and then I forgot. It was on that same house party that we had a curious conversation about driving a car. It started because she passed so close to some workmen that our fender flicked a button on one man's coat.

"You're a rotten driver," I protested. "Either you ought to be more careful or you oughtn't to drive at all."

"I am careful."

"No, you're not."

"Well, other people are," she said lightly.

"What's that got to do with it?"

"They'll keep out of my way," she insisted. "It takes two to make an accident."

"Suppose you met somebody just as careless as yourself."

"I hope I never will," she answered. "I hate careless people. That's why I like you."

Her grey, sun-strained eyes stared straight ahead, but she had deliberately shifted our relations, and for a moment I thought I loved her. But I am slow-thinking and full of interior rules that act as brakes on my desires, and I knew that first I had to get myself definitely out of that tangle back home. I'd been writing letters once a week and signing them: "Love, Nick," and all I could think of was how, when that certain girl played tennis, a faint mustache of perspiration appeared on her upper lip. Nevertheless there was a vague understanding that had to be tactfully broken off before I was free.

Every one suspects himself of at least one of the cardinal virtues, and this is mine: I am one of the few honest people that I have ever known.

Chapter 9
(Excerpt)

After two years I remember the rest of that day, and that night and the next day, only as an endless drill of police and photographers and newspaper men in and out of Gatsby's front door. A rope stretched across the main gate and a policeman by it kept out the curious, but little boys soon discovered that they could enter through my yard and there were always a few of them clustered open-mouthed about the pool....

I called up Daisy half an hour after we found him, called her instinctively and without hesitation. But she and Tom had gone away early that afternoon, and taken baggage with them.

"Left no address?"

"No."

"Say when they'd be back?"

"No."

"Any idea where they are? How I could reach them?"

"I don't know. Can't say."

I wanted to get somebody for him. I wanted to go into the room where he lay and reassure him: "I'll get somebody for you, Gatsby. Don't worry. Just trust me and I'll get somebody for you—"...

I think it was on the third day that a telegram signed Henry C. Gatz arrived from a town in Minnesota. It said only that the sender was leaving immediately and to postpone the funeral until he came.

It was Gatsby's father, a solemn old man very helpless and dismayed, bundled up in a long cheap ulster against the warm September day. His eyes leaked continuously with excitement and when I took the bag and umbrella from his hands he began to pull so incessantly at his sparse grey beard that I had difficulty in getting off his coat. He was on the point of collapse so I took him into the music room and made him sit down while I sent for something to eat. But he wouldn't eat and the glass of milk spilled from his trembling hand.

"I saw it in the Chicago newspaper," he said. "It was all in the Chicago newspaper. I started right away."

"I didn't know how to reach you."

His eyes, seeing nothing, moved ceaselessly about the room.

"It was a mad man," he said. "He must have been mad."

"Wouldn't you like some coffee?" I urged him.

"I don't want anything. I'm all right now, Mr.—"

"Carraway."

"Well, I'm all right now. Where have they got Jimmy?"

I took him into the drawing-room, where his son lay, and left him there.

Some little boys had come up on the steps and were looking into the hall; when I told them who had arrived they went reluctantly away.

After a little while Mr. Gatz opened the door and came out, his mouth ajar, his face flushed slightly, his eyes leaking isolated and unpunctual tears. He had reached an age where death no longer has the quality of ghastly surprise, and when he looked around him now for the first time and saw the height and splendor of the hall and the great rooms opening out from it into other rooms his grief began to be mixed with an awed pride. I helped him to a bedroom upstairs; while he took off his coat and vest I told him that all arrangements had been deferred until he came.

"I didn't know what you'd want, Mr. Gatsby—"

"Gatz is my name."

"—Mr. Gatz. I thought you might want to take the body west."

He shook his head.

"Jimmy always liked it better down East. He rose up to his position in the East. Were you a friend of my boy's, Mr.—?"

"We were close friends."

"He had a big future before him, you know. He was only a young man but he had a lot of brain power here."

He touched his head impressively and I nodded.

"If he'd of lived he'd of been a great man. A man like James J. Hill. He'd of helped build up the country."

"That's true," I said, uncomfortably.

He fumbled at the embroidered coverlet, trying to take it from the bed, and lay down stiffly—was instantly asleep....

The morning of the funeral I went up to New York to see Meyer Wolfshiem...When I left his office the sky had turned dark and I got back to West Egg in a drizzle. After changing my clothes I went next door and found Mr. Gatz walking up and down excitedly in the hall. His pride in his son and in his son's possessions was continually increasing and now he had something to show me.

"Jimmy sent me this picture." He took out his wallet with trembling fingers. "Look there."

It was a photograph of the house, cracked in the corners and dirty with many hands. He pointed out every detail to me eagerly. "Look there!" and then sought admiration from my eyes. He had shown it so often that I think it was more real to him now than the house itself.

"Jimmy sent it to me. I think it's a very pretty picture. It shows up well."

"Very well. Had you seen him lately?"

"He come out to see me two years ago and bought me the house I live in now. Of course we was broke up when he run off from home but I see now there was a reason for it. He knew he had a big future in front of him. And ever since he made a success he was very generous with me."

He seemed reluctant to put away the picture, held it for another minute, lingeringly, before my eyes. Then he returned the wallet and pulled from his pocket a ragged old copy of a book called "Hopalong Cassidy."

"Look here, this is a book he had when he was a boy. It just shows you."

He opened it at the back cover and turned it around for me to see.

On the last fly-leaf was printed the word SCHEDULE, and the date September 12th, 1906. And underneath:

Rise from bed................ 6.00 A.M.
Dumbbell exercise and wall-scaling...... 6.15 – 6.30
Study electricity, etc............ 7.15 – 8.15
Work.................... 8.30 – 4.30 P.M.
Baseball and sports............. 4.30 – 5.00
Practice elocution, poise and how to attain it 5.00 – 6.00
Study needed inventions.......... 7.00 – 9.00

GENERAL RESOLVES

No wasting time at Shafters or [a name, indecipherable]

No more smokeing or chewing

Bath every other day

Read one improving book or magazine per week

Save $5.00 [crossed out] $3.00 per week

Be better to parents

"I come across this book by accident," said the old man. "It just shows you, don't it?"

"It just shows you."

"Jimmy was bound to get ahead. He always had some resolves like this or something. Do you notice what he's got about improving his mind? He was always great for that. He told me I et like a hog once and I beat him for it."

He was reluctant to close the book, reading each item aloud and then looking eagerly at me. I think he rather expected me to copy down the list for my own use.

A little before three the Lutheran minister arrived from Flushing and I began to look involuntarily out the windows for other cars. So did Gatsby's father. And as the time passed and the servants came in and stood waiting in the hall, his eyes began to blink anxiously and he spoke of the rain in a worried uncertain way. The minister glanced several times at his watch so I took him aside and asked him to wait for half an hour. But it wasn't any use. Nobody came.

About five o'clock our procession of three cars reached the cemetery and stopped in a thick drizzle beside the gate—first a motor hearse, horribly black and wet, then Mr. Gatz and the minister and I in the limousine, and, a little later, four or five servants and the postman from West Egg in Gatsby's station wagon, all wet to the skin. As we started through the gate into the cemetery I heard a car stop and then the sound of someone splashing after us over the soggy ground. I looked around. It was the man with owl-eyed glasses whom I had found marvelling over Gatsby's books in the library one night three months before.

I'd never seen him since then. I don't know how he knew about the funeral or even his name. The rain poured down his thick glasses and he took them off and wiped them to see the protecting canvas unrolled from Gatsby's grave.

I tried to think about Gatsby then for a moment but he was already too far away and I could only remember, without resentment, that Daisy hadn't sent a message or a flower. Dimly I heard someone murmur "Blessed are the dead that the rain falls on," and then the owl-eyed man said "Amen to that," in a brave voice.

We straggled down quickly through the rain to the cars. Owl-Eyes spoke to me by the gate.

"I couldn't get to the house," he remarked.

"Neither could anybody else."

"Go on!" He started. "Why, my God! They used to go there by the hundreds."

He took off his glasses and wiped them again outside and in.

"The poor son-of-a-bitch," he said....

Questions for Discussion

1. In Chapter 3, what did Nick, the narrator, observe regarding the party and the party-goers? What was the priority obsession of the majority party-goers? Were they careful or careless people?
2. The man with owl-eyed spectacles makes his appearance in both Chapter 3 and Chapter 9. What does he do in these chapters? How is he different from other party-goers?
3. What's the implication of Gatsby's change of his name? Would he be regarded as a self-made man typified by Benjamin Franklin? Why or why not?
4. What is the meaning of the title? In what way is Gatsby great? Do you think the title given by Fitzgerald is sincere or ironic?

Chapter 6

From 1941 to the Present
World War II and American Postmodernism

6.1 World War II and Its Aftermath

The United States didn't join the Allies in opposing the Axis powers of Germany, Italy and Japan until December 7, 1941, when Japanese bombers attacked America's Pearl Harbor naval base, located in Honolulu, Hawaii. After years of the most devastating conflict the world had ever seen, America dropped two atomic bombs on Japan in August 1945, bringing World War II to an abrupt end.

After the war, the United States and the Soviet Union, the two superpowers in the world, became tense rivals in a worldwide struggle for supremacy. This rivalry resulted in the Cold War. The post-war era saw the world undergo many dramatic changes. As former colonies of European powers declared independence one after another, colonialism came to an end, and the world entered the postcolonial era. With the fall of the Berlin Wall in 1989 and the dissolution of the Soviet Union in 1991, the Cold War was supposedly at its end. Despite the arrival of the postcolonial and post-Cold War eras, the colonial mentality and Cold War mindset persistently exist.

Since the world stepped into the 21st century, the realities of today's world are too complex to be described. The wide use of computers and the on-going so-called Information Revolution embodied by internet-related technology are profoundly transforming people's worldviews and attitudes. People in general feel that they live at the center of a globalized world. This feeling enhances both a sense of close-knit togetherness and a sharpened sense of difference.

| From 1941 to the Present | Chapter 6 |
| World War II and American Postmodernism | |

6.2　Domestic Circumstances in the United States

World War II brought great changes to the United States.

Above all, the war effort had required the United States to produce a great deal of goods badly needed in the war and thus dramatically boosted American industry. Moreover, the devastation in Europe immediately after the war allowed American industries to dominate world markets, helping the wartime economic boom continue throughout the 1950s.

Though postwar Americans did not seem as disillusioned as they had been after World War I, there were grave crises: the United States got involved in the Korean War (1950 – 1953) and the Vietnam War (1954 – 1975), and the involvement was nothing but a manifestation of the Cold War mentality. The Korean War was the first large-scale war that America had ever fought without a sense of victory. The Vietnam War frustrated America even more; it seemed a life-swallowing machine without success in sight. In addition, America, as well as the rest of the world, lived under the mushroom cloud of the atomic age. A keen sense of anxiety accompanied the United States when the nation was playing an imperialist role in the world. This anxiety was not only demonstrated in its foreign policies, but also translated into fear-based domestic politics. McCarthyism, also known as the Red Scare, was the modern version of the Salem witch-hunt, persecuting artists and writers in the name of fighting communism and of questioning "un-American" activities.

Another new phenomenon World War II brought to America was the rising Civil Rights Movement, a "freedom struggle" by African Americans in the 1950s and 1960s to gain equality. In theory, the American Civil War in the 1860s had officially abolished slavery, but it didn't end discrimination against blacks, especially in the South. After Reconstruction (1865 – 1877), the Southern states created a legal system of discrimination against blacks known as Jim Crow Laws, which largely nullified① the rights of citizenship

---

①nullify: officially state that something has no legal force

previously granted to blacks by federal law, and this situation persisted well into the 20th century. During World War II, African Americans made enormous contributions to the final victory. With one million black men and women serving in the military in segregated units and many more working in defense industries, as the war ended, blacks saw themselves as waging a "double victory" campaign to secure democracy abroad and equality for themselves in their own country. They naturally were unwilling to return to second-class status. On the other hand, the mainstream society was aware of the black people's contribution, and could no longer enforce segregation and other forms of prejudice as easily as before. The Civil Rights Movement went far beyond fighting to win equality for blacks. It also prompted gains for other ethnic populations, for people with disabilities, and for women, etc. The surge of a new wave to feminism was highly comprehensible. During World War II, with three million men in uniform, the vastly expanded workforce had comprised increasing numbers of women. After the war ended, many women were reluctant to return to homemaking, so that gradually women emerged as a political force on behalf of rights and opportunities in the workplace.

All these factors accounted for why the 1960s was exceedingly turbulent, seeing many large-scale protests organized by Civil Rights activists, feminist activists, and anti-Vietnam War activists. These social activities produced new conditions and new ideas, but meanwhile the stormy 1960s also saw the assassinations of heavy-weight leaders, for instance President John Kennedy was assassinated in 1963 and Martin Luther King in 1968, four years after receiving the Nobel Peace Prize.

With the dissolution of the Soviet Union, the United States was considered as the only superpower in the world. To achieve global hegemony, under the guise of protecting human rights and democracy as well as fighting terrorism as a reaction against the "9/11 attacks" in 2001, the United States waged many a protracted, unjustified war across the world. These wars caused horrible humanitarian disasters, destroyed sovereign order, and brought about new chaos.

6.3 The Ideas of Existentialism and Deconstruction

After World War Ⅱ, the two most influential philosophical ideas in the United States were existentialism and deconstruction.

Informing and inspiring a whole generation of American writers and artists in the 1950s and 1960s, existentialism is, strictly speaking, a philosophy formulated in the first half of the 20th century, with Heidegger, Sartre, and Camus being the three main exponents. Of the three, Sartre is generally regarded as the formulator of its main version. The foremost principle of existentialism is that existence precedes essence. With this principle, the existentialists reverse the main tradition in western philosophy and the tradition of Christianity. According to Platonism-Christianity, what man ultimately becomes is the unfolding of his innate nature or essence; this essence of man reflects a pre-existent eternal and absolute Spirit or Idea. But the existentialist philosophers hold the view that there is no such Spirit or Idea, and that there is no pre-established essence of man, and that each individual man is what he makes of himself by a succession of actions taken with the freedom of choice in a specific physical and historical context, and that the world, by itself, is purposeless and thus absurd. A modern man often feels the absurdity of the world, mainly as the effects of alienation due to capitalist modernization. The Beat Generation writings most prominently manifest the influence of existentialism in the US, just as the Theatre of Absurd does in Europe and the UK.

The father of deconstruction is the French thinker Jacques Derrida, whose ideas were brought to America by means of a series of university conferences and academic publications. Derrida asserted that western philosophy from Plato had been logocentric[①] and the western philosophical systems had been based on binary structure.[②] This "logocentric" tradition of thought had attempted to establish grounds of certainty and truth by

---

[①] logocentric: regarding words and language as a fundamental expression of an external reality
[②] binary structure: a structure that is composed of, or involving two things

repressing the limitless instability of language. Derrida argues that the stable self-identity which we attribute to speech as the authentic source of meaning is illusory. Influenced by Derrida and his associates, such as Michel Foucault, Gilles Deleuze, Judith Butler, Jean Baudrillard, and Julia Kristeva—who have been collectively called post-structuralist philosophers (deconstruction and post-structuralism are often coterminous[①]), American people realized that what was accepted as absolute truth usually depended on rhetoric rather than fact, and that the so-called fact itself was constructed by intellectual operations, for example, the Vietnam War had been presented to the American people through slogans rather than realities.

6.4 American Postmodernist Literature

Like American Modernism, American postmodernism was part of the international postmodernism phenomena.

American literature since World War II is so diversified that it is difficult to make generalizations about it. After the war, it seemed that all Americans, men and women, majority populations as well as minority populations, aspired to pursue personal freedom and individual self-expression. Finding a voice became any person's first task in seeking to be heard.

The rich diversity of literary productions after World War II makes it very hard, even dangerous, to define the main features of American post-modernist literature. However, to facilitate the reader to form a rough picture in the mind, let's try our best to do the job.

War Fiction Writers World War II offered prime material for a number of writers' work shortly after the war, for instance, Norman Mailer's *The Naked and the Dead* (1948), James Jones's *From Here to Eternity* (1951), Irwin Shaw's *The Young Lions* (1948), and Herman Wouk's *The Caine Mutiny* (1951). None of these authors glorify war. Then, Joseph Heller, in his *Catch-22* (1961), cast World War II in satirical

---

①coterminous: having the same boundaries or extent in space, time, or meaning

and absurdist terms, arguing that war is laced with insanity. Thomas Pynchon, in his *Gravity's Rainbow* (1973), presented a complex, brilliant case parodying and displacing different versions of reality, and Kurt Vonnegut became one of the shining lights of the counterculture during the early 1970s following publication of *Slaughterhouse-Five* (1969).

The Beat Generation Writers The "Beat Generation" refers to a group of American poets and artists in the late 1950s, with the core figures being Allen Ginsberg, Jack Kerouac, and William S. Burroughs. It has been widely believed that the word "beat" originally meant "beaten down," but later also connoted a musical sense, a "beatific" spirituality, and other meanings. Living in the climate of post-World War II, the Beat Generation writers rebelled against American mainstream cultural values and middle-class tastes in their writings. They rejected materialism, militarism, consumerism, and conformity of the 1950s in search of "beatific" ecstasy. Their loose styles favored spontaneous self-expression and recitation to jazz accompaniment. The principal works of the group were Ginsberg's *Howl* (1956), Kerouac's *On the Road* (1957), and Burroughs's *The Naked Lunch* (1959). The opening phrase of Ginsberg's *Howl* reads "I saw the best minds of my generation destroyed by madness," which best epitomizes the Beats' criticism of the time. They thought that the joylessness and purposelessness of modern society was sufficient justification for both withdrawal and protest. The Beats had a strong influence on the "counterculture" of the 1960s.

The Massive Emergence of Ethnic Writers The post-World War II era witnessed the increasing number of ethnic writers. The literature by African American writers experienced a new surge, with the most impressive black writers including Ralph Ellison (best known for his novel *Invisible Man*), Alice Walker (best known for her fiction *The Color Purple*), and Toni Morrison, the first—also the only—black American woman who has been awarded the Nobel Prize for Literature in 20th century. Jewish American writers get both national and international recognition, with the best-known of them being Saul Bellow, Bernard Malamud, Isaac B. Singer, and Philip Roth. Other groups of ethnic writers were immensely impressive, too. For instance, Chinese American writers (such as Maxine Hong Kingston, Amy Tan, and Gish Jen), Japanese American writers, Mexican American writers, etc. Inspired by the new historical atmosphere, the ethnic writers portrayed in their works how the characters strive to seek their identity in a difficult world.

The Flourishing of Female Writers As a result of the women's rights movement, the post-World War II years saw the appearance of increasing number of female writers, either feminist or non-feminist, white or ethnic. No other period in American history had seen so many female writers creatively working in the literary arena.

The Blooming of Southern Literature Following the Southern Renaissance of the 1920s and 1930s, as a result of American Civil Rights Movement, post-World War II Southern literature grew thematically. More female and African American writers' work began to be accepted as part of the Southern literary canon. One of the most highly praised Southern novels of the 20th century, *To Kill a Mockingbird* by Harper Lee, won the Pulitzer Prize when it was published in 1960. Another famous novel of the 1960s is *A Confederacy of Dunces* written by John Kennedy Toole in the 1960s but not published until 1980. It won the Pulitzer Prize in 1981 and has since become a cult classic. Southern poetry bloomed in the decades following the Second World War in large part thanks to the writing and efforts of Robert Penn Warren and James Dickey. Tennessee Williams (1911 – 1983) was one of the most important dramatist that emerged in the South after World War II.

The Blooming of American Drama Following the great success of Eugene O'Neill (1888 – 1953), American drama continued to flourish after World War II. Two post-World War II playwrights who established reputations comparable to Eugene O'Neill are Tennessee Williams and Arthur Miller (1915 – 2005). Tennessee Williams came from the Southern State of Mississippi. His best known plays are *The Glass Menagerie* (1945) and *A Streetcar Named Desire* (1947). Arthur Miller was born in New York. He is especially remembered for *Death of a Salesman* (1949), the Pulitzer Prize for drama winner, and *The Crucible* (1953), a dramatized and partially fictionalized story of the Salem witch trials that took place in the

Puritan Massachusetts Bay Colony in 1692. Miller wrote *The Crucible* as an allegory for McCarthyism in the early 1950s, when an anti-Communist crusade① led by U. S. Senator Joseph McCarthy and others ruined innocent people's lives.

New Attention Paid to Native American Writers Native American writers received new attention from mainstream culture. In 1969, N. Scott Momaday (b. 1934) became the first and only American Indian to win the Pulitzer Prize in fiction for his novel *House Made of Dawn*. Published during a time of heightened cultural awareness in the late 1960s and early 1970s, *House Made of Dawn* not only produced a tremendous impact on the development of Native American literature, but also brought attention to other gifted American Indian writers, such as Vine Deloria Jr. (1933 – 2005), whose *Custer Died for Your Sins: An Indian Manifesto* (1969) helped generate unprecedented national attention to Native American issues, Leslie Marmon Silko (b. 1948), whose most well-known novel *Ceremony* (1977) tells the story of a World War II American Indian veteran returning home from the war to his poverty-stricken reservation, and James Welch (1940 – 2003), whose *Fools Crow* (1986) received several national literary awards. The most distinguished Native American writers in the contemporary period include Louise Endrich (b. 1954), whose novel *The Plague of Doves* was a finalist for the Pulitzer Prize for Fiction in 2009 and Sherman Alexie (b. 1966), who has been considered as the most widely read American Indian writer in the United States.

New Directions in Poetry American poetry was transformed remarkably after World War II with Allen Ginsburg's *Howl* and Robert Lowell's *Life Studies* (1959). Allen Ginsberg was one of the leading figures of the Beat Generation, also one of the leading figures of the San Francisco Renaissance. His *Howl*, with its open, experimental form and strong oral emphasis, is a radical departure from the well-shaped lyric. Robert Lowell, a Bostonian, has been credited as the precursor of the so-called Confessional poetry, which explores and exposes the extreme moments of a person's

---

①crusade: a vigorous campaign for political, social, or religious change

individual experience, such as personal trauma, mental illness, insanity, etc. It has been claimed that Lowell was, in part, inspired by the work of Ginsberg. Other significant poets of the Confessional school include Sylvia Plath (1932 – 1963), Anne Sexton (1928 – 1974), and John Berryman (1914 – 1972). Apart from the Beat Generation and the Confessional school, two other parallel schools are Black Mountain school and New York school. Generally speaking, the poetry after World War II is wild, disquieting, and orally stylish, dramatizing individual predicaments and stressing angers. American poetry moved increasingly farther from European traditions.

Joseph Heller (1923 – 1999)

Joseph Heller is best remembered for his fiction *Catch-22*, a representative work of black humor. In fact, to talk about Joseph Heller is to talk about *Catch-22* and black humor.

Heller was born into a Jewish family in New York City, where he received his high school education. In 1942, at age 19, he joined the U.S. Army Air Corps. Two years later he was sent to the Italian Front and served as a bombardier[①] in the Mediterranean. His experience as a bombardier during World War II provided the inspiration for *Catch-22*, a satire on war and bureaucracy.

The novel is set in World War II. The protagonist Yossarian and his comrades are in an Air Force squadron stationed on an island in the Mediterranean Sea. Yossarian's main antagonist is Colonel Cathcart, whose goal in life is to become a general. Yossarian wants to stop flying missions so he does not get killed, yet Cathcart's aim is to continue raising the number of required missions in order to impress his superiors. He uses Catch-22's unfair, illogical rules to keep the men flying. This creates a constant conflict between Yossarian and Colonel Cathcart. Yossarian's tent-mate, whose name is Orr, practices crashing every mission before successfully escaping to Sweden in his last practice. Yossarian witnesses the death of Snowden, his pilot, and the death of Nately, his friend. Mentally

---

①bombardier: the member of a bomber crew who is responsible for aiming and releasing bombs

troubled by these deaths, Yassarian refuses to fly any more missions. He visits Doctor Daneeka and pleads with him to ground him on the basis of insanity, but the doctor tells him that he can't do that on account of the army regulation Catch-22. In desperation, Yossarian wanders the streets of Rome and encounters every kind of human horror—rape, disease, and murder. He is eventually arrested for being in Rome without a pass, and his superior officers, Colonel Cathcart and Colonel Korn, offer him a choice: he can either face a court-martial① or be released and sent home on condition that he must state his support for their policy. Although he is tempted by their offer to send him back home, Yossarian chooses another way out—he decides to desert the army and flee to neutral Sweden, getting rid of the dehumanizing machinery of the military once and for all.

Catch-22 is a perfect example of black humor. Heller agrees that he attacks not only the absurdity of war but, in general, "the humbug, hypocrisy, cruelty, and sheer stupidity of our mass society." Now, the phrase "Catch-22" has become a synonym for an absurd and self-contradictory dilemma.

Catch-22

Chapter 5

(Excerpt)

... Yossarian ... decided right then and there to go crazy.

"You're wasting your time," Doc Daneeka was forced to tell him.

"Can you ground someone who's crazy?"

"Oh, sure. I have to. There's a rule saying I have to ground anyone who's crazy."

"Then why don't you ground me? I'm crazy. Ask Clevinger."

"Clevinger? Where is Clevinger? You find Clevinger and I'll ask him."

"Then ask any of the others. They'll tell you how crazy I am."

"They're crazy."

---

① court-martial: a court consisting of commissioned officers and in some instances enlisted personnel for the trial of members of the armed forces or others within its jurisdiction

"Then why don't you ground them?"

"Why don't they ask me to ground them?"

"Because they're crazy, that's why."

"Of course they're crazy," Doc Daneeka replied. "I just told you they're crazy, didn't I? And you can't let crazy people decide whether you're crazy or not, can you?"

Yossarian looked at him soberly and tried another approach. "Is Orr crazy?"

"He sure is," Doc Daneeka said.

"Can you ground him?"

"I sure can. But first he has to ask me to. That's part of the rule."

"Then why doesn't he ask you to?"

"Because he's crazy," Doc Daneeka said. "He has to be crazy to keep flying combat missions after all the close calls he's had. Sure, I can ground Orr. But first he has to ask me to."

"That's all he has to do to be grounded?"

"That's all. Let him ask me."

"And then you can ground him?" Yossarian asked.

"No. Then I can't ground him."

"You mean there's a catch?"

"Sure there's a catch," Doc Daneeka replied. "Catch-22. Anyone who wants to get out of combat duty isn't really crazy."

There was only one catch and that was Catch-22, which specified that a concern for one's own safety in the face of dangers that were real and immediate was the process of a rational mind. Orr was crazy and could be grounded. All he had to do was ask; and as soon as he did, he would no longer be crazy and would have to fly more missions. Orr would be crazy to fly more missions and sane if he didn't, but if he was sane then he had to fly them. If he flew them he was crazy and didn't have to; but if he didn't want to he was sane and had to. Yossarian was moved very deeply by the absolute simplicity of this clause of Catch-22 and let out a respectful whistle.

"That's some catch, that Catch-22," he observed.

"It's the best there is," Doc Daneeka agreed.

Yossarian saw it clearly in all its spinning reasonableness. There was an elliptical precision about its perfect pairs of parts that was graceful and shocking, like good modern art, and at times Yossarian wasn't quite sure that he saw it all, just the way he was never quite sure about good modern art or the flies Orr saw in Appleby's eyes. He had Orr's word to take for the flies in Appleby's eyes.

"Oh, they're there, all right," Orr had assured him about the flies in Appleby's eyes after Yossarian's fist fight in the officers' club, "although he probably doesn't even know it. That's why he can't see things as they really are."

"How come he doesn't know it?" inquired Yossarian.

"Because he's got flies in his eyes," Orr explained with exaggerated patience. "How can he see he's got flies in his eyes if he's got flies in his eyes?" ...

Chapter 40
(Excerpt)

There was, of course, a catch.

"Catch-22?" inquired Yossarian.

"Of course," Colonel Korn answered pleasantly, after he had chased the mighty guard of massive M. P. s① out with an insouciant② flick of his hand and a slightly contemptuous nod—most relaxed, as always, when he could be most cynical. His rimless square eyeglasses glinted with sly amusement as he gazed at Yossarian. "After all, we can't simply send you home for refusing to fly more missions and keep the rest of the men here, can we? That would hardly be fair to them."

"You're goddam right!" Colonel Cathcart blurted out, lumbering back and forth gracelessly like a winded bull, puffing and pouting angrily. "I'd like to tie him up hand and foot and throw him aboard a plane on every mission. That's what I'd like to do."

---

① M. P.: Military Police
② insouciant: indifferent

Colonel Korn motioned Colonel Cathcart to be silent and smiled at Yossarian. "You know, you really have been making things terribly difficult for Colonel Cathcart," he observed with flip good humor, as though the fact did not displease him at all. "The men are unhappy and morale is beginning to deteriorate. And it's all your fault."

"It's your fault," Yossarian argued, "for raising the number of missions."

"No, it's your fault for refusing to fly them," Colonel Korn retorted. "The men were perfectly content to fly as many missions as we asked as long as they thought they had no alternative. Now you've given them hope, and they're unhappy. So the blame is all yours."

"Doesn't he know there's a war going on?" Colonel Cathcart, still stamping back and forth, demanded morosely without looking at Yossarian.

"I'm quite sure he does," Colonel Korn answered. "That's probably why he refuses to fly them."

"Doesn't it make any difference to him?"

"Will the knowledge that there's a war going on weaken your decision to refuse to participate in it?" Colonel Korn inquired with sarcastic seriousness, mocking Colonel Cathcart.

"No, sir," Yossarian replied, almost returning Colonel Korn's smile.

"I was afraid of that," Colonel Korn remarked with an elaborate sigh, locking his fingers together comfortably on top of his smooth, bald, broad, shiny brown head. "You know, in all fairness, we really haven't treated you too badly, have we? We've fed you and paid you on time. We gave you a medal and even made you a captain."

"I never should have made him a captain," Colonel Cathcart exclaimed bitterly. "I should have given him a court-martial after he loused up that Ferrara mission and went around twice."

"I told you not to promote him," said Colonel Korn, "but you wouldn't listen to me."

"No you didn't. You told me to promote him, didn't you?"

"I told you not to promote him. But you just wouldn't listen."

"I should have listened."

"You never listen to me," Colonel Korn persisted with relish. "That's the reason we're in this spot."

"All right, gee whiz. Stop rubbing it in, will you?"

Colonel Cathcart burrowed his fists down deep inside his pockets and turned away in a slouch. "Instead of picking on me, why don't you figure out what we're going to do about him?"

"We're going to send him home, I'm afraid." Colonel Korn was chuckling triumphantly when he turned away from Colonel Cathcart to face Yossarian. "Yossarian, the war is over for you. We're going to send you home.

You really don't deserve it, you know, which is one of the reasons I don't mind doing it. Since there's nothing else we can risk doing to you at this time, we've decided to return you to the States. We've worked out this little deal to—"

"What kind of deal?" Yossarian demanded with defiant mistrust.

Colonel Korn tossed his head back and laughed. "Oh, a thoroughly despicable deal, make no mistake about that.

It's absolutely revolting. But you'll accept it quickly enough."

"Don't be too sure."

"I haven't the slightest doubt you will, even though it stinks to high heaven. Oh, by the way. You haven't told any of the men you've refused to fly more missions, have you?"

"No, sir," Yossarian answered promptly.

Colonel Korn nodded approvingly. "That's good. I like the way you lie. You'll go far in this world if you ever acquire some decent ambition."

"Doesn't he know there's a war going on?" Colonel Cathcart yelled out suddenly, and blew with vigorous disbelief into the open end of his cigarette holder.

"I'm quite sure he does," Colonel Korn replied acidly, "since you brought that identical point to his attention just a moment ago." Colonel Korn frowned wearily for Yossarian's benefit, his eyes twinkling swarthily with sly and daring scorn. Gripping the edge of Colonel Cathcart's desk with both hands, he lifted his flaccid haunches far back on the corner to sit with both short legs dangling freely. His shoes kicked lightly against the yellow oakwood, his sludge-brown socks, garterless, collapsed in sagging circles below ankles that were surprisingly small and white. "You know, Yossarian," he mused affably in a manner of casual reflection that seemed both derisive and sincere, "I really do admire you a bit. You're an intelligent person of great moral character who has taken a very courageous stand. I'm an intelligent person with no moral character at all, so I'm in an ideal position to appreciate it."

"These are very critical times," Colonel Cathcart asserted petulantly from a far corner of the office, paying no attention to Colonel Korn.

"Very critical times indeed," Colonel Korn agreed with a placid nod. "We've just had a change of command above, and we can't afford a situation that might put us in a bad light with either General Scheisskopf or General Peckem. Isn't that what you mean, Colonel?"

"Hasn't he got any patriotism?"

"Won't you fight for your country?" Colonel Korn demanded, emulating Colonel Cathcart's harsh, self-righteous tone. "Won't you give up your life for Colonel Cathcart and me?"

Yossarian tensed with alert astonishment when he heard Colonel Korn's concluding words. "What's that?" he exclaimed. "What have you and Colonel Cathcart got to do with my country? You're not the same."

"How can you separate us?" Colonel Korn inquired with ironical tranquility.

"That's right," Colonel Cathcart cried emphatically. "You're either for us or against us. There's no two ways about it."

"I'm afraid he's got you," added Colonel Korn. "You're either for us or against your country. It's as simple as that."

"Oh, no, Colonel. I don't buy that."

Colonel Korn was unruffled. "Neither do I, frankly, but everyone else will. So there you are."

"You're a disgrace to your uniform!" Colonel Cathcart declared with blustering wrath, whirling to confront Yossarian for the first time. "I'd like to know how you ever got to be a captain, anyway."

"You promoted him," Colonel Korn reminded sweetly, stifling a snicker. "Don't you remember?"

"Well, I never should have done it."

"I told you not to do it," Colonel Korn said. "But you just wouldn't listen to me."

"Gee whiz, will you stop rubbing it in?" Colonel Cathcart cried. He furrowed his brow and glowered at Colonel Korn through eyes narrow with suspicion, his fists clenched on his hips. "Say, whose side are you on, anyway?"

"Your side, Colonel. What other side could I be on?"

"Then stop picking on me, will you? Get off my back, will you?"

"I'm on your side, Colonel. I'm just loaded with patriotism."

"Well, just make sure you don't forget that." Colonel Cathcart turned away grudgingly after another moment, incompletely reassured, and began striding the floor, his hands kneading his long cigarette holder. He jerked a thumb toward Yossarian. "Let's settle with him. I know what I'd like to do with him. I'd like to take him outside and shoot him. That's what I'd like to do with him. That's what General Dreedle would do with him."

"But General Dreedle isn't with us anymore," said Colonel Korn, "so we can't take him outside and shoot him."

Now that his moment of tension with Colonel Cathcart had passed, Colonel Korn relaxed again and resumed kicking softly against Colonel Cathcart's desk. He returned to Yossarian. "So we're going to send you home instead. It took a bit of thinking, but we finally worked out this horrible little plan for sending you home without causing too much dissatisfaction among the friends you'll leave behind. Doesn't that make you happy?"

"What kind of plan? I'm not sure I'm going to like it."

"I know you're not going to like it." Colonel Korn laughed, locking his hands contentedly on top of his head again. "You're going to loathe it. It really is odious and certainly will offend your conscience. But you'll agree to it quickly enough. You'll agree to it because it will send you home safe and sound in two weeks, and because you have no choice. It's that or a court-martial. Take it or leave it."

Yossarian snorted. "Stop bluffing, Colonel. You can't court-martial me for desertion in the face of the enemy. It would make you look bad and you probably couldn't get a conviction."

"But we can court-martial you now for desertion from duty, since you went to Rome without a pass. And we could make it stick. If you think about it a minute, you'll see that you'd leave us no alternative. We can't simply let you keep walking around in open insubordination without punishing you. All the other men would stop flying missions, too. No, you have my word for it. We will court-martial you if you turn our deal down, even though it would raise a lot of questions and be a terrible black eye for Colonel Cathcart."

Colonel Cathcart winced at the words "black eye" and, without any apparent premeditation, hurled his slender onyx-and-ivory cigarette holder down viciously on the wooden surface on his desk. "Jesus Christ!" he shouted unexpectedly. "I hate this goddam cigarette holder!" The cigarette holder bounced off the desk to the wall, ricocheted across the window sill to the floor and came to a stop almost where he was standing. Colonel Cathcart stared down at it with an irascible scowl. "I wonder if it's really doing me any good."

"It's a feather in your cap with General Peckem, but a black eye for you with General Scheisskopf," Colonel Korn informed him with a mischievous look of innocence.

"Well, which one am I supposed to please?"

"Both."

"How can I please them both? They hate each other. How am I ever going to get a feather in my cap from General Scheisskopf without getting a black eye from General Peckem?"

"March."

"Yeah, march. That's the only way to please him. March. March." Colonel Cathcart grimaced sullenly. "Some generals! They're a disgrace to their uniforms. If people like those two can make general, I don't see how I can miss."

"You're going to go far." Colonel Korn assured him with a flat lack of conviction, and turned back chuckling to Yossarian, his disdainful merriment increasing at the sight of Yossarian's unyielding expression of antagonism and distrust. "And there you have the crux of the situation. Colonel Cathcart wants to be a general and I want to be a colonel, and that's why we have to send you home."

"Why does he want to be a general?"

"Why? For the same reason that I want to be a colonel. What else have we got to do? Everyone teaches us to aspire to higher things. A general is higher than a colonel, and a colonel is higher than a lieutenant colonel. So we're both aspiring. And you know, Yossarian, it's a lucky thing for you that we are. Your timing on this is absolutely perfect, but I suppose you took that factor into account in your calculations."

"I haven't been doing any calculating," Yossarian retorted.

"Yes, I really do enjoy the way you lie," Colonel Korn answered. "Won't it make you proud to have your commanding officer promoted to general—to know you served in an outfit that averaged more combat missions per person than any other? Don't you want to earn more unit citations and more oak leaf clusters for your Air Medal? Where's your 'sprit de corps?' Don't you want to contribute further to this great record by flying more combat missions? It's your last chance to answer yes."

"No."

"In that case, you have us over a barrel—" said Colonel Korn without rancor.

"He ought to be ashamed of himself!"

"—and we have to send you home. Just do a few little things for us, and—"

"What sort of things?" Yossarian interrupted with belligerent misgiving.

"Oh, tiny, insignificant things. Really, this is a very generous deal we're making with you. We will issue orders returning you to the States—really, we will—and all you have to do in return is..."

"What? What must I do?"

Colonel Korn laughed curtly. "Like us."

Yossarian blinked. "Like you?"

"Like us."

"Like you?"

"That's right," said Colonel Korn, nodding, gratified immeasurably by Yossarian's guileless surprise and bewilderment. "Like us. Join us. Be our pal. Say nice things about us here and back in the States. Become one of the boys. Now, that isn't asking too much, is it?"

"You just want me to like you? Is that all?"

"That's all."

"That's all?"

"Just find it in your heart to like us."

Yossarian wanted to laugh confidently when he saw with amazement that Colonel Korn was telling the truth.

"That isn't going to be too easy," he sneered.

"Oh, it will be a lot easier than you think," Colonel Korn taunted in return, undismayed by Yossarian's barb.

"You'll be surprised at how easy you'll find it to like us once you begin." Colonel Korn hitched up the waist of his loose, voluminous trousers. The deep black grooves isolating his square chin from his jowls were bent again in a kind of jeering and reprehensible mirth. "You see, Yossarian, we're going to put you on easy street. We're going to promote you to major and even give you another medal. Captain Flume is already working on glowing press releases describing your valor over Ferrara, your deep and abiding loyalty to your outfit and your consummate dedication to duty. Those phrases are all actual quotations, by the way. We're going to glorify you and send you home a hero, recalled by the Pentagon for morale and public-relations purposes. You'll live like a millionaire. Everyone will lionize you. You'll have parades in your honor and make speeches to raise money for war bonds. A whole new world of luxury awaits you once you become our pal. Isn't it lovely?"

Yossarian found himself listening intently to the fascinating elucidation of details. "I'm not sure I want to make speeches."

"Then we'll forget the speeches. The important thing is what you say to people here." Colonel Korn leaned forward earnestly, no longer smiling. "We don't want any of the men in the group to know that we're sending you home as a result of your refusal to fly more missions. And we don't want General Peckem or General Scheisskopf to get wind of any friction between us, either. That's why we're going to become such good pals."

"What will I say to the men who asked me why I refused to fly more missions?"

"Tell them you had been informed in confidence that you were being returned to the States and that you were unwilling to risk your life for another mission or two. Just a minor disagreement between pals, that's all."

"Will they believe it?"

"Of course they'll believe it, once they see what great friends we've become and when they see the press releases and read the flattering things you have to say about me and Colonel Cathcart. Don't worry about the men.

They'll be easy enough to discipline and control when you've gone. It's only while you're still here that they may prove troublesome. You know, one good apple can spoil the rest," Colonel Korn concluded with conscious irony. "You know—this would really be wonderful—you might even serve as an inspiration to them to fly more missions."

"Suppose I denounce you when I get back to the States?"

"After you've accepted our medal and promotion and all the fanfare? No one would believe you, the Army wouldn't let you, and why in the world should you want to? You're going to be one of the boys, remember?

You'll enjoy a rich, rewarding, luxurious, privileged existence. You'd have to be a fool to throw it all away just for a moral principle, and you're not a fool. Is it a deal?"

"I don't know."

"It's that or a court-martial."

"That's a pretty scummy trick I'd be playing on the men in the squadron, isn't it?"

"Odious," Colonel Korn agreed amiably, and waited, watching Yossarian patiently with a glimmer of private delight.

"But what the hell!" Yossarian exclaimed. "If they don't want to fly more missions, let them stand up and do something about it the way I did. Right?"

"Of course," said Colonel Korn.

"There's no reason I have to risk my life for them, is there?"

"Of course not."

Yossarian arrived at his decision with a swift grin. "It's a deal!" he announced jubilantly....

Questions for Discussion

1. What manifestations of black humor do you identify in the excerpts? What Catch-22 instances have you found around in real life?
2. Considering the thing that Colonel Cathcart and Colonel Korn proposed to have a "glowing press releases" composed for Yossarian, who had actually behaved in a cowardly fashion during the campaigns, what's your comment on the detachedness of any writing and the reality it means to refer to?

Toni Morrison (1931 – 2019)

Toni Morrison, the first African American recipient of the Nobel Prize for Literature, plays a central role in putting fiction by and about African American women at the forefront of the late 20th century literary canon.

Morrison was born to a working-class family in Ohio. She received her BA in English from Howard University in 1953, and then her MA in English from Cornell University in 1955. From then until her death, she worked as an educator and editor, in addition to being a writer.

Her first novel is *The Bluest Eye* (1970). Set in Lorain, Ohio, it relates the tragic life of the black girl Pecola, who was born to a poor, dysfunctional African American family and grew up during the years following the Great Depression. Due to her mannerisms and dark skin, she was consistently regarded as "ugly." As a result, she longed to have blue eyes, which she equated with "whiteness," so that she'd be as beautiful and as beloved as those blue-eyed, blonde children.

Morrison is a highly productive writer. Among her prolific work, *Beloved* (1987), the winner of the Pulitzer Prize, has been widely regarded as her best novel. Set in the middle of 1870s, *Beloved* shows a mother (Sethe) being haunted and eventually destroyed by the ghost of her daughter (Beloved) whom she had killed eighteen years earlier rather than leaving her to be taken by a vicious slave-master. Told in a style of magical realism,[①] this novel is central to Morrison's canon because it involves so many important themes and techniques, such as love and guilt, a rebuilding of history, and history's role in clarifying the past's influence on the present.

The short story "Sweetness" which follows was published in *The New Yorker* in 2015 as a prelude to her novel *God Help the Child* (2015).

Sweetness

It's not my fault. So you can't blame me. I didn't do it and have no idea how it happened. It didn't take more than an hour after they pulled her out from between my legs for me to realize something was wrong. Really wrong. She was so black she scared me. Midnight black, Sudanese black. I'm light-skinned, with good hair, what we call high yellow, and so is Lula Ann's father. Ain't nobody in my family anywhere near that color. Tar is the closest I can think of, yet her hair don't go with the skin. It's different—straight but curly, like the hair on those naked tribes in Australia. You might think she's a throwback, but a throwback to what? You should've seen my grandmother; she passed for white, married a white man, and never said another word to any one of her children. Any letter she got from my mother or my aunts she sent right back, unopened. Finally

---

[①] magical realism: a literary genre or style associated especially with Latin America that incorporates fantastic or mythical elements into otherwise realistic fiction

they got the message of no message and let her be. Almost all mulatto[①] types and quadroons[②] did that back in the day—if they had the right kind of hair, that is. Can you imagine how many white folks have Negro blood hiding in their veins? Guess. Twenty per cent, I heard. My own mother, Lula Mae, could have passed easy, but she chose not to. She told me the price she paid for that decision. When she and my father went to the courthouse to get married, there were two Bibles, and they had to put their hands on the one reserved for Negroes. The other one was for white people's hands. The Bible! Can you beat it? My mother was a housekeeper for a rich white couple. They ate every meal she cooked and insisted she scrub their backs while they sat in the tub, and God knows what other intimate things they made her do, but no touching of the same Bible.

Some of you probably think it's a bad thing to group ourselves according to skin color—the lighter the better—in social clubs, neighborhoods, churches, sororities, even colored schools. But how else can we hold on to a little dignity? How else can we avoid being spit on in a drugstore, elbowed at the bus stop, having to walk in the gutter to let whites have the whole sidewalk, being charged a nickel at the grocer's for a paper bag that's free to white shoppers? Let alone all the name-calling. I heard about all of that and much, much more. But because of my mother's skin color she wasn't stopped from trying on hats or using the ladies' room in the department stores. And my father could try on shoes in the front part of the shoe store, not in a back room. Neither one of them would let themselves drink from a "Colored Only" fountain, even if they were dying of thirst.

I hate to say it, but from the very beginning in the maternity ward the baby, Lula Ann, embarrassed me. Her birth skin was pale like all babies', even African ones, but it changed fast. I thought I was going crazy when she turned blue-black right before my eyes. I know I went crazy for a minute, because—just for a few seconds—I held a blanket over her face and pressed. But I couldn't do that, no matter how much I wished she hadn't

---

①mulatto: (*usually offensive*) the first-generation offspring of a black person and a white person
②quadroon: (*usually offensive*) a person of one-quarter black ancestry

been born with that terrible color. I even thought of giving her away to an orphanage someplace. But I was scared to be one of those mothers who leave their babies on church steps. Recently, I heard about a couple in Germany, white as snow, who had a dark-skinned baby nobody could explain. Twins, I believe—one white, one colored. But I don't know if it's true. All I know is that, for me, nursing her was like having a pickaninny① sucking my teat. I went to bottle-feeding soon as I got home.

My husband, Louis, is a porter, and when he got back off the rails he looked at me like I really was crazy and looked at the baby like she was from the planet Jupiter. He wasn't a cussing man, so when he cussed me and said, "What is this?" I knew we were in trouble. That was what did it—what caused the fights between me and him. It broke our marriage to pieces. We had three good years together, but when she was born he blamed me and treated Lula Ann like she was a stranger—more than that, an enemy. He never touched her.

I never did convince him that I ain't never, ever fooled around with another man. He was dead sure I was lying. We argued and argued till I told him her blackness had to be from his own family—not mine. That was when it got worse, so bad he just up and left and I had to look for another, cheaper place to live. I did the best I could. I knew enough not to take her with me when I applied to landlords, so I left her with a teen-age cousin to babysit. I didn't take her outside much, anyway, because, when I pushed her in the baby carriage, people would lean down and peek in to say something nice and then give a start or jump back before frowning. That hurt. I could have been the babysitter if our skin colors were reversed. It was hard enough just being a colored woman—even a high-yellow one—trying to rent in a decent part of the city. Back in the nineties, when Lula Ann was born, the law was against discriminating in who you could rent to, but not many landlords paid attention to it. They made up reasons to keep you out. But I got lucky with Mr. Leigh, though I know he upped the rent seven dollars from what he'd advertised, and he had a fit if you were a

---

① pickaninny: (*offensive*) a black child

minute late with the money.

I told her to call me "Sweetness" instead of "Mother" or "Mama." It was safer. Her being that black and having what I think are too thick lips and calling me "Mama" would've confused people. Besides, she has funny-colored eyes, crow black with a blue tint—something witchy about them, too.

So it was just us two for a long while, and I don't have to tell you how hard it is being an abandoned wife. I guess Louis felt a little bit bad after leaving us like that, because a few months later on he found out where I'd moved to and started sending me money once a month, though I never asked him to and didn't go to court to get it. His fifty-dollar money orders and my night job at the hospital got me and Lula Ann off welfare. Which was a good thing. I wish they would stop calling it welfare and go back to the word they used when my mother was a girl. Then it was called "relief." Sounds much better, like it's just a short-term breather while you get yourself together. Besides, those welfare clerks are mean as spit. When finally I got work and didn't need them anymore, I was making more money than they ever did. I guess meanness filled out their skimpy① paychecks, which was why they treated us like beggars. Especially when they looked at Lula Ann and then back at me—like I was trying to cheat or something. Things got better but I still had to be careful. Very careful in how I raised her. I had to be strict, very strict. Lula Ann needed to learn how to behave, how to keep her head down and not to make trouble. I don't care how many times she changes her name. Her color is a cross she will always carry. But it's not my fault. It's not my fault. It's not.

Oh, yeah, I feel bad sometimes about how I treated Lula Ann when she was little. But you have to understand: I had to protect her. She didn't know the world. With that skin, there was no point in being tough or sassy,② even when you were right. Not in a world where you could be sent to a juvenile lockup for talking back or fighting in school, a world where

---

① skimpy: scanty
② sassy: bold, impudent

you'd be the last one hired and the first one fired. She didn't know any of that or how her black skin would scare white people or make them laugh and try to trick her. I once saw a girl nowhere near as dark as Lula Ann who couldn't have been more than ten years old tripped by one of a group of white boys and when she tried to scramble up another one put his foot on her behind and knocked her flat again. Those boys held their stomachs and bent over with laughter. Long after she got away, they were still giggling, so proud of themselves. If I hadn't been watching through the bus window I would have helped her, pulled her away from that white trash. See, if I hadn't trained Lula Ann properly she wouldn't have known to always cross the street and avoid white boys. But the lessons I taught her paid off, and in the end she made me proud as a peacock.

I wasn't a bad mother, you have to know that, but I may have done some hurtful things to my only child because I had to protect her. Had to. All because of skin privileges. At first I couldn't see past all that black to know who she was and just plain love her. But I do. I really do. I think she understands now. I think so.

Last two times I saw her she was, well, striking. Kind of bold and confident. Each time she came to see me, I forgot just how black she really was because she was using it to her advantage in beautiful white clothes.

Taught me a lesson I should have known all along. What you do to children matters. And they might never forget. As soon as she could, she left me all alone in that awful apartment. She got as far away from me as she could; dolled herself up and got a big-time job in California. She don't call or visit anymore. She sends me money and stuff every now and then, but I ain't seen her in I don't know how long.

I prefer this place—Winston House—to those big, expensive nursing homes outside the city. Mine is small, homey, cheaper, with twenty-four-hour nurses and a doctor who comes twice a week. I'm only sixty-three—too young for pasture—but I came down with some creeping bone disease, so good care is vital. The boredom is worse than the weakness or the pain, but the nurses are lovely. One just kissed me on the cheek when I told her I was going to be a grandmother. Her smile and her compliments were fit for someone about to be crowned. I showed her the note on blue paper that I got from Lula Ann—well, she signed it "Bride," but I never pay that any attention. Her words sounded giddy. "Guess what, S. I am so, so happy to pass along this news. I am going to have a baby. I'm too, too thrilled and hope you are, too." I reckon the thrill is about the baby, not its father, because she doesn't mention him at all. I wonder if he is as black as she is. If so, she needn't worry like I did. Things have changed a mite from when I was young. Blue-blacks are all over TV, in fashion magazines, commercials, even starring in movies.

There is no return address on the envelope. So I guess I'm still the bad parent being punished forever till the day I die for the well-intended and, in fact, necessary way I brought her up. I know she hates me. Our relationship is down to her sending me money. I have to say I'm grateful for the cash, because I don't have to beg for extras, like some of the other patients. If I want my own fresh deck of cards for solitaire,① I can get it and not need to play with the dirty, worn one in the lounge. And I can buy my special face cream. But I'm not fooled. I know the money she sends is a way to stay away and quiet down the little bit of conscience she's got left.

If I sound irritable, ungrateful, part of it is because underneath is regret. All the little things I didn't do or did wrong. I remember when she had her first period and how I reacted. Or the times I shouted when she stumbled or dropped something. True. I was really upset, even repelled by her black skin when she was born and at first I thought of ... No. I have to push those memories away—fast. No point. I know I did the best for her under the circumstances. When my husband ran out on us, Lula Ann was a burden. A heavy one, but I bore it well.

Yes, I was tough on her. You bet I was. By the time she turned twelve going on thirteen, I had to be even tougher. She was talking back, refusing to eat what I cooked, primping② her hair. When I braided it, she'd go to school and unbraid it. I couldn't let her go bad. I slammed the lid and

---

①solitaire: any of various card games that can be played by one person
②primp: to dress, adorn, or arrange in a careful or finicky manner

warned her about the names she'd be called. Still, some of my schooling must have rubbed off. See how she turned out? A rich career girl. Can you beat it?

Now she's pregnant. Good move, Lula Ann. If you think mothering is all cooing, booties, and diapers you're in for a big shock. Big. You and your nameless boyfriend, husband, pickup—whoever—imagine, *Oooh*! *A baby*! *Kitchee kitchee koo*!

Listen to me. You are about to find out what it takes, how the world is, how it works, and how it changes when you are a parent.

Good luck, and God help the child.

Questions for Discussion

1. Who is the narrator of the story? What's the advantage of the first-person point of view in relating this story?
2. Who or what is to blame the most and the least in the story? Please expound your argument.
3. What does this story say about race, colorism, and motherhood?

Maxine Hong Kingston (b. 1940)

Maxine Hong Kingston is a distinguished Chinese American writer. She is best known for her debut work *The Woman Warrior: Memoirs of a Girlhood Among Ghosts* (1976), which received the National Book Critics' Circle Award for nonfiction.

Born in California to parents who had emigrated from China, Kingston is the eldest of six children of the couple. She grew up helping in the family-run laundry and listening to her mother telling stories about old China. She adopted the last name of her husband, Earl Kingston.

Kingston studied at the University of California at Berkeley during the turbulent middle sixties. Before publishing her debut in 1976, Kingston was an unknown. *The Woman Warrior* became an immediate success and has entered the American mainstream readership. Though it draws on Kingston's autobiographical facts, it is by no means an autobiography. Rather, it is fictionalized autobiography, freely mixing memories, stories, Chinese legends, and psychological fantasies to present the difficulties Kingston has gone through in her upbringing as an ethnic-minority female, and how she has become a woman warrior like Hua Mulan (spelled as Fa Mu Lan in the book). Unlike conventional autobiography, the book tells, in its five chapters, the stories of her female antecedents including her paternal aunt "no-name woman," her mother Brave Orchid, her maternal aunt Moon Orchid, as well as the legendary Chinese heroine Mulan and the Chinese poetess Cai Yan (spelled as Ts'ai Yen in the book). All these women shape her growth one way or another.

Kingston's second success came from *China Men* (1980), a recipient of National Book Award for nonfiction. Kingston had originally conceived of *The Woman Warrior* and *China Men* as one long book, but ended up deciding to preserve an overall division by gender. *China Men* depicts the stories of her male family people, especially her father and the earlier male forebears who came to America and worked on building the railroads, and in the final section, she writes about her brother who served in the U.S. Navy during the Vietnam War.

Tripmaster Monkey: His Fake Book (1989) is presented more deliberately as a novel. Its hero is a Chinese American young man named Wittman Ah Sing. It is an extended, picaresque account of Wittman's adventures as an aspiring playwright who imagines himself to be an incarnation of the legendary Monkey King Sun Wukong. Combining magic, realism, and black humor, *Tripmaster Monkey* is about a young male Asian American's search for a community in America.

The Woman Warrior: Memoirs of a Girlhood Among Ghosts
White Tigers
(Excerpt)

When we Chinese girls listened to the adults talk-story, we learned that we failed if we grew up to be but wives or slaves. We could be heroines, swordswomen. Even if she had to rage across all China, a swordswoman got even with anybody who hurt her family. Perhaps women were once so dangerous that they had to have their feet bound. It was a woman who invented white crane boxing only two hundred years ago. She was already an expert pole fighter, daughter of a teacher trained at the Shao-lin temple, where there lived an order of fighting monks. She was combing her hair one morning when a white crane alighted outside her window. She teased it with her pole, which it pushed aside with a soft brush of its wing. Amazed, she dashed outside and tried to knock the crane off its perch. It snapped her pole in two. Recognizing the presence of great power, she asked the spirit of the white crane if it would teach her to fight. It answered with a cry that white crane boxers imitate today. Later the bird returned as an old man, and he guided her boxing for many years. Thus she gave the world a new martial art.

This was one of the tamer, more modern stories, mere introduction. My mother told others that followed swordswomen through woods and palaces for years. Night after night my mother would talk-story until we fell asleep. I couldn't tell where the stories left off and the dreams began, her voice the voice of the heroines in my sleep. And on Sundays, from noon to midnight, we went to the movies at the Confucius Church. We saw swordswomen jump over houses from a standstill; they didn't even need a running start.

At last I saw that I too had been in the presence of great power, my mother talking-story. After I grew up, I heard the chant of Fa Mu Lan, the girl who took her father's place in battle. Instantly I remembered that as a child I had followed my mother about the house, the two of us singing about how Fa Mu Lan fought gloriously and returned alive from war to settle in the village. I had forgotten this chant that was once mine, given me by my mother, who may not have known its power to remind. She said I would grow up a wife and a slave, but she taught me the song of the warrior woman, Fa Mu Lan. I would have to grow up a warrior woman.

The call would come from a bird that flew over our roof. In the brush drawings it looks like the ideograph for "human," two black wings. The bird would cross the sun and lift into the mountains (which look like the ideograph "mountain"), there parting the mist briefly that swirled opaque again. I would be a little girl of seven the day I followed the bird away into the mountains. The brambles① would tear off my shoes and the rocks cut my feet and fingers, but I would keep climbing, eyes upward to follow the bird. We would go around and around the tallest mountain, climbing ever upward. I would drink from the river, which I would meet again and again. We would go so high the plants would change, and the river that flows past the village would become a waterfall. At the height where the bird used to disappear, the clouds would gray the world like an ink wash.

Even when I got used to that gray, I would only see peaks as if shaded in pencil, rocks like charcoal rubbings, everything so murky. There would be just two black strokes—the bird. Inside the clouds—inside the dragon's breath—I would not know how many hours or days passed. Suddenly, without noise, I would break clear into a yellow, warm world. New trees would lean toward me at mountain angles, but when I looked for the village, it would have vanished under the clouds.

The bird, now gold so close to the sun, would come to rest on the thatch of a hut which, until the bird's two feet touched it, was camouflaged② as part of the mountainside....

After I returned from my survival test, the two old people trained me in dragon ways, which took another eight years. Copying the tigers, their stalking kill and their anger, had been a wild, bloodthirsty joy. Tigers are easy to find, but I needed adult wisdom to know dragons. "You have to infer the whole dragon from the parts you can see and touch," the old people would say. Unlike tigers, dragons are so immense, I would never see one in its entirety. But I could explore the mountains, which are the top of its head. "These mountains are also *like* the tops of *other* dragons' heads," the old people would tell me. When climbing the slopes, I could understand

---

① bramble: a rough prickly shrub or vine
② camouflage: conceal, disguise

that I was a bug riding on a dragon's forehead as it roams through space, its speed so different from my speed that I feel the dragon solid and immobile. In quarries I could see its strata, the dragons' veins and muscles; the minerals, its teeth and bones. I could touch the stones the old woman wore—its bone marrow. I had worked the soil, which is its flesh, and harvested the plants and climbed the trees, which are its hairs. I could listen to its voice in the thunder and feel its breathing in the winds, see its breathing in the clouds. Its tongue is the lightning. And the red that the lightning gives to the world is strong and lucky—in blood, poppies, roses, rubies, the red feathers of birds, the red carp, the cherry tree, the peony, the line alongside the turtle's eyes and the mallard's. In the spring when the dragon awakes, I watched its turnings in the rivers.

The closest I came to seeing a dragon whole was when the old people cut away a small strip of bark on a pine that was over three thousand years old. The resin underneath flows in the swirling shapes of dragons. "If you should decide during your old age that you would like to live another five hundred years, come here and drink ten pounds of this sap," they told me. "But don't do it now. You're too young to decide to live forever." The old people sent me out into thunderstorms to pick the red-cloud herb, which grows only then, a product of dragon's fire and dragon's rain. I brought the leaves to the old man and old woman, and they ate them for immortality.

I learned to make my mind large, as the universe is large, so that there is room for paradoxes. Pearls are bone marrow; pearls come from oysters. The dragon lives in the sky, ocean, marshes, and mountains; and the mountains are also its cranium.① Its voice thunders and jingles like copper pans. It breathes fire and water; and sometimes the dragon is one, sometimes many.

I worked every day. When it rained, I exercised in the downpour ...

Menstrual days did not interrupt my training; I was as strong as on any other day. "You're now an adult," explained the old woman on the first one, which happened halfway through my stay on the mountain. "You can

---

①cranium: the part of the skull that encloses the brain

have children." I had thought I had cut myself when jumping over my swords, one made of steel and the other carved out of a single block of jade. "However," she added, "we are asking you to put off children for a few more years."

"Then can I use the control you taught me and stop this bleeding."

"No. You don't stop shitting and pissing," she said. "It's the same with the blood. Let it run." ("Let it walk" in Chinese.)

To console me for being without family on this day, they let me look inside the gourd. My whole family was visiting friends on the other side of the river. Everybody had on good clothes and was exchanging cakes. It was a wedding. My mother was talking to the hosts: "Thank you for taking our daughter. Wherever she is, she must be happy now. She will certainly come back if she is alive, and if she is a spirit, you have given her a descent line. We are so grateful."

Yes, I would be happy. How full I would be with all their love for me. I would have for a new husband my own playmate, dear since childhood, who loved me so much he was to become a spirit bridegroom for my sake. We will be so happy when I come back to the valley, healthy and strong and not a ghost.

The water gave me a close-up of my husband's wonderful face—and I was watching when it went white at the sudden approach of armored men on horseback, thudding and jangling. My people grabbed iron skillets, boiling soup, knives, hammers, scissors, whatever weapons came to hand, but my father said, "There are too many of them," and they put down the weapons and waited quietly at the door, open as if for guests. An army of horsemen stopped at our house; the foot soldiers in the distance were coming closer. A horse-man with silver scales afire in the sun shouted from the scroll in his hands, his words opening a red gap in his black beard. "Your baron has pledged fifty men from this district, one from each family," he said, and then named the family names.

"No!" I screamed into the gourd.

"I'll go," my new husband and my youngest brother said to their fathers.

"No," my father said, "I myself will go," but the women held him back until the foot soldiers passed by, my husband and my brother leaving with them.

As if disturbed by the marching feet, the water churned; and when it stilled again ("Wait!" I yelled. "Wait!"), there were strangers. The baron and his family—all of his family—were knocking their heads on the floor in front of their ancestors and thanking the gods out loud for protecting them from conscription. I watched the baron's piggish face chew open-mouthed on the sacrificial pig. I plunged my hand into the gourd, making a grab for his thick throat, and he broke into pieces, splashing water all over my face and clothes. I turned the gourd upside-down to empty it, but no little people came tumbling out.

"Why can't I go down there now and help them?" I cried. "I'll run away with the two boys and we'll hide in the caves."

"No," the old man said. "You're not ready. You are only fourteen years old. You'd get hurt for nothing."

"Wait until you are twenty-two," the old woman said. "You'll be big then and more skillful. No army will be able to stop you from doing whatever you want. If you go now, you will be killed, and you'll have wasted seven and a half years of our time. You will deprive your people of a champion."

"I'm good enough now to save the boys."

"We didn't work this hard to save just two boys, but whole families."...

When I could point at the sky and make a sword appear, a silver bolt in the sunlight, and control its slashing with my mind, the old people said I was ready to leave. The old man opened the gourd for the last time. I saw the baron's messengers leave our house, and my father was saying, "This time I must go and fight." I would hurry down the mountain and take his place. The old people gave me the fifteen beads, which I was to use if I got into terrible danger. They gave me men's clothes and armor. We bowed to one another. The bird flew above me down the mountain, and for some miles, whenever I turned to look for them, there would be the two old people waving. I saw them through the mist; I saw them on the clouds; I saw them big on the mountain top when distance had shrunk the pines. They had probably left images of themselves for me to wave at and gone about their other business.

When I reached my village, my father and mother had grown as old as the two whose shapes I could at last no longer see. I helped my parents carry their tools, and they walked ahead so straight, each carrying a basket or a hoe not to overburden me, their tears falling privately. My family surrounded me with so much love that I almost forgot the ones not there. I praised the new infants.

"Some of the people are saying the Eight Sages took away to teach you magic," said a little girl cousin. "They say they changed you into a bird, and you flew to them."

"Some say you went to the city and became a prostitute," another cousin giggled.

"You might tell them that I met some teachers who were willing to teach me science," I said.

"I have been drafted," my father said.

"No, Father," I said. "I will take your place."

My parents killed a chicken and steamed it whole, as if they were welcoming home a son, but I had gotten out of the habit of meat. After eating rice and vegetables, I slept for a long time, preparation for the work ahead.

In the morning my parents woke me and asked that I come with them to the family hall. "Stay in your night clothes," my mother said. "Don't change yet." She was holding a basin, a towel, and a kettle of hot water. My father had a bottle of wine, and ink block and pens, and knives of various sizes. "Come with us," he said. They had stopped the tears with which they had greeted me. Forebodingly I caught a smell—metallic, the iron smell of blood, as when a woman gives birth, as at the sacrifice of a large animal, as when I menstruated and dreamed red dreams.

My mother put a pillow on the floor before the ancestors. "Kneel here," she said. "Now take off your shirt." I kneeled with my back to my parents so none of us felt embarrassed. My mother washed my back as if I had left for only a day and were her baby yet. "We are going to carve revenge on your back," my father said. "We'll write out oaths and names."

"Wherever you go, whatever happens to you, people will know our sacrifice," my mother said. "And you'll never forget either." She meant that even if I got killed, the people could use my dead body for a weapon, but we do not like to talk out loud about dying.

My father first brushed the words in ink, and they fluttered down my back row after row. Then he began cutting; to make fine lines and points he used thin blades, for the stem, large blades.

My mother caught the blood and wiped the cuts with a cold towel soaked in wine. It hurt terribly—the cuts sharp; the air burning; the alcohol cold, then hot—pain so various. I gripped my knees. I released them. Neither tension nor relaxation helped. I wanted to cry. If not for the fifteen years of train, I would have writhed on the floor; I would have had to be held down. The list of grievances went on and on. If an enemy should flay me, the light would shine through my skin like lace.

At the end of the last word, I fell forward. Together my parents sang what they had written, then let me rest. My mother fanned my back. "We'll have you with us until your back heals," she said.

When I could sit up again, my mother brought two mirrors, and I saw my back covered entirely with words in red and black files, like an army, like my army. My parents nursed me just as if I had fallen in battle after many victories. Soon I was strong again....

I led my army northward, rarely having to sidetrack; the emperor himself sent the enemies I was hunting chasing after me. Sometimes they attacked us on two or three sides; sometimes they ambushed me when I rode ahead. We would always win, Kuan Kung, the god of war and literature riding before me. I would be told of in fairy tales myself. I overheard some soldiers—and now there were many who had not met me—say that whenever we had been in danger of losing, I made a throwing gesture and the opposing army would fall, hurled across the battlefield. Hailstones as big as heads would shoot out of the sky and the lightning would stab like swords, but never at those on my side. "On *his* side," they said. I never told them the truth. Chinese executed women who disguised themselves as soldiers or students, no matter how bravely they fought or how high they scored on the examinations....

I stood on top of the last hill before Peiping and saw the roads below me flow like living rivers. Between roads the woods and plains moved too; the land was peopled—the Han people, the People of One Hundred Surnames, marching with one heart, our tatters flying. The depth and width of Joy were exactly known to me: the Chinese population. After much hardship a few of our millions had arrived together at the capital. We faced our emperor personally. We beheaded him, cleaned out the palace, and inaugurated the peasant who would begin the new order. In his rags he sat on the throne facing south, and we, a great red crowd, bowed to him three times. He commended some of us who were his first generals.

I told the people who had come with me that they were free to go home now, but since the Long Wall was so close, I would go see it. They could come along if they liked....

I touched the Long Wall with my own fingers, running the edge of my hand between the stones, tracing the grooves the builders' hands had made. We lay our foreheads and our cheeks against the Long Wall and cried like the women who had come here looking for their men so long building the wall. In my travels north, I had not found my brother.

Carrying the news about new emperor, I went home, where one more battle awaited me. The baron who had drafted my brother would still be bearing sway over our village. Having dropped my soldiers off at crossroads and bridges, I attacked the baron's stronghold alone. I jumped over the double walls and landed with swords drawn and knees bent, ready to spring. When no one accosted me, I sheathed the swords and walked about like a guest until I found the baron. He was counting his money, his fat ringed fingers playing over the abacus.

"Who are you? What do you want?" he said, encircling his profits with his arms. He sat square and fat like a god.

"I want your life in payment for your crimes against the villagers."

"I haven't done anything to you. All this is mine. I earned it. I didn't steal it from you. I've never seen you before in my life. Who are you?"

"I am a female avenger."

Then—heaven help him—he tried to be charming, to appeal to me man to man. "Oh, come now. Everyone takes the girls when he can. The families are glad to be rid of them. 'Girls are maggots in the rice.' 'It is more profitable to raise geese than daughters.'" He quoted to me the sayings I hated.

"Regret what you've done before I kill you," I said.

"I haven't done anything other men—even you—wouldn't have done in my place."

"You took away my brother."

"He was not an apprentice."

"I free my apprentices."

"China needs soldiers in wartime."

"You took away my childhood."

"I don't know what you're talking about. We've never met before. I've done nothing to you."

"You've done this," I said, and ripped off my shirt to show him my back. "You are responsible for this." When I saw his startled eyes at my breasts, I slashed him across the face and on the second stroke cut off his head....

The swordswoman and I are not so dissimilar. May my people understand the resemblance soon so that I can return to them. What we have in common are the words at our backs. The idioms for *revenge* are "report a crime" and "report to five families." The reporting is the vengeance—not the beheading, not the gutting, but the words. And I have so many words—"chink" words and "gook" works too—that they do not fit on my skin.

Questions for discussion

1. From whom did the narrator learn the story of "Fa Mu Lan"? In what way is her Fa Mu Lan different from the Chinese legendary heroine Hua Mulan?
2. The narrator was trained first in tiger ways, then in dragon ways. What different feelings did she have with regard to the two ways? What might these two creatures symbolize? Explain.
3. Should Kingston be criticized for misrepresenting Chinese history and Chinese legends? Why or why not?